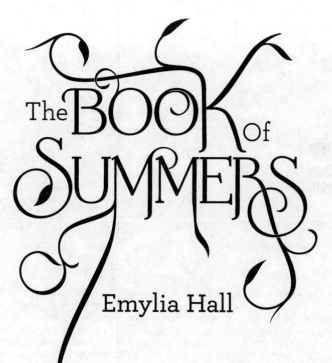

The BOOK of SUMMERS

Emylia Hall

MIRA®

ISBN-13: 978-0-7783-1411-0

THE BOOK OF SUMMERS

Copyright © 2012 by Emylia Hall

JUN 0 4 2012

Printed in U.S.A.

First Printing: June 2012
10 9 8 7 6 5 4 3 2 1

For Robin & Family Hall

When you are old and gray and full of sleep,
And nodding by the fire, take down this book,
And slowly read, and dream of the soft look
Your eyes had once, and of their shadows deep.
—W. B. Yeats
When You Are Old

Prologue

It is on white nights like these, when the snow outside is pushing at the shutters, and the windows are licked with frost, that Marika takes down the book. She turns the pages and she disappears, into all the sun-filled days.

There's Erzsi in the early mornings, when soft light kissed away the dew and tempted them all outside, with blushed cheeks. There she is in the late afternoons, when a ruder heat descended, flattening them, sending them sprawling— on the yellow lawn, in the forest pool, beneath the canopy of acacia trees. There she is in the slow-ebbing evenings, when the spent sun dipped toward the faded hills, and they lounged on the terrace, basking in the last of the glow.

Marika looks at the pictures, and, fleetingly, she feels them looking back.

Her relationship with the book is curious. She made it herself, with searching fingers and ink-smudging tears, with paint and glue and snippets and fragments. She took photographs when no one knew photographs were being taken, so the pictures within its pages appear like whispered secrets. The cloth cover is painted with flowers, swirls and strokes of bright white, blooms that haven't faded. Unlike the real flowers, the ones outside that twine the veranda, and wither and die as night falls. She remembers mixing the colors, the crick in her neck as she bent awkwardly over her square canvas, how she'd heard Zoltán's gentle laugh as he spotted her tongue peeping from her lips in concentration. The lettering was an afterthought, and as such the words are arranged haphazardly between the petals in a lilting, lifting scrawl: *The Book of Summers*. A name that came from the delight of the first, and the anticipation of all the others to come.

Marika loves and hates the book in almost equal measure. For when she turns the pages she is a time traveler. When she turns the pages she is bound in chains.

The photographs thrum with life, and tempt her closer. She smells coconut cream streaked on pale skin to ward off scatterings of freckles. She smells wood smoke lingering in hair, as though there had been a dance through licking flames. She smells cherry sherbets with a taste like a sweet prickle. She dips her head over the pages, caught too much in the moment, and now the only scent she can catch is a papery one. Dry and musty and lifeless.

She hears a voice calling her name. She closes the book and sets it back on the shelf. She goes back to the life she has now. The life she chose, once, above all else. And all that is lost stays between the pages of the book.

CHAPTER ONE

Friday morning began as English summer mornings often do, with a shy but rising sun and wisps of cloud that were blown away by breakfast. My father was visiting, so I should have known it was never going to be an ordinary day, despite its early promise. It was the first time that he was seeing my London home for himself, and I was no newcomer to the city. I was seventeen when I decided on art college, and with the utter resolution that it had to be London. I wanted to lose myself, and it seemed just the place in which to be lost. I can remember the day I left home twelve years ago, my father standing by the car in the train-station parking lot, one gnarled hand raised in farewell, the other already feeling in his pocket for his keys. Then the *put-put* of the exhaust as he passed me at the station entrance, how he didn't see me that time, for he was hunched over the steering wheel like someone who was already late. I watched him go, the only family I had.

Family. A word that has always sat so uneasily with me. For other people it may mean rambling dinners with elbows on tables and old jokes kneaded and pulled like baking dough. Or dotty aunts and long-suffering uncles, awkwardly shaped shift dresses and craggy mustaches, the hard press of a well-meant hug. Or just a house on a street. Handprints pushed into soft cement. The knotted, fraying ropes of an old swing on an apple bough. But for me? None of that. It's a word that undoes me. Like the snagging of a thread on a sweater that runs, unraveling quickly, into the cup of your hands.

Since college I've lived on both sides of the river, in boxy flats and sprawling town houses. These days, my home is a neat Victorian terrace in Mile End, with a straggle of garden and a displaced gnome. My roommate, Lily, sings Frank Sinatra in the bath and has a jet-black bob, shiny like treacle. Our street is in the shadow of a clutch of tower buildings, and there's a long-abandoned Fiat three doors up, its back window cracked like a skating pond. I once saw a cat stretched out on the pavement, black and white and dead all over, an image I've never quite cleared from my head. Another time there was a flock of pigeons pecking at a roast-chicken carcass as I stepped out of my front door. I hurried past pretending I hadn't seen, like a twitchy citizen turning a blind eye to a crime. But just five minutes on my bicycle and I can be stretched out in Victoria Park, on a raft of newspapers and books. I go to a café where if the sun's beaming the owner gives me a free cup of coffee and I sit beside her at a rickety table as she smokes cheap cigarettes in her blue apron. All in all I feel settled here. It's a place where I feel I can welcome my father, without more complicated feelings budging their way in.

He was always older than the other fathers, and he made

me giggle when I was small, saying he had been born ancient, with glasses sliding down his nose in his crib, knees already wrinkled. When other dads shouted and laughed, wore Levi's jeans and made makeshift waterslides on summer days, my father was in his study, shirtsleeves rolled to the elbow, lost in books. I would slip away and seek him out, guided by the soft closing of a door or the creak of a stair. He'd touch a finger to my cheek and call me his Little Betty. I'd cling to the ridges of his corduroys.

At breakfast times I used to spread marmalade on his toast and present it to him, flushed with care. He opened the new cereal boxes, wrestling with the plastic inner, shaking cornflakes into my bowl, stealing one for himself. He ironed my school dresses on a Sunday evening and hung them carefully on rose-patterned hangers, with their backs still creased. And sometimes I would come home and find an offering on the kitchen table, always in the same bottom corner. A storybook. A newly ruled notepad. A bouquet of three, sharp-pointed lead pencils. We would make tea and read nonsense poetry together, me going to bed dreaming of Quangle Wangles and a beautiful pea-green boat. We'd gotten along famously, with all the appearance of happiness.

Nowadays, we have new terms. Simply this: there are some things we talk about, and some things we don't. As long as the boundaries are observed, all is well. It makes what could be a complicated relationship into a very simple one. This understanding of ours didn't evolve gently over time; instead, it began with rushed descent, hurried by splashed tears and spilled promises, when I was sixteen years old. Ever since, we've been quietly complicit. And we get along just fine.

He's never been the sort to just pop in to London on a whim. Our infrequent visits are planned well in advance and I always go to see him in Devon. *I'm not built for London, Beth,* he's always said, and I've found it a relief that he's not one of those enthusiastic parents who is forever making suggestions and proposing plans. Lily's mother permanently scours the paper for exhibitions and new plays, looking for excuses to come and visit. She comes every couple of months and Lily turns into a tourist then. The two of them tumble through the door with crammed shopping bags. They catch taxis and go to the ballet. They eat at talked-about restaurants and sometimes invite me to join them for dessert. Lily's mother also attacks our domestic space with relish. She scrubs our sink so it looks like silver, and replaces our gnawed toothbrushes with pert bristled ones. She buys us giant packs of toilet-paper rolls and cans of soup, as though we were remote hill folk that might one day be snowed in. I observe such events with interest. I wonder what it would be like to have the lives of your parents so entangled with your own. Lily's mother's embraces extend to me, as well, but somehow her inclusive acts make me feel lonelier than I ever did before. Before I realized I needed a new toothbrush, or a slice of cheesecake from a fancy restaurant.

So it came as a surprise when my father telephoned three days ago to say that he was coming to see me this very weekend. *Would I be around on Friday? Would I be free?* he'd asked. This was new territory, and he entered it with a sideways glance and a fretful edge. As chance would have it, I had the day off. I work in a gallery and so I often have to do weekends, but that week I was gifted a rare Friday and Saturday of freedom. I'd had visions of a lazy breakfast at the pavilion in the park, a bicycle ride along the canal path, an afternoon in a sunny beer garden with friends who never worked weekends, but still celebrated them no less rampantly. *Of course I'm free, Dad,* I'd said, though, affecting an easy tone. *Come anytime.* I'd offered to meet his train at Paddington and he'd laughed vigorously, saying that he wasn't decrepit yet. I stole in and asked him then, *Is everything okay?* And he said, *Of course it is.* Then he added, *I just want to see you.* And it sounded simple enough at the time— unexpected, but just about believable. After I'd hung up the phone, I couldn't help feeling a queer mix of elation and worry. I decided to temper both through avoidance. I lost myself in recipe books. Instead of spending the next three days imagining all the possible scenarios that might have provoked his visit, I baked, I cooked and I dusted, feeling more daughterly than I had in a long time.

An impromptu spirit was clearly in the air, for Lily announced she was going sailing for the weekend with her new boyfriend, Sam. I pictured her windblown and salty, laughing at the breeze. I was disappointed that she wouldn't be at home. My father would have enjoyed meeting her, and I'd have appreciated the way she'd have taken the conversation and steered it along in an effortless way.

Will that chap Jonathan be with you? he'd asked on the telephone, and I'd had to remind him that Johnny and I had broken up six months ago. He easily forgot things like that, and for my part I downplayed them, if I played them at all. Johnny had taught geography and had a disheveled beard and laughing eyes. We spent nearly two years together, and in that time I'm not sure I ever got to describe myself as his girlfriend, something I somehow never minded. One day he told me he was leaving to travel South America and asked me if I wanted to go with him. I thought about it as he talked of crashing waterfalls and jungles so deep and thick that they were black as night by day. But in the end I turned him down more easily than I'd thought was possible. We made love that night for the last time, Johnny collapsing onto my chest afterward, me closing my eyes and folding an arm about him, as if he were the one that needed comforting. As if I was the one leaving. And on the last morning, he took my chin between his finger and thumb and looked into my eyes. *If only you'd let me really know you,* he said. Then, with more assurance, *I think I got closer than anyone, Beth. I think I knew you better than you think.* I'd closed my eyes, and when I opened them again I could see that I wasn't to be his puzzle anymore. He was as good as gone.

In trying to decide what to do with my father while he was with me, I thought immediately of the gallery. It's just off Brick Lane and I love the space I work in. The vast, glass panes let the best of the sunlight in, and inside there's an organic feel, lending the impression that you've fallen into a sun-filled glade in an otherwise dark and tangled wood. When I was a student, I always believed that art was there to show people something new, not something old, and this has stayed with me. For the past week, though, we'd been running an exhibition comprising the work of three landscape artists. Their gentle, pastoral subjects were not our usual fare, but Luca, the owner, had one day woken up with a yearning for something "kinder," he'd said, that "harked back to altogether simpler times." I could imagine my father enjoying the work, peering close to the canvas to admire a swell of hillside, or a blooming tree in the middle of a pancake-flat field. He'd see something of Devon in the pictures and feel at home, perhaps. And I would be pleased to show him my place of work at last. He'd never seen it, and I'm sure he imagined it was all dismembered mannequins and incoherent spray paint, the kind of thing he saw now and again in the supplements of Sunday papers.

For the evening I'd bought some films, old black-and-whites with stuttering soundtracks and footsteps in the dark. Settling down in front of the television was one of the things we'd always done together, conversing aimlessly and gratefully about whatever we were watching. And for our supper I'd made a huge pan of chili and bought tortillas from a Mexicán shop in the Bethnal Green backstreets. He hadn't said if he was staying, but I'd folded towels and fresh sheets in anticipation. I'd cleared up the junk mail that carpeted the communal hallway, and put a bunch of tulips on the table in the kitchen.

There's a sad kind of poetry in the unsuspecting. For every catastrophe that befalls us there was a time before when we were quite oblivious. Little did we know how happy we were then. If only we could learn to celebrate the ordinary days—the ones that begin unremarkably, and continue in unnoteworthy fashion. Days like yesterday, and the day before, when the irksome things were slight and passing—the fuzzy edges of an early morning headache, the spilling of a little coffee as I stirred in the sugar, the sudden recollection that I had cookies baking in the oven and their sweet smell had turned a touch acrid. These are the days to prize. The days on which to pause, to give thanks. And in doing so to acknowledge that we're ready, we're poised. If the skies were to fall, we'd have a chance of catching them.

My father arrived just after midday. I heard the idling of an engine outside and spied his taxi from the window. I ran downstairs, skidding on the landing in my socks, reaching the door just before he rang the bell.

"Dad!"

He moved to kiss me, but had bags in both hands so we bumped each other clumsily. I reached to take some of his load but he shook his head.

"No, you go on. I'm all right. Where are we going, up these stairs?"

I looked at him with new fascination, the way we always do when we see people out of their natural habitats. I was almost surprised to see clothes that I recognized—his camel-colored coat that was too warm for the weather, his blue cotton shirt that was frayed at the collar but remained a favorite. In the living room I stood back from him, shy almost, and watched as he set down his bags. A navy suitcase, a reusable bag with a turtle on it, the kind that have replaced plastic bags in greener supermarkets, and a string bag that appeared to be filled with newspaper packages.

"Are you staying the night?" I asked.

"I wasn't sure," he said. Then added, "But I could, of course, if you wanted me to. Oh, you're looking at this lot. It's vegetables mainly, from the garden. I thought you'd like them."

He started going through the string bag, drawing out bundles of radishes and a plump lettuce.

"I got up early this morning to pick them," he said. "There's some new potatoes here, too."

The vegetable patch was another of our common grounds. When I was small I'd help him sow and dig, my knees pointed and muddy, my hands swallowed by a giant pair of cotton gardening gloves. As I'd grown older, and my visits home had been more sporadic, he'd made it his duty to appraise me of developments in the garden. Whether it was frosty grass splintering underfoot or slippery mud, a slither of moon in the sky or full sun, we'd always walk down to the bottom of the garden, soon after my arrival home.

With my arms now loaded, I went through to the kitchen. "You can stay if you want," I said. "I mean, you've come all this way. And you've never been before. And, well, it'd be nice, wouldn't it?"

"My ticket's a flexible one," he said. "I can go back on any train."

I knew how meticulous he was, and that all possible trains between now and tomorrow afternoon would be noted down in his minute and precise handwriting, on a piece of paper, folded in his pocket. He'd have asterisked the slow trains, the ones that trundled through Wiltshire or stopped in Bristol. But his apparent flexibility was novel, and I approved of it. I was beginning to relax, believing in the spontaneity of his visit, after all.

I called back through to the living room. "Do you want to go to the gallery? We have an exhibition on that I think you'd like, and you'll get to meet the people I work with, too. Then we could have some lunch somewhere, and then come back here in the evening for dinner. But it's up to you. I mean, we can do anything, really."

"Oh, I don't mind, Beth. It's just nice seeing you," he said. "Is there a cup of tea going?"

I walked back into the living room, carrying a plate of biscuits. "Kettle's on. Look, I baked, maple-and-walnut cookies. They're a bit burned at the edges, but…"

He was picking up the bag with the turtle on it, and he jumped when I came into the room. He set it back down.

"Beth…" he said.

I'd heard him say my name like this before. Countless times, each of them years and years ago.

"What?"

"Before anything else, there's something I need to give you. Perhaps you want to sit down."

His voice hit the low notes, with a tremor at the last.

"What is it?" I said, and was surprised at how calmly the words came out.

He turned back to the bag and picked it up again. It seemed to take a considerable effort, as though it was immensely heavy. His fingers tightened on the handle, and I thought then how clawlike his hand looked, the skin tight over the giant knuckles, the sharp thumb. His face had turned gray, his eyes swam with apology. And I knew then that there was a reason for him coming to London so suddenly, after all. It wasn't just to see me, or just because he'd wanted to. We weren't those kind of people, those happy and spontaneous types who did that sort of thing. I wish he'd kept me fooled for longer. We could have prolonged the spell that way, even if its hold was thin as mist.

"Something came in the mail for you," he said, "and I thought I'd better bring it right away."

He held out the bag to me. I stared at the cartoon green turtle printed on its side, with its round eyes and stumpy feet. The words *a friend for life* were stamped beneath it. I looked back at my father.

"What is it?" I said.

"I don't know, Beth. I haven't opened it."

He looked pained as he spoke, and I felt a sudden flare of anger. A heat in my chest that flickered, then settled. I pulled at the string of my necklace with its tangle of charms, my fingers twisting the silver chain. I met his eyes, and he blinked first. He shrugged. "I just thought it might be important," he said quietly.

I set the bag on the floor and knelt down beside it, reaching inside. I drew out a parcel wrapped in brown paper, book-heavy. I turned it over, and saw a smeared postmark and a clutch of foreign stamps. *Magyarország*. Hungary. A place that once, a very long time ago, meant *summer* to me. The handwriting was faintly familiar, spiky and picturesque, every word a mountain range a mile high. It was addressed to Erzsébet Lowe.

Erzsébet Lowe. Two words, a name. Sandals that left a tread of flower patterns in the dust. Eyes wide like saucers, pushing through fronds in the hidden woods. And later, sharp elbows and long legs, a sunburned chest and kisses by a dark pool. Tears that stung and rattling breath. A shattered mirror and a sudden escape. Unless I stopped them, the fragments of my Hungarian summers would come skittering back; first as paper pieces, blowing in the wind, and then a maelstrom.

I had to be resolute. Erzsébet Lowe no longer existed. She was a figment, a fading trace of breath on a pane, a pattern of tea leaves, swirled and disappeared. Long lost, long gone.

I glanced up at my father. He was staring down at me,

his hands loose by his sides. His face was wrung of all color and creases streaked his cheeks.

"Why did you bring it?" I said, dropping the parcel back into the bag, snapping upward. "Why did you think I'd want it?"

"I'm sorry, Beth, but I thought it had to be important. Not the kind of thing to just forward in the mail."

The word *important* smacked of cold formality. It was a static word.

"None of it's *important*," I said. "You should have just trashed it."

I saw it then as it might have happened. The parcel taken to a post office and pushed under the glass, a heavy-set woman in a creased blouse licking the stamps and slapping them haphazardly. Tossed into a sack, as the sender, a dark shadow, turned to leave. A package, bound with worn string, crossing the continent in a jet plane's hold, to sit propped in the porch in Harkham, a snail leaving a sticky trail behind it. Then the final leg, a train to London, my father sitting in the back of a taxicab as it rumbled through East London streets, the weight of the thing in his lap. His hands closed around it, protective, fearful.

This was how the past traveled toward the present. Such was its journey.

I stood, wiping my hands on my dress as though it was dusty.

"So you came here to give me this?" I said. "Why couldn't you have told me that was why you were coming? I'd have said don't bother. I don't want it. Whatever it is, I don't want it."

"I didn't think it was just a parcel," he said. "It's been such a long time since anything with that postmark came to the house, Beth. I just thought I should come...."

"But you never come, Dad. You've never seen this place, not once. I don't mind about that. It's how it is, it's fine. But honestly, of all the wasted trips. Please take it, just take it away with you. I don't want it."

"I didn't want to upset you. I really didn't. It was rash of me to come."

"It wasn't rash, it was normal. For other people, it would have been normal. But not for us, Dad. I should have known that there'd be a reason behind you coming. But *this?* Why couldn't you just say? Why couldn't you have told me what was going on? Instead of pretending you were just swinging by on a social visit, with a bag of radishes, for God's sake."

"I didn't know how to tell you, Beth. I knew what it would mean to you."

"Dad, why is it, that after all these years, we still get it wrong? Nothing's changed, not one thing."

"Would you rather I went?" he said.

"What, home?"

"Yes."

I considered it, and felt an old familiar feeling turning in my stomach. Guilt and sorrow, mixed.

"Well, you only came to give me this, and now it's given. But, I mean, you *could* stay. We could just pretend that everything's okay. That you didn't lie about why you were coming. That you didn't just give me something that is completely irrelevant but is now going to be stuck in my head for, oh, I don't know, forever. We could do that, yes."

My voice was extraordinarily high-pitched, as though

I was a stringed instrument tightened beyond all reason. I clapped my hands to my mouth to stop myself talking.

He took the bag from my hand. I saw the tiredness in his face then, the lines about his eyes like cracks in plaster. He picked up his suitcase. I imagined it contained his neatly folded pajamas, a change of shirt, a pair of balled woolen socks. Things that he'd need in case he stayed the night, after all. What had he thought? That after the parcel I'd want the comfort of his presence? That we'd walk in the park and look at paintings and eat chili and watch films, then say good-night on the landing, and all would be well?

We stared at each other. He opened his mouth to say something, then hesitated. He closed it. The time to speak, to make things different, had been and gone and neither of us had taken it.

"Do you want a cab to the station, then?" I said, already reaching for the telephone.

"If that's best, Beth. I'm sorry."

I hesitated. "It came out all wrong before, but we could pretend. We're good at it, aren't we? Pretending? We could still have a nice day."

He shook his head, and I didn't know if it was in disagreement or a deeper, broader, altogether older sense of despair. I shrugged, and slowly but deliberately I began to dial.

The taxi came quickly, far more quickly than I expected. On a Friday lunchtime I thought we'd have had at least twenty minutes, but the doorbell was ringing inside of five. I saw him downstairs. On the pavement he hugged me, and for just a moment I hung on to him, but then he was stepping away and reaching for the taxi door. He'd be thinking of the running meter, the impatient driver, the car waiting to pass on the opposite side of the road. My father was a man who bowed easily to such influences, cracking and bending like a bean stem.

"Goodbye, Dad," I said.

He climbed inside and I closed the door, slamming it louder than I had meant to. I tapped the glass and waved. Then I stood watching as the cab drove off, saw the shape of his head in the back window, already disappearing. He would be back in Devon by midafternoon, just as the sun was pouring through the crooked boughs of the apple tree on the back lawn. It would be as though he had never come at all.

I looked quickly up at the small strip of London sky and blinked fast, an old trick, to catch the tears before they started. I went to push my hair back from my face with both hands but found I was holding the turtle bag. I couldn't remember it being proffered and I couldn't remember taking it. But that was my father. Wily, in a beaten sort of way, like a fox dodging hounds.

"Oh, Dad," I said, "why can't we ever just talk to each other?"

I couldn't even imagine his reply.

I trailed back inside, slamming the front door behind me. The apartment was shining, with all its freshly vacuumed carpets and scrubbed surfaces. The tulips beamed at me from the table. I took the plate of cookies and threw them in the bin, one hitting the edge and scattering into crumbs at my feet. Then I stood and looked at the turtle bag, where I'd dumped it in the corner of the kitchen. I sank down to the floor, and watched it. As though just by looking, I could turn it into something else entirely.

★ ★ ★

I know this much; the old hurts never go. In fact, they're the things that shape us, they're the things we look to, when we turn out roughshod, and messy at the edges. I don't know how long I sat staring at the bag, but my legs stiffened and my neck creaked and I knew I had to leave the house. In a fit of unmediated wistfulness for the day that might have been, I found myself treading the path that my father and I would have taken. I caught a bus to Bethnal Green. The high road was mellow enough, at that time of day. It wasn't Sunday morning, when the place was rammed with gray-eyed street traders, peddling toothpaste and broken records. When clusters of girls giggled into their palms and old East End boys trod the pavements, getting squashed okra on their shoes. Nor was it nighttime, dark hours where fried chicken smoked the air, boys with rolling gaits owned the streets and squeaking microphones gave away karaoke spots, stages hogged by big bellies and bigger hair. The afternoon was simply sunny, and there was the crackle of people going about their business, with calm and uncomplicated steps.

As I walked, I stared down at my feet in their flip-flops, my toes already graying from the urban grime. An image suddenly came to me of my father back in his luscious Devon garden, a sweet breeze sending ripples through the beanstalks. He'd have his sleeves rolled to the elbow and would be digging, furiously. He always dug in times of strife. But I realized I was speeding time. He'd more likely still be stuffed into a railway carriage, fidgeting with his mustache as noisy children scattered toys on the table across from him, and podgy-armed women chattered into their telephones. *My father.* Thinking about him—his regret, his discomfort, his anxiety—stopped me thinking about the other thing. The invading parcel, and all the things it brought with it. Its matted strings of cobwebs. Its smell of the past.

I got to the gallery in twenty minutes and walked straight in, the door clanging like an old-fashioned grocer's.

"Hi," I said, then, "it's lovely and cool in here."

"Hey, Beth! Where's your dad?"

Kelly had only been with us for three months. She was from Wisconsin, twenty years old, and was impossibly chirpy all of the time. She had a halo of blond curls and today she wore a red silk scarf knotted at her neck, looking like a busty pinup from an old calendar.

"Long story," I said, in what I hoped was an easy dismissal. I knew Kelly hadn't quite got me figured yet, for I struggled to match her easy charm and endless stream of confidences. "He couldn't make it in the end," I added.

I dropped my shoulder bag by the counter and, with my hands in my pockets, walked over to the walls. Kelly made as if to join me, but was fortunately diverted by the clanging of the door and the arrival of two hipster Japanese tourists, with elaborate hair and a fistful of guidebooks. She rushed to welcome them, and I moved quietly off.

Why *had* I come here? To somehow remind myself that I had a place and I had purpose? But turning up at work on your day off just raised questions, even in the guileless. I turned my attention to the pictures, my fingers curled tightly in my jeans pockets. I'd been at the opening a week ago, helping to pour wine and offering elaborate hors d'oeuvres. And I'd spent the best part of the week surrounded by the paintings, as their keeper, their chaperone.

I imparted the details of their background to those who were curious—moving from picture to picture, with nods and feathery fingers, pointing out the brilliance of the sky, the rhythms of the water, the many textures of bark. But it was only on that afternoon, as Kelly rattled on spiritedly with our visitors and I drifted farther and farther away from them, that I began to really look at the pictures, and demand something else of them. It was as though I wanted to know that somewhere, away from frame or lens or eager eye, the places they showed continued to exist. That their origins could be found, if finding was what someone wanted to do.

In that moment, I thought of another artist. Zoltán Károly. You could plot his paintings with a pin on a map for he had always painted the world he lived in, just as he saw it. I hadn't thought about his paintings for a very long time. Like everything else they had been forgotten. I hadn't thought about the landscape that inspired them, either, nor the place he called home: Villa Serena. The name tripped from my tongue with such ease, its rolling consonants and impossible prettiness, but it had a sting in its tail. A bitter twist that belied its picturesque sound. *Zoltán Károly.* I thought then of the way he signed his pictures, the spiky letters of his name in the bottom corner of the canvas. Suddenly I knew that it was his writing on the parcel from Hungary. And as soon as I allowed it this smidgen of recognition, all my attempts to forget the day's intrusion fell away. I felt the fast-rushing avalanche of memory, I heard its roar, and while I could flee from it, I knew that in the end it would catch me up. That no matter how hard I fought to keep my head, its force would be too strong and I'd succumb, falling into its startling white depths.

I pushed past the tourists and Kelly, and hurried into the back office. In the bathroom I stared hard at myself in the small pane of mirror we had propped above the sink. My breath came in rapid gasps. I appeared as no more than a mussed outline, any woman's figure marked by edges only, and it was then that I knew that I was crying, the tears falling unchecked down my cheeks.

Zoltán had written to me, after all these years. And of all the thoughts that scrambled on top of one another, the one that persisted, the one that rose above all others, was this: Why him? Why him and not her?

It was a late night, in the end. I stayed at the gallery in the back room, pretending to get on with some forgotten and urgent paperwork. By the time Kelly had closed up, all I knew was that I didn't want to be alone. I went with her to meet some of her friends, guys and girls I didn't know, and they were each as merry and easy as her. We hopped from bar to bar, throwing down cocktails with abandon. Through a mouthful of crunching ice and a strawberry-stained smile, Kelly asked me again what had happened to my father. I said that something had come up and he simply "couldn't get away." For a moment it made him sound like a time-stretched businessman, and I balanced a moment on this idea. I pictured myself friendly with his secretary, being sent tickets to fancy events in the mail. Us both being quite different people, really. Then I remembered the wilting vegetables and the hessian bag with the turtle, the look of anguish that marked his face as I'd said, *We're good at it, aren't we? Pretending?*

By midnight I'd had enough of everything and everyone.

I said quick goodbyes and slipped away. I eschewed taxicabs and night buses, favoring the echo of my feet on the pavement, the even stares of urban foxes and the throbbing bass of passing cars as metronome for my pace. It took me forty minutes to walk home and if Lily had been there she would doubtless have admonished me for my lack of caution. But I was returning to a house that was empty, yet pulsing with a presence that was stronger than any single person. So I'd taken the long way home.

Certain lights always seem eerie to a wandering imagination. When I walked into my living room, I stopped uncertainly in the half-light and seemed to float outside of myself. Across the street an upstairs window framed two people tangled in a kiss. I snapped the blinds shut and went to curl up on the sofa, drawing my legs up underneath me. Going to sleep was out of the question, and so I sat reflecting, becoming the night, my surface made of the dazzle of a kiss, the bars of light that sifted through a hastily pulled blind.

I must have fallen asleep because much later I awoke, crick-necked and dry-mouthed, and the dawn light of a new morning was warm on my face. The fingers of my left hand were leaden and prickling. I had dreamed of nothing. Literally. Vast empty spaces from which everything was missing. I should have been relieved, having feared scrabbling, confused ramblings, but instead it felt like a portent. Hollowed, I stretched and yawned.

I got up and went through to the kitchen, barefoot, my clothes crinkled. The early sun lit the kitchen so it was soft and pale and not quite there. I opened the window and a chirruping chorus of birds, invisible but riotous, greeted the rise of the day. I ran my hands through my hair, finding knots where I had shifted restlessly in the night. As I rubbed my eyes yesterday's makeup smeared my hands, leaving dusky smudges on my fingers. I felt in sudden need of cleansing, rushing water and toothpaste, sweet-smelling soap and puffs of talcum powder.

I filled the kettle, set out my coffeepot and went through to the bathroom. The water of the shower ran cold at first and I emitted a breathy scream, but I bared my teeth and clenched my fists with a savage staying power. Afterward, I groped for a towel, and wrapped myself in it.

In the hallway, my feet left dim prints on the wooden boards, like a beach wanderer. I rubbed the ends of my hair dry as I walked into my bedroom to get dressed. Not quite dry, I pulled on a vest and my old denim shorts, frayed cotton skimming my thighs. Needing strong coffee, suddenly and sharply, I went into the kitchen.

Since I had woken up, first stretching in that bright and restless dawn, my every movement had been consciously avoiding my father's aborted visit, and the package that sat in the corner, watchful, waiting. I needed a plan for the day and I needed it fast. Perhaps I could dig out my camera and walk the waterways like a hobbyist. There was a pub where I could drink a cider sitting on the grass at the water's edge, daisies pressing my palms. All I had to do to escape was get out of the house, and walk quickly. My camera clunking reassuringly against my side, holsterlike.

But before that there was coffee. I sat at the table with my back to the open window. I crossed my legs, rested my chin in my hands and my elbows on the table. The shopping bag was on the floor just beside the door. I twitched, then stood, and poured my drink. I wrapped my hands around the mug

and breathed its scent, eyeing the bag again, over the rising
steam. It was quiet in the kitchen—the birds outside sang
with less of their early exuberance, the traffic murmured,
the inhabitants of my street rolled in their beds and hit their
snooze buttons. The clock on the wall said half past seven.

I balanced on my tightrope, and thought of other people,
and what they were doing. I tried to locate and place myself,
rooted in the order of things. So I began. Lily would be with
her boyfriend, waking to damp canvas and the rubbery scent
of an airbed. Kelly and her friends from the night before
would be rolling in their beds still, their mouths slack from
sleep, the woolly edges of their hangovers not yet formed.
Johnny? He would be wrapped in the arms of another girl,
no doubt, her hair spilling across his burly chest. My father?
The old interloper. I couldn't help including him. He always was an early riser, so perhaps he'd be creaking about
the house, watching his morning egg boiling on the stove,
a thin plume of white spilling from its cracked shell. He
would maybe tut, and press his knuckles hard against the
sideboard. And then the others. The ones I never thought
about, much less spoke about. The thought of them being
anywhere, doing anything, was inconceivable. For hadn't I
erased them? Didn't they cease to exist? I saw her then, as
she might be. *Marika*. Standing at the window in the early
morning haze of an Esztergom morning. Her dark hair
pulled back in a girlish ribbon, a red enamel mug of coffee,
tar black and sweetened with sugar, held in her hand. She'd
be pushing seventy, but later she'd still ride a bicycle along
the rutted track, stopping to buy pastries made with crumpled apricots from the baker's on the square. Cat-calling to
the neighbors. Laughing, without effort. Smiling, without

care. *Marika.* How could she still be real? Didn't forgetting let you lose a person, once and for all?

I made a sudden decision. I set down my coffee, got up and approached the bag. I reached into it and took out the parcel. I placed it on the table, and looked at it. Its bright stamps jumped, the handwriting, bold and spiky, seeming to climb up from the paper like the detail of an elaborate pop-up book. I watched it as though it was an unpredictable and living thing, with my muscles tensed, ready to move if it flew at me. Except it had to be dead, a dried husk, like a bug on its back, its legs taut and folded. For it had blown in from the past, cobwebs dragging, dust choking, with its old string and creased paper.

I reached over and pulled it toward me, turning it over in my hands, feeling its weight. Then I unlaced the string so it shrugged off at all four corners. I picked at the sticky tape with my nails, and ripped the edges. I placed my palms flat on its surface, and waited a moment, before folding the paper back. As I did so, I fancied I caught a waft of old scent, biting like wood smoke. The taste in my mouth had a metallic ring to it, and I realized I was biting hard on my lip, a thin smudge of blood on my finger as I touched it. Annoyed with myself, at my tense muscles and overactive imagination, I tore open the rest of the wrapping without ceremony, letting it drop purposely and carelessly to the floor. Inside was a further wrapped parcel, and an envelope with *Erzsébet* written in the same jagged hand. I made myself open it casually, with indifference, the paper fudging and ripping messily. It was a letter, on thick parchment paper, cream colored and written on one side only.

Just as I had guessed, it was from Zoltán, Marika's partner. The man she met just weeks after my father and I had returned to England without her, all those years ago. His was a name she rolled about her tongue as she introduced him, tasting the newness of it, the freedom of it. *Zoltán*. A painter. She told me she fell first for his robust and pulsing landscapes, then quickly afterward for him. It must have seemed, to nine-year-old me, like she never spared the details. As though she told me everything there was to know, the whole gritty truth of it, drawing my hands toward her and filling them with jewels of her own making.

In the letter, Zoltán had tamed his painterly scrawl to write carefully and precisely. It would have been a long time since he'd spoken any English, and he'd have needed a dictionary, because Zoltán always seemed as though he never knew any sad words.

I began to read.

Dearest Erzsébet,

It has been such a long time since we heard from you. I am so very sorry that it is with such news that I now write. Marika passed away. It was a heart attack, sudden and fast. On July 10, a Saturday, a day of such unbearable heat that we swam early at the forest pool and slept in the afternoon with the shutters closed. She died in the cool of late evening, as I laid the table for supper and she fetched a bottle of wine. Until that moment, it was a day like all of our days. Like the ones you will remember, fondly, I hope. I have scattered her ashes on the land she loved, at the tree with arms like a man, you know the one, with the fields running until the horizon. She loved you for always, Erzsi. You must

know that. And, Erzsi, you are welcome here, as you always were and always will be. I wait to greet you.
(Old) Zoltán Károly

I didn't realize I was holding my breath until a wordless sound climbed in my throat and fought to escape. My chest tightened to a gasp.

I had imagined the moment of her death before. Sometimes with the prickle of fantasy, mostly with the emptiness of dread. The first time I was just a child and afraid of my own thoughts. But my intentions were honorable. I missed her, and I wanted to mourn with a respectable and honest grief. I imagined picking spring flowers and laying them at a grave, a single tear on my cheek. Later, years later, as I walked between high-rises, I saw falling axes and silver pistols, with a sudden drop and scream. But always the same full stop. These were the fantasies. Death would happen one day, of course, but not that day, not that year, just some time in the dim and distant future. The same future that lasted forever.

It was impossible to believe that she was really gone. Leaving a creased sheet and a thick-stemmed wineglass smudged with ruby kisses. A pair of sandals, their insides rubbed black and shining, askew in the hallway. Funny, that the things that came to mind were motionless objects, left behind. When nothing about her was static. *You only have one life,* she'd said to me once, breathily, her eyes flashing. But it wasn't true. She had had several.

A heart attack. Perhaps it was poetic justice? That uncertain heart, that mad and dashing thing that caught in her chest and sent her in all directions and only sometimes the right one. She was always too much. Her head didn't come into it, only ever her great and feeble heart. And so finally her body had had enough, and turned in upon itself. She would have spontaneously combusted, the licking flames about her feet leaving a black hole in the carpet. A noisy death, of color and light and then…nothing.

Marika. My mother.

Time passed, and I realized I had been sitting quite still, hunched at the table with the letter in my hands. I clapped my hands to my cheeks to rub some life into them, and then I saw the other parcel. I had quite forgotten it. I took it carefully in my hands and turned it, running my fingers over its surface. Then I tore it open. Inside was a book, clothbound with a hard cover. Someone had painted bright white flowers all over it, crowding its edges, and I recognized them, even by the quick and stylized strokes. *Hajnalka*. A Hungarian word that in English meant *morning glory*. They looked like spinning tops, ablaze with light and movement. On the first page a title had been written, against sky-blue paint. *The Book of Summers*. Just four words on a page, the edges of each letter splayed with an artful brushstroke. Despite the whimsical penmanship and the soft new-washed blue, the words spoke clearly of ownership. A definite time and a certain place.

I put my hands together in a sort of temple, and dipped my head. I wasn't praying but I was wishing, with my lips pressed to my fingers. *Please,* I said, *please can this not matter?* But I knew already that it would. And that it always would.

I opened it at random, and saw a picture of myself. My face was pushed close to the camera, one hand shielding the sun from my eyes, and a burst of it, bright like a burning star above my shoulder. I must have been wearing some kind of hat, meshed straw maybe, for my face was dappled with split shadow. And I was laughing, my brown nose wrinkled, my eyes shining. I was fourteen. I know I was fourteen because there was a tiny scratch on my chin and I remembered the cat that did it. A wild cat that I'd found skulking at the edge of the track, picking over dried melon skins, with a skinny rib cage and tottering legs like a drunken ballerina. I'd scooped her up fearlessly, laughing as she spat and scratched. I'd nuzzled her head until she softened. She'd followed me everywhere that summer, a piebald shadow, twining and tripping at my legs. I'd fattened her up on pieces of ham and chicken from my own plate, smoky sausages smuggled from the hot coals. I'd called her Cica, which was Hungarian for *kitten*. It sounded so pretty, *tseet-tsoh,* like a tiny Oriental empress or the song of a lark.

I realized then that I'd tried so hard to forget the big things, and that all the little things had gone, too. Cica. My small shadow.

I turned the page, and the next, flicking quickly through the rest of the book. There was an order to it, a structure. Each section was dated, beginning with 1991, written in the same painted looping hand, all the way through to 1997. Not a summer missed, for seven years. There were no footnotes to any of the pictures, no neat handwritten annotations, just page after page of photographs. Different settings, but always the same place I knew: faded green hills, banks of dark forest, a green glade pool, endless cornfields, a run of lawn and a big house made of red wood and pale stone. And different times—first delicate light, the full heat of high noon, flat-baked afternoons, thundery evenings, black nights pricked with fireflies.

So this was how I came to see myself again, in quick-flicking snatches. Ten years old, sunburned and uncertain, but grinning with a sort of triumph. Eleven, twelve, thirteen, standing in tall grasses with the sun in my eyes, in a yellow bathing suit at the edge of a forest, slumped in a hammock, with one bare foot swinging. Fourteen, fifteen, posing with a badminton racket like a Wimbledon champion, holding up a giant sweet corn with butter on my chin, lounging on blankets, my skin baked brown and freckles on my shoulders. And sixteen, when my hair was at its longest, sweeping the cups of my bikini, and my bangs falling languidly into my eyes.

Marika, Zoltán, even Tamás, whom I've never allowed myself to think about, the people of those Hungarian summers were there, too. Not as the shadowy, shrinking outlines I had made of them, but seen red-cheeked and flame-haired, laughing and kissing and holding, and always pictured with me. Marika's face taunted from the page, with her hair so like my own, the brave hook of nose, the smiling, smiling mouth.

Had it been like that? For a time, perhaps. But left unwatched, the camera could lie, after all. Proffering a fractional moment caught in time, with no sense of the before or after, nor all the things that made it so. A false imprint that cheated memory.

The book was not signed and there was no note slipped inside its pages, but Marika's fingerprints were all over it. Only she could make everything look just the way she wanted it to, drawing veils and wafting smoke. Perhaps the book could have been put together naturally, year by year, for her to take down and look at by the fire, on freezing winter nights when the snow banked outside the windows. And that Zoltán had simply come across it and wanted me to have it, hoping it would stir some feeling that might remain in me still. But it seemed unlikely. Instead, I saw it as artifice, designed to dredge sentiment from me with a petty trick of the light. To prompt me to sigh, *Ah, these were still the days, and they mattered, after all.* Typical, that Marika should needle this from me, wanting the last laugh, even in death.

The first tears of old grief, of new grief, too, rose and pushed at my eyes. I began to weep angrily. I slumped on the table, *The Book of Summers* cradled in my arms.

To think that these precious terrible things, carried by my poor father, little knowing what he was doing, could so easily have gone unopened. I'd pushed them to a corner and tried to carry on as though I'd never seen them. Brushing questions under the corner of a rug, and treading on it, to be sure.

Now, I know this: some would say a photograph disserves memory, coating it in rigidity, like an icy blast from a Snow Queen's wand. The mind cannot see past the fixed expressions and frozen poses, and so the rest fades. But what if everything, this "rest," has been locked away, and the sighting of a single image proves the turn of the key. Surely that lid would fly open at the slightest touch? A Pandora's box of delights and dismays, spilling out and upward.

Every family has its stories, but I can't help feeling that us Lowes have more than most. Tight-lipped and yearning, we kept them from one another. We must have thought that we were each alone. But now I know that we were bonded, after all; for each of us had lost what we loved, leaving only memory. Memory that seemed, paradoxically, to be too much, and never enough. Today, I could tell any number of these stories, but I won't. For, selfishly, there is only one that really matters to me. It is not my father's loss, nor is it my mother's. It is mine, and I possess it wholly. Knowing that in doing so, it possesses me.

I thought of the pictures in the gallery, and the Villa Serena landscape I knew so well. In Zoltán's hands it was conjured in a vivid palette, but nothing was as bright as its reality. Simply, it was a place suffused in color and light. The place that Marika, my mother, shared with me. A place where once I ran through wheat fields, bloodred poppies catching at my legs. Where I dived into a lake as big as a kingdom, my belly sweeping the bottom, my hands turning dark stones in the muddied sand. And where I lay beside her on a faded sweep of lawn, our elbows crooked at right angles behind our heads, swallowed whole by the blue sky. Hungary, the land of my dreams, my hidden place. And my eyes, my lips, the very tip of my chin would proclaim that I loved Marika still. I always had, I never hadn't.

CHAPTER TWO

I always knew that my mother was different from my father and me. *She's blown by different winds,* he used to say, but that made her sound flimsy, and I knew better. She snapped like a firecracker when she was mad, and cried the Danube when she was happy, but she always did exactly what she wanted. She was tall and proud and relentlessly foreign, with a scarlet stain for lips and hair like a flock of ravens.

I think of her and all I see is red. Red for passion, because whatever else I can say about her, I cannot doubt her ardor. Red for her favorite flower, poppies, meaning remembrance, but also bloodshed. She stitched rows of tiny poppies to the hems of her skirts, and to the cuffs of blouses. And red for *Beware!* A warning that should have been flashed to anyone who came near.

I used to think that it was all because she was from another country, and we weren't. Then I met other Hungarians, and there was never anyone remotely like Marika. What it meant was that right from the beginning, my father and I were thrust together. Not through a deliberate alliance, more by bent of not being her. *You and your father are two peas in a pod,* she used to say to me, and she made it feel like an insult, the way she popped the last word from her lips.

Once when I was very small, no more than five, I remember trying to fall asleep on her chest, but the beating of her heart beneath my cheek threw me off-kilter. I lost my own rhythms and began to gasp. And sometimes I caught her looking at me, as though I was a puzzle she was trying to figure out. I dared to glare back, to make sure she knew that she, too, was indecipherable. Even later on, when I grew to like the same things as her—fireflies in the garden at sunset and Hungarian dances, Zoltán Károly's landscapes and cold cherry soup—there was always a distance between us. It was as though we just weren't meant to be.

So it made sense that events culminated as they did, for in the end we let each other go. The natural order was, I suppose, restored. That is what I've always told myself, on nights when I've woken tangled in bedsheets, my forehead damp. When I've found myself craving the sound of her voice, her whoops and hollers, sent from one room to the next without a care for walls or doors. Or the feeling of her hand in mine, and her rings, shining like licked toffees, leaving their indent in my skin. I've always said that everything happens for a reason, and such empty reasoning comforted me once. But it can't work anymore, not now. Instead, my mind scrambles and flits, like mosquitoes caught in a curtain. I haven't seen or heard from her in fourteen years. The only thing I know for certain, now, is that she is dead.

She left for the first time when I was nine years old, during our one and only trip to Hungary as a family. That was twenty-one years ago, almost to the day. It was a vanish-

ing act that had nothing of magic about it and I remember
thinking that things would never be as bad again. I was
wrong, of course.

In 1990 I was called Erzsébet, a name that meant Elizabeth in Hungarian. *Er. Zshe. Bet.* It was spoken like a deep
draft, a ripple, then a bubble popping. The trickle of rain on
a pane of glass, a sudden run and drop. For shortening, only
the wistful part was taken: Erzsi. A tooth missing, with a
gentle wind rushing through the gap. Now I am called Beth.
And I have enjoyed the fact that the *th* would fox Hungarians. I've taken a certain pride in being unpronounceable.

Back then, I still called my mother *Mother*. I hadn't yet
decided that *Marika* was more appropriate. That would happen little over a year later, a rebellion I would thrill to and
one that she surprised and slightly annoyed me by never
minding.

I knew the facts of her Hungarian life. I can't remember ever being sat down and told them sequentially; there
were no pages turned in picture-book fashion, but I knew
her story nonetheless. She was born in Hungary, a mewing
creature wrapped in a sheepskin blanket. When she was ten
years old Soviet tanks rolled in on Budapest, so her parents
spirited her away. She left her country and her friends behind, trailing behind her mother and father, all the way to
England, with its box hedges and lumpy mash. She spent her
youth in the darkened rooms of houses belonging to other
homesick Hungarians. She sat with her long limbs crossed
and watching, her fingers twirling her rangy braids as old
men told old tales of the old country, their stories shot with
liquor and clouds of smoke. She'd worn a tin brooch in the

shape of a heart pinned to her chest and red and green ribbons in her hair.

Once she showed me a photograph of my long-dead grandparents, a tiny square of black and white with two stiff figures nudged into its frame. The woman had a shock of white hair, the man wore a hat tipped low over his face, and they both had coals for eyes. She kept the photograph in her underwear drawer, and it carried a waft of fresh cotton, masking its old and cobwebby scent. She let me see it only once or twice, guarding it like a jealous secret.

England took her and brought her up, sent her soft rain and the city of Oxford, with its orderly quadrangles and lofty spires. She worked here and there in libraries, wandering between the stacks with a faraway look in her eyes, stamping books with a ferocity, coming home with ink-smudged thumbs. She said she always wanted something else and now it makes a sort of sense. Perhaps it was easier to lose who you were, if you never really knew in the first place.

We decided to travel to Hungary the year after the Berlin Wall came down. We'd watched it happen on television, seen people balancing atop it, as though thronging the uppermost tiers at a football game, their fists punching the sky. The Berlin night looked unreal, as pickaxes rang out and stone crumbled under bright lights. I remember the word *Freedom* spray painted in white, and the look in my mother's eyes as her lips repeated the same in Hungarian: *szabadság*. She saw the fierce bravery of revolution, the ragged, heartfelt acts of people that believed in change. Beside her on the sofa in our Devon cottage I felt the pressure of her elbow in my side; I watched her feet arch in her pink slippers. I had a mug of tomato soup and I hid my face in it. My father got up to make tea.

The following spring, a letter arrived. It was in a crumpled cream envelope, one corner ablaze with foreign stamps. My mother fell on it and devoured its contents with a hunger it seemed she'd forgotten she had. She carried it about, tucked in the pocket of her apron, or marking the pages of a book. The envelope became mottled with her prints. She said it was from old friends of her parents, inviting her, and us, to stay with them at their house by a lake called Balaton.

"We must go," she said, "our history is important."

History, to me, meant drawings of men with spears, great ships sped along by a hundred oars and a trip to see the famed shrunken head in Exeter Museum. It looked like a clod of compost, or a gnarled root kicked across a forest floor. Distant, remote things, that you paid an admission to see, then walked away or closed the book on. History didn't follow you around. It had no claim on you.

Right away it was as though there was another force within the house. A foreign force, disrupting all the usual rhythms, bringing with it silty wafts of lake water and distracting rhapsodies of glee and woe. My mother became muddled and distant. Supper was often late, and one evening the soup was spoiled with three handfuls of chopped chili instead of peppers. It ended up on the garden, a spicy shock for the worms, and as recompense we were given giant sandwiches filled with fish paste and a handful of potato chips for decoration. I didn't mind, I liked fish paste, but my father raised an eyebrow and turned the sandwich over in his hands before proceeding to eat in very small, tight-lipped bites. Later I heard him saying that my mother's head was

full of only one thing now, and there was no room for anything else in it. I wondered at this proclamation, not sure if
this was what he really thought, as he seemed to voice his
opinion to no one but the cuff of his sleeve or the middle
pages of the newspaper.

Once the trip was confirmed for the summer holidays,
my father begrudgingly turned to what he liked best—
meticulous planning. I wandered into the sitting room
where he sat, poring over a map that seemed to cover the
entire dinner table. He had a magnifying glass, and was
making small, tightly written notes in a leather-back notebook. I slid into a chair and rested my elbows on Poland.

"The Iron Curtain," I said, by means of announcing my
arrival. "I doubt it's a curtain at all."

He looked up. "We can't possibly imagine it, Erzsi."

But I could. I saw the remnants of the Iron Curtain as
tattered shards waving, giant eyelets reaching to the sky and
filings that carried on the wind, leaving their ugly taste in
your mouth. I resolved to carry peppermint candies.

It was funny how time worked. Three weeks later, and
we were plunged into a landscape that seemed a million
miles from the orderly lines on my father's map, and the
markings I'd traced with my fingertip from the safety of
our sitting room. We rumbled through French towns and
blasted down the German autobahn, traversed dashing riv-
ers and swept through mountain pastures, finally winding
up in the dusty Austrian border country. As we crossed into
Hungary, our Western plates aiding our progress past the
mustachioed border guards, my mother twisted in her seat

to face me. The sides of her neck were red and that meant nerves or excitement or both.

"This is Hungary, and it's home," she said.

I gave her a small smile and gazed miserably from the window. *Home?* It was nothing like. We were in a wholly different land. A place where heavy-headed ponies pulled ramshackle carts, and stacks of painted pottery were piled at the sides of the road like a dropped load. I saw a straggle of low-flying storks fly by, strange-looking birds with hunched wings, their long legs trailing behind them. I found myself missing the polished sheen of Austrian villages, with their well-behaved geraniums and fancy shoe shops. And France, with its giant supermarkets that smelled of cheese and spit-roasted chickens, and garage cafés where you could eat a plate of stick-thin fries overlooking the forecourt. But more than anything else I longed for Harkham. Home was the blue door of our cottage with the lion-head knocker, the creak of the floorboard on the third stair, the cookie tin with roses on the top shelf of the larder. How could my mother so easily forsake such essential things? I thought of the clothes I didn't pack, my gym shoes under the bed, the blue butterfly net by the back door. And my parents, sunk in a sofa side by side, watching a wall tumble down on television.

As we arrived at Lake Balaton I remember squealing. I'd been craning forward in my seat for the last ten miles, searching for a flash of blue, and suddenly it was upon us. The Hungary we had been promised, the Hungary we had been told about in the mornings, as I was made late for school, and in the evenings, as suppers burned on the stove. Balaton, at fifty miles long and ten across it was more sea than lake. A terrific expanse of shining water, bigger than a dream. The shoreline was filled with endless one-of-a-kind dwellings, low-rise hotels, 1960s-built apartment blocks with yellowing screens and faded awnings and private houses with homemade *zimmer frei* placards advertising rooms in German. There were cafés with sun umbrellas spotted with the logos of exotic soft drinks, shaded terraces with twisted vines and wicker fencing and newly built pizza parlors with Western-sounding names. Kiosks sold newspapers packed with tiny type, high-bouncing rubber balls and Day-Glo ice cream, and watermelon vendors drove pickups with their giant green moon fruits piled high in the back.

We stayed at a *nyaraló,* which is Hungarian for *holiday house.* I remember first wrapping my tongue around the word. My mouth fell slack as I rolled the loose consonants. A catching in my throat meant that I was saying it right and I coughed. The *nyaraló* belonged to Zita and Tibor Szabó, the old friends who had written to my mother.

I thought of our arrival. My father batting away a fly and mopping his pink brow, my mother's toes scrunching in the soil as she breathed in the perfumed air. She'd spent the summers of her childhood at Balaton, and always talked of the vast expanse of water, *the Hungarian sea.* I pictured a young Marika, running long-legged toward the lake, her slapping sandals throwing up the dust.

The lake house was set back from the road in an unbroken row of holiday rentals and weekend dwellings in a place called Balatonfenyves. It was a pointy house, the shape a child might draw in quick strokes of crayon. Tucked behind a line of scrawny firs, it had a rusted red roof, steeply tiled, with whitewashed walls of scratchy concrete. There was a first-floor balcony made of dimpled yellow glass panes, where we hung our dripping swimsuits and garish towels to dry at the end of every scorching day. To the front there was crazy paving, the cracks smattered with weeds and dotted with rogue flowers. In the long hours of the sun-heavy afternoons I hopscotched my way across those slabs, the concrete shining white, my shadow leaping. And the garden, a plot slung to the side and behind, ending in a tangle of dislocated corn stems and drunken, lolling vines. I came to own that patch, scouting through the tall grasses. I marked my name in cool scattered ashes.

We spent a little under two weeks at the lake house, and yet it has stayed with me, unshakably, down the years.

I wondered if the inflatable whale was still in the garden shed, its skin patched from a puncture repair kit. Once, I'd scrambled onto its broad and slippery back and floated on the lake's shining surface, in the early morning light. I called to my mother and father as they stood on the bank until I drifted behind the tall reeds and they were gone. No sound but for the passing churn of a pedalo's paddles, no sight but for a distantly thrown Frisbee splicing the sun.

And the smell of the place. It lingers still in the creases of my skin. Dried paprika and frying meat, the strange detergent in the bathroom and the stale heat when the French doors were shut at bedtime.

Zita and Tibor Szabó knew my mother when she was a girl, living in an apartment block in Budapest, just steps back from the waters of the Danube. Marika said she remembered eating great bowls of fish soup with them at her parents' kitchen table. Zita would bring round slices of her world-famous honey cake folded in her apron, sticky crumbs settling in the creases. Tibor and her father would crack walnuts together, sitting side by side on the narrow balcony. They spat shards of shell to the courtyard floor below, and now and again tossed her one, little Marika catching it like a kiss—woody tasting with a metallic edge. To me, they sounded like the oldest of memories, cloudy but nascent.

The Szabós almost looked like English old people, but then not quite. As though at the last minute someone had grabbed a pair of scissors and chopped them strange haircuts, and raided a trunk of odds and ends to dress them. Zita had white hair that ran to her shoulders and wore long cotton housecoats and clumpy sandals. Tibor was tall as a giant and seemed to like it best when he was in his swimming trunks, shiny black ones, with his belly ballooning above the waistband. His head was prickled with blond stubble, and his chin was smooth as a baby's. They were kind and sweet to us, going about humming and singing and pinching our cheeks with a familiarity that amused me and embarrassed my father. Marika, on the other hand, was besotted. She glowed in their presence, at once humbled and entranced, as though they held a secret that she hoped to one day learn.

To welcome us to Hungary, the Szabós organized a small party. They invited friends of theirs, most of whom knew my mother as a small girl and remembered her parents with sad smiles and faraway looks. Zita and Tibor took great pride in the nine or ten people they had mustered, and my mother was touched. She clasped both of their hands and dropped kisses on their cheeks, with ferocity. The old people cooed like dumpy pigeons.

The most irritating of the guests was a woman called

Marcie. My mother had known her as a tiny child, and Marcie didn't look as though she had grown up a lot since then. She'd lived in the apartment below my mother's, and they'd played together in the shared courtyard, twirling their jump ropes and ducking between rows of laundry, their cries bouncing off the four walls that surrounded them. Marcie was tiny, a shrimpy-looking person with a mop of yellow hair and a pink mouth like a cherry. She was noisy, too, and swept my mother along with her as though they were old accomplices. She insisted on them clinking glasses at every opportunity, and when she wasn't crowing she was whispering furtively, cupping her hand to her mouth in cartoon fashion. And she almost entirely ignored my father and me.

It wasn't just any party, it was a *szalonna* party. The point was to sit in a circle, toasting fan-shaped pieces of fat over a roaring fire. Everyone had their own stick, and just as the fat was glistening and ready to drop, you took a piece of bread and dropped it onto it, shaking paprika and salt and pepper, then eating it quickly, with your mouth burning. The grown-ups soothed their tongues with liquor, see-through stuff in bottles with homemade labels that sent them breaking into raucous song and tears popping from their eyes.

My mother was sitting on the other side of the fire, in the thick of the Hungarians and with Marcie beside her, crossing and knocking their sticks above the flames. She was the beautiful one, the elegant one, whose laugh was clean and clear and rose above the others. I couldn't help feeling that she was surrounded by people that felt they could lay claim to her. And, in turn, I saw my mother lay claim to them. In their company she seemed to stand for something beyond the girl of ten years old, the one who left Hungary years ago. *She* was the one who had come back. They had but a passing interest in her little English daughter and gentle husband. Together they talked of long-lost friends and replayed old jokes. They shrieked with laughter and wrapped their arms around one another, embracing my mother as one of them. I watched from across the fire. I saw my father drop his piece of *szalonna,* and root around in the ashes with his stick for it, one hand swiping at mosquitoes. I prayed no one else had spotted him in this failure. I felt like shouting at the top of my voice, but what would I say? That the normal rules were simply not being followed? That no one should be this happy this quickly, or this busy, with their kisses and toasts and sighs as though it was a day of celebration, when it wasn't at all? It was a day like any other. *What was everybody doing in England?* I wondered. Nice, everyday things probably. Visits to the duck pond and the renewal of library books. Sucking orange lollipops but wearing jeans because the sun wasn't quite shining.

I've always believed that it was at the *szalonna* party that my mother decided she wanted to stay on in Hungary. That her life should be there, not at home in Harkham with us. Because afterward, life at the lake house seemed to alter its course. There were still the swimming trips, the lounging in rickety deck chairs beneath the spread of the pine trees, the hot and dusty walks to the shop to buy giant watermelons and packets of cherry sherbets. But there was something else in the air. Zita and my mother engaged in long and muttered conversations in the kitchen, over the heat of the stove. Their voices would rise, then quickly fall as I appeared in the doorway, even though I couldn't understand a word that they were saying. My mother walked around looking chastised and childlike. She chewed the ends of her hair and ran from rooms.

My father and I kept our distance through all this. We went swimming at the lake. As we paddled and splashed our way through the warm water, the gray mud oozing between our toes, I decided it was a good time to ask him something that had been bothering me.

"Is Mum sad?" I said.

"Sad? No. Why do you say that? I don't know if sad is the word. Although it's very emotional for her, I suppose, coming here like this, after all this time. She's always felt a great connection with Hungary. I think she's wanted to come back here her whole life. This was her childhood, you know, Erzsi. You never forget your childhood."

I watched my father. He always spoke quietly and deliberately, but now more than ever. And he appeared to be talking more to himself than to me. It was in the way he nodded as he spoke, the way he turned his hand to find the right words.

"We need to give her some space," he said. "I think that's the modern term." There was something in his tone that I seized on.

"She seems different," I said.

"She's always been different," he said with a quick, sharp laugh. "Come on now, Little Betty, show me your front crawl."

I started to swim for him, but my stroke was a frantic doggy paddle as my mind whirred. My mother *was* different and I wasn't imagining it. Her hair looked darker and looser, her eyes deeper. And her voice was unrecognizable, as it lifted and jumped and garbled successions of incomprehensible phrases. She'd even forget sometimes and turn to my father and me, throwing us the same strange words. Anybody could see that something in her had altered. My father was the same at least, but out of his depth. He even looked vulnerable, his pale legs in shorts that still held the store-bought crease, his neck and forearms burned a rude red from the sun beating through the windshield as he drove us safely and cautiously all the way to Hungary.

A shout from the shore broke this thought. I listened to the voice, at first not recognizing my name being called, Erzsébet, each syllable rendered unfamiliar, weighed down by a foreign tongue. My feet reached for the bottom and found it. Zita and my mother were standing at the jetty, waving to us. I imagined them tangled in one of their debates, taking their arguments to the lake path, and looking to the pair of us for distraction. And so we gave it to them. My father and I waved back, then we waded to the bank, our giant steps throwing up the water so that it fell around us like silver rain.

Over the days that followed we increasingly swapped conspiratorial looks, our own bond tightening as my mother was lost to the Szabós. My father muttered, *These crazy Hungarians,* when no one was looking, and I had to shush him, shaking my head until the garden spun. I saw my father rest a gentle hand on my mother's arm once; I heard him say, *We don't have to stay. I know they're your parents' friends but if it's all too much…* As though he was trying to draw her back to our side. But she looked at him as though he'd spoken nonsense or suggested the most ridiculous thing. She said, *What are you saying, David? Are you all right?* As though he was the one who was going mad.

It was decided that we would spend a few days at Balatonfüred, a spa town across the lake. *To break up the stay,* my father said. There was no irony to his remark, not then. Zita and Tibor waved us off from the veranda, Zita dabbing a handkerchief to her eyes, Tibor already turning back toward the house. I found their sadness melodramatic, but surprised myself by shedding hot tears as soon as the engine started. We rumbled onto the lake road and I stared hard out of the back window. No one noticed I was crying.

Why did we ever bother to go to Balatonfüred? Did my mother think that she might feel different, if she was in a different place? I never asked her, even when I had the chance. Perhaps by then it seemed irrelevant. Looking back, it just felt like she was trying to give us the slip, in the clumsiest fashion. And we kept on tagging along, doggedly trying to enjoy ourselves on holiday, but failing miserably. The happiness I enjoyed was made of stolen moments, the warm kiss of the lake water around my middle, the syrupy juice when I bit into a melon, the first *Wiener schnitzel* I ever had, huge and golden, draped across my plate. The bigger picture set me uneasy. I didn't trust it, but I didn't yet know why.

Balatonfüred was famous for a wine festival that took place along its elegant tree-lined promenade. When we got there the waterfront was ringed with crowds, and the air was thick with music and laughter. I was presented with a huge sweet corn on a stick, salted and smeared with butter, and a coil of sausage striped with bright mustard. We flitted through the crowd, my father and I holding hands, hurrying to keep up with my mother. She made friends easily, delighting people with her English-accented but fluent

Hungarian. In the end she stopped turning to my father and me to translate her conversations. She forgot us. My father could tell that I was growing restless, so he asked if I wanted to go down to the water and look across to the lights on the other side. I tapped at my mother's elbow, asking if she wanted to come.

"No, you two go," she said, pulling her hair out of her eyes. "I'll just be here."

"Please come," I said.

She shook her head. She smiled, and reached a cool hand to touch my cheek.

"You're very warm, Erzsébet. I think you've had too much sun."

"I feel a bit funny," I said.

"Go to the water," she said, "there might be some breeze there."

She clasped me suddenly to her. I let myself be hugged and said into her hair, "Will you be here?"

"Yes. Be careful. And stay with your father."

We went down to the water's edge, but I didn't like the lake at night. The masts of boats clinked and the water threw up strange shadows and there was a twitchy breeze that wasn't there by day. We didn't stay long. But by the time we'd rejoined the party, my mother was nowhere to be seen. We guessed she'd wandered off and got caught in a new crowd. We expected to see her swept up in the arms of a sweet old Hungarian, or tickling the chins of some pudgy babies, but she was nowhere. We combed the promenade, up and down, but in the end the only thing to do seemed to be to return to the guesthouse.

The lamp above the guesthouse's front steps was lit and

a ring of moths and midges spun below it. My father felt in his pocket for the key while I turned and looked to the side. I don't know what it was that drew my eyes, for it was dark in the garden, the only light coming from the small lamps that dotted the edges of the lawn. But I was aware of something. A presence, on the terrace. I stared hard and then tugged at my father's sleeve. It was the undeniable outline of my mother. She was sitting with her back to us, facing the view that by day was full of the tops of trees, hotel rooftops and the strip of lake beyond. By night it was all nothingness, and it looked like she was staring off the edge of the world.

"Go on inside," my father said softly. "I'll catch up with you."

The next morning the three of us breakfasted together on the terrace. I sat opposite my parents, watching them over my slice of bread and chocolate spread. I turned a muddy smile to them both, but neither were looking at me. My mother appeared darker than usual, something about the eyes, and her hair hung in wet twists from her morning shower. Beside her, my father was a pale ghost, with just a flush of red about his throat, like sunburn or a kept-in anger.

If I was older or braver, I thought, I'd say, *You gave us quite a scare last night, Mum.* I'd assume the offhand but pointed way that adults seemed to manage. But I didn't dare. Because something wasn't right that morning. The night before had not yet been left behind. It was in the way my mother stirred sugar into her coffee, her spoon clattering, a little slopping onto the cloth. And the way she sat very still as she drank, one finger slowly tucking a strand of hair behind her ear.

It was my father who spoke in the end.

"Here's the plan, Erzsi. You and I are going to have a day at the beach. Marika has some things to do in the town, so it'll be just the two of us. How's that?"

Marika. He never called her that. At least, not when he was speaking to me, not when what he meant was *your mother.*

"You don't mind, do you, Erzsi? If I go off on my own?" she asked.

"Can't you come with us?" I asked.

My mother shook her head, said, "I'm sorry," as her fingers circled at her temples.

My father stood, the feet of his chair screeching on the paving. The sound appeared to alarm him because he jumped and looked suddenly pale.

We went to the beach, paying our few forints to go behind the iron railing and sit on a well-trimmed lawn, as a lifeguard in red shorts and a white shirt patrolled lazily. Viewed from the busy beachside, the lake looked different, and not at all like the stretch of water by the Fenyves house.

"I don't know if I want to go in," I said, watching the shallows as they teemed with children and adults, splashing and jostling. "I think I'd like to just sit here."

"Oh, come on," my father said. He took off his shirt and put his hands on his hips. "I'm all set."

I thought how pale he looked, his chest like uncooked chicken, whereas everyone around us was baked and roasted. But I slipped my hand into his and together we walked toward the water. *We're two sore thumbs,* I thought. *We don't belong here at all.*

We went back to the guesthouse a little after three o'clock.

My mother surprised us both by waiting for us in the hotel lobby, sitting on one of the padded wicker chairs. She had a bag at her feet.

"Hello," she said, rising as we came in.

"We had the cotton candy," I rushed, "and an ice cream. I had melon flavor, and one with raisins in it."

"Did you?" she said. "And was it wonderful? Did you love it?"

"I felt sick afterward," I said. "But maybe that was the sun. What's that bag?"

"Yes, what's that bag, Marika?" said my father.

My mother flicked her eyes to the receptionist, who disappeared into the back office, folding her arms across her boxy chest. "I'm…taking some time away. I… It's as I said last night, and this morning, I can't…help it."

"You didn't say anything this morning," I cried.

"David, it's everything I said. I have to do this. I'm sorry, I'm so sorry."

She looked like she would cry then. She drew herself up, so her chest and shoulders were higher than usual, so her neck stretched with long cords. She pinched the end of her nose. It wasn't how a mother should look.

"I didn't think you meant it," I heard my father say. "You've said it all before, a hundred times."

"I meant it."

"But you didn't say anything!" I cried again, flicking my head from one to the other, wondering why they couldn't hear me.

I saw my father wipe his hands on his shorts. "I'm not doing this here," he said as the reception telephone began to ring.

"There's nothing more to do," said my mother to him. "I'm really very sorry."

I turned and walked a few steps away. I stayed indoors but faced the screen door, and pushed my nose up against the green mesh of the mosquito net with its frayed edges. I looked out onto the guesthouse garden, with the twisting path and the spotlights set at the edges. I listened to the ringing telephone, and the silence of my parents, and counted paving slabs, white in the sun. I remembered the fierce whisper that had woken me up one night at the lake house. I'd tossed and turned in the night, sleeping only fitfully. I'd heard the hushed voice, saying, *You could never be happy here. I don't think you could be happy anywhere, and you know it, too.* Then I'd been swallowed back up by the night. In the morning I'd forgotten all about it. But I remembered it now, with startling clarity.

"Erzsi?" my mother said in a soft voice. "Could you come outside with me, please, darling?"

I waited a moment, before I turned around, and when I did I saw that both my parents' faces were wet with tears. Their cheeks were shining and their mouths were slightly open. In a different light they'd have looked almost happy. But I wasn't confused anymore. I knew exactly what was happening. I nodded and followed her outside. Placing my feet just where hers had been, as though she'd left prints.

Simply, Hungary was her home and she missed it. That was how she explained it to me, at the time. I remember us both sitting on a swing seat in the guesthouse garden, my mother rocking it gently back and forth as she spoke. I was curled into her side, like a tiny baby, hanging on for dear life, with wet cheeks and a puckered mouth. But even then, I knew I wasn't being treated like a baby, because she had graced me with something like the truth. I recognized it, and felt grave in its presence. She cupped my face in her two cool hands and said, "You're nine years old, Erzsi. I can't lie to you. You have to know I love you and that will never change. It's just that Daddy and I…don't fit anymore. But here, I fit. It's a place I love and I need to be here. Can you understand that? Your father can't, you see."

I'd been able to neither nod nor shake my head, for it was clamped gently but firmly by my mother's palms. Instead, I blinked, rapidly, and tears scuttled down my face. But my chest swelled, for she was taking me into her confidence. She was counting on me to understand her, where my father could not. That hadn't happened before. I wiped my tears with the back of my hand.

She told me that she remembered every tiny detail of her life in Hungary, and she couldn't live anymore with all that memory just fighting to get out. She said it was like being stuck indoors on a beautiful sunny day, with your face pushed to the window. In the end you'd have two choices: turn away and make do with the gloom, or break the glass and run for it. We both knew that she was definitely the glass-breaking type.

We agreed that I was to visit all the time. I told my father this, as I recounted our conversation to him, curled under the top sheet of the big double bed later that evening. When we were still there but she had gone.

"We didn't say goodbye, she wouldn't let me. Because 'goodbye' means an end, doesn't it? And she said it wasn't, she said this was just the beginning."

"I said goodbye," he croaked.

"We said *szervusz*. You know, it means *hello* and *good-bye* in Hungarian. It means both. *Szervusz*. She said she'd write all the time and we'd be like pen pals. She said…she said we'd be best friends. That's what Mum said…." I lost my voice in tears.

My father stood over by the window, his arms folded across his chest, his neck bent. A ragged bird man. I wanted him to gather me up in his wings, but he wasn't moving. He was staring out of the glass. I heard him say, "Why she bothered bringing us here, I'll never know." The view before him was of the lake, shining like a mirror held to the sun, its water glistening with splintered diamonds. He drew the curtains against its glare and the room turned to darkness. I closed my eyes and joined it.

It seemed impossible that we could leave my mother behind in Hungary, but we did. We drove all the way home to England without her. I sat in the front seat, where she normally was, with my hands folded in my lap. Through Germany, I discovered I could hold my breath for the count of thirty elephants at a time. And that if I wound the window all the way down the wind would swipe the tears from my cheeks and dry my eyes. I thought of my mother and father at home in Harkham, and all the things I'd been aware of but thought that that was just the way it was. My mother's crashing doors, my father's retreats to the garden shed. The snipes at the supper table, that always missed their mark because either they didn't notice or didn't care. Somewhere in Austria my father put on an Elvis Presley cassette and we sang along, chock-full of faux cheer. In his rallying, my father was uncharacteristically full of voice. Just before the ferry port we traipsed around the aisles of one of the supermarkets I liked, the one with a tusked elephant for a logo, and he bought me a plastic fountain pen and a giant bag of chewy sweets that locked my jaw and made my gums sting. He drank a bottle of beer standing in the parking lot, and missed the bin when he threw it. It covered the ground in green glitter and when he stooped to pick up the bigger pieces I don't know why but I pretended not to notice that his finger dripped red onto the toes of his shoes.

The white cliffs of Dover were smudged gray. We drove in convoy with the other cars from the ship, following arrows pointing this way and that. A giant poster advertising a chocolate bar greeted us with the headline Welcome Home. The bottom corner panel was missing, a fierce onshore wind tearing at the loose edges. The *e* of *Home* flapped.

"Now that we're back in England, there will be questions, Erzsi," my father said.

I shifted in my seat and glanced across at him.

"People are like that," he went on. "They won't be able to help themselves. But you mustn't fret, Little Betty. You must let me answer them."

He took a hand from the wheel and squeezed my knee. I mustered a smile.

"Okay," I said, and in a sweep of worry, suddenly school loomed large. I needed a new skirt for the fall. My pencil case had a hole in it. We would have to work out where to buy these things from. I made a crisscross on an old scar on my hand and concentrated very hard on watching it fade. I made another.

We drove through funny little terraced streets where French fry wrappings blew along the pavements. We climbed a hill and the town began to fall away. The scarred cliffs, the restless gray sea, the craggy, soaring gulls, all receded.

"Questions, questions," he said, drumming his fingers. "For an inquiring mind, I have a distinct dislike of certain questions."

I looked straight ahead, my marked hand smarting. "I dislike questions, too," I said. "Distinctly."

I remember that on the afternoon we returned, the Devon skies opened to deliver a summer downpour. Rain lashed against the window of the living room, and my father and I huddled together on the sofa. We wore our pajamas and dressing gowns; our sun-bleached holiday clothes were discarded in the laundry basket. We ate hot buttered toast for supper, and lit all the lamps for coziness. Later, we pushed some dominoes around the kitchen table. My father opened his mouth to talk and I prepared myself to listen, my heart pounding. But he was only blowing on his tea, the steam rising in front of his spectacles.

The telephone rang the day after we'd returned home. We were sitting side by side at the dining-room table, the pieces of a giant jigsaw puzzle before us. It was an English village scene, and a row of stone cottages was taking shape, with a patch of sky behind. We both jumped at the sound of ringing. My father carefully laid a piece of chimney before getting up to answer it. I watched him walk across the carpet, his slippers making no sound, fearing that with every slow step the telephone would cut out. That he'd be too late. I dropped the piece of blue sky I was holding.

"Hurry, Daddy!" I cried.

After what seemed like an eternity, my father opened the door and beckoned to me. He placed the receiver in my hand, very carefully, as though it might shatter, and then went into the dining room, closing the door softly behind him.

I stood with my feet pointed in, like a crooked ballet dancer.

"Hello?" I said, as though peeping into a deep hole.

I shut my eyes, and my mother's voice sounded at once very close and dreadfully far. But her words seemed to wrap themselves around me, curl under my armpits and tuck behind my ears, with a gentle music. It was a different sort of mother that spoke to me. A honeyed version, laying words like garlands. I curled into the chair in the hallway and put my lips very close to the receiver. I tried hard not to cry, in case my tears fell into the telephone and cut off the connection. My cheeks ached after a while, from all the beaming.

When I went back in, I struggled to contain myself with my father. I wanted to tell him the stories I'd been told, the things my mother said. I wanted to cry, *She loves me, she loves me.* But instead I took my seat at the table and bent over the jigsaw. He turned to me, squeezing my fingers with the lightest of touches. I picked up my piece of sky again, and with a triumphant "Look!" slotted it into place.

If only we'd left things there. My mother in Hungary, my father and I newly allied. If only we'd picked ourselves up and found a way to get along without her. Then all the years that followed would never have happened. Or, if they had, they'd have been different. Perhaps they would have mattered less. But, as it was, her absence filled our house. She was everywhere. I carried her about with me, my head and heart creaking with her weight. And by night, she stole in and visited my father, too. Tempting and soothing, with equal breath.

She might have left us, you see, but she never went away.

Morning had broken and outside the window Saturday was everywhere, unapologetic with its backfiring exhausts, its passing thrum of music, its shouts and hollers. The world, it seemed, stopped for no one.

My apartment felt claustrophobic suddenly, its walls inching closer, its ceiling bowing low. I needed to be outside, somewhere where there were people, but I could remain distant from them, surrounded by noise, but alone with my thoughts. I picked up *The Book of Summers,* and hugged it to my chest in an uneasy press. Against me, it rose and fell with every breath I took, as though it was part of me, as though I couldn't shake it off if I tried. With heavy movements I rose from my chair and went to the door. I scooped my bag from the floor where I'd dropped it last night, and still carrying the book in my arms I left the house. Stepping into the bright morning light as though it was just another summer's day, I made for the park.

Would this be how I conjured her? By laying a blanket on still-damp grass, beneath a sagging chestnut tree in a city park. By turning the pages of a book she'd made, and losing myself one by one, in every summer that we'd had together, at the villa in the hills. After so many years of tightening latches against her tapping, turning my head from shadows that shifted at the edges of my sight. Trying so very hard to forget, thinking that remembering was the worst thing

I could do. Would this be how I mourned her? Now that she was really gone?

I leaned my back against the trunk of the tree and opened the book.

CHAPTER THREE

In the picture it is 1991 and I am ten years old. I am standing by a tree, one arm reaching up and holding loosely to a branch. I am pitched into shadow but the light falls in bright patches at my feet. Behind me there is a house, bathed in sunshine, its white walls luminous. It is the same house that appears in all the pictures. It is Villa Serena. I am posing, and although my face is darkened I am smiling. It is an odd smile, tight-lipped, and my chin is tipped. But the shape of me, the arm thrown up in studied nonchalance, the awareness of the looming house, throws light of a different sort on the scene. Just as an angler holds a giant fish to the camera, and a hunter poses with one foot on his kill, I, too, am pictured with my prize. The house shines brilliantly behind me, bold and undeniable.

It was as though I imagined that somehow I'd tricked the fates by being there, that the doing was all mine, when really it was my father.

As I looked at the page, I plummeted. I can't remember being in the photograph. I don't recall how it felt, to stare down the camera with the winning, hard-edged smile that my lips formed in that split second. And I have no recollection of the shade that the tree brought, or how my toes might have twitched in the warm sun at my feet. But I believed what I was seeing, and I knew it to be true. Once, in this same life, I was really there.

I turned the page, and as I did so, I caught myself looking at my hands. These same fingers touched the bark of that tree, I thought, twenty years ago, and yet they bore no traces. With the book upon my knee, it struck me that the passing of time was a magical, fearful sort of thing.

I hadn't seen myself at ten since I was, more or less, that very age, glancing in mirrors. My father's house always had paintings on the walls, not photographs. He'd never developed the reel of film he took from our first trip to Hungary, and I always understood why. For a long time, though, I ached to see those pictures, and painted them in my mind as I struggled to sleep or stared at the blank page in my school notebook. As the years passed and I strengthened my resolve, my childhood fell to time. And I drew a lid on it, as one might the contents of an old chest, pushed to the corner of an attic. If you had asked me yesterday what I had been like at ten I would have shrugged. The usual things. I would not have added "secretive," though I would have thought it. Nor would I have mentioned "steely, hard-edged, like a sharpened stone." Or "unhappy." Unhappiness, I was sure, had been my silent, constant bedrock.

But in the photograph, I didn't look like any of those things.

I looked happy.

A postcard came unstuck, its glue long dried out. In its

top corner it said *Esztergom, Hungary,* in an ornate font. The image was taken low over the water, and the foreground was of the river Danube, its surface glistening. The sky above was a loaded blue-gray, and to me it looked as though a lightning storm was threatening, the town's deep summer stupor shortly to be split and soaked. The sunshine on the water had a hint of neon. I recognized the dome of the basilica, a perfect bonnet, and the castle walls below it. Pearly, red-topped houses lined the shore. From that angle, Esztergom appeared like an island, but I knew it wasn't. We could drive there in five minutes from Villa Serena, my head stuck out of the window like a dog's. I once ate a lollipop standing by the castle walls, orange ice melting on my tongue. And in the basilica I bought a postcard of the pope, because he looked like Hebert Smythe, who ran the store near our house. Marika had erupted in laughter when I'd told her this, and I remember my delight in knowing that I could still amuse her. I'd hopped on the spot, my hand looking for hers as my own tinkling laugh was lost in her guffaw.

I pressed the edges of the card down, but it refused to stick again.

As the weeks passed since she left, our Harkham life found a new rhythm. The first days of our return seemed to belong to another time altogether. Then, the air in the cottage had been thick with our loss. I couldn't speak for long without choking on my words and my eyes stinging, as though the smoke of her swirled out from under the skirting boards. My father sat with his hand covering his mouth, his nostrils flared wide, and I knew he was feeling it, too. I would fall against things as my legs failed me—the arm of the sofa, the apple tree's rough trunk, my father's hip. I clung on to what I could. And I kept hearing noises, my head jerking on its loose string. *Was that the telephone? A knock at the door? My name called: Erzsébet?*

When my father wasn't looking, I crossed my fingers, squeezed my eyes and willed her to appear. In bed at night I pressed my palms tight together and made all the promises I could think of. And she came to me, as she said she would. Her voice over the telephone, her words in letters. I held on to her by the thread she gave me. And in the meantime, my father tried his very best.

In September, soon after school had started back, there was a party, where pink and white balloons dangled in the high corners of the room and a table was set for little girls with paper napkins and yellow bows. I was invited, along with six other classmates. A table with a flowered cloth was piled high with gifts, and I saw my own gift somewhere near the top. It was wrapped in brown paper with a big red ribbon. I'd tied it myself, my father lending his finger so I could make the bow. And he had helped me choose it from a dazzling array in the toy shop. It was a board game, Scrabble, which he had taken in his hands with enthusiasm.

"I think this might be just the thing," he'd said.

"Do you think so?" I'd replied uncertainly, wondering if the long-lashed doll dressed in pink dungarees wouldn't perhaps be better. Or a luminous jump rope, for jumping in the dark.

"Well, it's your choice, Erzsi," he said, "but it is such a fun game."

"That's true," I said, although I'd never played.

At the party I'd presented it to Catherine, the birthday

girl, and I was shy at the giving of the gift, twisting into a
half curtsy as I turned away. Now it was on the table with
all the others.

A cassette of birthday songs was put on, and Catherine
capered about the living room as her mother handed her
presents to open, and her friends gathered around. I twisted
the corner of my T-shirt as my own gift was selected. I concentrated hard as Catherine shook it, rattled it, thrilling at
the noise of the pieces moving inside.

"Careful, darling," said her mother.

"She won't break it," I said, flushed with the secret of its
contents, "not easily, anyway."

The careful wrapping was torn and Scrabble was revealed. I beamed.

"Oh," said Catherine, "a game," and reached out her
hand for the next gift.

"Aren't you going to say 'thank you'?" said Catherine's
mother, then turning. "Thank you, Erzsi, that's very kind
of you."

I nodded and twisted my hands in my lap.

The party rushed on, and soon Catherine was seated in a
heap of discarded wrappings, torn paper with poodles and
sailboats and spirals of cut ribbons. Gifts were held up and
cherished, a pair of slippers like ballet shoes, a video with
sing-along tunes and a toy microphone. My Scrabble was
left on the floor, half-hidden by discarded wrapping. Afterward, as everyone moved to the garden, I stayed behind
to retrieve it. I set the box on the table, removing a stray
piece of sticky tape that had attached itself to it. I glanced
around, then took off the lid, fished among the letters and
pocketed one. I ran outside to join the others.

That evening, my father collected me from the party and drove me home. He asked me if my friend had liked the game.

"Oh, yes," I said, "she thought it was lovely."

"Ah, good," he said, pleased. "A good idea, then. I'm glad."

"A very good idea," I said.

Glancing across at him, I surreptitiously felt in my pocket. My fingers closed around the little square letter I had taken. "Thank you for choosing it, Dad," I added.

It was an *M*. *M* for Mother. *M* for Marika. I doubted that Catherine would miss the piece. I wouldn't have taken it otherwise. In Scrabble, it was worth just three points.

I believe my father spoke to Marika no more than three or four times that first year. One of those was on a Sunday afternoon, and I remember every detail of it. I was curled on the sofa reading, with a blanket tucked around my legs for there was the first chill of autumn outside and it was drafty in the sitting room. We had a big fireplace and every so often a breath of wind would stir the dust in the grate. I heard the telephone ring and knew it was Marika, for my father closed the door behind him and his voice hit the low tones that were reserved for all things concerning her. I marked my place in the book and struggled up so that I was sitting neatly, waiting to be called to the phone. I quickly thought of new things to tell her since we'd last spoken, that I had come third in my class in a history test, that I had finished reading her copy of *Robinson Crusoe,* that I'd used up the last of her shampoo from the bathroom cupboard, and where did she buy it from, the one with hazelnuts on the label that smelled sweet like treacle? I crossed my legs and tried to order all of the other things I wanted to say, but in the moment my mind went blank. My head throbbed unhelpfully. I suddenly heard raised voices in the hallway. I imagined our porch had been stormed, and my father accosted as he sat in the telephone chair. I grabbed the blanket for protection and ran to the door. I opened it very quietly and carefully, and through the chink saw my father bang down the receiver and smack the flat of his hand hard against the wall. *Slap!* There were no intruders, there was no fight.

"Daddy?"

"Erzsi!"

He wheeled round, his face aghast to see me.

"Why were you shouting?" I said. "Where's Mum gone?"

He came and knelt down in front of me, as though I was much smaller than I really was. He brushed my cheek with the knuckle of one finger, as if he was wiping away a tear when I wasn't crying, not yet.

"I'm sorry," he said. "Erzsi, I'm sorry. I didn't mean to alarm you."

"Why couldn't I speak to Mummy?"

"Next time," he said. "Next time."

"What if she doesn't call again?"

I fell into him and buried my nose in the wool of his sweater. He wrapped his arms around me in a hug but he held me gently, as though I might break if he squeezed too hard. We stayed like that, not moving, until he carefully peeled himself away. I stood with my arms by my sides like a toy soldier.

"Erzsi, if there's one thing I know about your mother, it's how much she loves you."

"But she didn't want to speak to me," I said.

"She did, of course she did. She was calling for you, not me."

"So why didn't I speak to her?" I said.

"Erzsi, that was me. I'm so sorry. I just don't know what's best. I don't know how to make you happy. I don't know..."

I went back into his sweater, and my tears wetted his shoulder. I heard him say, "Sorry," over and over, and rub my back in slow circles. Around and around.

I knew then that he must miss her, too. That for all his show, she had torn a hole in his life, as well. Perhaps he was only coping better because he knew what it was like to be without her. He can't have been married to Marika all of his life. But me? I'd never known a day without her. As he gripped me tightly, I wanted to turn to his ear and whisper, *Tell me about the day you met.* I imagined them courting as school sweethearts. Him scratching her name on the underside of a desk. Her whispering his name in girlish circles. But I knew I could never ask a thing. Would never ask a thing. It was much better to make up our own answers sometimes, and content ourselves that way. My father's hand on my back had slowed, then stopped. After a while it was as though he'd forgotten I was there, so I wriggled gently free of his grip. His lips still moved. *Sorry.* I wondered if he made up his own answers, too, and decided he probably did.

Later we sat side by side on the sofa, eating slices of toast smeared with jam. He'd lit our first fire of the winter and the wet logs hissed and smoked. We were trying to feel cozy. I kept my ears pricked for the ringing of the telephone, but

I had to wait nearly a week before she'd call again. In the time between, my father did everything he could to make amends. He baked cookies from a recipe that he tore out of the newspaper. In the oven they ran into one giant splodge that was burned all along the edges, so he considered the venture a failure but I was delighted by it. I broke off huge misshapen pieces and spilled crumbs all over my school shirt. Another time he woke me up early one morning and we went mushrooming in the misty fields behind the house. I carried a basket and felt like a fairy-tale character with my hands warm in red mittens as around us the world still slept. Afterward, he fried our spoils on the stove and we ate them on top of slices of toast, all before school. On a different day he even tried telephoning my mother for me, but the phone just rang and rang and rang. I imagined the whole of Hungary pulsing with our unanswered call.

When our telephone finally rang again we both knew it had to be her. My father let me answer and disappeared into the kitchen. He came back just to bring me a cup of sweet tea, kneeling down to set it beside me as I sat cross-legged on the floor. Then he tiptoed back down the hall, closing the door behind him, as quietly and carefully as if replacing the lid of a tomb.

Something seemed to shift in him, as the year turned. He saw me devour Marika's letters, and hug the receiver to my chest after I'd spoken to her. He observed the simple joy I got from the things she sent—a postcard of the Danube that I tucked into the pages of a schoolbook, a picture of a poppy field that I propped beside my bedside lamp. But when he gave me the airplane ticket, I still couldn't believe it. I never thought he'd really let me go.

We were sitting at the kitchen table, the remains of our supper on our plates, with a Sunday evening stretching before us. He'd produced it from his pocket, and I'd gasped, as though he were a magician who'd conjured a rabbit. *It's all arranged,* he said. *She's desperate to see you.* And I knew how difficult it would have been for him, but he had done it all the same. I felt love soar inside me, a rush of hot air, and in that moment it was for him, not her. My poor father. In the face of victory, I was humbled. I turned the ticket in my hands and saw the word *Budapest* loom large. It sounded terribly far away. My single seat, 12B, sounded awfully lonely. I started to cry, and he must have thought he was seeing shades of Marika in my tears of joy. He called me a silly thing and dropped a kiss on the top of my ear.

For months I'd lost myself in longing and it had felt safe, the yearning. Now that I was to get my wish I was awed. It was as if I knew that in going to Marika's Hungary, nothing would ever be the same again. Was this how she had once felt? I remembered one windy day when we'd walked together in the fields behind our cottage. It was after the letter had arrived from the Szabós, and after my father had agreed that we would go on holiday. The ground was soft beneath our feet, the grass soggy from April showers, and I sank a little in my Wellingtons as we climbed the hillside. At the highest point of the field Marika stopped suddenly, as though someone had called her name. She flung out her arms, threw her head back and yelled. No specific words, just one long roar, like a charging army. Just at that moment the hood of my coat blew forward onto my head and over my eyes. I struggled to pull it back and turned to see her standing quite still, wiping her mouth with the

back of her hand. The same wind that had torn at my coat
had drawn tears from her eyes. They ran this way and that
down her cheeks. And it took from my mouth the words I
tried to find for her, blowing them clean away. The cows
in the field beside us regarded her with sluggish suspicion.
She noticed their stares, and after a moment she laughed.
Without a word she grabbed my hand and pulled me along
with her. Together we pelted down the hillside, my feet
tumbling over each other in an effort to keep up. We were
complicit, and the moment for worrying about why she was
yelling had passed. We ended up at the bottom in a heap,
our cheeks bright as firelight.

    I worried that I wouldn't recognize her. There was so
much I could remember, but they were the tiny things, like
the way she tapped her spoon on her teacup after stirring in
two sugars—*tap, tap*. The blue band she would pull from
her hair and wear tight around her wrist, snapping it back
and forth when she was thinking, leaving a perfect circu-
lar mark. The dress she wore the day she left, the shape it
made her, as smooth-silhouetted as a sugar shaker. But as
to how she actually looked, the tilt of her chin, the shape
of her shoulders as she turned in a crowd, I was afraid that
I'd forgotten.

    People could change in a year. I knew I had. At ten years
old I was the third tallest girl in my class when I used to be
somewhere in the middle. My hair was a little shorter than
before, cut by my father with a pair of kitchen scissors, and
I had a new sweater on that she wouldn't have seen. It had
been a Christmas present, and had blue and white stripes
like a sailor. For traveling, I had a case that ran on wheels

and was black and square like a magician's box. I pulled it behind me, as if a strange sort of pet.

I was escorted through Arrivals by an attendant from the plane, with a silk scarf tied at her swan-white throat. She'd been with me since London, and had mopped my tears after I said goodbye to my father. She'd placed a hand on my shoulder, and I'd glanced down at it, saw her perfect nails painted bubblegum pink. My father had waited behind the barrier as I stood on tiptoes and handed over my passport. He was still standing there when I went through the X-ray machine, and was there still, as I took my little bag off the conveyor belt and put it back on my shoulders. I'd turned and waved one last time and he stood there behind the glass with one arm raised, the flat of his hand wide open, five fingers saying goodbye.

In the Budapest airport, I watched the people gathered waiting, leaning on the railing, their faces lit with anticipation. There were small children twining their parents' legs, and old men hunched over sticks. There were young women with mops of red-dyed hair, and older women with wide hips and flowered housecoats. I looked for my mother's face in the crowd, imagining her pushing to the front, straining to catch a first glimpse of me, but I couldn't see her.

The itch of tears was just starting at the back of my throat and behind my eyes when I saw her hurrying in through the entrance doors. I held my breath, for she looked exactly the same as she always had. Just as she had by the red umbrellas, that last night she rocked with laughter down by the lakeside. Just as she had at home in Harkham, saving pretty weeds from under my father's trowel, or hanging laundry to dry, laughing as she got tangled in flapping sheets. She hadn't seen me yet, and as I watched her my heart banged in my chest until I worried it would explode with relief and with trepidation. She was late, and anxious, I could tell by the way her legs skittered, her car keys jangling in her fingers, one hand pulling through her hair.

It was then, in that moment, that I decided she would be Marika. There was a girl at school who called her parents by their first names—Caroline and Marcus—and I thought it horrifying and brilliant. Watching her then, as though behind a window, I couldn't conceive of calling out "Mum!" or even whispering it into my sleeve. *Mum* had been someone who'd darned the elbows of my school sweaters, made lumpy porridge and placed a cool hand on my forehead after I sneezed. *Mum* had suggested walks on bright days, put clutches of spring flowers by my bed and sang along to the kitchen radio. She couldn't do those things anymore, now that she had chosen Hungary. She was *Marika*. The taste of it on my lips was alien, but nothing compared to the dreadful, empty ring of *Mum*.

"Erzsi! Erzsi, it's you!"

I was bundled up into a hug and my nose pressed hard against her cheek. She smelled of cooking, a sweet spicy smell that I remembered from the summer before. So she hadn't readied herself with meticulous care, soaped and spritzed in anticipation of my arrival. Instead, she'd simply stepped from her new life, carrying all of its fumes about her.

"Oh, Erzsi," she said, and kissed my hair.

"Lunch smells good," I said, and she laughed at that, pulling me closer again.

"Oh, can you smell it? I didn't have time to change. Come on, let's go. I hate airports. Let's get you home."

And I followed her, my hand held tightly in hers. It was only when we were out of the doors and treading across the parking lot that I realized I hadn't said goodbye to the lady from the plane, with her pointy hat and shiny scarf and painted lips. I hadn't given her as much as a backward glance. I thought of how she had smelled, a colorful bouquet of scent that made me feel cleaner and brighter just for catching it. She didn't drag the smell of foreign kitchens with her. It made me think of something Marika used to say: *they'll have to take us as they find us.* She said it if people were coming around to the house and there was no time, or inclination, to neaten things. It had a scrappy pride about it. Now it seemed *I* was to take Marika as I found her. As I climbed into the front seat of her car, a cranky-looking thing, I decided that was exactly what I would do. Because despite the new smell and the old clothes, the lateness and the brisk hug, I was as much in love with Marika as I'd ever been. I looked across at her and felt such a swell of happiness to be beside her again that I thought I might explode. It didn't matter that she'd been late to meet me. Or that she rammed her keys in the ignition and looked over at me and laughed as if this was just another day. She was perfect.

As we left the airport, I stared out of the window at the bright Hungarian afternoon. I let the sunlight climb inside me and lull my racing heart. Five minutes into our journey, five minutes of silence broken only by the rattling sounds of the old car, Marika swung across a lane of traffic to a symphony of horns. She pulled over at the side of the road. She turned off the engine and the car shook as a truck thundered by. She sat for a moment with her hands in her lap and her head dipped. I twisted in my seat, scared that she had gone mad. I put out a tentative hand and touched her arm. She turned and looked at me with such intensity that the backs of my arms prickled and my stomach pitched. My mouth tried to speak but no words came. Marika's eyes were brimming and her red lips were held apart. She had a look of the dragon about her, fire breathing and fantastic.

"Oh, Erzsi," she said in a rush, "I don't know what to say."

And she didn't need to say anything, because then she fell on me, kissing me until my cheeks stung, pulling me so that my arms bent at awkward angles. My knee pushed the gear stick and Marika's elbow sounded the horn. I felt sure that with so much life inside it the car would power up of its own accord and blast wildly into the traffic, killing us both. I shut my eyes tight and surrendered to her grip. For this was love, of the desperate, thieving, glorious kind. Not only the suggestion of it, like the gently pecked kisses of my father, or the feel of his palm lightly on the crown of my head, but an avalanche of blinding, unstoppable, actual love. I let Marika sweep me up and carry me with her for as long as she wanted.

Afterward, we drove on. I felt damp and ached slightly, from the kisses and the tears and her fierce hold. But I was smiling, a true smile that spread across my face and robbed me of any nervous energy. I slumped comfortably in my seat as Marika drove us away from the city and toward the Pilis hills. Budapest was to remain a mystery, just as it had the previous year. I had seen only pictures, of a giant, gray snake of river and bridges like elongated accordions, guarded by lions with stony faces. But I was glad we weren't going, because I thought it would be too easy to lose someone in a city's crowds. Instead, we were headed to the countryside, to Zoltán Károly's house near Esztergom.

Marika had told me about Zoltán. She had written it in a letter and her pen had pressed lighter on those lines as though the nib was merely dusting the page. The words could be missed if you weren't reading carefully. But I had my nose pressed to the page and my fingers pinching the paper tightly. I had breathed in every line of Marika's letters, and heard her voice sound each word in my head. She wrote of Zoltán like this:

I have met a man, Erzsi, something I never looked for or expected, or even, really, wanted. But I do believe in fate, you see. We all have to trust in something. He is a good man. An artist. With a wonderful laugh. And he lives in the countryside, at Villa Serena, surrounded by fields and flowers and forests. I have begun to share my life with him. And he, in turn, has done the same. I call Villa Serena my home, too, now. It is strange, how quickly some places can become a home, even when they are new to us. I hope you will feel the same when you come. I don't know what it is, the place, the people, and something else, something magic. Perhaps it's fate again. But it all combines to somehow be… right. I think you will love it here as much as I do. It's a place to run wild in, to feel the sun on your skin and have the soles of your feet grubby, only washed by water from the stream. We'll stay up late and watch the fireflies. Spot glowworms on the lawn and listen to the nightingales sing. You can do what you like at Villa Serena, Erzsi, it is all here for you. That much I promise. It's a place of freedom. A place for both of us. And I know you will like Zoltán, but only in your own time. I will ask nothing of you here, Erzsi, only to smile and know that you are loved. That much I can promise you.

It was funny how after this letter, it was Villa Serena that my head was full of, not Zoltán. I wanted to be shown a glowworm, to see a firefly against the black of a Hungarian sky. I believed her, that the soles of my feet would be dirty and I'd catch the sun on my skin, because those were the kind of things she had always trusted were good and true. I remember her once hitching up her skirt and wading into an icy river, whooping with delight as her legs turned pimply, then blue. *It's so invigorating, Erzsi!* I also remember my father peering over his plastic cup of coffee, watching her, the edges of his mouth turned down. And another time, when she wanted to remember if she could cartwheel, doing it there on the lawn in Harkham, a perfect whirl of legs and arms and falling hair, ending up in a crumpled but victorious heap in the hedge at the bottom of the garden. She'd held up her grass-stained palms and laughed, and I'd clapped my hands in glee. My father was cross later and said that she could have broken her wrist, but she'd laughed it off and said how wonderful it had felt, to be upside down and spinning around.

I'd only thought of Zoltán later, as I lay in bed and pulled the covers over my head. He sounded like a warrior, a primeval character with a spear and a loincloth. What did he

do when Marika cartwheeled? Pound his chest in apprecia-
tion? Launch a volley of arrows toward the sky? I wondered
if my father knew about him, and decided that he probably
did. These days my father's step had a weary tread about
it and he wore a defeated air, like the coat with the ripped
elbows that he pulled on to go out to the garden. Aunt Jessica told me not to worry, though. She said he was as fine as
he'd ever be, and that it was *just his way*. She was his older
sister, so I supposed I had to trust her. When Marika was
at home, Aunt Jessica had rarely visited; the two of them
never saw eye to eye. I heard Aunt Jessica calling her *a selfish woman* once, another time the word *foreigner* was said,
through gritted pearly teeth and wafts of perfume. Marika
rose to her disapproval every time; she never could turn the
other cheek. On the rare occasions that my aunt visited,
Marika used her extra-hot paprika in the goulash soup she
made, and filled the house with gypsy music that made the
cobwebs tremble, when most of the time she seemed happy
enough with Cole Porter and a cheese sandwich. Her effect
on my father was less pronounced. He simply stayed quiet
when she was around, retreating to the garden or slipping
behind the pages of a newspaper. So I didn't really like heed-
ing her advice; I felt like a traitor to everyone.

Even if my father was fine, I wondered why I wasn't an-
grier at the thought of Zoltán and his house with its fields
and forests and my mother running through them. Had I
been bewitched by talk of fate? I did always love a fairy
story. At home, I'd twisted into a ball under my covers,
hedgehoglike, and thought of Marika. She had, I'd decided,
told me the truth. She had trusted me, placed Zoltán and
his house gently into the palms of my hands and asked that

I hold them carefully, because they were important to her. And I liked being trusted with the truth. From hundreds of miles away and with a few lightly scratched lines she had made me feel like I was the most important person on earth. And that Villa Serena was waiting for me.

Marika drove quietly, her sunglasses hiding her face. Her hair was pulled into a ponytail, a parting cleaved as distinctly as a woodsman's chop. She wore a cotton sundress with giant poppies on it, and the skirt was pulled up around her knees as she drove. I noticed how much browner she was. I looked down at my own pale arm, and decided I very much wanted to be brown, too.

"Erzsi, we can stop and get a cool drink soon. There's a roadside kiosk coming up. Would you like that?"

"I'm okay, thanks."

"Are you sure? It's getting very hot. And I wanted to get a few things to take down with us—a watermelon, for one. Do you remember the watermelons, Erzsi? We had them at Balaton."

I hadn't heard the word *Balaton* spoken by anyone, except myself, in a whole year. My father shuffled and shifted and had taken to approaching all words with caution. And even Marika had avoided it in the cards and letters that she sent with unbending regularity. She wished me Merry Christmas and drew bells and snowflakes and said that in Hungary it was celebrated on Christmas Eve, and it was an angel that brought the gifts. She sent me a postcard of a cowboy dressed in flowing skirts, standing balanced on the backs of two galloping horses, his legs parted. It said Puszta on the front in rounded, flattened pink letters, and this was another word I carried with me, and possessed, like *Balaton*.

"Erzsi, love. I haven't said very much to you, have I? I'm sorry. I had so much I wanted to say, but none of it seems to matter now you're here. Only that I love you. Isn't that how it is? I mean, are there things you want to ask me? There's nothing I wouldn't tell you, Erzsi."

And it seemed enough. It was enough. She loved me. I had dozens of questions that back home had seemed so huge that they followed me wherever I went. They bounced off the mute walls and waited for me around corners, they were there when I pulled my covers to my head at night, and there in the bubbles when I hid in the bath. They opened up like endless horizons and chased behind me down tight alleyways. But they faded here, like the paint on Marika's car, from red to pink. I was in Hungary. Marika loved me, and she was beside me. We were driving on a summer's day; we would buy a watermelon, and a cool drink with a straw. I, too, would blend in. In a few days my skin would turn brown, and I'd wear a skirt with flowers on it. I felt alive to possibility. Maybe that was the way things worked in Hungary, if you were awake to it. Maybe that was what had happened to Marika the summer before. It was very easy to become someone else if no one tried to stop you.

I wished my father could see me now. Because whenever I talked about Marika at home, he took on a worried look, his furrowed brow running deeper than usual. Perhaps he thought she was still slippery, and liable to take off if you tried to catch hold of her. Or maybe he thought she'd shed us too easily, like a caterpillar shaking off its chrysalis, never looking back on the sad old shape it used to be. But I never thought any of those things. I heard the love in her voice; I saw the way her pen scratched its letters, made its kisses at the bottom of the page, like row after row of unruly cross-stitch. And every time I had to wait to hear from her, his face darkened; I saw it, the shadow passing. And I knew then that he must miss her, too, in his own way.

My first sighting of Villa Serena was over the skinny back of a goat. We had turned onto a stony dirt track, and bumped slowly along it. We followed its winding path beside a stream, past fields of stubble and dense foliage that dripped with shining pink flowers. I'd wound my window all the way down, the flat heat of late afternoon filling the car, when I came face-to-face with the animal's quivering muzzle. I cried out and Marika jumped on the brakes and the goat looked at us with curiosity in its big milky eyes.

"Ah, it's Jimmy! He's out again. Isn't he lovely, Erzsi? Don't you just love his face? Pet him, he won't hurt you."

"A goat," I said, "a wild goat."

Marika laughed. "Jimmy's about as wild as a pussycat. He belongs to the Horváths. They live just below us. And look, you can see the corner of the house there, see, behind the trees? Up there? Oh, look, here's Tamás now. Hey, Tamás!"

Marika sounded her horn and the goat dipped his head and pulled up a mouthful of long grasses. I reached out an uncertain hand and patted his bony back through the window. Over the tops of the trees I could just about see a triangle of red roof, a flash of white. Then I turned, and all of my attention was caught by the approaching boy. He was sauntering down the road ahead, with his hands pushed into his pockets. He was small and blond and wearing nothing but a pair of blue football shorts. He waved when he saw us and broke into a run.

"Hello, Marika *néni*."

He stood on Marika's side of the car and bent down.

"Tamás, this is Erzsi, whom I told you about, all the way from England." She spoke slowly, in clear, measured English.

"Ah, yes. Hello. I am Tamás. Pleased to meet you."

Tamás. The way he said it sounded really quite like *Thomas,* which is what it was in English, but with a clash at the end. A noisy, more spirited version of the same name. He reached in across Marika and held out his hand to me. His arm was even browner than hers, the color of hazelnuts. I shook it, and it was easy to count how many times I had shaken hands before. About three. When I met Tibor Szabó last year, when the headmaster handed out the awards at the end of the school year and after a tennis game, at the net, two schoolgirls with limp wrists. This was completely different. His hand was hard and rough and warm. It wasn't sweaty like the headmaster's, or crushing like Tibor's giant bear paw. It fitted neatly in mine.

"Jimmy and Erzsi have been making friends," said Marika. "You should show her your other animals. She's here for the week."

He smiled, and I smiled back. Jimmy was caught by the scruff of his neck and turned expertly around. The two of them, boy and goat, stood to the side so we could pass by. Tamás waved and called out, "See you!"

"How does he speak English?" I asked, turning in my seat.

"He learns at school. And he's just one of those sort of boys, very bright. I'm not sure you get them in England the same. He really wants to learn. He'll love having you here to practice with. He's your age, you know."

"So, he's a neighbor?"

"He's *the* neighbor. There's an older brother, too, Bálint, but he's cut from a different cloth. He's not around much. But István and Ági, his parents, are very sweet. They haven't two beans to rub together but that's how it is here, Erzsi. You'll have to get used to that."

"But he was wearing football shorts."

"Of course, he's football mad."

The engine groaned reluctantly but Marika stamped on the accelerator in her brown sandal and we shot up the final section of track, between lolling wooden gates. We ground to a halt, dust rising, parking on white gravel beneath dark trees. And there I saw Villa Serena laid before us. I was thrown by its beauty, expecting a weary cottage or a sagging longhouse, the type we had seen at the roadside on the way there. Instead, it was a house that beckoned in welcome, and I struggled to undo my seat belt so I could get at it. Marika had said it was built in the style of a hunting lodge, and while I didn't exactly know what that meant I thought it sounded exotic and adventurous, like something from a fireside story. It was built on two levels, with a wooden balcony that ran the length of the first floor, with columns of red wood reaching all the way to the tiled roof. All the windows were shuttered, and the walls were painted bright white. It stood at the far end of a vast, flat lawn, a winding path of slabs dotting across it. Behind, the wooded hills rose steeply to the forest beyond and below it the fields fell away to waving grasses, pale earth, a tangle of bristling undergrowth. The road we had taken to get there had disappeared and lay somewhere among the trees below. Villa Serena was in a world all of its own.

"Is this it?" I asked, panicking suddenly that I was mistaken.

"This is it," said Marika.

Zoltán drank cups of red wine before midday. He wore baggy blue trousers that tied with a string at the waist. And he had a way of looking at you that made you feel like you knew more about the world than you actually did. Those were the things I learned about him in my first days.

"So, you are Erzsi," he said, looking down at me, his eyes twinkling blue, his hair a thatch of gray. "I have heard so very much about you. You are even prettier than Marika said."

"I'm ten," I said, as if that explained everything, and he took my hand, laughing as though he thought I was funny, as well as pretty. "So, come on, Ten. Come in and help me find you a drink."

He spoke English lustily, in a loose drawl that had none of Tamás's precision about it. Rather the words tumbled out and they happened to be in English, but could just as well have been something else. Hungarian or Russian or German. I wanted to be shy around Zoltán but he wouldn't let me. He placed a hand on my shoulder and steered me alongside him. Later I'd realize this was his way; he enlisted you, got your help with something, like lifting a corner of a table or hunting for a shoe or snapping some ice cubes into a glass. As though you were just the person he was looking for, and now that you'd come along everything would be all right.

I followed him inside, brushing through the bead curtain that hung in the doorway and for a dread moment my heart skipped back to the Szabós' lake house. But I needn't have worried, for Villa Serena's bead curtain, and the green-gauze mosquito nets at the windows that I was yet to notice, were where similarities between the two houses began and ended.

In the hallway I noted the unruly heap of shoes beneath the coat pegs. Giant, flattened sheepskin slippers that must have belonged to Zoltán, a pair of silvery strappy shoes that I knew were Marika's, tennis shoes with trailing laces like licorice, a grand and polished pair of black riding boots. Above the mountain of shoes, coats and hats were hung. I counted several straw boaters, a floppy sun hat and a bright yellow raincoat. It was chaos, but everything seemed to have its place. Zoltán steered me onward into the kitchen, chuckling at the look on my face.

The kitchen was white and light, with a tile floor the color of russet apples. In the middle of a huge table there was a bowl of grapes, glinting like rubies. Zoltán took a jug of lemonade from the fridge and filled a glass to the top. He handed it to me and I took a long drink, emerging with my nose wet. He put his hand back on my shoulder and took me back outside and onto the balcony.

"Your house is really nice," I said, glancing back over my shoulder at the staircase and the entrance to the room leading off from the hall. I wanted to explore every inch of it, leaving my prints just as Marika had done.

"Thank you, Erzsi. It is, isn't it? We want you to feel at home here. It's very important to Marika, and to me, too. I've never had a little English girl come to visit before. It's quite an excitement."

"I'm half-Hungarian," I said.

"So you are." He smiled. "So then, the balcony. And

the view! Do you paint? Your mother can paint—did you ever know that about her? We will find you some brushes. Yes, we will set you painting here. How can you not, when faced with this?"

And that was how I first really appreciated the view from the house, with Zoltán beside me, our hands shielding our eyes. I could tell his mind was shaping things, a frizzle at the thought of getting started, already sketching the rounded moons of hills, the grizzle of undergrowth, the slap of sky. Beside him, I placed my palms on the warm red wood of the balcony and squinted up at the blue. From behind me I heard Marika talking to herself as she set about making lunch, knocking and banging and now and again a snatch of song, tripping from her mouth. She was acting differently, like last year all over again, but this time it suited her. She seemed blissfully happy. Or was I misremembering? How is happiness measured, anyway? In Devon it was through everyday things, the enjoyment of a cup of tea sitting on the step in the sun, the spotting of a clutch of snowdrops shining on wet earth. But at Villa Serena it smacked of flight, open skies and far-off horizons. Marika was winged. And she'd started painting? That was definitely new. I gripped the balcony edge and tried to see again what Zoltán was seeing, but all I could think of was how pale the sun made everything. At home the sky would cough with dusty clouds and our garden was full of trees that went black in the rain. Villa Serena was sun-bleached, but Marika seemed more colorful than ever.

We ate our meal at the table on the terrace, a white cloth flapping in the breeze. I had a plate of slimy ham and bullet-holed cheese, peppers the color of bananas and thick slices of bleeding tomatoes. I surprised myself by being hungry and eating every last scrap, mopping the last of the tomato juice with my bread. Afterward, as Zoltán dozed in his chair with a straw hat pulled down over his eyes, Marika gave me a tour of the house.

The living room smelled of beeswax, with a hint of wood smoke. The floor was made of intricately woven wooden strips, and there were two enormous leather sofas the color of blackberries. Curtains at the windows hung like tapestries in a gallery, showing twirling strings of fruit, bulbous grapes and fig leaves. The furniture was antique and heavy and looked like it had been there forever. But despite the museum pieces, it felt like a home. The shining wood asked for my touch; the embroidered cushions that were piled on the sofas invited the press of my head against them. There was a vast and furry rug made from the pelt of an unknown animal, and instead of scaring me it demanded to be danced upon in bare feet. I was drawn toward a feature that occupied one corner and appeared to be built into the very structure of the house. It was taller than me and with three sides of shiny forest-green tiles. A traditional wood-burning stove, a *kemence*, Marika said. I gazed into it, watching as my reflection shifted in the glossy tiles, and I imagined it burning hot in winter as outside snow fell thick and fast. The rooms had about them a whiff of ancient Hungary, where cavalier horsemen with baggy trousers and billowing shirts came home hungry, where the woods were hunted and plundered and the spoils eaten over crackling fires. It was romance and mystery and I was smitten.

There were paintings on the walls, brightly splashed canvases, and before I saw the jagged *ZK* initialed in every cor-

ner, I knew them to be Zoltán's. There were other pictures,
too. A startling painting of a wolf, with a sneering look and
hunched shoulders, his feet wide and splayed.

"Isn't he wonderful?" said Marika, joining my side.
"That's by János Papp, a friend of Zoltán's. In fact, he and
his wife, Margit, are coming tomorrow—you'll meet them
then."

The brushstrokes had a frenzied touch to them and I
didn't like it. I moved on to look at an intricate pencil
drawing of a mountain landscape, mounted in a gilt frame.
I pretended to study the lines of the fir trees, when I was
really thinking about the wolf artist and wondering why
new people had to visit the day after I'd arrived. Marika
tugged me on to explore the rest of the house.

It was Zoltán's place in every way. His clothes and shoes
were cluttered in the hallway. A sheaf of papers from a gallery in Berlin lay strewn on top of the dresser. A pair of
reading glasses lay folded in the middle of the table, rim-
less and delicate. But Marika was there, too, her belongings scattered casually about the house. Her book lay upside
down on the table with its spine cracked, and the beads of
her necklace were spilled on the windowsill. I wondered
if she thought she was staying forever. It didn't seem possible, somehow.

We went upstairs, Marika walking ahead of me carrying my case that until then had sat on the veranda. My bare
feet slid on the wooden stairs, and halfway up I saw a pair
of antlers on the wall. I stood on tiptoe and ran my fingers
over their surface, wondering if they were real. I hurried
after Marika, glancing back over my shoulder, half expecting them to twitch and toss, with the ghost of an angry stag.

In contrast to the stately sitting room with its dark furniture, upstairs was light and bright and full of sunshine.
The bedrooms in the roof had wood-paneled ceilings and
caramel-colored boarded floors. Marika threw the door
open to what was to be my room with some ceremony, and
I crowded in behind her. It was simple and rectangle shaped
with a low bed in the corner with white linen covers and
a rug on the floor made of blues and yellows. There was a
bedside table with a lamp, its base carved from the root of
a tree, its edges curling and uneven. A tin cup was stuffed
full of forget-me-nots.

"Do you like it, Erzsi?"

I took my case from her and opened it. I began to set out
my things, my pajamas under the pillow, the book I was
reading beside the bed. I hummed a little.

"Erzsi?"

"I love it," I said. "I really love it."

That first night I took a long time to fall asleep. My room
was set high under the eaves and it was hot, the wooden
walls and roof trapping and holding the heat of the day.
Scant breeze came from a small and rounded window that
was pushed open to the dark sky. The mosquito netting was
bumped perpetually by bloated moths and eager midges.

In bed I lay very still, like a starfish, no one limb touching another. I had the sheet drawn loosely about my waist.
Outside, the night echoed and roared in a way it never did
in Devon. In Harkham, when the lights went out there was
a heavy silence, but at Villa Serena, the night erupted all
around me. The barking of dogs was a distant but endless exchange of greetings and gruff song. I pictured them chained

in farmyards, stalking the edges of lawns and howling in
porches, in nighttime conversation. I heard the faraway
clanking of ominous machinery, and I imagined waking to
a churned landscape, the woods and fields worked over in
the night. It was probably a farmer coming home from the
pub on a giant tractor, his headlights swaying. Then there
was the high-pitched whine of a mosquito that had found
its way into the room. I propped myself up on my elbows
and listened in the dark, slapping at my legs in anticipation
of its bite. But beneath it all ran the steady chirrup of cicadas that made the surrounds of the house fizz with a hidden life. This last was an exotic lullaby to my ears and was
the sound I took with me as I finally dropped into sleep.

The following morning the early sun bleached me wide
awake. I pulled back up the cool sheet that I had kicked
down in the night and lay cocooned for a moment, listening. Mornings had a character of their own, as well.
There was birdsong, for the house was surrounded by forests. Later, Marika would pick out the sounds of skylarks
and nightingales, and I would lie listening to their sweet
and soaring warbling, feeling as though I had stumbled on
a magical hidden truth. The hills caught and held sounds
for miles around, then threw them back again and again.
That same day I would stand tiptoe on a hill and yell, my
arms thrown out behind me, making my first echo, tall as
a giant. Then there were all the noises of a house awaken-
ing, Villa Serena's morning symphony. The low chatter of
Hungarian voices on the radio, the knocking of the giant
metal coffeepot, Zoltán's humming as he stomped down
the steps to his studio. At home, my father had developed
the knack of slipping soundlessly through the house. There

was a floorboard that creaked on the landing, and our kettle pitched to a whistle when it boiled, but they were the exceptions. Although he always awoke before me I never knew if he was up. I would come downstairs in my dressing gown and peer into rooms, jumping to see him at the kitchen table, eating toast with his back to the window. Or I'd catch sight of him outside, shoveling earth at the bottom of the garden or carrying beanpoles with long strides. He'd just raise a hand, or say *Good morning,* his voice barely a whisper, as though there was a baby in the house he didn't want to wake. At Villa Serena, Marika and Zoltán shouted around corners and called through rooms. They banged and crashed and laughed and I hurried out of bed quickly, not wanting to miss anything, afraid of being left behind.

I arrived downstairs tangled in my sheet like a toga, my hair muddled from sleep. And Marika leaped up when she saw me, and cried, *Jó reggelt!* in a joyful voice. Mornings were there to be celebrated, dawn was greeted with a whoop. She had been like that at home in Devon, but more erratically, like a wind that switches. Sometimes she would wake up moody and shake cereal into my bowl with ferocity, the milk splashing onto the tablecloth, but the glorious morning greetings, when they came, had always made my heart sing. There, at Villa Serena, I reveled in them. They became part of the order that so quickly established itself. A routine of happy chaos that, despite my brief stay, I learned to follow rigorously.

My first breakfast at Villa Serena was a raspberry cake. I arrived in the kitchen, fingers twisting in my nightclothes, and saw it on the table. It had white icing that rolled down the edges and ran onto the plate, a slanting surface like uneven paving, and ERZSI written out in raspberries, my favorite fruit. As Marika came over I sank my head into her apron and flour speckled my hair. She hugged me tight. After a while I emerged grinning, and hungry. I sat down to an enormous slice and picked off all the berries that made up *E*. Marika sat opposite, her hands clasped around her coffee cup.

"I can't believe it's cake for breakfast," I said, through mouthfuls.

"I can't believe you're really here," said Marika.

We looked at each other, me with sticky sweet lips and Marika through rising steam. She tipped her head on one side and held out her hand.

"Pinch me, Erzsi."

I set down my fork, and instead of pinching her I took her hand in mine. I rubbed her fingers, feeling each one as though counting them, the bumps of the knuckles and the smooth of her rings.

I felt magic at that moment, as though I was blessing Marika's table just by being there. It didn't feel like I was the one that had been left behind, wet-cheeked and red-eyed. Instead, I was a fairy princess visiting a faraway land, and my arrival had been greeted with disbelief and joy. I smiled a raspberry smile and got back to my cake.

The wolf artist arrived at lunchtime, in a blaze of crunching tires and spitting gravel. I watched from the balcony as he and his wife, Margit, strolled across the lawn. Marika danced forward to meet them, Zoltán ambled behind. I stayed stock-still until I was summoned.

They all talked together in English, which I realized was

for my benefit and felt honored. Later on, after a long lunch of grilled meat and heaped sauerkraut, I heard Margit say to Marika that she liked children, *but only from a distance.* Marika had laughed in reply. I sat smarting, feeling hot from my head to my toes, until Zoltán rescued me. He clapped a hand to my shoulder and said that János wanted to see the horses in the next-door field, and would I go with them? I left Marika and the suddenly hateful Margit, and the three of us walked down the track.

I liked János better, as he whistled to the two chestnut horses and they trotted to the gate. He stooped low and blew on their muzzles and they blinked slowly. I climbed on the gate and patted their necks, dust rising at my gentle smack.

"Did you paint the wolf?" I asked.

János smiled and I saw a glint of gold tooth.

"Erzsi has a very good eye," said Zoltán, and I took the compliment without knowing quite what he meant. "I think she has all the makings of an artist herself."

I nodded modestly, although I really wanted to tug at his arm and say, *Do you think so, really, Zoltán?* For praise from Zoltán was something precious and I wanted to understand its origins. If I was doing something right I wanted to do more of it. But it was as if he understood me without me saying a word, for he dropped a hand onto my shoulder and spoke again.

"Erzsi is a romantic, János, just like Marika. She appreciates the beauty of things."

I beamed. I'd never heard anyone say it before but he was right. I did. And, as long as I was in Hungary, to be just like Marika was everything I wanted.

As we walked back to the villa I glanced at the Horváths'

house as we passed but there was no sign of the blond boy, Tamás. It was a shame, for I thought I had a certain swagger about me, walking between the two men, my arms swinging loosely by my sides. Me, the romantic.

As I went to bed that night, Marika came in to say goodnight.

"You were very good today with János and Margit," she said.

"I didn't like that Margit," I said.

"She's a jewelry designer," said Marika.

"But she doesn't like children, does she?" I said, watching her from under my lashes.

"And I shouldn't think they like her, either," said Marika, and we both giggled.

I went on to sleep soundly, dreaming of riding the chestnut horses, my mouth bursting with gold teeth.

That first week at Villa Serena passed both quickly and slowly, in jilted rhythms. Some days stretched before me as endless as the horizon, days where I trod the paths in the woods for hours before lunchtime, when I lay on the lawn on a blanket, the rays of the sun nudging me into sleep. Then a long and happy evening, pulling meat from skewers with my teeth and gulping lemonade, my elbows planted firmly on the table. Endless days.

Then there were the days that scurried from first waking, and I felt desperation with every passing hour that time was marching onward and there was nothing I could do about it. I wasted whole mornings fretting that it would soon be the afternoon. Then I'd run headlong into the night with the evening chasing me, finally going to sleep in my hot

attic room with a sense that I'd done nothing that day, but
it had passed all the same.

And I felt both at home and an alien, in equal measure. I
liked Zoltán, and never once did it enter my head to com-
pare him with my father. He was quite simply a different
entity altogether. He spent the days in his studio, wandering out with a smile and a cup of wine, placing a hand on
my head and teasing out a laugh. And Marika was so happy
to have me there that I swelled with relief, leaping aboard
whatever plan she floated. Sometimes I caught myself just
looking at her. She and Zoltán had a camera, a giant, heavy
thing with a leather neck strap. If they were around, then it
was never far away, and I felt important, posing, staring into
the lens and losing myself for a moment in its black hole.

It seemed mean that while my mind was contented, my
body was plagued. The sun was largely good to me, eventually turning my skin a sweet honey brown, but it savaged
me, too. My shoulders and back were ruby streaked with
sunburn. My nose peeled and freckles erupted. One afternoon, when I had been exploring the surrounding fields
in full sun, I returned to the house feeling dizzy and sick.
I was made to lie upstairs with a cool compress and a piece
of cloth hung across the window to shed some dark. I woke
again in the early evening with the memory of a headache
and a feeling of inadequacy, that I couldn't stay the pace.
And the mosquitoes fed on me with a raw delight. I always
remembered to apply lotion in the evenings, and put on
clothes with long arms and legs, but I was frequently caught
out during the day by the shadowy woods with their small
clouds of bugs that spun back and forth in waiting. Marika
and Zoltán were never bitten, but they burned citronella

candles for me and I grew to associate the zesty scent with gratitude, but also with a sense of failing. When I went home to England my ankles were dotted with bites and I had scabs on my arms from my itching and a slight redness about my tan. But I'd grinned through it all, proclaiming a wonderful time. My father simply nodded and bought me a green bottle of soothing aloe that he set beside my bed.

After János and Margit's visit there were no more visitors during my stay, something I was glad of. I liked being on my own with Marika, and Zoltán, too. There was, however, Tamás. And although I didn't see a lot of him that first summer, our brief exchanges read back in my head like the best kind of poetry, where every gesture is weighted with meaning.

After meeting him on my very first day, I was to see Tamás twice more. You could say that the first came about all because of Zoltán's bicycle. It had been in his shed for years, with rusted spokes and trails of spiders' webs. But one morning he brought it out shining, its frame wet and soapy from a quick spritz. The tires were newly pumped, the saddle lowered, and it was ready to be ridden. I took it down to the track and clambered onto it, my toes only just brushing the ground at full stretch. Just as I was wondering whether I could cope with this fresh challenge, I caught a glimpse of Tamás's blond head nodding farther down the lane. He was walking with his hands in his pockets, his feet kicking at the dust. He had a string shopping bag on his shoulder; I guessed he was walking to Esztergom. I decided that this was a good opportunity to show off my daring ways, so I set both feet on the pedals and off I went, the handlebars twisting as we met with bumps and dips. He shouted a greeting

as I whizzed by, before we disappeared from sight around
the corner and on down the lane. But with too much speed
and too little control I shuddered and juddered. I took my
feet off the pedals to gain a footing but all they could do
was flail uselessly in the air. Off balance, the cycle tipped up
and sent me sprawling in the dust. I wasn't too badly hurt,
a graze on my knee and a knock to my elbow, but I began
to cry with a short-lived and shocked intensity. I scooped
myself up and limped hurriedly on, pushing the cycle beside me. Where there was a break in the undergrowth I
slunk quickly to the side and hid within the loose tangle of
a bush, dragging my bicycle in with me, and dabbing at my
knee with a handful of grasses. I held my breath and prayed
that he wouldn't see me. Boys, in my experience, were no
good at times like this.

Two years ago, when I was eight, I'd fallen off the top
rung of the jungle gym at school. I'd been hanging upside
down, showing off the monkey skills I'd honed among the
Harkham apple trees, and my summer dress had dropped
over my head. Two boys in my class, James and Kieran, had
started shouting and laughing, saying they could see my
underwear. In the hullabaloo I'd lost my grip and fallen,
landing with a thump on the daisy-studded school lawn. I
remember everything going very quiet, except for one girl's
crying. Then I realized it was me, and I cried louder. The
boys had scattered instantly, and it was girls that smelled
like cotton and bubble gum that had gathered around me,
with their caressing words, gentle presses and whispered assurances. I was sent home early, with a bump like a fresh-
laid egg on the back of my head. The next day I was given
a note by Kieran, folded over and over so that it was gray

along the edges. It said, *Sorry you fell, Erzsi. I didn't mean to laugh. I like you a lot,* and somehow it only made me feel worse. As though I was falling all over again. Only this time, the ground seemed even farther away, and my landing patch uncertain.

From my spot in the bush I heard footsteps. Tamás's easy saunter had been replaced by running feet. I hid in my lair. I heard the footsteps slow. I peered through the briars and saw the outline of him. He was in touching distance.

"Erzsi, are you okay?"

He was talking to me through the bush. My sore knee was forgotten in the realization of this fact. For a moment I didn't answer. He hadn't run away or pretended not to see; he had deliberately sought me out. And not only did he want to know if I was all right, he knew my name. As though it was a name he'd known all along and he'd just been waiting to say it. *Erzsi.* It sounded nice from the mouth of a Hungarian boy.

"Tamás?" I said. Because it was the only thing I could think of saying. Then, with greater inspiration, I added, "Yes. I'm fine."

"Are you hurt?"

"Hurt? No. Not me."

"But you fell?"

"Yes, but it was nothing. Nothing much."

"Why are you hiding?"

"I'm not. I mean, I'm not *hiding.*"

"Do you want me to get Marika?"

This was a strange idea. I certainly didn't want to see Marika at that moment.

"No, thanks," I said. "I'm going home soon, anyway."

I could see the blue of his T-shirt through the twigs and brambles. I couldn't see his face, but I could picture it. His lashes were as long as a girl's and he had the best suntan of anyone I knew. I remembered this from the day with the goat. A Hungarian boy, I said to myself again. Honestly something quite different from anything I'd ever known.

"How come you speak such good English?" I asked, speaking very quickly, as though I'd seem less curious that way.

"Do I? I never had anybody to practice with before," he said. "Not until now."

Not until now. Three words that seemed to change the way that everything around me looked. As though the future had been brought a little bit closer.

"Marika said I should come and see your animals," I edged.

"Why do you call her Marika?" he said.

"Because I do," I said. A little bit prickly. I imagined his eyebrows shooting up at that.

"Well, see you, then," he said. And he didn't sound annoyed, just matter-of-fact.

"Oh," I said, rustling as I shifted my position. "Are you going?"

"I think so."

"Oh."

"Do you want to come?" he said.

I wanted to say, *Yes, please.* Wherever it was he was going. But instead, I thought of my grazed knee and the limp it'd surely give me. My tear-smeared cheeks, and the leaves caught in my hair. And he might ask me more about Marika. About why she was here and I was there. Perhaps

Tamás could guess what I was thinking, because after my long pause he went on his way, anyway, calling, "Goodbye, English Erzsi," as he went. I was left hugging myself, in a strange muddle of disappointment and delight.

When I was sure he was gone, I wandered back to the villa. I limped only slightly, and pushed the bicycle along beside me. I gripped its handlebars lovingly, glad, now, of it having bucked me off. I thought of the picture of me that Tamás might have in his head. Me flying past, my hair streaming, free as a bird. Or perhaps the crescent of my smile, seen through the leaves of the bush. Either way, I hoped he held on to some image. Something to make me seem as real for him as he was for me.

The next time I saw him was on the forest path, and it was the day before I was due to return home. I was walking with Marika, the kind of walk we often did that first stay, where she pointed out things on the forest floor or high in the trees and I trotted by her side, exclaiming. We drew our delight from the flipping of a slow worm in the dust, or a toad dragging itself along laboriously on its belly. I asked questions about the markings on skin, bright feathers under a wing and the names of the wildflowers that dotted the edges of the paths. Neither of us mentioned going home. I clung to her hand and she held tightly to mine.

We rarely met anyone else on these walks, except Tamás that one time. Which made it seem like it was meant to be. He was strolling along at a casual pace and it was hard for my own steps not to falter when I saw him. But then I re-membered that Marika knew nothing about our meeting in the lane, so I kept calm and quietly observed him. For the first time we could see each other properly, without a goat or bush obscuring. His hair was wet and hung darker and longer. He seemed taller than I remembered, too. I noticed that the football shorts he wore had a tiny diamond pattern stitched along the hem, and that he wore a watch on his wrist that had a plastic blue strap that looked like it might disintegrate at any moment. I felt his eyes on me. I hoped he didn't notice my ugly grazed knee, like a smattering of bran flakes, and instead was distracted by my denim shorts that I thought were particularly cool, with their red studs at the belt and frayed edges. There was so much to notice about another person, I thought, a fact that I hadn't particularly considered before.

Marika asked him if he'd been at the forest pool, and if he'd had a nice swim. He said yes, and showed all his white teeth and said, turning to me, that it was *wonderful,* and he pronounced it *whon-der-fool* and the word sounded better than I'd ever heard it before. I thought about saying, *Spoken to anyone else in a bush lately?* and imagined us collapsing in laughter together. I'd have enjoyed the look of bewilderment on Marika's face. But instead we simply smiled quietly at each other, and then Marika chatted to him in Hungarian a little. Then he said goodbye and he reached out his hand to me. We shook. And it felt different this time. On the day with the goat it had felt somehow special, but now it wasn't enough. I wondered if it counted as holding hands and was sad to conclude that it probably didn't. I realized then that that was the Goodbye. I really was going home tomorrow and I hadn't even seen his house or animals or let him practice his English on me. Probably because I hid in the bush and snapped about Marika, and now he thought I was just odd.

As we carried on walking, Marika said that his mother had been unwell so it wouldn't have been a good time for me to have visited, but I could see the animals next year if I liked, the goat again and the three sheep and the chickens with red hats. I smiled. So there would be a next year, then.

But coming again next year meant going away that first year. And all of the eternity that lay between the two visits. I chewed hard on the inside of my mouth. After a little while I spoke.

"Can I go swimming next year, as well?" I said. "At the same place as Tamás?"

Marika laughed in that lilting songbird way of hers, which I took to mean *yes*. But I was grave. Swimming made me think of Balaton, and I was desperate for a new memory to replace it. A forest pool with Tamás would be a good new memory.

We walked a different way home, a longer way, and it seemed like Marika wanted to put off our return as much as I did. Getting back to the villa would mean moving my sandals from their spot in the hallway and folding up my sun hat that hung on a peg beside hers. It meant the checking of airline tickets, seeing the word *London* printed and it looking like just a set of foreign letters, not a place near home. And worst of all, a telephone call to my father, where Marika would sit hunched over the receiver and speak in a voice that sounded stretched like old elastic. We delayed all of these things and went home through the cornfields.

From a distance, they looked perfect, a golden, gently undulating sea. I wanted to dive in and have my body shimmer with gold dust as I floated.

But we walked in, sedately. Our waists were tickled by

the stems. Suddenly Marika broke into a run and I followed behind her, my feet kicking at the clods of dry earth. We spread out our arms and our fingertips stroked our wake. Then Marika stopped suddenly, and put her finger to her lips, turning. We heard the distant churn of a tractor. It grew louder, and Marika pointed at a slice of red metal that flitted behind the trees at the field's edge. She flapped her hands, and the two of us dropped to our bellies, hidden by the corn. I covered my mouth with my hand, stifling a laugh, as Marika poked me in the ribs. We were robbers hiding in a maze, stowaways that had leaped into the sea. We kept as still as we could, only our shoulders shaking in mirth. When the tractor had passed, Marika breathed out in a loud draft. But we stayed in our corn den, chins resting in palms, facing each other.

"Don't you want to keep having fun?" I asked. "Don't you want me to stay here so we can keep having fun? Or come home with me—we can have fun at home, too."

"Oh, Erzsi."

Marika reached out and tucked my hair behind my ear. She smoothed my cheek with three of her fingers, and they felt cool like water. It wasn't an answer, a stroked cheek and patted hair.

"You know," she said, "that until you come here again, we're all waiting for you. Not just me, but these fields, the house, that toad we nearly stepped on back there in the woods. We're all here, waiting. Because we're yours now. We belong to you. You've a whole other world here, Erzsi. And every summer, the sun won't shine until you come. Not for us."

I dropped my chin at this, and a tear rolled down my

cheek. This small patch of Hungary in the hidden hills was mine. Balaton and all that had happened was far away and I pushed it back until it offered only a flicker of memory. I was filling my head with new things to replace the old, and Marika fit in this landscape, with her cakes that spelled out names and easy gait through the cornfields. And I fit with her. Not in perfect tessellation but well enough for there to be a next year.

In my lying position, I unwittingly smelled the Hungarian soil. It was ground into my fingernails and dusted the soles of my shoes. And it was Hungarian sun that had browned my skin and lightened the tips of my hair. I would be carrying the place back with me, unawares. I knew I would count the days until I returned.

And I did count the days, each and every one of them. It was as though I had an advent calendar that spanned the year, and the window with the double flaps and the promise of a joyful scene inside was the day I went to Hungary.

And I remember now how it was to feel like this. When promise and hope came out of sadness, and were precious for it. I don't remember in a distant way, where only the fact of *having felt* remains. Nor does it begin quietly, with a tickle in the pit of my stomach. Instead, it is a blow that lifts me from my feet and suspends me in midair. My feet kick and then, suddenly, I stop. The time for hope and promise has gone, and all these days have passed. There can be no more, and I know this.

CHAPTER FOUR

I looked up from the book, and saw with some surprise that the world around me was much as I'd left it. The pointed roof of the Victoria Park pavilion was visible just beyond the trees. The cloudy heads of willows bowed together, consolingly. A siren pitched and wailed some streets away, and a Dalmatian ran fast across the grass, his ears blown back in his haste, spots flying. A father with two small girls either side of him cut across the path in front of me; they were all three in on the same joke, giggling chaotically, as their hands, which held one another, jumped and their feet hurried. I imagined them late to meet their mother, their waiting ice creams turning to dribble at the pavilion café. There would be kisses and friendly recrimination for the father's tardiness. More laughter and hiccups. Then all four would stroll back across the park together, on their way home. I always did this, made stories of other people's lives. Not consciously. Just accidentally, as though I couldn't help it. As soon as I fell into the book again I knew these sights and sounds would be lost to me, and so for a moment I reveled in them. They were part of the life I had now, not the one I'd lost. The life that was just fine. So I clung to them.

It is 1992, and in the picture I am eleven years old. I am on the lawn in front of Villa Serena, reading. I am lying on a piece of material that is crinkling underneath me. It is printed with yellow flowers and looks like an old curtain or a snatch of tablecloth. Perhaps the grass is damp and it is morning still. The soft light suggests it. I am on my belly, and have one leg kicked up coquettishly, the flat of my foot laid bare to the sky. My back is a smooth dip, and I am wearing a white cotton dress that is wrinkled and easy. I am holding a book loosely in my hands but I cannot see what I am reading.

It is that rare sort of photograph, the kind where the picture is taken without the subject being aware. Without the presence of monument or occasion or posturing companions, it is simply a fragment of time. A girl reading on a lawn, on a summer's day. I look more closely. My face bent reading is not so very different at eleven to how it is now. Smaller and finer and lighter, but still a version of me.

A daisy, fragile stemmed and with dusky petals, was slipped between two sheets. I peered closely at it, afraid of breaking its spindly edges. I looked again at the picture of me lying on the lawn, surrounded by patches of daisies. I wonder if she'd plucked it from that very spot, crept up behind me while I was lost in my book and tiptoed away, spinning her prize between her fingers. Marika always loved flowers. She treated them all as though they were magnificent gifts, whether humble roadside weeds, or spidery forest blooms. She placed them in jam jars, egg cups, wine bottles, and set them all about the house. But I never knew she pressed them. I never imagined her saying to herself, *One day I'll look at this again and marvel that it's beautiful still.* She appeared to live too much in the moment to care for how things would look in the future.

I had spent the waiting year in preparation. I had practiced my swimming, turning my childish splashing into a smoother, sleeker stroke. On Tuesday evenings I used to go with a girl in my class to the pool near the school, and her mum would drop me home afterward. Later, I'd eat my supper across the table from my father, sniffing at the chlorine on my wrists and thinking of the day that I would dive in a perfect arc, the surface splitting and applause breaking out from the bank behind. I was also working on the art of riding my bicycle without my hands. I'd managed it once, with the front wheel twisting like a frisky pony, all the way down the middle of the lane beside our cottage. I thought of Zoltán's bicycle in the shed and how much I had grown in a year. Perhaps my feet could touch the ground now and make riding it altogether less of a hair-raising experience.

I was growing adept at conjuring Marika. I held not just the memory of her with me all the time, but the promise, which was somehow brighter and more reliable. It was strange, how swiftly she had, in my mind, assumed a new identity, one that was tied inextricably to the house in the hills. And one that included me, in a way that I'd never felt before. I longed to be there with her, but accepted that that was for the summer. I would lie on my back in my bedroom in Harkham and stare at the uneven ceiling, seeing the clean white walls of Villa Serena, the milky stones that studded the track below, the pale sorbet we ate from cut-glass bowls on the terrace with the sun glinting off our spoons. I had always been a master of reverie, but my daydreams were no longer the idle sort.

One wet afternoon in the early spring Aunt Jessica came for tea, and I made the mistake of telling her that I was excited about going to Hungary again that summer. She smacked her cup back into its saucer and pursed her lips, so that I could see all the cracks in her pink lipstick. My father came back into the sitting room at that moment, a plate of cookies in his hand. He had crumbs down the front of his sweater and I smiled at him, liking the thought of him sneaking cookies in the kitchen before Aunt Jessica could eat them all. He winked back.

"It's not right, David," she said, her hand reaching for a bourbon.

"Erzsi's happy," he answered, sinking into the opposite armchair.

"Well, so long as *Erzsi's* happy," she said, through a cookie. For a moment I thought that was a nice thing for Aunt Jessica to say, but then I caught the look on my father's face and realized that perhaps it wasn't. It didn't make sense that my aunt should be more angry with my mother than my father was. It never occurred to me that she was angry with everybody.

Later, as she left, my father and I watched her walk to the front gate, her shoulders hunched against the drizzle. She turned to wave, and we waved back.

"Interfering old bat," he muttered as she got into her car.

I collapsed against his side, rolling with helpless laughter.

Marika met me at Budapest Airport, just as before. We drove to Esztergom, down the same roads that looped

through forests and streaked by chalk-dusted towns. In the
car I bubbled with excitement at the week to come, sitting
beside Marika and asking every question I could think of.
Was the woman who worked in the bakery that sold the
poppy seed twists the same? You know, the one with the
sticky-out ears and yellow hair? Yes, yes, she was. Were
the two horses still there, with the chestnut coats and
white manes and soft lips that brushed up carrot pieces
from the flat of your hand? Yes, they were. And the bicycle
in the shed, if I wanted to ride it, could I, all the way down
the dusty track and maybe onto the road, if I was careful?
Yes, I could. I didn't mention Tamás; I didn't want to jinx
anything. Instead, I thought about the football stickers that
I had packed deep in my case. Two brand-new packets that
I had swapped my sandwiches for with a boy at school.

It was a summer with the hidden pool at its heart. I think
now of its cool depths, its sunlit surface, the smart cracking
of pigeon wings in the sky above as we lay floating like lil-
ies. The dream of a pool in the woods had stayed with me
the full year. I had convinced myself of its location; otherwise, why would Tamás be walking that way, his hair
dripping wet? I got to see the pool for myself on the second day of my stay, but not quite in the manner that I had
anticipated.

It began with Marika announcing over breakfast that it
was a fine day for swimming. I was sitting beside her on
the terrace bench, eating a ham roll and drinking tea from
one of Zoltán's wine cups. The outsides of our knees were
touching, and I nudged a little closer. The day was already
warming up, the shadows on the lawn slipping ever back-

ward, the heat haze breaking on the far horizon. I chewed carefully, choosing my words with precision.

"I'd love to go swimming. I remember now, last year, that boy I met had been swimming in the woods, hadn't he?"

"Tamás? Oh, what a good memory you have. No, I wasn't thinking of that. In Esztergom there's a swimming pool. It's quite nice, there's a deck area for bathing and you can buy ice creams, and *lángos*. Oh, Erzsi, have you ever had a *lángos?* It's a wonderful fried pancake thing, huge, and delicious. I must buy you one."

I know my face dropped because I made no attempt to hide it. In fact, I might even have exaggerated my disappointment, because although we'd been a year apart, I knew that Marika easily missed things.

"I hope," she said, turning to me, "that we're not dull for you, stuck out here in the middle of nowhere. I mean, it's not so very different from being at home in Devon, in some ways."

If there wasn't so much between them, after all, why Hungary and not Harkham? I bristled; my face needed no encouragement in its adjustment, and Marika caught it instantly.

"I mean, no, oh, I'm sorry, I don't mean that. It's very different, of course it is. I couldn't be happy there anymore, Erzsi, you know that. Here, I feel light. I feel right. Oh, God, I sound like a terrible poet, but really, you know what I mean. I know you do, you're a clever girl."

I set down my cup on my empty plate and folded my arms across my chest. I felt uncomfortable when Marika sought words to reassure me about her new life. All they did was drop into my head and rattle about like loose change.

I had made my own peace, in the simple press of her hand in mine, the taste of a cake she placed before me, the moments when our sighs fell light and synchronized. In the things we shared—a joke, a settee, a hairbrush. And in our laughter, when we both erupted and the sound rang out as one, tangled as stitches. I had all the proof of love I needed.

"I would like to go swimming," I said, "but not in the town. I want to go to the other pool, the one in the woods. You said I could go with Tamás, last year when I was here."

"Did I? I don't know, Erzsi. I don't know how safe it is. It's just a pond, really, full of weeds and all kinds of nasty things. It sounds nicer than it really is, I promise."

"Please, Marika."

And that was the first time I'd said her name out loud, using it as anyone else would. As anyone except her daughter, that is. There was a hardness in my mouth that wasn't there before, and I ran my tongue across my teeth, not liking the taste. Marika looked at me and nodded briskly.

"If that's what you'd like, of course, Erzsi. It might be nicer than I remember. Did you want to go this afternoon?"

And I felt it then, a slight shifting of power. I wriggled in my seat and was glad of my arms across my chest. I gripped myself tightly, my thumb digging the inside of my elbow.

"And what about Tamás? You said before that I should go with him, maybe that would be safer?"

Marika shook her head. "Tamás isn't here. He's visiting his grandparents in Debrecen for the week."

Debrecen. I hated the place instantly. I imagined Tamás stuffed on a sofa between two creased old people, looking bored and twitchy. It wasn't fair.

"It's all right, Erzsi. Zoltán and I will brave it with you.

It'll be good to get him out of his studio, breathing some fresh air. He's been festering these past few weeks, preparing for an exhibition. Come on, do you want to see the paintings? They're wonderful."

And with that the day was made and the week before me fell to ashes. The problem with make-believe was that it brushed up hard against reality. I had spent the year planning and plotting, reliving and reimagining. Perhaps it had been a delusion all along that I could be as happy there as I pictured.

Before I left, my father had tried to dampen my spirits, in that quiet way he had. I knew he was trying to be kind, thinking ahead to the trouble to come, rather than putting the mockers on things. *The mockers.* Marika had always jumped upon that word, hurled it at my father like a spear. *Oh, don't go putting the mockers on everything, David!* And I had laughed along, silly old Daddy, worried old Daddy, because it was such a funny word. The mockers. Like a big pair of swampy green hands descending. It was only later that I translated it, hearing her put it another way. *Oh, stop sucking the life out of everything, David.*

In the weeks leading up to my visit I'd struggled to contain my excitement. I'd talked about Marika, the jugs of lemonade, the walks we took, the laughs we had, and my father would reach down and cup my chin in his hand. He'd hold me steady, until my voice petered out. Then he'd say, *Slow down, Erzsi, slow down.* And I knew how she must have felt then. The mockers. But the difference was, maybe he was right.

I had only peeped into Zoltán's studio once the year before. Perhaps I had been considered too much of an unknown quantity to be allowed near the paintings. Marika had shown me some of her own pictures and my mouth had dropped. She had a lust for chaos and a disdain for geometry. *It's abstract,* she'd said. *What do you think?* At first I'd never imagined her painting at all, but as soon as I saw her pictures, they were so much like *her* that it made a sort of sense. As though she'd dipped a brush into her soul, and swept it across the pages of a sketchbook, in slapdash but spectacular fashion. She closed the book shut and said, *Let me show you some real art.*

Zoltán's studio occupied most of the ground floor of Villa Serena, and it had its own entrance. Unlike usual houses, the living room and kitchen were on the first floor, and the bedrooms were all tucked upstairs under the rafters. This way, Zoltán could be cocooned in his own world. If he'd been working late at night, then he'd clatter up the steps to the main house and throw open the front door, stamping his feet on the mat, mosquitoes and moths blowing in behind him, spinning about his head. I tried to make sure I was already in bed if he worked through to nightfall, to avoid the unwelcome visitors that accompanied his bold entrances.

Marika knocked and opened the door, poking her head in.

"*Szervusz!* Can we come in?"

Zoltán had a paint-smeared cotton apron tucked into his belt. His sleeves were rolled to the elbow and he wore a look of intent. His thick gray hair stood on end, his fingers having constantly run it through with smudges of oils and white spirit. He smiled, and his tanned face relaxed.

"Please! Please, come! Is that Erzsi, too? Yes, yes. Come on in."

The studio was a chaotic place of work, the tools of a trade apparent at every turn. The back wall was covered in shelves like struts on ladders, each home to bottles and jars and boxes, bouquets of paintbrushes, clear potions and piles of books teetering on the edges of tables. An old sofa, the sort that never would have made it into the main house, sagged in a corner, springs wheezing from its underside, its foam hanging like entrails. A paint-splattered sheet was bunched up in a corner of it, and a chipped mug balanced on the arm. Taut and creamy canvases were leaning against the walls, and three separate easels each held a painting of such color and vivacity that despite wanting to explore every corner of the room I couldn't tear my eyes from them.

I had seen Zoltán's paintings before, for there were three hanging in the house, two in the living room and one in the hallway. My favorite was a picture of his grandmother, a woman with a headscarf and a perfectly tipped crescent of a smile. But there was something about seeing the work in progress that appealed to me far more than a perfectly hung creation. I trod carefully toward the first canvas. It showed a village, a street of huddled cottages bent and leaning, that reminded me of gingerbread houses in a twisted wood. Their walls were bright, as Hungarian walls were, mustard yellow, dusty red and minted green. Rooftops sagged with red tiling that skittered and jilted haphazardly. The ground was dusty and uneven, with ragged grass at the sides. A tree swept into the center of the picture, heavy with blossom, and behind was a sky of every kind of blue. I stared at it, wanting to be in that street more than anything, my feet gently shuffling in the dust, my senses full of the color and light and scent of blossom, falling like confetti onto the flats of my upturned hands.

"It's the village I grew up in," said Zoltán. "I haven't been back there for twenty years, but I see it just like that. I paint from memory. Far clearer and brighter than the real thing."

"I'd like to go there," I said, edging closer.

"Do you like this one, Erzsi?"

Marika stood by a canvas that was less than half-finished. The paint was in thick daubs, every stroke distinct. It showed a small house, with white walls and a red roof tucked in a clearing in a forest. Behind, the sky was a fierce, burning pink. Rounded humps of yellow bushes crowded the edges.

"It's very colorful," I said, then realizing that sounded limp, added, "is it somewhere else you know?"

"Of course. It is my cousins' house. I used to play there, as a child. I think the places where we spend our childhood stay with us, Erzsi. They become our comfort and our inspiration, when we are old and gray. Perhaps this house, these hills, will be that for you one day."

"I hope so," I said. But really I was thinking more about the here and now than the distant and improbable future. I was thinking about Tamás leaving his grandparents' house early. Because he'd suddenly remembered that Erzsi, All The Way From England was at Villa Serena. I must have had a wistful look on my face because Zoltán tipped his head on one side, in that way he had.

"Go on," he said, "you've heard enough of me talking. Go and play in the sunshine."

"Will you swim with us this afternoon?" asked Marika. "Erzsi wants to go to the woods."

"No, that is something for you women. Only women's bodies should grace a pool like that. It is beautiful, Erzsi."

"Zoltán sees beauty in everything," said Marika, smiling. "His view of the world is wonderfully distorted."

"And don't you share it with me, this world?" he said. "How can it be distorted when there are two of us in it?"

I wandered back outside, leaving Marika and Zoltán together. They often forgot that I was there, something I liked on the whole because it meant that I was blending in. But occasionally it disconcerted me, making me feel younger, or older, than I really was. I went and sat down on the lawn at the edge of the terrace and stretched my legs out. I saw the view before me expand in simple brushstrokes and exaggerated color, just like Zoltán's paintings. I felt a prickle of longing for a world so bright and full of charm. It was as though they lived at the end of the rainbow.

We left for the pool that afternoon, when the sun was high in the sky. Even the surrounding fields seemed to sigh and shift, lazily. I had spent the rest of the morning reading in the shade of the terrace, drinking iced tea, holding each ice cube on my tongue for as long as I could bear. I had made my peace with the disappointment over Tamás. I didn't want to waste my precious days wishing for something that couldn't come true. Even I knew better than that. I crunched ice and listened to a bumblebee's drone coming from the patch of blue flowers by my feet. I watched the slow climb of a blue tractor on a far hill, enjoying the way its cranking rhythms came at me from behind, with the steep echo of the hills. Inside, Marika was singing. And she was making gingerbread, my favorite kind, chewy and soft, its top studded with almonds and smeared with honey.

We would pack squares of it in our bag with us, to eat after the swim.

When she was ready we walked together across the lawn and scrambled up the bank that led to the woods. I carried a red towel rolled under my arm, and beneath my dress I wore a yellow swimsuit. It was brand-new, from a mail-order catalog that had arrived by chance on our doormat in Harkham. I had spent a long time looking at the girls' things in the Summer Wear section, lusting after the tennis shoes that were available in five pastel shades, the frilly skirts with pictures of tiny sailboats teasing the hemline, and the swimsuits, in all their rainbow shininess. When my father telephoned to order the yellow one, its name Sunny, order code XF347, I'd stood beside him to make sure he got it all right. A week later it arrived in a slippery blue package with my name on it, and I'd pranced about our dark cottage wearing Sunny XF347, only faltering when I knocked my knee on the side of the card table. My father agreed that the suit was *just the thing,* and I felt good about wearing it then, in Hungary, knowing he had telephoned for it and paid by saying numbers into the receiver. That he was somehow still involved, as I hurried through the forest on my way to trying it out.

I wondered briefly what he was doing without me. Whether he'd remembered to watch our favorite detective show. And if he had, whether he sat nudged up on his side of the sofa, even though he could have stretched out and had it all to himself. I wondered if he still bothered poaching an egg for breakfast when it was just him. I hoped he did. I liked the thought of him cutting into the perfect yolk and mopping it with bread. Shaking salt first, then pepper to finish.

We passed the point where last year we'd seen Tamás, and cut onto a rough etching of a path. Clambering up a steep hill, our feet slipped on the clover and the ground was loose underfoot. We forged forward, briars snatching at our legs, until we hit a tighter, snaking path that could have been a rabbit run or a shoot for deer. The woods smelled thicker and deeper here. Above us canopies of oak and beech mingled. Around us were crooked trunks in drunken poses, with their roots tangled and branches listing. Marika panted slightly and drew her hand across her brow as sweat pricked her skin. I scuttled to keep up. I felt light-headed and my mouth hung open. Marika stopped to point out a giant orange slug like a wet and pickled alien fruit. I slapped my skin as flies descended. I began to wonder if a sunny blue swimming pool with white lines on the bottom and a kiosk selling lollipops and cola might have been a better idea, after all.

But then we came upon the pool. It appeared suddenly below us, lying deep in shadow and quiet as a tomb. After barely a moment's pause we slithered and skidded down the bank toward the water's edge. With one arm I clutched my red beach towel; the other was stretched out for balance.

Seen from above, partly obscured by foliage, it had looked like a small dark pond. Up close it was much larger, a pool that reflected the color and motion of everything around it—the blue sky, the green trees, the bright light. It had sprung up from the forest floor and remained a part of it. Willow trees trailed their fingers in the water. Trunks twisted with ivy stood like columns lining the edges. We stood on a flattened bank of wiry grass, broken only by sprays of buttercups that dusted our feet yellow.

"Wow," I whispered.

"It's nicer than I remembered," agreed Marika.

We were startled by a sudden splashing at the far end, and I jumped and clung to Marika's arm. I thought a giant stag might be rising and crashing toward us. Or a wet-backed bear rearing up and swinging its claws. But instead it was a certain yellow-haired boy. I squeezed Marika's arm unselfconsciously, and she nodded. She was seeing what I was seeing, too. He swam toward us in a fast crawl, droplets of water catching the light. He reached the middle of the pool and trod water, waving.

I couldn't tell if he was taller, or browner, or more pleased to see me than last year. But I knew one thing for certain. That at the hidden pool in the woods, magic was possible.

"Hey! Hello!" Tamás called from the water.

"Tamás! You're not away? At your grandparents'?" cried Marika.

"That's tomorrow! Are you coming in? Hey, Erzsi! You're here! You can jump, it's deep water. You can jump in!"

And so I did, without so much as a second thought. I slithered out of my dress, letting it drop to the floor, and I kicked off my sandals. Then I ran and leaped, far and high, one hand clutching my knees, the other my nose. I hit the water with a perfect splash, as though a frame in a comic book with an arc of water and letters across the page: S-P-L-A-S-H! I rose up spitting pondweed, my eyes streaming, my ears clearing to hear the sound of clapping from all around. Tamás in the water, Marika on the bank, the woods throwing back the joyful noise again and again. I kicked onto my back and lay floating, basking, deciding that that was happiness, right then. That was what it meant to be really, truly happy.

We spent the whole afternoon at the pool, until the sun dipped below the trees and we shivered in the water. Marika came in, too, and swam lengths with grace and speed. Tamás and I perfected our cannonballs, accompanying them with yells like wild things. He taught me how to swim down toward the bottom, and then skim along the stones eellike, rising back up toward the light only when my chest was bursting and stars were pricking at my eyes. We gasped and splashed together, rolling onto our backs, our chests heaving.

"I never had so much fun swimming before," I said as I floated, turning my hands in small, cupped circles. Tamás was beside me, and now and again parts of us bumped, our feet or a shoulder. It was like there were different rules in the water. When he'd been showing me how to swim un-derwater I'd just about mastered it, and he swam up behind me and tickled me. I'd struggled and laughed and swallowed water, bursting up and out, coughing and choking. If a boy had done that to me at home I'd have been furious. So per-haps it wasn't just the water that changed things, then.

"I wish I wasn't going to Debrecen," said Tamás as he floated beside me. "It's better here, now."

"Now?"

I paddled with my hands and dipped my head a little lower, felt the cooling water moving through my hair. *Now that you're here,* I willed him to say.

But "Yes, now," was all he said.

The sun had moved around and the shadows fell longer. Marika was lying on the bank and she called to us both then. I rolled onto my front and swam to the side, hearing Tamás's splashing stroke behind me. I got out reluctantly, wrapped myself in my towel and picked a handful of buttercups to remember the day. My fingers were shriveled and white and I wanted them to stay that way. Tamás stood dripping in his blue shorts, and said he ought to run ahead; he was expected at home.

I studied him while I could, from under the cover of my wet bangs. There was a sharpness to his features, a wiliness to his look. And his body was hard and deliberate looking, not like the pudgy boys in my class with dimples in their elbows, or the brittle ones that looked as though they could snap in a sharp breeze. Altogether, he was a perfect sort of boy.

"Are you away all week?" I asked boldly, my teeth chattering a little in the shade that fell.

"Yes. Until next Tuesday."

"Well, have a good time," I said, already at eleven affecting a cool demeanor.

"Yes, I did," he said, and smiled before waving, then disappeared through the trees. I didn't know if he had misunderstood me, but I held on to those words just the same. I watched the space he had left for a moment, then turned to Marika.

"Well, that was fun. Shall we go now?"

On our own far more leisurely walk home I handed Marika the bunch of buttercups that I had gathered.

"These could be for you," I said.

She took them, burying her face into the blooms. Then she dropped a kiss onto my head, light as a butterfly.

"That was brave, jumping in like that," she said. "I thought you were a more cautious girl."

"I wouldn't," I said, "normally." Then I added, "But nothing's really normal here, is it?"

Marika laughed.

"You understand, then. We are not so very different, after all, you and I."

And those words stayed with me, all the walk home and over our supper at a candlelit table and into my bed as I nestled in the rafters. To my frustration, they nudged out thoughts of Tamás. It was what I had wanted, to be not so very different from her. But it was the "after all" that nagged at me, like a ragged nail or a loose tooth, and I worried at it. For it meant that she had always thought of me as different, in the past. *Your father's daughter,* she used to say, and before it hadn't ever meant anything more to me than the sum of its parts. But now that she had chosen to make a life without him, for me to be *like* him reminded me that I was left on uncertain ground.

I wanted to ask her in what ways she thought we were similar, because I could think of some. I knew we both loved watching the flames shoot up when another log was put on the fire. We got excited about Christmas at the beginning of November, and cried when the tree was put out for the trash collectors after the holiday was over. And if we ever saw a dragonfly we'd stop whatever we were doing and follow its path, a blue-green piece of magic, bobbing and zipping like no other creature.

I wanted to ask her, *What else?* But I daren't. I couldn't risk her smile, feel the ruffle of her hand in my hair and hear her say, *You and me, Erzsi? Why, we're like chalk and cheese.*

★ ★ ★

One afternoon I tapped at the door of Zoltán's studio. He called, "Come in," in English and I wondered for a moment how he knew that it was me and not Marika. But she, of course, would have swept in without warning, throwing greetings and kisses in every direction. If he had been less used to her, his brush would be sent skidding across the canvas at her arrival, chimney pots and tree trunks would need to be sponged over and reworked. Or turned into something else altogether, the bright wing of a passing bird, or a sudden explosion of twisting vine. But Zoltán always met her vigorous currents head-on, with open arms and a smile that knew no buffets. I pushed open the door and peered in.

"Can I watch for a bit?" I whispered.

He looked suddenly piratelike; his painting smock had slipped and his shirt was open to his furry chest. A brush was jammed between his teeth, snarling his face in a way I hadn't seen before. But he whipped the brush out and beamed, and the Zoltán I knew was with me again.

"Erzsi! Of course! It is my pleasure. Give me one moment and then I am yours."

He gestured to the sagging sofa and I slid onto it, curling my legs underneath me. His pictures were full of vivid flourishes, yet his hand was slow and steady. I watched him, quite mesmerized. I decided that when next I couldn't sleep I would think of Zoltán painting. I would picture the set of his back and the crook of his arm and the gentle *dab, dab, dab* of paint on canvas.

"So, Erzsi!" He set down his brush and turned around. "What are we going to do today, make a little art?"

"I paint at school on Fridays," I said, "flowers and fruit

and once you had to do the person sitting in front of you so I did Sally Bryan."

"And how was this Sally Bryan, did you make her beautiful?"

I thought of Sally's gentle smatterings of freckles that in my hands had turned to a nasty orange rash. I thought of her perfect golden braids that I knew her mother did for her every morning, sitting at the table in their shiny kitchen, and how I had turned them into mustardy, knotted ropes. I put my hand to my mouth, my cheeks turning pink with the memory.

"I made her mad. Afterward, that is. She said she'd never seen anything so ugly in her life. She tried to rip it up but our teacher said it was actually quite good, just not very complimentary to the subject. Is that right, 'subject'?"

My words were lost in Zoltán's bellow of laughter. He beckoned me over to a spare easel and clipped a fresh sheet of paper to it. He rooted in a drawer and came out with a box of pastels; they were well-used and stubby, and the packaging was sun-yellowed, as though they'd been sitting in the sun glaring in from the window for a very long time before being stowed away. I took them reluctantly.

"Here, you have every color of the rainbow," said Zoltán.

"We used pastels at primary school," I said.

"So, show me what you can do," he said. He went behind the easel and dragged a stool into a patch of sunlight. He perched on it and thrust his chin high, stuck his hand on his hip. "So," he said, "draw me, and if I look anything like your Sally girl, then there is no ice cream for you later."

And so I began.

Zoltán didn't laugh when I'd finished; instead, he studied his portrait for some time, murmuring to himself. Then he turned to me.

"Very good, my little Picasso."

"You can keep it," I said, my bottom lip wobbling through my smile. "It's a present."

He asked me to sign my work, and as I bent to do so I asked him the question that I'd been holding on to all afternoon.

"Zoltán," I said, "do you think I'm the sort of girl to run and jump into a pond?"

He didn't answer right away, and so I went ahead and wrote my name in quavering capitals. I straightened up and handed it to him, then stood waiting. He gently wiped some pastel dust off my cheek with the corner of his apron.

"I think you're a girl who can do anything she wants, Erzsi," he said.

Together we walked outside—Zoltán carrying his portrait carefully so the bright dust didn't smudge, me walking in his footsteps, my heart beating fast. Two happy tears had escaped from my eyes, and when I put up my hand to catch them my fingers came away, smeared like the colors of the rainbow.

The remaining days of that summer's stay took on a steady rhythm. It was a visit characterized by small details, the minutiae of time well spent, as though after the days at the pool and in the studio my senses had been heightened to all the little things. The sparkly silver color of my toenails after Marika had painted them, and my hair—braided by her when it was wet from the bath, so that later when I shook it out under the sun, I wore a halo of tight curls. What else? A hot-dog sausage, its split skin glistening, with a perfect blob of muddy mustard beside it, eaten off a paper plate under the shade of a plane tree. A chocolate bar that had a bear in dungarees on the wrapper, that tasted sweet and smoky, like toasted marshmallows. János the wolf artist visited without Margit, and he showed me how to draw an elephant in one continuous line, without taking my pen from the paper. I signed it and gave it to him to keep, looking for the glint of gold as he smiled.

One day we went into Esztergom and stood looking at the giant green copper dome of the cathedral, then walked by the lazy river like regular tourists, licking ice creams, mine from the bottom up as the tip of my cone snapped off in my fingers. Zoltán pointed out Slovakia, a whole other country just across the water. We looked out over distant hills, and he told me of a time when Hungarian kings hunted in the woods, and I pictured volleys of arrows trailing red, white and green ribbons. Another time we went to the market, where stalls lined a street of mustard-colored houses with uneven tiled roofs. I stared at a pile of tomatoes heaped that shone like snooker balls, and helped Marika select red and yellow peppers shaped like witches' noses, all bulbous and crooked. We admired the lengths of *házi kolbász*, homemade sausage, and I tasted a slice off the end of a knife, held out by a woman with hands swollen like balloons. I chewed and chewed and when no one was looking I took a piece of obstinate gristle from my mouth and let it fall from my fingers, onto the street behind me.

After such visits I appreciated the joy of driving home afterward, bumping up the dirt road, calling out to the chestnut horses as we passed them in their field. And retreating into our house, for it was our house; I had left my mark on it. My things were strewn about, just like Marika's. A paperback I had finished, then added to a shelf in the hall, a pencil I had brought with me that had rolled under one of the sofas in the living room and I had purposely left there. Some loopy writing in the bathroom mirror that showed itself again when the mist rose: *I Was Here.*

Nothing bad happened to stir the days. I didn't say "Marika" out loud again, and the only time I came close to alarm was when Marika mentioned Marcie.

"You remember Marcie, don't you?" she'd asked as she peeled potatoes at the sink. She bent to rub an itch on her nose with her forearm, as her hands dripped muddy water.

Did I remember Marcie? With her mop of white bright hair, her heavy spectacles and her childish shrieks, she was forever imprinted on my mind. I saw her shape, all elbows and sharp shoulders, pushing closer to Marika as they sat around the Szabós' fire, whispering like schoolgirls with a secret.

"She's not coming here, is she?" I asked.

"Next week she is, just for the day. She and Zoltán have known each other for years."

"What about Zita and Tibor?" I asked, my head full of the *szalonna* party that first summer at Balaton, the impassioned chatter and whispering. "Do you see them much?"

"Not really." Marika hesitated, pursed her lips and blew at a wisp of hair that had fallen across her face. "Zita and I, we had a bad falling out, unfortunately. I don't think she altogether approved of what I wanted to do with my life. Not that it's any business of hers. But I hope to see them again perhaps one day. And if you'd like to, Erzsi, I know they'd be delighted."

"I like it when it's just us," I said, biting my tongue.

"I thought you did," said Marika, "that's why I rear-ranged Marcie's visit."

I felt a rush of relief like a sudden and welcome breeze. "Can I help peel?" I asked.

It was as though we moved together in a bubble, a delicate thing of beauty spun over the hills of Esztergom. Each one of us knew better than to press our fingers to its edges.

We only returned to the pool once more, the day before I was due to go home. It was so hot that to retreat into the shade of the woods was a great relief. And to plunge into the pool was heaven itself. Zoltán came with us that time. I caught sight of his bottom, bare like a hairy peach, and wished I hadn't. Marika regaled him with the story of my glorious first leap. I tried to replicate it, but was never able to go quite as far, or as high, again.

I remember saying goodbye to Villa Serena that year, more so than any other. I visited every room and whispered farewell, already mourning my own absence. I ran a hand over the green tiles of the stove; I curled my toes in the animal-skin rug. I kissed my finger and rubbed it on the tips of the antlers in the hall. I took a moment on the balcony, at my spot by the tall column and the snaking blue flowers, and leaned against the warm, red wood. I imprinted the view behind my eyes. The row of pine trees that staggered on the far slope, the thinly gauze-wrapped sun that dipped so low, the snatch of the Horváths' tin roof, Tamás's house, glinting like a mirror held to the sky.

I heard footsteps behind me. Marika was standing with her hands clasped.

"You must be looking forward to seeing your father?" she said.

Her voice whistled a little, like air coming out of a balloon.

I shook my head. "Of course," I said, "it's not that."

"What is it, Erzsi?"

"I don't know. I feel funny. It's like, the end of something."

"And the beginning of something else. You'll be back. We'll be waiting for you, remember?"

She pulled me to her, always more rough and tumble than other mums. She covered me in kisses, laughed and wiped my eyes and then her own. And then she took my elbow and steered me gently toward the waiting car. Like a time machine that would spirit me back to my other life.

CHAPTER FIVE

I was sitting on my blanket on the grass. My feet were rooted on the ground. In front of me was a clear stretch of park, rimmed by trees and tracked by paths. The sky came all the way to the treetops, then spun off uninterrupted, a rare thing in this patch of town. My small back garden, just minutes away, offered views of satellite dishes, soot-smeared chimneys and ill-conceived attic extensions, while in the near-distance high-rises skulked. It was all right as a place for coffee drinking on bright mornings, a sly cigarette on the back step or a crowded party, but when I really wanted to feel the space of outdoors, when I wanted my eye to carry to the horizon and then go on climbing, I came to the park. Here, I could almost believe that the land stretched away endlessly, on and on, cut only by oceans as it wound the curve of the earth. There was a time when I could slip easily between worlds, when it didn't matter where I was or what I saw, for I was constrained by nothing, flighty and fancy-free. With every step I took in the Devon lanes, leaves squelching underfoot and musty wafts filling the air,

I was transported to the dusty paths that carved through the hills around Villa Serena. I was able to blow back and forth without ever needing to shut my eyes so that I could travel. Nor was it an effort to remember, because I lived all my days in a curious mix of past and present and future. As though I was somehow infused with all the things that mattered, and carried them always with me.

In recent years, if I've looked back on this time, with shy glances and fretful stares, all I've seen is a sorry little girl waiting for her summer holidays to scoop her up and away to her fanciful land. A hopeless existence, living for a dream that was never real. I've stared from the misted windows of red buses and dawdled in snaking supermarket lines, thinking about the innocent fool I was.

But now? Now, timidly, tentatively, I was perhaps beginning to believe again. A little more with every page I turned. I sank lower on the blanket and shifted the book on my knee. It was midmorning and the sun was warming up, a gentle summer's day promised. The canal path would be ringing with bells as bicycles jolted past, pub gardens would be filling, early barbecues would be setting up, blankets thrown down in full sunlight. The park was growing a little busier, even as I watched. A man with smart glasses and new jeans just sauntered by with a newspaper, eyeing me as he passed. Two women in summer dresses walked past laughing, their elbows knocking. I probably looked for all the world like a studious girl caught in a good book, an arts student wrapped in reverie, a little away from the rising hubbub of a summer Saturday. But I was neither. I was traveling, to places strange and familiar.

In the picture it is 1993 and I am twelve years old. I am

on the dirt road that ran up to Villa Serena. I recognize it, because of the field of tall grasses that falls away behind me, and the sentry line of firs marking its edge. It was the second to last corner, the one you'd have to round before catching the first glimpse of the crooked gable. It was the corner after the stretch that ran beside the stream, the corner I had sailed around on Zoltán's bicycle, where water spilled over stones that were flat and round like pennies.

The image is crowded with sunshine. We are bleached, the scene and I. I'm standing by a gate with the field behind me, and its grasses are a watery green, yellow at the tips. I'm standing on stubbly ground, and my legs are long and coltish, my feet bare and brown from smudged tan and stained earth. I look a strange mix of modern girl and fairy queen, with strings of daisies caught in my hair and ragged garlands around my neck. I am wearing my yellow swimsuit, although it no longer hangs a little baggy, and a pair of cutoff denim shorts with jagged edges and straggling ends that sit just above my knees. Both of my hands are thrust deep into my pockets. My face is turned up to the camera, and I am laughing. It's an uneven laugh, unstaged. Whoever was taking the photograph must have said something funny, and I broke just as the shutter went.

It was because of the simple thing that I was beginning to believe in the memory of it all. The fact I could remember making the twisted garland of flowers that I was wearing around my head in the picture. I knew that it split three times, and I held my breath as I made dints with my thumb in the delicate stems. I could remember how when the sun shone directly on the yellow of my bathing suit it looked like gold dust. And I could remember exactly what we did after the photograph was taken. Marika and I climbed to the very top rung of the field gate and balanced. We held out our arms and threw our heads back and shut our eyes. And beneath us the world spun dangerously, beautifully.

I look at the picture again and I want to know this girl, draped in wildflowers, with her sides splitting.

It would be better to know her and love her than to have been her and forgotten. But she is nothing but a wisp, blown in from the pages of a dusty fairy tale. The old-fashioned kind that carries with it a hint of darkness, with nothing as it seemed.

It was a summer that began brilliantly. After much nagging my father had said that I could extend my stay to two weeks. After two years of successful one-week visits he felt safe that I would return home to him, untainted. A little browner, a little brighter, sometimes with alarming pockmarks from bites, but no obvious bad habits. And he seemed pleased how easily I appeared to slot back into life at Harkham. I made my bed and tucked in all the corners; I expressed interest in the progress of the hip-high broadbean stems. I circled the detective shows in the TV listings, and we still watched them together on chilly winter evenings. When the two-week stay was granted I ran upstairs and buried my face in my pillow and cried soundlessly, until my cheeks stung. Two weeks was a wonderful lifetime. I was growing more Hungarian by the day. Tears of joy were a definite symptom; I just had to keep them to myself.

My father and I never really spoke about Villa Serena. When I returned home from my trips he'd give me a brisk hug and prepare a pot of tea, saying, "So, do you want to see what's come up in the garden? The peas will be ready in a day or two." And for my part, I guarded my time at the villa closely. It was my secret life. With no incitement to describe it to anyone else I remembered it exactly as I wanted. I had a great faculty for replay, holding a single shining moment for as long as I wanted. I cheated time and space, living the same experiences over and over again, my head a treasure trove on even the darkest English days.

Occasionally my father would say, "I suppose she's all right, then?" the words squeezed from him reluctantly by conscience or politesse, and I would nod and be sure to ask an enthused question about when the corn on the cobs might be ripe enough to eat, or whether he thought the pink sky meant that rain was coming.

When my father appeared indifferent in this way, I tried hard to imagine a time when he and Marika had needed each other. When neither was complete without the other. They'd seemed to shrug each other off so easily, two planets that shifted into separate solar systems with infinite ease. But I knew it hadn't always been that way, because I found a card once. It was tucked inside the pages of a poetry book on the bottom shelf of the bookcase in the hall. I came across it on one of the days when I was exploring my whole house afresh. It was a rainy-day game, when I'd creep about, investigating every crooked beam and space beneath the baseboard. When I'd open books I'd never touched before, and peep behind curtains. I never knew what I was looking for, only that I'd know it when I saw it. My explorations turned up some interesting things. For one, a broken piece of pottery—Chinese-willow pattern with a blue bridge and ladies in cracked dresses—that was behind the dresser in the sitting room, beneath a pelt of dust. What else? A mother-of-pearl button that shone like treasure when turned in the light. And the card, the love card. It was written to my father and it was from Marika. It was dated 1983, so I would have been a toddler still, with pudgy knees and a bowl haircut. I guessed it for a Valentine's Day card, for it was ruby red and on the front a small white heart was painted. Inside was her florid handwriting, her ink pen blobbing in her haste to set her love down on paper. *Dearest David,* it said, *just remember, "they do not love that do not show their love."* The quote marks looked like wriggling tadpoles. I did not recognize it as Shakespeare, nor did I recite it back with pause or reflection to try and decipher it. Instead, I saw her lovely, reckless handwriting, the word *love* written not once but twice, and I imagined fanfares and rose petals and kisses dabbing the air like perfume. My parents twined in romantic bliss. Although I knew they had stopped loving each other, to know that they had once was reassuring. It was a history that made a sense out of me. The only both-ersome thing was that the poetry book belonged to Marika. It was called *Ariel,* a lovely airy-sounding name, and I'd seen her reading from it before, with her chin propped on her knees like a schoolgirl. As I slipped the card back inside its pages, I wondered why the card was kept in her book, not one of his. Had she changed her mind and not given it to him, after all? Or had he not prized it enough in her opinion, so she picked it up from where he'd dropped it and saved it for herself, like reclaimed treasure?

I think of that card again now, with its hand-painted heart of ragged brushstrokes.

They do not love that do not show their love.

It is a poetry that haunts. As though Marika is judging us still, and is right to.

On my third visit to Villa Serena I felt like an old hand as I walked up the path, my case bouncing behind me. Everything was the same; it was as though I'd never been away. Marika walked ahead, her long skirt skimming the heads of the daisies. She wore a set of jangling bracelets on both wrists, so her every movement was accompanied by music. Her long dark hair was braided and hung down her back like a swaying rope. She'd kissed me on both cheeks as I'd arrived at the airport, a smart, snapped ritual of a kiss that I hadn't had from her before. It had made me feel grown-up and continental, even if I'd secretly longed for a stifling hug with my toes lifting off the ground. Perhaps she had been unnerved by my appearance. I had grown again, and beneath my T-shirt was the tentative rising of two small breasts. I no longer wore my hair in braids but in a high ponytail, pulled tight and bouncing. Or loose so it fell over my shoulders in a glossy spread that smelled of shampoo and the coconut shine that I rubbed in the ends, a gift from a more glamorous friend at school. At home I had started listening to music; I danced on my bed to radio tunes and pressed lipstick kisses onto squares of toilet paper, feeling grown-up and naughty. But I still climbed trees and talked to myself, tramping through the copse behind the house. I still poked in hedgerows with sticks, and jumped through puddles if it rained. And I always picked flowers and set them in egg cups beside my bed, going to sleep dreaming of a house with a red roof and wooden arches. And swimming again with Tamás. Floating side by side.

"Erzsi! Welcome!"

Zoltán stepped from the side of the house and jabbed the air with a pair of metal tongs in wild greeting. I waved and hurried toward him. He wore an apron, blue and white striped like a butcher's, and a pair of flannel trousers that were rolled to the knee. On the breeze I caught the scent of barbecuing meat mingled with smoke and ash. My stomach grumbled. I hadn't eaten since my father's mottled cheese sandwich on the way to the airport and I was starving. But then it pitched, turned by the memory of a barbecue, with its heat and smoke and a giant lake rising behind. I felt sick and gripped the handle of my suitcase. It was foolish, because Zoltán often barbecued at Villa Serena. We'd sit elbow to elbow on the terrace, quite happily, our fingers greasy and our mouths aflame. Perhaps it was the journey from Budapest that was making me queasy. The hot sun had beaten through the windscreen all the way, pulling my eyes into a squint. Or maybe it was the early start, my father gently shaking me awake at five o'clock, when the light in my room was thin and shadows on the wall formed the jagged arms of the apple trees from our lawn.

I fought my face into a smile and decided I'd change out of my England clothes and wash my face at the little sink in my room. After a long drink of iced tea from a tall blue glass, the one with the scratched remains of flowers about its rim, I knew I would be ready.

I exchanged kisses with Zoltán, glad of their rapid formality, then rushed past Marika and up to the room I knew was mine, taking the stairs two at a time, my case thrashing behind me.

I had just changed into shorts and a vest when there was a tap at the door.

"Erzsi? Can I come in?"

Marika opened the door and stood just inside the room with her feet together and her arms folded. One hand pulled at her plait.

"How are we? Are we okay?"

It was a strange use of the plural, and I wondered if her grasp of the English language was slipping after all this time submersed in Hungary. Or perhaps she intended to implicate herself in my condition. Maybe she understood that she and I and Hungary were a knotted bundle.

"I'm fine," I said, taking a brush to my hair and yanking it through. "Just tired."

"I haven't done this yet," said Marika, and came to me with her arms wide like wings and scooped me up in them. My face pressed into her neck and I smelled cinnamon, warm apples and wood smoke, but from a winter's hearth, not a summer's grill. I screwed my eyes up tight and pushed harder into her.

"I can't breathe," I said in the end, and we pulled away, doubled with chirrupy laughter.

"Erzsi, you're growing up." She stood back, appraising me, her face lit with pride. She set her hands on her hips, her head on one side. "You're not a little girl anymore."

"It's only because you haven't seen me for a year. Dad thinks I'm still eight years old, I'm sure of it."

"And how is your father, Erzsi?"

My father was distracted. He poured milk into his tea

until it ran white, and trod muddy footprints across the
carpet before cursing under his breath and dropping to his
knees to scrub at them. He made a whole day last on just a
few words spoken, and only some of them to me. I decided
he'd perhaps be glad to be on his own for a bit. Perhaps
that was my problem. I was thinking too much about my
father. Just two days ago I had found him in his study with
a handful of photographs. He'd pushed them under some
papers as I came in, but I saw a flash of blue water or big
sky on one of them. I thought right away of Balaton. His
face wore a guilty expression, his eyes were cast down. He
looked about a hundred years old. *What are you looking at?*
I'd asked, quick as a whip. *Nothing,* he'd replied in a voice
that snapped. *Nothing that matters, anyway,* he added softly.
I wanted to say, *Everything matters, Dad,* but I couldn't. My
throat felt rusted, as if the words would flake if they came
at all. I'd left the room quietly.

Then just yesterday, as I set my suitcase down in the hall,
he'd clasped his hands to my shoulders and I'd felt the press
of each one of his fingers. *You'll have a good time, won't you?*
he'd said, a little wildly, his hair on end. *Of course I will,* I'd
said. *I always do.* And I saw the relief then. He loosened his
grip and patted my head. *Good girl,* he said. He made having a good time feel like an achievement.

"He's fine," I answered.

"Please do give him my regards," said Marika, with solemnity, handling the words delicately, as though a foreign
language. "I do think of him, I do…" Then she clapped her
hands together, laughing as she ran headlong back into safe
territory, "Oh, Erzsi, listen to me. Zoltán had a wonderful
idea! Would you like to hear it? As you're here for longer,

and I'm so very happy that you are—it was good of your father to let you come, it really was—but as you're here for longer, what do you say to making some trips?"

"Trips?"

"Yes, day trips. Or for a couple of days even, we could stay away. It's just that all you ever do when you're here is rattle around this house and the fields and the forest and I know you like all that but there's the whole of Hungary to see. It'd be an adventure, Erzsi. You've barely seen Budapest. Heavens, we hardly even go to Esztergom when you're here. I want to show you more. You know, on the river Danube you can take a boat and sail all the way to a wonderful little place called Szentendre. It's an artists' town. Zoltán sells some of his pictures in a gallery there. What do you say? Does that sound fun?"

I sat down on the edge of my bed and placed my hands on my knees. I remembered last year, when I called her *Marika* out loud, and when she had stuttered and made the mistake of saying it was just like Devon there. How, then, I had tipped my chin and wielded a little power, a new wand in an uncertain grip. Earlier that year I had learned about the idea of "playing people." It was a girl called Ginny in my class at school who'd taught me. She had red hair and a gap between her teeth like a tunnel through rock. She said her parents had split up, and that she spent alternate weekends with them. Her green eyes were shot with glee as she told me that she had learned to make sure that all her sentences started with, "Mum always lets me…" or "Dad said I could…" Through such tactics she won extra helpings of ice cream, late nights at the movies and expensive shopping trips. Once she threw open the doors to her closet and showed me all her new dresses, shining like a neon rainbow. I couldn't stop myself from gaping a little.

"Wow, Ginny," I'd said, "but wouldn't you swap it all, just to have them back together?"

"No, idiot," she'd snapped, and pushed her hand on my face to quiet me, a little too hard for my liking. "I hate them," she'd said.

I'd gone home with my nose tingling and a resolution to ignore Ginny from then on. That evening I sat across the table from my father at supper and we ate muddy pools of oxtail soup with silver spoons.

"I think it's bedtime for you, Erzsi, after this. You've a test tomorrow, haven't you?"

It was only eight o'clock. It was still light outside; I could hear the birds chattering. I had planned to go to the bottom of the garden after dinner and watch the rabbits. Tuck in behind my favorite holly bush and wait for them. And I had a new letter from Marika that I had been saving. I wanted to read it outside, under the same sky, with the same pale moon, low and rising. But I blew on my soup and nodded. There wasn't any point in upsetting him, he didn't deserve that. But Marika? Marika was different.

"Well—" I looked at her and kneaded my hands together "—I really, really like it here. And the time always goes so quickly, anyway, without going anywhere else."

"But, Erzsi, there's so much of Hungary you're not seeing."

"I've been to Balaton," I said, "and I didn't much like it. Neither did Dad." I dipped my head but then forced myself to look up. I met her eyes and held them. Marika looked away first.

"Balaton's very beautiful," Marika began, not able to help herself. "I think if you were to see it again…"

"No way," I said, standing, "no way. You *would* say that. I wouldn't go back there if you paid me. It's a dump, and I hate it."

I was shouting, and I could feel a swell of tears rising. I hadn't ever shouted at Marika before, and it felt like something snapping, that couldn't be mended again. I clenched my fists and thought of Ginny and her selfish resolve. But even Ginny broke when pushed. I'd had the print of her hand on my face to prove it. For the first time I wondered if anything she had said was even true. What if she was lying, and instead of reigning victorious she spent her days curled in a ball, crying. All her gifts scattered about her.

I panicked. I didn't know what I was supposed to do next. But Marika wasn't waiting to see. She turned and slammed the door behind her, leaving the space where she had stood and hugged me peculiarly vacant, the sunlight making the dust dance.

I threw myself back on the bed. I had gotten it so horribly wrong. Now I would be sent back to England, my two weeks over before they had even begun. I rolled onto my front and wept messily.

"Erzsi, Erzsi, stop it."

I hadn't heard her come back in. I turned slowly, my arm wiping my face, and saw her standing just inside the doorway, holding something in her arms. I wriggled up and pushed my hair out of my eyes. I sniffed noisily.

"Would you look at this? Just for a moment. I'd like you to see it."

Marika's voice was soft but frayed. I looked at her face,

ignoring what was in her arms, and saw that her eyes were red at the edges, her cheeks scarlet with pinched color. I went to her and draped my arms around her, let my head rest against hers.

"I'm sorry," I whispered, "I didn't mean it."

"Look, Erzsi. Look what I have."

She turned around the bulky object she was holding and I saw that it was a canvas. A painting. And it was almost entirely blue. The color of cornflowers and the color of the night sky. The color of the stripes of the sweater I wore on my first visit, and the color of my tongue after eating a blueberry ice pop. It was Lake Balaton, a sweep of sky and a stretch of bank, made of Zoltán's brushstrokes. The water was one blue where the sun sprayed, and another blue where it nudged the bank in the shallows, and blue again where it ran on endlessly toward a different horizon. All blue, blue, blue. I looked at the picture and the picture looked back. I had been there; I had swum in those waters. And it had been beautiful, for a time.

"Why are you showing it to me?" I whispered.

"Because it's beautiful. Life is beautiful, Erzsi. And it's far too short for regrets. You're too young to understand, but one day you will. We must learn to always take the good of a place."

"Is that what I should do? I came, didn't I? I came to Hungary."

"Yes, you did. And I'm so very glad of it."

"And I love it here. I love the villa, and the hills. I really do. I hate going home, every time I hate it. But..."

"Would you like to keep this painting here in your room, to look at?"

"I don't know."

"I just think, I don't know…it's so beautiful. I think it's one of Zoltán's best. He would be pleased if it were hung in here, for when you come."

I looked at Marika and she proffered it to me, as a gift. I took it and held it in front of me, my arms outstretched.

"Just think about it. And come downstairs when you're ready. We have the most wonderful feast waiting. Zoltán's been cooking all day. There's plenty of sausages, pork steaks, and I've made a potato salad with those little gherkins."

"Thank you," I whispered.

As Marika left the room I stood holding the painting, drinking it in. My heart thumped in my chest like somebody else's anger. I set the picture carefully against the wall and went downstairs.

After my discordant arrival, we enjoyed a peaceful afternoon. Zoltán went inside for a siesta, I found a patch of grass to lie in and propped my chin in my hands and Marika fetched a book, a giant hardback with a sun-yellowed spine. She draped herself on a lounger, tucked just inside the shade of the veranda. I watched her as she stretched her long legs and crossed her ankles and I noticed the freckles on her chest and her collarbones shining brown. She wore a white cotton blouse that was half unbuttoned, with embroidered flowers like snippets from a gypsy headscarf at the cuffs. Her silver bangles glittered in the sun. Her braid lay over one shoulder, and I noticed a red poppy head with a blackened ink blot at its middle, twined under the band that held it in place.

"What's that flower in your hair?" I said.

"Oh, a poppy. Zoltán put it there. He's always decorating me. You should watch out, Erzsi. You'll wake up and find yourself bound in daisy chains."

"You look like a gypsy woman," I said. "Where did you get your blouse from?"

"I made it, I sewed all these little flowers, only don't look too closely as the stitching is terrible."

"You never made handmade clothes before," I said.

"Oh, I did. I used to make your dresses when you were very small. And I've knitted scarves before. But I always managed to use itchy wool so they were never very popular. Would you like a blouse like this one, Erzsi?"

I considered it. I liked the exotic look of Marika. She belonged there, with her blackened tresses and their flash of red, her embroidered blouses and rumpled skirts. She looked as though she should be sitting on the steps of a horse-drawn caravan, one painted with swirling flowers and pulled by a clod-footed pony the color of a magpie. I imagined myself sitting with her, similarly adorned. Then I saw myself in Devon, waiting for the bus to town on a Saturday in a raincoat and black sneakers.

"Maybe," I said. "Can I go up to the forest?"

It had become a tradition on my first day to scout the land, making sure that everything was as it should be. The tree on the ridge with arms like a man surrendering. The silver brook with the gangly pond skaters. And my favorite part, the skidding run back down to the lawn from the woods above, where every step revealed another section of the house like a jigsaw puzzle, first a chimney stack, then a glimpse of tile, or Zoltán in his canvas work shirt passing on the balcony. I felt like a loping giant as I ran toward Villa Serena, my arms spread.

"Of course. But be careful, though, Erzsi. Don't go where you're not supposed to. The Horváths have been hunting beyond the woods."

"Hunting? Which Horváths? All of them?"

"István, I suppose. And Bálint, no doubt. It's their own land, of course, but the shots crack awfully close to the house sometimes."

I thought of István and Ági, Tamás's parents. I'd passed them on the dirt road and always greeted them with shyness, embarrassed at my own curiosity. I couldn't stop staring, at Ági's bowl haircut the color of a pumpkin and the scuffed white clogs she wore. István beside her was built like a bull, with a thick neck and sun-wrinkled skin. His sleeves were perpetually rolled to the elbow, his arms like two giant hams. He always winked as he said hello, and Ági would nod, the sides of her mouth twitching. But Tamás's parents had a practical, no-nonsense air about them. Did they hunt their supper? I imagined a skinny wood pigeon as the Sunday roast, Tamás with a napkin tucked in his T-shirt, licking his lips at the prospect. Somehow it didn't seem likely.

"I won't get shot, will I? By accident?" I said.

"Of course not, just be careful."

She waved her book at me and I clambered up from the grass where I lay. I wiped my hands on my shorts and set off across the lawn.

I didn't like the idea of people with guns lurking in the forest. I knew I would balk at every shadow, turn each time I heard a crunch of twig or rustle in the grass. To distract myself I thought of the football stickers that I had brought out with me for a second time, that I had been too shy to give last year. Their edges were folded and the players had probably changed teams by now, but perhaps they would still be welcomed.

I trod cautiously through the forest, listening for unfamiliar sounds. It was as noisy as it ever was, the boughs above exploding with birdsong, the insects humming, the frantic rustle as a deer pounded through the foliage in sudden exit. If my favorite part of the forest walk was the run back down to the villa, my second favorite was the View. The View was a moment, as well as a place, that part of my walk when I reached the highest point of the forest, and the thick trees gave way to tumbled hillside as far as the eye could see. It was yellowing and stubbled with bent grasses and old shrubs, and a view that looked far and away to a thin smudge of horizon. I would emerge from the trees blinking and gaze toward another part of Hungary altogether, an unknown land. Esztergom lay behind me somewhere, a place easily recognized by its silver twist of river and bulging cathedral dome, as did the road we took from the airport, a straight sweep with the flat roof of a car factory beside, and lines and lines of shining vehicles in reds and blues and silvers. These landmarks did not belong in the View. Instead, there was the soft bump of neighboring hills, studded with slant-roofed huts and sweeps of vineyard. Then the endless run of fields, tripped with pale trails of dust and loose stones, spreads of long-stemmed flowers, their heads yellow and heavy, and bright bursts of ornamental-looking trees mixed in with oceans of beech and oak. The hum of heat hung overhead, paling the landscape, dousing the horizon in a haze of light.

I wanted to slip into the clearing reverently. But as I pushed the last stubborn fronds aside and dipped my head to pass under a hazel branch, I caught a flash of color and froze. Someone had found the View. I stayed where I was, hidden by branches, and squatted down to peep. It was a man and a woman, or a boy and a girl; I couldn't tell their ages. The man was tall and angular. He wore just a pair of jeans and his chest and arms were skinny and brown, muscles popping like crooked bones. The woman was blond haired and pale with a loose cotton dress that had slipped off her shoulders, showing a swell of breast. They were entwined and their hands were everywhere as they kissed each other. I crouched with my hand covering my mouth, my breath hot in my palm. I was sure I couldn't be seen and they were oblivious to their surroundings, lost in each other in a way that I had only seen by accident on television.

Then things changed again. They dropped to the floor in a strange and seamless movement as though the ground had come up to meet them. The man seemed to suddenly have more sets of hands, for he was gathering mops of the girl's yellow hair, so it spilled through his fingers, while simultaneously pulling at his jeans. The girl's dress had fallen low, and he was dragging it down farther still. As he knelt, one of his hands went behind her, and for a moment she was suspended, held by the curve of his arm. I was close enough to see a button fly off, caught its twinkle as it rolled into the grass. I was close enough to see a patch of darkened skin on the man's back, a mottled birthmark or old sunburn. I was close enough to see the inside of the girl's mouth as she tipped her head back, a flash of pink tongue and white teeth. I'd never seen a face like that before. And then they were rolling, and this time it was the man that faced me, his face lifted toward the sky. He looked younger than I'd thought, after all, about seventeen or eighteen, with flattened hair and a wet mouth. And then he saw me. He looked right into my eyes, as though he'd known I'd been there all along. His face changed, from abstract to horribly real, a grin twisting his lips. He tipped his head in acknowledgment, just as though we were passing each other on the track, not at all as though there was a half-naked girl beneath him, who at this point had not seemed to notice that anything had changed. When he called out to me—as I knew he would, for I saw it in the teasing shimmer of his eyes—his voice came all slurred and breathy, and so loud, in the clearing.

"What are you looking at, little girl?"

My heart thumped so loudly in my chest that I feared it'd burst right through me. I gasped and struggled up from my crouching position. My legs were stiff and I was clumsy. The grasses around me rustled. The girl tried to turn her head. The man laughed. He broke away, and got to his feet in one deft movement. Pulling at his jeans he began to come toward me, his belt swinging loose, the sun winking off its metal clasp.

I turned then and ran, not caring how much noise I made, my feet skidding on the uneven ground, brambles catching at my arms and legs. I ran until I was sure no one was following me, and I could stop for a moment and steady my breathing. But my heart rattled still. Because he had tried to chase me, for three or four strides he had definitely been coming toward me. And all the time the girl had been shouting something in a crackling voice, like the leaves underfoot as I ran.

As soon as I got my breath I ran on, hurtling back down

the woods toward Villa Serena. I burst onto the lawn with
red-hot cheeks and my hair damp at the nape of my neck.
Marika was still reading on the lounger. She waved absently
as she saw me. I hurried inside and shut myself in the bathroom, locking the door. I washed my hands and face and
pulled my hair back into a ponytail. If Marika or Zoltán
asked, I would simply say that I'd played around at the edge
of the woods, but never far from the garden.

My face in the mirror was a marvel, red slowly settling
itself to pink. Fear had sent blood pounding to the surface.
I splashed more cool water on my cheeks. I couldn't get
the man's face out of my head. I'd had a clear view as he
came toward me, brown eyes and sharp cheekbones and hair
tucked behind ears. Then I realized who he looked like.
It was Tamás. An older, meaner, uglier version of Tamás.
Marika had once talked about there being an older brother
who was *cut from a different cloth*. Bálint. I hadn't understood
what she meant by that phrase but now I did. If you were cut
from a different cloth you could do things in the woods with
a girl that looked like they hurt. You could chase someone
just for being in the wrong place at the wrong time. And
your little brother, who seemed so good, could grow up to
be just like you, without even knowing it. And then I realized something else. That he had spoken in English. Not
in Tamás's precise and delicate way, or Zoltán's lusty drawl,
but English nonetheless. Which meant he knew who I was.
Which made things even worse than they had seemed five
minutes ago, when they were already bad. I stared hard at
my face in the mirror and blinked rapidly. Crying was no
help at all. There were no excuses I could make for him, no
way I could paint the picture so it was less incriminating.

And wasn't I just as bad for being there in the first place? Wasn't it my fault, just as much as his?

After that, I really did stay close to the house and garden for the next few days. The woods had changed somehow. I kept thinking about what I'd seen. The glimpse I'd had of a different kind of world that I wasn't sure I wanted to know existed. I shook my head and tried to fill it with different things. I know I got under Marika's feet a little because she told me so with a laugh, as she stepped around to reach the stove. I helped her make an enormous pan of goulash that lasted for three meals. My job came at the end, frantically cutting dough fragments to cook as dumplings on the goulash's red-hot surface. I asked her to read sections of her book out loud to me, and she did so, reluctantly at first, then with gusto. We were transported to eighteenth-century France, where women hid behind fans and carried miniature dogs with squashed faces. I trailed Zoltán, too, taking my spot on the studio sofa, folding Budapest newspapers across my knees as though I were reading them, looking learned. I watched him paint a sky the color of rock pools with a red sun swirling in the middle of it. I tracked the progress of a fat-bellied fly knocking the windowpane before seeing it zip off in a jagged path. I made daisy chains, great lengths of them, and wore them as bracelets, necklaces and headdresses. And once, when no one was watching, I snuck upstairs and looked at the painting of Balaton, which was now hanging on the white back wall of my bedroom. I let it swallow me until I felt the rustling breeze in my hair and the warm water about my ankles. Until I squinted at the sun, reflected brighter than ever before. Until I felt like I'd fall in.

After three days like that I threw myself down by Marika's feet and made a proposal.

"Can we still go on a day trip?"

"A day trip?"

"Or for a couple of days? Like you said? I think you're right. I don't think I've seen enough of Hungary. I'm fed up with these fields. I'm bored."

But I wasn't bored. I had never been bored. I could sit down on a patch of grass and find entertainment to last me a whole afternoon. But I knew it would touch a nerve. Marika had always grown bored easily.

"I could tell you were restless. Poor thing. Well, Erzsi, I think it's a wonderful idea. But it's Tamás's birthday tomorrow. I saw his mother in the lane and he's invited you to a barbecue."

"What, all of us?"

"No, just you. It's for children. You don't want us adults hanging around. His brother, Bálint, is doing the barbecue, so you won't even have the dear old Horváths bumping around. What do you say?"

"His brother? I thought you didn't like him. I thought you said he was bad."

"Did I? Oh, I don't know, perhaps when he was younger he was difficult. Teenagers, Erzsi, just you wait. And I know you haven't seen Tamás yet this year but you two do seem to get along, and he always asks about you."

"Does he?"

"Of course he does."

I wanted more information. I wanted to know what these questions were that he asked, and if he came expressly to ask them, of if they were just chance occasions in the street, or at the market. Did he stand twitching on the veranda, his arms folded and his feet shuffling, or did he throw a casual question over his shoulder as he picked a watermelon from the kiosk on the high road? But more than anything I wanted to know if Bálint and Tamás were the kind of brothers that told each other everything. And laughed together with dirty looks. I snapped the daisy chain that I had been working on and folded my hand around it.

"I don't think I want to go," I said. "I'll be the only one speaking English. No one will talk to me."

"Oh, Erzsi, don't be silly. You were asked especially. I think it'd be rude not to go."

"But if we went away somewhere it wouldn't matter. We could just say that we had it planned."

"Why do you suddenly want to go away? Erzsi?"

I dropped my head. Several different answers flitted rapidly through my head, like slippery fish through shallow water, but I didn't think I had the heart to share any of them. So I answered obliquely, in flattened tones.

"I just want to. Sometimes people just want to do things."

Marika nodded and I knew I had my way.

Our timing turned out to be poor. The day started unusually gloomily, and without the sun bursting through the windows we slept longer and later under the cover of cloud. Zoltán had elected to stay behind as he had work to do, but he was nonetheless determined to send us off with a good breakfast, so he fried eggs and English-style bacon. The bacon was more like fatty chunks of ham with blackened rind, but fried to a crisp it tasted delicious. Meanwhile, Marika misplaced a precious earring, and there was a great

search for it which involved checking under the floorboards
and in the far corners of each room. Finally, there was an
argument about the route to take, where Zoltán and Marika
spread a map over the kitchen table and both insisted they
knew a better way, their fingers jabbing at the paper until
I feared it'd tear. Then they went to the balcony and I saw
through the blinds that they were kissing, not wanting to
part on bad words.

Marika and I finally left at midday, bumping slowly down
the dirt road with the car windows wound down low. Just as
the first arrivals for the birthday party were on their way up
the lane. Tamás was with them, taller than last year, his skin
just as brown. Red shorts, this time, and a white shirt that
was creased at the shoulders. Marika looked at her watch.

"He must have met his friends from the bus," she said.
"Oh, and I never did let them know you couldn't come.
How rude."

I sank low in my seat. The car had to slow to a crawl to
get past the children without crushing toes or knocking
elbows. They stood with their backs to the hedgerow on
either side, peering in at us. Five of them and Tamás. Four
boys and two girls, both of whom were wearing short cotton dresses and had gold earrings that caught the sun. I reminded myself that I was Western and glamorous. Erzsi All
The Way From England.

"Hello!" Tamás waved. He peered into the car. "Hello,
Erzsi. Welcome! Are you coming this afternoon?"

I just stared, and the words I tried to say stuck like glue
to my teeth. Marika spoke in Hungarian and laid her hand
on Tamás's arm as she did so. He looked disappointed, I
could see that. The face was the same in English and Hun-

garian. He bent into the car again, and with the conversation having turned to Hungarian I felt safe in studying
him. He looked a little changed, but not a bit like the man
in the woods. Except perhaps the shape of the nose, and
something about the texture of the hair. He smiled at me.

"I wish you to get well soon, Erzsi."

I raised my eyebrows, glanced across at Marika. "Thank
you," I said. "And, oh… Happy birthday."

We drove on, and I saw in the side mirror that they were
watching us, the six children in the lane on their way to
a party. I felt sad suddenly that I wasn't a part of it, after
all. That my official status as a friend of Tamás's, an exotic friend, All The Way From England, was not to be ce-
mented. I thought of everybody else making a fuss of him.
Gobbling hot dogs streaked with ketchup and Coca-Cola
from paper cups, and dancing to music from a stereo on the
patio. But I was thinking of English parties. At Tamás's, the
sullen, dangerous brother would be sweating over the grill.
If he saw me he'd surely tell everyone I'd been caught spy-
ing. Make me feel silly or worse. And what if the girl with
the yellow hair was there, her face still flushed, her clothes
rumpled and even torn? I wouldn't be able to look at her.

"What did you say to him?" I asked suddenly. "What
did you tell him?"

"Oh, God, I don't know," said Marika. "I panicked. I felt
sorry for him. I said I had to take you to the doctor's because
you felt sick. Sorry, Erzsi, I didn't know what else to say."

We were pensive rather than carefree as we headed for
Szentendre, the town on the Danube that Marika had mentioned. A place of houses like frosted party cakes by a wide
slice of river. Zoltán's pictures were in a gallery there, and

he had described it to me, with its white arches and a tiled floor the color of the ocean, set on a steep and cobbled street. We were going to visit, to tell them our names and enjoy whatever treatment that afforded us. I had high hopes of lemonade taken in a shady courtyard, and Marika played along and told me she longed for sweet wine in a crystal glass and salted cashew nuts eaten from a hand-painted bowl. We would stand with our hands held behind our backs and peer learnedly at the paintings. But meeting Tamás had left me morose, and every mile we drove took me farther away from him and toward the possibility that I'd made a mistake. We avoided the main roads and passed through rambling forests and villages one street long, their houses set side-on with gardens falling behind and tangerine-footed geese padding at the verges. Once we slowed to let a swineherd and his charges pass, their crumpled snouts knocking at our tires. We saw two children riding stout ponies bareback, their hands making fists in the white manes. I thought again of the girl in the woods and Tamás's brother's hand closing around her hair. I broke out in a sudden sweat and looked to Marika. I wanted her to say something, anything. She turned to me.

"Erzsi, I feel terrible. Here's me trying to make you go to a party you don't want to and I'm sitting here having missed three of your birthdays. How dreadful of me. I didn't think. Is that why you didn't want to go?"

"No," I said. "I hadn't even thought of it. Really. Anyway, you didn't miss them, you sent me lovely cards. And that bag with the stars on it, and the picture book of Hungary."

"Cards," repeated Marika. "Yes, I suppose I did. If only

your birthday was in the summer, you could have spent it here."

But I liked having it in May. May brought with it sunny evenings and sweet blossoms. The hedgerows were spotted with wildflowers and I could sleep with my window open at night, watching my curtains lift in the breeze and pretend I was high up in a tree house. And birthdays were one day when my father seemed to brighten, shaking off his dogged quietness like a giant waking. He'd buy a cake from the baker in the next village and set it in the middle of the table. He'd make sandwiches—cheese and cucumber, corned beef and crinkly lettuce—then cut them into triangles and heap them on a plate, far too many just for two of us. And he'd put on a record as we had our tea, our old cottage shaken by "California Girls," me sipping my tea wondering what it would be like to drink a case of some-one, as Joni Mitchell seemed to do. It was a far cry from the parties of my friends, with coordinated dance moves across a carpet freed from furniture, florid paper plates and pointed pink shoes, but I loved it.

"However," said Marika, "there are always *névnaps*. Perhaps we could do something with that."

And so Marika told me what it meant to have a name day in Hungary. It was strange, to think of everyone across the country with the same name as you celebrating at the same time. I preferred the randomness of birthdays, the feeling of the stars aligning themselves the day you were born. But the concept intrigued me nonetheless.

"So children in Hungary get two sets of presents, then? That's not fair."

"Well, you have to remember, Erzsi, that children here

aren't spoiled the way that English children are. Tamás didn't get a great heap of gifts this morning. Birthdays are, in fact, less important than *névnaps*."

"He didn't?"

"People are poorer. You really don't know what it's like. We're sheltered here, in our Esztergom valley, but go to the towns, Erzsi, the cities, people don't live all that well. Life isn't always easy here."

"When is my name day?"

Marika just scratched her nose.

"But better to be poor and free," she went on. "That's what Zoltán says. And we do live well, in our way. He makes enough from his paintings. He really does very well. More tourists are coming now, Erzsi—you'll see today in Szentendre, people from Germany and Austria—and they will pay far more for a beautiful landscape than we could have imagined before."

"But when is my day? Is it in the summer?"

Marika took her eyes from the road and turned to me. She tapped her fingers on the steering wheel and I heard the *clack-clack* of her silver rings.

"I think it's in the autumn, Erzsi. Or the winter. We'll have to look it up when we get home. But listen, I have an idea. We could just adopt you a name, couldn't we? A summer name-day name, so we have something to celebrate while you're here."

"I don't want to be anybody else," I said.

"Well, then—" Marika hesitated "—we'll have to think of something. Don't worry, it'll be something wonderful. I know it."

I didn't think anything needed thinking of. I was fine

as I was, with a birthday in May and a summer holiday to Hungary.

"I've got it!" Marika smacked the horn with her hand as she proclaimed triumphantly, "Wishes! Three wishes, one for every birthday I've missed! What do you say?"

"Like in Aladdin?" I said.

"Exactly! Think of me as your own personal genie."

Her face cracked wide with glee, her mouth open, and a flick of red tongue was visible as she laughed. Part of me wanted to be carried along in her excitement, tell her to blare the horn again and stick my head out of the window and shout, "Three wishes!" to anyone who passed. My mother the maker of magic, with whom anything was possible. She, whose heart pounded in her chest, beneath warm brown skin and a blouse embroidered with Hungarian flowers. Hadn't her own great wish come true? To live in Hungary again, despite the trappings of a life back home? She'd pulled it off, and still kept me by her side. Perhaps she was a genie, after all.

"Okay, three wishes," I said, "but only if you promise they'll come true."

"I promise, I promise."

I made my wishes from that moment, not choosing all that carefully, just taking the things that happened to be in my head.

"First, then, is that you'll never make me go to the Horváths' house, if I don't want to."

"Oh, Erzsi."

"I mean, I like Tamás, but I don't want to see his family or his brother and things. I don't like visiting people, not understanding when they speak Hungarian at me."

I felt like a traitor. A traitor to the forest pool and learning to swim underwater. A traitor to football stickers and practicing English. But the creased and shining face of Bálint loomed large in my imagination and made me shudder.

"I'll never make you do anything you don't want to, Erzsi. So, all right, no visits to the Horváth house. Although it's a shame. They have a lovely farmyard with all sorts of animals, and you never have been to see them. Do you remember Jimmy the goat, from your first time here?"

"My second wish…" I continued, "is that for lunch today, all we have is ice cream. One of those glass cups where they pile it all in and dribble sauce on top and perhaps even an umbrella."

"Oh, Erzsi, you'll be sick. But yes, absolutely, your wish is granted. Ice cream for lunch."

I didn't have to think hard about my third and final wish, as the words of it were always just phrased near the edges of my lips, tucked behind so they were never quite said. But I felt the taste of them always, like anticipation tinged with the fear of disappointment. Sweet, salty and flat.

"And I wish, I wish that I could come here, every year, for the rest of my life. And stay for longer when I want to. And that the sun will always shine and we'll always be happy when I'm here and that nothing will ever change."

Marika pulled over then. She swung off the road and bumped the car onto the edge, grasses brushing its metalwork. We had been here before, the first time she picked me up at the airport. I knew what was coming. She leaned across and pulled me over in a ragged hug, the sort that squeezed my breath and ended in soggy kisses. I smelled cinnamon again and a zesty kind of spray-on scent applied especially for the trip to town. I knew then that my third wish had been the One. The one I really meant, with all my heart, and the one that Marika could make come true. And it had a snatch of magic about it, as all good wishes do, Marika reaching to the stars and drawing them toward her in a pattern that meant our happy fates were decided.

In the end, the day had been perfect. We ate our ice-cream lunch at an iron table set on cobbles by a fountain that dribbled and gurgled green water. We visited the gallery and saw Zoltán's pictures and our steps had a strut about them, for we knew and loved the artist. We were given mints to suck like cool pebbles and I was mesmerized by one picture with a little brown-haired girl that looked just like me, lying on her front, watching the fields drop away before her in an endless stretch. Later, we sat on a bench by the river Danube and ate dusty paprika crisps from a big red bag, licking the salt and spice from our fingers. And on the drive home we saw a horse and cart carrying a gypsy family. Six dark figures wearing sweaters and long clothes in the hot sun. I watched with curiosity from my open window and swapped stares with a girl of my age or younger who was sitting astride the back of the cart, a stick in her hand. She had seashells wound into her hair and eyes like sweet toffees. I smiled and waved. She smiled back, and I saw two rows of perfect teeth. She waggled her stick in the air as we passed, and I twisted in my seat to watch her grow ever smaller.

Tucked in my bed that night, beneath the Balaton painting, I relived each of the things that made the day. The big and the little. I thought about the gypsy girl and her easy smile. The salty taste of the paprika crisps on my lips and

the toy town streets of Szentendre. And the wishes. I lingered longest on the third wish, the big one, the one that
had made Marika pull the car over and gather me up in
her arms.

As I shut my eyes and rolled toward sleep, I felt again her
fierce embrace. Marika had hugged me as though she was
the one who needed to hold on to me tightly. When, really, anybody could see that it was the other way around.

Emboldened, I woke up the next morning with an idea.
One which Marika met with instant disapproval, and then
as if she hated to be the one to say no, proffered a new idea,
all of her own.

"I think we should give Tamás a present," I said, "because we missed his party."

"That's a nice thought, Erzsi. What would you like to
give him? We could go to the supermarket and get some
candies? You could fill a jar with them?"

"I was thinking I'd give him my painting," I said.

I was eating breakfast and so was speaking with a mouth
half stuffed with bread and jam. Marika pretended not to
have heard me properly, but I knew she had, because I saw
the look that fell across her face like a smack.

"Pardon, Erzsi? Did you say, *your painting?* Which do
you mean, have you been doing some painting with Zoltán again?"

"Not one I made. I mean the lake painting. The one
that's in my room. My painting."

"Oh, Erzsi! Oh, Erzsi, no! That's a lovely idea, honestly, it
is, but you can't do that. It's much too much to give someone. It's one of Zoltán's best. You saw in Szentendre yes-

terday how much his work can sell for. And really, more
importantly, I think he'd be terribly sad if he thought you
wanted to give it away. He meant it to be for you."

"I didn't think of that," I said quietly. I took a sip of black
tea and let my bangs dip over my eyes.

"But I think it's wonderful that you'd like to share it.
Why don't we invite Tamás over for tea and then you can
show it to him while he's here? I'll get some *traubisoda* and
one of those cherry cakes, and you can wish him happy
birthday and show him the villa. He's never been inside,
you know."

"Okay," I said in a hushed voice, "but only Tamás, not
the other Horváths."

"Only Tamás," said Marika, clapping her hands together.
"Of course."

He came at three o'clock that same day, walking across
the lawn with easy steps. I watched him through the green
gauze of my mosquito-netted window. He was wearing a
pale buttercup-colored shirt and had it buttoned all the way
up to his chin. And football shorts. He didn't look even the
slightest bit English.

Marika poured us fizzing glasses of grape soda and cut
thick wedges of cake. The pair of them spoke in Hungarian and I lined up the cherry stones on the edge of my
plate, wondering what the point of him coming was if we
weren't going to speak in English. Wondering also if Bálint
had said anything to him about seeing me in the woods.
Then I felt his finger tapping on my arm and jumped, my
cheeks blushing as pink as the icing on the cherry sponge.

"I would like to see Zoltán-*báci*'s painting of Balaton—
your painting—could we?"

I nodded. Marika had gone over to the sink and was clattering cups. "It's in my room," I said. "You haven't been
upstairs here before, have you?"

He shook his head. "No. I've never been in a girl's bedroom. Not Hungarian or English or even half and half."

Marika ran the tap noisily. I jumped up, scraping my
chair. "Oh, haven't you? It's no big deal."

I beckoned to him and then began to walk out of the
room. Hearing his bare feet on the tiled floor behind me,
I broke into a run, a laugh escaping as I heard his own step
quicken. We arrived at the top of the stairs panting slightly.

"Ready?" I said.

"Ready."

For someone who'd never been in a girl's bedroom before Tamás didn't spend a whole lot of time exploring. He
walked very neatly over to the wall with the painting on it
and stood to view it with his hands loosely knotted behind
his back, his lips pursed as though he was in a Szentendre
gallery. Knowing he was coming I had tidied my room
that morning, tucking my teddy bear beneath the covers—
now obvious only if you were looking for him—and hiding my nightdress beneath my pillow. I had no books or
toys or keepsakes scattering all corners as I had at home in
Devon. The treasures of my Villa Serena room were not of
the visible kind.

"Do you like it?" he asked, turning from the picture.

"Of course I like it. Zoltán painted it. I love it."

"I mean, do you like Balaton?"

I thought of Marika and Tamás's mutterings in Hungar-

ian when we were downstairs. And Tamás's earnest stance
as he looked at the picture, his sudden seriousness. Suddenly,
I felt like he knew more than I wanted him to. Not about
Bálint; the importance of that had suddenly faded. A miracle, which I'd only appreciate later. No, it was of my very
presence in Hungary that I now thought of. The things that
had brought me to these hills where he lived. The things
that, somehow, made me *me*. He'd turned to face me now,
and his hands weren't stuffed in his pockets or folded beneath his armpits. Instead, they hung loosely by his sides,
and his face was open and questioning. But there was no
judgment, no joke ready to burst from his lips, or discomfort scribbled in red across his cheeks. Perhaps he knew just
enough. He smiled and scratched his arm.

"It's not really as blue as Zoltán has painted it," I said. "I
remember thinking it was blue at first, but then sometimes
it looked gray or green or black. I prefer it like this—" I
waved my arm "—to the real thing, I think."

Tamás nodded. "I would like to live in the world that
Zoltán paints," he said.

At first I thought he had muddled his English. But he
hadn't. It was clear as day.

"But you already do," I said.

We both looked back at the painting, our faces side by
side, peering at its canvas. I heard Marika shout from the
bottom of the stairs, something about our soda losing its fizz.
I made to move, but Tamás appeared not to have heard. I
glanced at him, sideways. I noticed that he had a very light
down on the side of his cheek, and that he had a tiny mole
on the lobe of his ear. Right in the middle, as though it had
been pierced by a careful hand.

"Was that Marika?" he asked, turning. For a moment my face was as close to a boy's as it had ever been.

"I don't think so," I said, barely audibly.

But then she shouted for us again and this time there could be no mistake. We bumped in the doorway as we both made to go downstairs at the very same time.

CHAPTER SIX

In the picture it is 1994 and I am thirteen years old. I am sitting at Villa Serena's breakfast table on the terrace in the morning light. A red tin cup is beside me, filled with the inky coffee we always drank, and a plate dotted with crumbs and a streak of yellow yolk. I can almost hear the songbirds stirring in the woods behind, and smell the sweet, damp morning before the heat dried and cracked the air.

My hair is mussed from my bed, and my bangs fall crook-edly into my eyes. I am lost in an oversize T-shirt with a zigzag of painted color on the front, a bold flash. I am leaning forward, and my elbows are on the table. My chin sits in one hand and my head is propped drowsily. I would have been woken by the sonorous clatter of Marika in the kitchen, her voice looping in over the violins and accordi-ons of old gypsy songs. I'd have heard the sizzle as eggs hit the hot stove, and Zoltán's gulping bellow of a laugh. I'd have pulled myself up, limbs weighty from sleep, and hur-ried downstairs. Not wanting to miss a moment.

My eyes are lifted to the camera, the edge of a smile

turning my lip. I would have imagined myself a late-waking starlet, some kind of disheveled ingenue, for there is a certain swagger to my innocent pose.

The photograph must have been taken early in my stay. My skin is still dewy and my nose unfreckled. I remember blowing into Hungary that year with a fierce bluster about me, determined to do better. All year I had bemoaned the squandered opportunities of my last visit, my awkwardness. Thirteen was to be a new start. Puberty did not yet have me in its clutches. There were no eruptions of pimples on my smooth chin, nor was I riddled with self-doubt. I had made resolutions. I would run through woods without shrinking and go to every party. Devon was too quiet, my father and I living side by side like chess pieces. I'd wanted to be rattled. I needed Marika.

I stopped at this picture even longer than the rest. I liked the fact that it was taken in the morning because it felt like the start of things. The day was waking and so was I, and somehow, there was promise in that. It was the beginning of another sun-soaked Villa Serena day. But I don't remember it. The only day I remember from that year is a rain-filled one, when water fell from the sky in great sheets. *Esik az eső.* The words came to me suddenly. It means *It's raining.* Said in Hungarian it has a gushing quality, and as I whispered it my mouth was full of *shhhhh* sounds. It was the first time I'd ever seen rain in Hungary, so it would have been the first time that I heard the words spoken, too. Odd, that after seventeen years, they should come to me at that moment. Not drip-dripping into my consciousness, but in a torrent.

My phone beeped with a message and I pulled it out,

seeing it was Lily. It's raining on the water. Wetter than ever, it read, not sure I'm having as much fun as I should be. Might be home early. I smiled. Lily was one of those people who had everything to be happy about but rarely was. It made me think of a Sunday night a month or so ago, when we were at home and her mother had just left after another stay. Lily was patting at her eyes, thinking that I couldn't see her. I asked what was wrong and she'd smiled sheepishly. *I always feel a bit sad when she goes,* she'd said. *I don't know why.* I'd given her a quick hug and poured us some wine, admired the new shoes that adorned her feet and heard about the play again that they'd seen last night. Truth was, Lily and her mother were close now, but she always said that she'd been a vile teenager. *I was horrific,* she always said, laughing. *I hated her with a fury and I'm sure she hated me back. It's the same with all teenagers, though, isn't it? We all hate our parents.* I'd made noises of agreement; generally, in life, I've found them easier. But looking at the picture of me at thirteen, I knew without a scrap of doubt that I had never hated Marika, not then. Not even close. Nor my father. In our strange, estranged ways, we had been good to one another.

I began to text Lily back, then stopped myself, not wanting to reenter the ordinary world. I turned off my phone and went back to the book.

There was a drawing tucked inside the page that I was on. It had none of Zoltán's artistry, or even Marika's florid touches. Instead, it belonged to a far more uncertain hand. And I knew it right away to be my own. Beneath the hesitant lines were the rubbed-out imprints of others, and I remembered making every one of them. There must have been twenty ghost drawings, each discarded beneath the one that survived. It had been so hard to get it right. And there were other lines all the way across it, creases, criss-crossing and haywire, and I remembered doing it, balling it up, meaning to throw it away. But someone had salvaged my picture and smoothed its edges. It was a drawing of a boy, and despite the inadequacies of the artist, I knew him right away and I was taken all the way back to the day of rain. I heard the words *Esik az eső*. I saw the shape his lips made as he spoke them, standing beneath the plane tree. And I remember how I repeated them, the way my lips moved, matching his.

The only interruption to our routine at home was oc-casional visits from Aunt Jessica. She came that June, when drizzle fell outside and our cottage was drenched in the summer cold season. I remember all the details of it. Her sitting on the edge of the couch, looking smug and joyless in a pale pink sweater and a string of pearls. The way she bustled about the kitchen, taking mugs and plates from the cupboard and washing them before she used them, click-ing her tongue with disapproval. The sound of my father's incessant coughing coming from the ceiling above.

He had caught his cold from me the week before, and taken it much worse than I had. I had nothing left but a sniffle, whereas he had been in bed for the past three days. I'd gone to the village shop to buy medicine and boxes of tissues that didn't rub his nose raw. I'd heated chicken soup and carried it up to him, the bowl sliding on the tray, knocking the slices of toast askew. And I'd taken the radio from the kitchen and set it on his bedroom windowsill, so he wouldn't miss his afternoon programs. Then the telephone rang and it was Aunt Jessica, and she spoke to him, and decided she was coming to stay. That we simply couldn't do without her. We'd avoided seeing her for nearly four months. She arrived that same afternoon with a flurry of importance and two supermarket bags crammed with groceries. The kinds of things we never bought and didn't like—Spam, canned pineapple and butterscotch candies.

"Apart from anything, this house is going to rack and ruin," she said as she scrubbed the countertop with a potion that left a fake strawberry smell. "Thank goodness I could drop everything and come."

I watched her from my spot at the kitchen table, my homework spread before me. I didn't think there was anything wrong with the house, but her tone was so insistent that I couldn't swear by it. I looked around me cautiously and reluctantly, as if spotting a crooked cushion or a bunch of wilting flowers in a vase would prove her right.

"Honestly, Elizabeth," she said, filling the sink with hot water, a bank of bubbles rising, "I really don't know what to do with the pair of you."

She always called me Elizabeth, as though she wanted to deny the existence of Marika and Hungary altogether. I pretended that it didn't rankle me.

"We're *fine*," I said, chewing the end of my pen. I bit too hard, and the plastic cracked. Blue ink dripped down my arm and onto the table.

"Really!" she crowed, and swept down on me with a sopping cloth.

I rubbed blue into my fingers and wiped them on my jeans.

"I'm going up to see Dad," I said. "I'll see if he wants a cup of tea."

"He doesn't," she said. "He needs to rest. Why don't you help me with supper? How about a bit of fish?"

"I don't really like fish these days," I said, wrinkling my nose.

"Well, what do you like, young lady? It doesn't pay to be fussy."

I bristled. "I like *gulyás,*" I said, "and *Wiener schnitzel.* And *cigánypecsenye.*"

She shook out a dish towel and sniffed it.

"I suppose they're things you have over there," she said, in clipped tones.

"In Hungary? Yes, that's right. Marika's an amazing cook."

She raised an eyebrow. "*Marika,* now, is it?"

I shrugged. "I've called her that for years. She likes it. It's her name."

"Very modern," she said, her nose twitching like a hamster.

"Only a month to go before I'm there again," I said, laying on my enthusiasm with extra lashings. "I can't wait."

"I'm surprised your father lets you gad about like that," she said.

"It's not gadding about, it's going to see my mum. We'd see each other all the time if we could. It's only because she's so far away. There's a girl in my class who spends every weekend at her father's house, now that her parents have broken up."

"Your father doesn't always think," said my aunt. "He never has. Even as a boy. He takes the path of least resistance. He's like one of those birds that stick their heads in the sand. What are they, emus?"

"He likes that I go to Hungary. He likes that it makes me happy."

"Your father doesn't know the first thing about happiness anymore, I'm afraid, Elizabeth. He's not even very good at pretending."

I dropped my broken pen and stared at her with my mouth open. I was ready to argue, to defend him, but something stopped me. Was my father unhappy? And if he was, had I even noticed? Or was it so very obvious that I'd come to ignore it. Taken it as a given, because trying to do anything about it seemed like too impossible a thing. Aunt Jessica started opening a can of tuna with brisk strokes, then stopped halfway through. She pushed her hands to her eyes, and I recognized the gesture. I'd seen my father try not to cry like that, as well—which I suppose was all the answer I'd been looking for. But then she was hastily back to normal, tidying my homework up for me and setting the table, complaining that nothing would ever get done if she didn't do it herself. Somewhere in the middle she slipped in that she was sorry for saying such a thing about my father. I didn't remind her again that I didn't like fish. I avoided looking at her, in case she did anything else difficult.

After he was better and Aunt Jessica was gone, we went back to normal, but I found myself watching my father, looking for some sign that my aunt was wrong, after all. But it was hard with him to tell if he was miserable or not. Where the lines lay between okay and not okay. He carried on doing the things he always did. Every weekend he went to the pub for a pint of ale, and he took me along with him. He'd sit and do the crossword in a corner of the bar as I drank lemonade from a bottle with a straw and tickled Larry, the pub dog, on the belly. He was friendly enough to the village ladies that he saw now and again in the shop, and they were kind to us in return. We were given a home-made fruitcake by one, and another left us a jar of black-berry jam on the doorstep every couple of weeks. They said his name softly, *David,* as though it was a word of comfort in itself. *David,* as someone might say, *there, there.* At home, we worked in the garden together side by side, me claim-ing the potatoes from under his fork, scrabbling like a pi-rate for treasure. In the evenings we watched our television shows and he helped me with my homework, especially math, his own subject. And every morning he saw that I got on the school bus as he drove off in the other direc-tion, where he taught prep school boys in a building that looked like a castle. We compared our days when we both got home. We always agreed that they were *fine,* then set about making supper.

On one of these still evenings, when the radio murmured from the windowsill and light rain patted the panes, I asked him outright. We were sitting opposite each other, sawing at lamb chops, when I set down my silverware and spoke.

"Dad, are you happy enough?"

He carried on chewing slowly and rhythmically, but I saw the way his brow knotted. His glasses shifted a little on his nose.

"It's just... I want to know, because... I'm not sure. Aunt Jessica..."

He set down his knife and fork and made a steeple of his hands. The tips of his fingers pinched white, and then

I knew that whatever he said it'd be the truth. In a very quiet voice, almost a whisper, he said, "I've had my happiness, Erzsi." I thought of a too-rich pie then, one that no one could manage seconds of. But he didn't have the look of a man who was well fed. He had no rosy cheeks, no belly round with joy. So that was that. I'd asked him and he'd answered, and I knew no more than I had before. I picked up my chop with both hands and began to gnaw.

We were at the restaurant in Esztergom with the elephant sign, a wrought-iron creature you passed under in order to enter. It was an exotic touch, and made me think of a Marrakech back alley or a Cairo bazaar, not that I had been to either. The frosted pink of the building and the dark stares of the waiters were excitingly foreign. Marika liked the place for its hot paprika chicken and huge banks of *galuska,* which were ragged twists of homemade noodles. I was old enough to take pleasure in the young waiter with his narrow hips and black hair that fell forward as he stooped to set the drinks. Zoltán liked the place for the deft manner in which his empty beer glasses were replaced with bright full ones. He always left with an uneven lope to his gait.

Marika and I'd stopped there for lunch after doing the grocery shopping for the week ahead. We were not normally that organized.

Traditionally, Marika would rattle off on Zoltán's old bicycle, coming back with whatever she could carry, a watermelon stuffed in the front basket and a loaf of bread trapped under the metal spring over the back wheel, its crust wheezing. She was absentminded when it came to shopping and rarely made lists, seeming to prefer the er-

ratic trips that brought back four bottles of wine and some
sunflowers, or a fish wrapped in brown paper and a string
of chili peppers, when what we really needed was butter
and cheese. In Harkham, shopping was a methodical process, each item checked off a list with a neat tick, always
on a Monday evening after school. The list read the same
each week, and the trip down the aisles was well rehearsed;
we were never tempted by special offers or new lines. The
Harkham kitchen was one that was always adequately, if
unthrillingly, stocked. At Villa Serena there was drama in
opening the fridge to find no milk but three cartons of
peach juice and a bottle of Hungarian champagne. When
searching for some bread it was not uncommon to come
across only a single stale roll dying under a mound of poppy
seed, but beside it a perfectly huge, fresh honey cake studded with almonds and cherries. My diet there was scatty
and eccentric but I never went hungry.

On that day, Marika had planned to cook a special supper, to celebrate my arrival. The three of us, she said, would
eat like kings, and now that I was a teenager, I could have
my first taste of Hungarian wine. We bought two bottles
of sweet *Tokaji* and it looked like liquid gold. The bottle
had an embossed label with a regal-looking crest that made
me feel grand just for looking at it. We also bought a parcel filled with hunks of red beef, a large sack of potatoes,
enormous red peppers and a cake with a hard top like a tof-
fee-colored skating rink. Afterward, flushed with success,
we sat in the courtyard at the elephant restaurant. Marika
pushed aside her plate and lit a cigarette.

"I didn't think you smoked," I said.

"Now and again," she said.

"Can I try it?" I asked, quick as a flash. "Now that I'm a teenager?"

She hesitated, and a look passed between us. I held my head high and she shrugged one shoulder. "I don't think you'll like it," she said, handing it across to me, her eyes like two slits.

I took her cigarette with caution, as though it would be hot to the touch or would burst spontaneously into flame. I put it to my lips, set it for a moment between them and held my breath. No puffing, no inhaling. I took it swiftly out and held it between finger and thumb, as I had seen people do.

"That wasn't a big deal," I said, but coughed a little, for effect. I handed it back carefully. So. I'd smoked. I had never been tempted to try it at home, as I saw the girls and boys in huddles at the top of the school field, frantically chomping mints and spraying clouds of perfume as they came back down to class. I caught the eye of the dark waiter who was hovering in the doorway and sat a little straighter, ran a hand though my hair.

"Oh, it's nothing to make a fuss about," said Marika. "And they're expensive and very bad for you. You'd have to be a fool to smoke." She stubbed it out and clapped her hands together with sudden efficiency. "Shall we go back?"

"You're not like other mothers, are you?" I said as I drew back my chair, the taste of the cigarette still on my lips. She didn't say anything and I wondered if I had offended her. I added, "I mean that in a good way."

She smiled and shook her head, her look somewhere between agreement and light despair.

In the car on the way to Villa Serena I considered asking about Tamás, imagined seeing her brow raise and a know-

ing smile appear. But thirteen was the age for crushes of
the silent kind. Instead, I let my arm hang out of the open
window and wiggled down in my seat so my bare feet rested
on the dashboard. I picked absently at a toenail. Marika
glanced across at me.

"What?" I asked.

"I know I say this every year, but you've really grown
up this time."

"Thanks," I said, pleased.

I enjoyed the myth of myself. She wouldn't have thought
me grown up if she had seen me a week ago in Harkham,
the night the wasps got into my bedroom. I'd shrunk to
the floor as they zipped back and forth, three of them together. I'd pulled a cover from my bed over my head and
ran from the room screaming. I'd hurtled into my father
and hid in his neck. He'd gently peeled me off and went in
to attack, afterward emerging heroically, wielding his slip-
per with the remains of the wasps in its tread. He'd made
us both tea after that, and we'd sat together on the sofa, col-
lecting ourselves. There were lots of times when I didn't
feel grown up at all.

We turned onto the dirt road and bumped along, tiny
stones pricking at the sides of the car with a metallic ping.
My hand swept the hedges as we drove, catching handfuls
of fern and ivy.

"Careful, Erzsi, there are nettles in there."

"I don't care," I said. "There's dock leaves, too."

"Ah, so there is," said Marika, and she drove fast up the
last stretch, me pulling my arm in just before we passed
the gatepost.

"That wasn't funny," I said.

"I did say to be careful."

"My arm could have come off."

"They'd have sewn it back on. The doctors are very good here."

"Are they? Great, then I could stay all summer. Recuperating. Tanning. I'd love to stay longer."

"Perhaps next year, Erzsi."

"Who do I need to ask, if I want to stay longer? Is it you or Dad?"

Marika hesitated, then said, "Your father, really. You know you can stay with me as long as you want."

"Can I?" I said. "Can I, really?" And I forgave the foot on the accelerator and the looming gatepost.

That night we dined together on the terrace. It was a fine evening, cool and clear, the heat of the day only a dim memory. Marika had labored in the kitchen, strands of hair sticking to her cheeks, her sleeves rolled to the elbow as she peppered the food with happy curses. It was dark outside by the time we ate. We lit citronella candles and Zoltán set a record playing. He gave me the sleeve to study as French jazz stirred the still air. Then he caught my hand and drew me into a dance, our feet slapping the tiles. He twirled me and I spun, laughing into the vines. Marika clattered out with a triumphant holler and placed a giant pot in the middle of the table. We took our seats and watched as a buttery mound of mashed potatoes arrived, and a plate of cucumber salad doused with sour cream and dusted with paprika. Zoltán lifted the lid on the pot and spooned out the *pörkölt,* a thick beef stew the color of mud, with clods of meat and glistening strings of onion. Our plates were piled high, the silvery slithers of cucumber dripping off the edges. Zoltán

poured the glowing wine into three glasses. In the candlelight it looked like magic caught and held. He handed me
one and I took it as I had the cigarette before, meticulously,
warily, as though the glass could shatter, the liquid spilling. He stood.

"With this supper we welcome Erzsi, once again, to our
home."

"Thank you," I said. *"Köszönöm."*

I said it shyly, the consonants hurried, in a stumble to
get it out and over with. Marika and Zoltán set down their
glasses and clapped their hands, and I basked in the applause,
my cheeks tightening. I realized it was the first time I had
spoken a Hungarian word to either of them. In the three
preceding summers I'd made a point of speaking English, a
combination of stubbornness and trepidation. With Tamás
I had taken a kind of delight in being the alien abroad,
never more English than when lost in the swell of those
foreign fields.

"Now this, Erzsi, is *Tokaji*. King of wines, wine of kings.
Egészségedre!"

And we clinked our glasses in a perfect ringing glance
and shouted, *Egészségedre!* I sipped my wine, and it tasted
sweet and strong, of sun-wrinkled raisins.

"It's a dessert wine, really," said Marika, "but Zoltán and I
don't care about things like that. What do you think, Erzsi?"

I swirled the wine against the side of my glass. "I think,"
I said, "that I like being thirteen."

We ate slowly and talked at length. But there were no
questions about school, or ambitions, or condescending
looks. No giant, nagging, gnawing conversations that re-

minded me of my nonadult status, my visitor status, my only half-Hungarian status.

Marika discussed life at Villa Serena and I listened eagerly. She talked of springtime, the hidden pool chock-full of frogs clambering on top of one another with their brown legs kicking in cartoon fashion. How one day a heron had sailed through the woods and landed on the lawn, sitting plum in the middle, hunched and regal looking, only taking off when she had scattered bread crumbs with too much exuberance.

"What have the neighbors been up to?" I asked, really meaning, *Frogs and things are all very well, but tell me about the boy next door.*

Zoltán began to laugh. I worried he'd seen through my question, but it wasn't that at all. He described how Marika had gotten into a fight with Bálint Horváth because she had seen him beating his father's horse. He said that she ran at Bálint and pulled his arm so hard that later their neighbor had rolled up his son's sleeve and showed off a perfect set of Marika's prints, in fading red. I thought of last year and the woods, and how Bálint had looked so tough and scarily agile, how he could have fought off Marika if he'd wanted. How he could have done anything, if pressed. What did this mean? That he wasn't so bad, after all? I wanted to know if anyone else had seen her scrapping, thinking only of Tamás. But all Marika could do was shake her head and say in wan tones that Hungarians could be very cruel sometimes.

"Not Hungarians, just Man," said Zoltán, and Marika covered his hand with hers.

"Is István Horváth a farmer? I mean, a proper one?" I rushed, before the conversation could move on.

"Not really. At least, he has a small farm, I suppose you'd call it. But he has a bad leg so he doesn't do a lot with it," said Marika.

"Why was Bálint hurting the horse?"

"Oh, I don't know. I don't expect it was doing what he wanted it to. He's got a short fuse. I've seen it before."

So have I, I thought.

"There's nothing wrong with the Horváths," said Zoltán. "István is a hard worker. But Bálint's a lazy sort, which is why he has no business taking anything out on a horse."

"Oh, look at us, Erzsi, you must think we're a pair of old gossips. But there's no one to talk about on this hillside except each other."

"Bálint's too old for school, isn't he?" I edged. "But Tamás goes to school in Esztergom, doesn't he? With lots of other boys and girls?"

"Oh, yes, I don't know how long Bálint stuck it out. But Tamás is a star student, by all accounts. He's only thirteen, and top of his class, his mother says. Oh and Bálint has a new motorbike, Erzsi. You'll hear it roaring up here, day and night. I don't know where he goes on it. But he's not at home helping his father, I know that much. But then, he's young. Who can blame him? Teenagers are supposed to be trouble, aren't they? Oh, Erzsi, we're being boring. Let's shut up. Tell us something new. Something exciting."

"I don't know if I can think of anything exciting," I said, disappointed that the conversation had turned away from the Horváths. I wanted to know more about Tamás at school. Who he sat next to in class, and whether it was a girl or not. And if he was nice to everybody, or just the ones he really liked. "I'm excited to be here, though," I added softly.

Zoltán laughed and filled his and Marika's glasses. He beamed at me, a look of indulgence. I could say anything and he would find it winsome, and I liked the way it made me feel. As if I was charming. Marika was leaning forward and had her chin propped girlishly in her hands. She smiled.

"What about boys?"

"Boys?" I shriveled a little and clutched the stem of my wineglass. The little I had had in it was gone, but it was useful to hold.

"When I was your age it was all about the boys. Of course I was exotic to them. I spoke English with a terrible accent and my clothes were borrowed and darned but they thought I was exciting. I'd say and do anything, which of course English girls never would."

I pictured her then, skinny and black-haired, only three years in the country. With her crooked, bewitching features, and a laugh that took hold and shook you. I wondered if we would have been friends, the young Marika and I. I decided probably not.

"I don't like boys very much," I said, wondering if my cheeks had gone as red as they felt. And then so as not to lie, I added, "All the ones at my school are stupid."

A call rose from the woods, dimmed with distance, and we turned simultaneously. There was a peal of faraway laughter, and I thought I saw a flicker of light between the trees.

"What is it?" I whispered. I realized I had caught at Zoltán's arm and I withdrew my hand quickly.

"Ah! Talking of boys. Tamás and his friends, they've been camping up there."

This was news, and I was both surprised and annoyed that it had not been broken sooner.

"What, in our woods?"

Marika said that the woods didn't really belong to them, and that the line of ownership zigzagged all over the place. I collected my thoughts. So, Tamás was outside, after dark and behind the house. If it was trespassing, it was the most exciting kind.

"Who are they, the boys he's with?"

"Just some school friends, I suppose. There's three of them. I saw Tamás the other day and he said it's their new thing, camping in the woods."

"What, by the pool?"

"I don't know—all over, I suppose. It's fun, when you're that age. They build fires and make camps out of what they can find. Tamás wanted to show me but it was too hot to be tramping about. I was wilting just out here on the veranda. Did you see any of them, Zoltán? The camps they made?"

"No, no," said Zoltán, "but no wonder old István's struggling if his boys are running wild like savages." He said it with glee, as though he, too, considered it an exciting idea.

"Bálint doesn't go, too, does he?" I asked. I'd seen quite enough of him in the woods, and despite the fact that there had been no repercussions, I wasn't sure what would happen if I ran into him there again.

"Oh, I doubt it," said Marika, "he's too old for playing in the woods. He'll be in Esztergom, chasing girls, no doubt."

I glanced at her, wondering if she somehow knew what I'd seen last year, with some strange and motherly sort of intuition. But then she said, "Boys that age, it's all they think about." Her casual tone, her underlying laughter—I resolved to stop thinking of Bálint as having done something wrong, and, well, stop thinking about it altogether. But then we heard a shout again, farther away this time. I stood.

"I'm going to look," I said, "just from the lawn."

I padded off the veranda in my bare feet and onto the grass. It bristled under my toes. The night had changed and felt warm and soupy now, with the suggestion of thunder at its edges. I walked to the last of the lawn, toward the blackness. At the bank that ran up to the woods I turned and behind me the shape of the house glowed invitingly. The windows were lit inside and the candlelight on the terrace showed the shapes of Marika and Zoltán leaning toward each other.

The forest had previously scared me a little when darkness fell, but that night it was alive and full of undefined promise. Part of me wanted to venture in, to hurry through the trees toward the leaping flames of Tamás's campfire and the jagged outlines of his den. See the boys turn in surprise and then welcome me, Tamás eagerly making a space for me beside the ring of stones. The other part of me dared not leave the bosom of the villa, with Marika and Zoltán and their gossipy chatter and zesty candles that kept away the mosquitoes that even then I could hear buzzing around my head. I swept the air with both hands, sobering now, at the thought of the bugs that would be feasting on me. I hurried back up the lawn, with a final glance behind me at the forest. I might not be brave enough at night, but my day tomorrow was made. I would pack a lunch and go looking for traces of their camps. Then perhaps I would chance upon Tamás, wandering down a path, whistling, with a bundle of sticks under his arm. And then any number of things could happen. Teenagers are supposed to be trouble, I said to myself, repeating Marika's line from earlier, and although I'd only held the position for three months, I was keen to make up for lost time. Something in me had answered the calls from the forest.

I awoke the next morning to pouring rain and vast disappointment. I could hear it falling on the roof like needles and I lay for a moment, not recognizing the sound. It had never rained at Villa Serena before, not while I was there. I rolled out of bed and went to the window, putting my hands to the pane in despair as rivulets ran down the glass and the world outside was sodden and gray. I looked across the flattened, dismal landscape, a clinging mist hugging the treetops and just a faint neon haze in the far distance, shimmering beneath the bank of gray cloud. The color gray didn't belong at Villa Serena. I had never seen it in Zoltán's palette, or in anything Marika wore. It looked like a different place altogether. I had taken the sun for granted and now it was gone and I mourned it vigorously. I willed the clouds to break.

Downstairs, Marika was sitting at the kitchen table, eating bread and jam. Her hair was piled in an extravagant twist, and she wore a vest the color of hydrangeas. I slid into a chair beside her and folded my arms across my chest sullenly.

"It's raining," I said. "It's not supposed to rain here."

"It's very much needed, Erzsi. Didn't you see how dry the ground was? It hasn't rained for weeks."

"But why rain now? Just when I've arrived?"

Marika stretched, and her long brown arms reached to the ceiling, her fingers wide like starfish.

"Oh, it's not the end of the world, Erzsi. It's only rain."

"I might as well be in England," I said.

"Yes, I should think it's perfectly fine and sunny there," said Marika, helping herself to another slice of bread and layering on the jam thickly. "A heat wave probably."

I sneered, willing her to rise to my childish insolence. But instead she teased me gently. I hadn't remembered her being like this back home. Here she was like elastic, popping back into shape no matter how much you pulled. Perhaps being a mother for just two weeks a year helped. I thought of her letters, doodles in the margin, underlinings and crossings out, and her telephone calls when they came. She was gabby as a schoolgirl. She licked her knife, then her lips.

"This jam is delicious. It's wild strawberry. I bought it at the market in Esztergom. Would you like some?"

I nodded, and she cut more bread, then found me a fresh knife and plate.

"Sorry for being grumpy," I said, unfolding my arms and setting my hands in my lap.

"You never were very good in the mornings." She stood beside me and placed a hand on my shoulder. She curled a finger through a lock of my hair. "But listen, the rain needn't stop you. Zoltán has a giant cape of a raincoat that would cover every inch of you. It's the color of sunflowers. You can go out and splash about in that. Or, you can forget there's a world outside and curl up and read in here. Whatever you want. It'll brighten up later, I'm sure."

I chose the raincoat. I still felt guilty for being sullen and wanted to impress again. I decided I'd walk to the end of the dusty road and back, and count the slugs drawn out by the rain. I presumed that Tamás and his friends would have abandoned their camp long ago. So I donned Zoltán's ridiculous garment and ventured out, the mud splattering my ankles, my only exposed part, with my face turned up to the shifting sky. On the path I looked back and waved at Marika, who stood watching me on the balcony. She waved, and I broke into a run and a scarcely concealed jump. I stamped in puddles and hollered to the clouds. My hood fell back and my hair was soaked until it hung in ratty tendrils.

On the path I thought I heard footsteps and turned beaming, hoping to see Marika, wet and laughing. But the path was empty, save for my own reflection in the rapidly filling pools. As the house fell behind me I made less show of enjoying the rain and dawdled, my hands sunk in the big yellow pockets. I wondered what Marika would be saying to Zoltán in my absence. Would she be in his studio, collapsed on the sofa, sighing about how ungrateful I had become, what a small life I lived, to be so upset by a turn in the weather? Would they laugh together, the pair of them? It was almost as though Marika had wanted me out of the house. They could close the studio curtains and do things, Zoltán setting down his paintbrushes and removing his apron. My teenage senses were heightening and I'd become aware of every touch and kiss that passed between them. I saw the shape of Marika beneath her dresses, and even, with a guilty horror, the swell of Zoltán's crotch in his raggedy trousers. Yesterday evening I had lain in bed tracing the shape of my lips with my tongue, wondering if they were pretty enough for kissing. It was strange to feel this way at Villa Serena. I had resolved to be free and easy but I was finding that I was easily undone. Perhaps more so than in Harkham, where nothing changed, including me. It was as though I saved up all my feelings for being in Hungary and let them take me, blowing me over the fields and into the forest in uncertain directions.

I stomped in a puddle and the muddy water splashed my bare legs. I wondered how long I had to stay outside in order to prove that I was having a good time.

"Hey, hello, Erzsi!"

I turned, and this time there was somebody else in the lane. Three somebody elses, in fact, but I only recognized Tamás.

"*Szervusz*," I said, remembering the fast applause at last night's supper table.

"*Szervusz! Szervusz, Erzsi!*" he cried, with what was magical enthusiasm.

I waited until they got to me, Tamás and his two friends with their feet smacking in the wet mud. I stood with my hands eating at the bottom of the giant pockets of the raincoat, suddenly feeling foolish and extremely yellow.

"You are a fisherman," said Tamás. Teasing, just like all the boys in all the world.

"And you're a bum," I said, eyeing his disheveled appearance. He was wet through, and his coat was a flimsy blue affair with ripped sleeves. I delighted in the fact that he wouldn't know the word, even though, given his appearance, he definitely should.

He shook his head and smiled but I was determined not to find this charming. He gestured to the two boys with him and said their names, Pál and Gábor. I found their faces weaselly and smirking. One was much taller than the others, his cheeks peppered with spots. They were both staring brazenly at me, and I began to flush.

"Pal is a kind of dog food in England," I said, in delayed retort.

Tamás laughed and I knew then that he was on my side still. He translated, and the other two smiled crookedly and pushed each other with the flats of their hands. Tamás said something else to them and they said something back and then shrugged and kicked at the mud. Then they said, *Szervusz,* and I realized they were going. They walked down the dirt road, shoving at each other, glancing backward at me.

"Are they your friends?" I asked, making sure that my tone was level. I wasn't smiling, although this was becoming much harder now that the other two had gone.

He shrugged, an infuriating gesture that seemed to mean anything and everything in Hungary. The rain pinged off the shoulders of his raincoat.

"How long do you stay for?" he asked, each word delivered in a precise, neat manner, like lines in a schoolbook. I could picture his arm shooting up to answer the teacher's questions while his stupid friends slid lower in their seats in the back row.

"Two weeks," I said. "I came yesterday, so it's only the beginning, really."

"What do you do when you are here?" he asked.

"What do I do? All sorts of things. We're always very busy."

"Last time, you were ill."

"No, I wasn't." Then I remembered. "Oh, yes, yes. But just that one day. I got better afterward."

"Last year you were here for my birthday. This year, I've already had it. So you're here later?"

"Yes. A little bit."

"What are you doing now?"

"Like you said, I'm going fishing," I said, thinking of my raincoat, and stuck my tongue out.

"Can a bum come?" he said, and my mouth gaped a little. I nodded.

We walked down the dirt road alongside each other. The rain was still falling and I let it, enjoying the feeling of it on my face. I ran my hands through my hair and wrung out the drops.

"Do all English girls like the rain?"

"Oh, yes, we're more used to it, I suppose." I wheeled away from him suddenly, my arms wide, and threw my head back as I ran. "It's so refreshing, don't you think?"

"If you say so!" said Tamás, and ran after me.

We didn't stop until we reached the end of the lane. There I fell back against the trunk of an old plane tree, panting. We both stood under its giant canopy, listening to the pitter-patter of rain on the jagged leaves and the woods behind us sighing with it, expelling gentle puffs of mist. We stayed quite still beneath the tree. There was a sweet, rich smell in the air, of damp earth and sweet, shining buds. I breathed it in as though inhaling the finest scent.

"It's beautiful," I said.

"*Esik az eső,*" said Tamás. "It's raining everywhere, except here."

And he leaned in then and kissed me. From out of the blue. Perhaps that was how it worked in foreign countries. All of the circling ceremonies are sidestepped. There was no sidling closer; no tentative arm slid around my shoulders. Just a kiss, falling from the sky. Even with our wet faces his lips were warm and soft. The kiss lasted only a second or two, no longer. But in that time I smelled sun-warmed wood and a taste like nothing I could describe. Then he stepped back and watched me from under his lashes, his hands shoved deep inside his pockets.

"You kissed me," I said. I couldn't move if I wanted to. One hand went to my lips and I tentatively touched them. "You kissed me."

"I wanted to see what it would be like," said Tamás.

"And?"

He paused. "It was better than Kati and Dora and Angelika."

I bristled. "Who else?"

"Stefanie."

"Better than Stefanie?"

"Stefanie is fifteen," said Tamás, as if that explained everything. He shrugged and I glowered. "But Stefanie kisses everybody, so, better than Stefanie."

I teetered suddenly, feeling as though I was peeping into a world that I knew nothing of. I'd always thought that the hills of Villa Serena stood still until I arrived each summer. I pictured Tamás then, on the bus to school, stuffed into the backseat beside Stefanie. I saw children sticking chewing gum to the ceiling and pulling it down in long strings, taking Walkmans out of bags and sharing earphones, drawing love hearts on the windows in the mist and laughing as Tamás and Stefanie kissed, as the bus jolted all the way to Esztergom.

"Do you wish I lived here?" I said.

"But you're English!"

"I'm half-Hungarian. I could live here just as easily as I

live in England," I said. "Then you could kiss me all the time."

He smiled, perfectly.

"Instead of all those other girls," I added.

He laughed. And I laughed with him. And it was a different sort of laughing to any I'd done before. But he didn't say anything to that, just smiled some more, and we didn't kiss each other again. I suddenly decided that I didn't know what else to say.

"I've got to go," I said.

I turned and ran back up the dirt road, my giant raincoat flapping behind me. I stopped on the corner and looked back. He was still standing there, just as I'd left him. I put my head down and ran home.

He stayed away after that. Perhaps because he wasn't interested in trying to kiss me again. After all, he had plenty of other girls to practice with, it seemed. Ones that didn't need to be the "only one." I laid low for the next couple of days, kicking about the house miserably. Occasionally I felt a prickle somewhere near my stomach and I remembered what it had been like to kiss him. Before I'd started asking questions that he had no intention of answering. Outside the rain still fell, and I watched it mournfully.

Two days after the kiss I went to the bathroom and when I pulled down my pants I had a shock. I sat for a long time on the toilet holding my stomach and crying a little, the funny prickle that I'd been feeling soaring to an ache. Marika tapped on the door and I let her in and she knew right away, and I loved her. More than I ever had. She got in her car and sped off to Esztergom and this time even though she didn't have a list she returned with exactly what was needed.

She put me to bed and brought me home-baked cookies, squidgy and bending from the oven, and a glass of pear juice. She sat on the end of my quilt for a while and told me how she had started on a school swimming trip—imagine that, for horror—and we laughed together at the dreadfulness of it all.

For supper that night we had schnitzels, golden and bread-crumbed with a heap of homemade fries the size of orange quarters. I wore an enormous sweater that belonged to Marika and smelled of her, and as I buried my nose in the sleeve I thought how lucky it was that this had all happened while I was with my mother. It was a fisherman's sweater made of thick blue wool and I thought of Tamás's joke about the raincoat, and wondered what he would think if he were to see me then. I decided it was a good thing that he was keeping away.

That night, after supper, when my stomach was round and full of food and only ached a little, I climbed into bed and Marika tucked me in.

"Listen, it's stopped raining," she said. "We'll have sun again tomorrow."

"I kissed him," I said. "I kissed him. Is that why it started?"

She held me very tight after that, and didn't say a thing. But her holding me was better, really, than any words might have been. After a while she said good-night and got up to go. She hesitated by the door and turned around.

"Was it your first kiss, Erzsi?" she asked.

"Yes," I said quietly.

She nodded, and looked sad. Only fleetingly, but I saw it, like a cloud flitting over the sun. My own eyes filled with tears and I sank under the covers so that she wouldn't see them.

It was only after she left the room that I realized she hadn't asked me who I had kissed. But then I supposed it had been obvious, right from the beginning. Right from the day with the goat.

After an eventful start, my spirit quelled a little, and I spent my days quietly. I didn't tear about the forest or run skidding down the dirt road, and I made sure to stay away from plane trees. One night when I took myself off to bed I found a brown paper package lying on my bed. Its folds weren't stuck shut, and I pulled them open to reveal a big and brand-new sketchbook with a beautiful purple cover, and a little black tin box containing pencils, an eraser with foreign writing stamped across it and a sharpener. I ran back downstairs to thank Marika but she looked blankly at me, and it was then that I noticed Zoltán smiling into his cup of red wine. I went over to hug him, and he patted my back with his hand and said that once an artist had their materials, all they needed was inspiration. *And I know you have plenty of that,* he said. For a moment I wondered how much he knew, if his studio had a view down the dirt road as far as the plane trees, but he was just splashing more wine into his cup and smiling at Marika as she kicked her feet up on the couch.

"But before inspiration comes, rest, Erzsi," he said. "Good night, angel."

I wished them both good-night again and went back upstairs, clutching my new things tightly.

With Zoltán's gift, I began to sketch, my arm folding around my work childishly whenever he or Marika approached. In painstaking lines I drew every tile of Villa Serena's roof, I turned my pencil on its side and shaded the veranda. I took some liberties with the morning glory and drew it so the flowers twisted up and out of the picture, the last flower drawn much larger than life. Later, I took my sketchbook behind the house, where a rough vegetable garden ran down to a sea of elder trees. I found a spot in the full sun, a patch of long grass tipped with gem-colored butterflies and bearlike bumblebees. Half-hidden, I set my pad on my knees and drew a face that I had seen, for fleeting seconds, every smallest detail of. I broke the point of my pencil coloring the black of his pupils. I was never happy with how I made the hair fall, making it limp when it was light, pallid when it was golden. The grass around me grew a coating of rubber shavings as I worked my picture over and over. My forearms and the top of my head grew hot and red. My lips were apart as I drew, set in studied concentration. In the end I balled up my attempt and stuffed it in my pocket. I had made him ugly, when he was beautiful. I had given him crooked features and a surly stare, when he was as symmetrical as the sun and shone just as brightly. I would try again tomorrow, and the next, until my patch in the grass bore the permanent imprint of my bottom, and I started each day by kicking away the old rubber shavings that lay like snow.

Marika suggested that the three of us go for a walk the day before I was due to leave. We took backpacks and

walked into the Pilis hills. They were scraggy old bags
with faded flaps and ragged straps that Zoltán had dug out
from a closet under the stairs. But I felt intrepid wearing
mine, and not a bit like I was going off to school. The para-
phernalia was split between us. I carried the hairy blanket,
padded round like a ball and stuffed in, making my back
hot, but I didn't complain because it was light. Zoltán and
Marika split a humongous picnic between them, their packs
stuffed with bruised peaches, a long-necked bottle of wine
and hunks of ham like fists. I put the giant bag of paprika
crisps in last, drawing the straps gently so as not to crush
them. They were a precious cargo.

The plan was to walk through the woods behind the
house, then cut onto a path we had never taken before, for
which Zoltán had a crumpled trail map. It was an adventure, made all the more exciting for the fact that Zoltán was
with us, a rare day away from his studio. He wore a faded
denim cap and a pair of ancient-looking binoculars around
his neck. He'd swapped his habitual bare feet for a pair of
walking shoes that looked faintly orthopedic and made me
giggle helplessly. Marika put her arm around his shoulders
and explained that he didn't get out much and had lost touch
with what people were wearing. We both laughed at that.
My father might have liked him then, in his ill-fitting garb.
But it was so strange to think of the two of them ever meeting that I didn't dwell on the thought.

Marika, for her part, looked trim and sporty. Gone were
her swirling skirts and embroidered blouses, replaced by a
cotton T-shirt and denim shorts. I wore the same and beside each other we looked like a mother and daughter in a

catalog. We laughed and pushed at each other. I felt light
as a feather.

"Onward, unto the forest!" bellowed Zoltán in an ex-
traordinary snatch of well-articulated, if archaic, English.
Perhaps it was a line from an old poem. Whatever, it gave
us all hearty purpose, and we struck forth, heads bent.

We were just getting to the end of the lawn when from
the corner of my eye I saw a figure standing at our gate. It
was Tamás. I hadn't seen him since, well, *that* day. His hand
was resting on the handle as though he was just about to
open it, an act that always drew a creak like a baying stork
and would surely have turned heads. But Marika and Zoltán were marching forward, looking in the direction of the
forest, hands shading their eyes as the sun glinted down
through the trees. I pretended not to see Tamás and followed behind them, but then I stopped and crouched suddenly, fiddling with an imaginary shoelace. As my head bent
and my bangs fell into my eyes, I snuck another look and
saw him standing there still. I noticed his hand move off
the gate and drop by his side, but he didn't call out. He just
watched us. Watched me. I saw that Marika and Zoltán had
reached the bank and were scrambling, their hands wound
in tufts of grass. If I didn't hurry forward they would turn
and look for me when they reached the top. So I walked
on. However, just before the bank I turned, deciding that I
had a wave and a smile in me, after all, but there was no one
at the gate and the dirt road was empty. Tamás had gone.

Had I imagined it? Could something be made to happen
just by wanting it enough?

The day's walk was spoiled for me after that. I could
have been traipsing through waist-high barley with noth-

ing but the splitting sun above, for all the attention I paid to my surroundings. Every detail was lost on me as Marika squatted and pointed to a jet-black dung beetle, or snapped a flower from its stem to turn beneath my nose. Even as Zoltán threw his arms wide to reveal a new and startling vista, then held up his hands to square it off and frame its heart. My head was elsewhere. I trudged along beside them, my feet moving and my mouth omitting occasional sounds.

"Oh, Erzsi," said Marika, "are you sorry to be going home?"

We were resting awhile, each sitting on a tree stump in a circle of firs. The light danced at our feet and the sound of a stream ran close. It was a beautiful haven, and I began to cry. I didn't realize I had started until I could feel my cheeks wet and my eyes smarting as though mosquito-bitten. Marika crouched beside me, draping her arm around my shoulders.

"I wasn't," I said. "I mean, I wasn't thinking about it. But now that I am, I don't want to leave. I really don't. Can't I stay? Can't I stay a few days more?"

Marika pulled me close to her and I disappeared for a moment inside her neck.

"Please will you let me, Mummy, please?" I said. I realized I'd called her *Mummy* and I never did. It was impulse, and I cried harder for it. She held me tight, and I was lulled that way, my breath matching the rise and fall of hers. When I sat up, my cheeks flushed and tingly, I saw that Zoltán had stood and moved away. He was rolling a pinecone beneath his foot, his hands planted in his pockets. Even after I had stopped crying and Marika had smoothed my hair, he didn't come back to us right away. I hoped I hadn't annoyed him somehow by being so pathetic.

Later, as we were walking toward home, dragging our feet a little, our trio straggling, he caught my elbow.

"Erzsi, please, don't be sad," he said.

I felt silly for making a scene before. I tried to look him in the face.

"It's just the time always goes so quickly," I said.

"For us, too, you know."

"And it's like I forget to count every second of every day until it's too late. If I ever remembered, I'd treasure every moment, from the very first step I take off the plane. But I always just get swept along and it feels normal to be here and then before I know it I have to go again."

I was gabbling, and in severe danger of crying again, which I really didn't want to do in front of Zoltán.

"I'm sorry," I said, rubbing my nose with my hand. "I'm sorry."

"You're sorry? Sorry for what? Erzsi, my darling, you are never to be sorry. Listen to me, you are welcome to come here whenever you like, you know. You are my friend, too, you see."

I wished Marika had heard him, but she was walking far ahead of us, whacking the undergrowth with a stick as though she was beating for bodies, her mouth set in a thin red line. As though she didn't want to be a part of my misery.

"Thank you, Zoltán," I'd said, and for a few steps he walked with his arm slung around my shoulders, tucking me into his side. Until the path narrowed and steepened, and each of us had to make our own way down.

Zoltán's words from the forest walk stayed with me. As did Marika's. She kissed me goodbye at the airport the next day and said, *Next year, we'll see you next year,* a promise whispered into my hair. The same words I'd said to myself as we drove past the Horváths' front gate. And like every year I resolved the next would be better. I belonged there, even though I was Erzsi, All The Way From England. And I had kissed a boy, underneath the leaves of a dripping plane tree.

CHAPTER SEVEN

Within my view, a casual game of football had started up.
A light breeze was stirring, carrying the shouts of the players with it. Boys and men with their shirts off ran around
in waves, the ball bobbing and soaring expertly, as though
on a string. I watched them absently, my eyes following the
game. I caught nicknames and admonishments, applause and
rallying cries. It struck me how very alive they all were, as
they dashed about chasing the ball and one another. How
their chests may be heaving and their eyes smarting but in
the microcosm of the game they had such purpose and feeling. I thought of Tamás as he might be now. I couldn't help
it, not when faced with football. Long legged and strong,
with a sheaf of hair the color of straw. Did he know, about
Marika? Wherever he was, whatever he was doing, had he
worn a jet-black suit and stood in line as the coffin passed?
Perhaps laying a gentle hand on Zoltán's arm, as beside him
the old man's steps faltered.

My insides buckled. Tucked inside the front pages of the
book was Zoltán's letter. I took it in my hand and I read

through it again. I imagined him as he might have written
it. Bent at the table on the terrace, in a crumpled denim
shirt with sleeves rolled to his elbows. His brush of thick
gray hair falling forward, his wire-rimmed glasses sliding
down his nose. Old Zoltán. He would be in his seventies
now, a face tanned and creased, with a pair of paint-smeared
thumbs. Playing French jazz records, studying the folds with
his brow crinkled. Chewing on cigars at dusk, watching
the dark come down to the woods' edge.

He should have forgotten me long ago, they all should
have. He must have written because he felt duty bound; otherwise, why would he? He never had before. Had Marika
whispered that he should, as she lay dying? I quickly admonished myself for this vanity, that I should think I was
ever in her thoughts. Before me I saw ashes blowing and
reforming, like vapor from a genie's lamp. A tiny puff of
cloud covered the sun for a moment, and the light in the
park faded a little, then it blew on and the sun burned as
brightly as before. I sat in shadow, the game forgotten.

In the picture it is 1995 and I am fourteen years old. I
am sitting on the edge of the veranda with my knees pointing. There is a carefulness to my pose, a stillness that goes
beyond the frozen photograph. The black-and-white cat,
the same one that I am cradling in the very first image in
the album, is crouching beside me. Her paws are together
and her tail swept low. We are new friends, still feeling our
way. My face is wiped clean with wonder as I watch her.
The sun falls in a puddle at my feet. A woman's leg is also
in the shot, long and lean and nut brown, with a slither of
red-leather sandal just showing on her foot. The rest of her

is cut off, a lapse in concentration from the man behind the camera, but it is undoubtedly Marika. We are sitting apart and the cat is between us. The receptacle of our strokes and whispers. Neither of us wishing to make too fast a movement. We do not want to ruin a thing.

We were never any good at asking questions in our family. I see that now. Not even with Aunt Jessica around. She clicked her tongue like she was playing the maracas, but she was never constructive with her interference. And my father seemed so ready to discard her judgment that I learned not to rise to it, either. Things could easily have been different, though. If we'd become friends, my aunt and I, sharing candies from her handbag and walking side by side at church events, I might have learned a lot. But I always sided with my father, and saw her as a slightly foolish old woman that clucked like a chicken and pecked around where she wasn't wanted.

I was fourteen when I learned from her that my parents had never been married.

"Plenty of people get divorces," I'd said, and that was what started it off.

It was a Saturday morning and my father had taken the car to the garage. Aunt Jessica was due to visit that afternoon, but instead she arrived early. I sat with her in the living room and tried to think of things to say. In the meantime, she talked at me.

"A friend of mine is going through a terrible time," she said, "divorcing, at the age of seventy. Imagine it! A dreadful thing, at any time of life, but so late on, well, I hardly see the point."

"Plenty of people get divorces," I said. "Just because you're old you still deserve to be happy."

"And do you think divorce makes people happy, Elizabeth?"

I wondered why it was that whenever my aunt was around we ended up talking about happiness. As though there was a ruling on it, you either were or you weren't, with no in between, and she was the great authority.

"Well, when I think of Dad and Marika..."

She sat back on the sofa and rearranged her pearls. She had large breasts and always stuffed them inside high-necked sweaters. Her pearls shifted, as her salmon-colored chest rose up and down.

"But, Elizabeth, they're not divorced."

"What?" I had a glass of Coca-Cola and it jerked in my hand as though someone had pushed me from behind. It slopped and fizzed on the carpet.

"You'll need to get a cloth for that," she said, pointing.

I rubbed it with the sole of my shoe and stared back at her, defiant.

"Of course they are," I said. "They've been divorced for five years."

"They've been separated for five years."

"Same difference." I shrugged. She was doing the thing she always did, assuming a high-and-mighty tone, as though she knew our business better than we did.

"You have to be married to divorce. Elizabeth, Marika and your father never got married. I don't know how you couldn't know that." She muttered this last bit into her chest.

I'd never seen a wedding photograph. There was no picture propped on the piano, with Marika haloed in white and my father with his hair combed down. Marika's hands were busy with rings, every finger glinting but none especially so, and my father's knuckles were bony and bare. I'd never heard them reminiscing, about a windswept Scottish honeymoon or a sun-dripped cruise to the Mediterranean. There was no china that we had to be particularly careful of. No sets of silverware that lived in glass cases, swathed in velvet. Was it true? That they weren't married? I had only ever assumed that they were.

"I'm sorry," she said. "I am. It wasn't my intention to confuse you."

"It's fine," I said quickly.

We both heard the sound of tires on the gravel outside. My father returning.

"I didn't come here to cause trouble," she said, shifting in her seat.

"You haven't," I said. "What does it matter now, anyway?"

I spent the rest of her visit doing my homework in my room. At teatime, there was a knock on my door. I had been waiting for it, listening out for the sound of the front door closing, the creak on the stair followed by the floorboards of the landing, then the pause before the knock and the slight drawing of breath.

"Come in," I said.

He sat down on the edge of my bed and placed his closed fists on his knees.

"I suppose we forgot that we weren't, and it never seemed like a thing that needed to be said to you," he said.

My desk was in the corner of my room, and I was facing away from my father. I stared at the wall in front of me, at a map of Europe I had stuck to it. There was a red heart-shaped pin a little way from Budapest.

"It never made a difference to the way we felt about each other or about you. We just...chose not to."

"It's not like I care," I said. I turned around in my chair, my arms wrapped around its back, holding on to the hard wood. "It's just funny that I think I always assumed, but at the same time I can't remember ever thinking about it."

"There's a lot of things like that," he said.

"Are there?" I asked suddenly.

"No, I mean, that's just how the human mind works. We have to make some assumptions. Otherwise, we'd question everything all the time and no one can live like that."

I nodded. I thought then that it was a long time since he'd stayed for more than a moment or two in my bedroom. An even longer time since he'd sat on my bed. I was suddenly aware of all the Hungarian things I had in there. Postcards that Marika had sent, a sketch that Zoltán had made of the view from Villa Serena, a length of red, white and green ribbon that Marika had wrapped my last birthday present with and was now tied in a bow around my bedside lamp. I was worried he'd think he had stumbled into a shrine. I didn't want him to feel outnumbered, so I stood and tapped his arm.

"Shall we go and have some tea, now that she's gone?" I said.

And that was that. I knew that we wouldn't speak about it again, not now. He put his hand on my shoulder as he followed me out. It was a touch so light that it felt like a ghost's.

Looking back, this was the moment when we might have really talked. But instead of a greater intimacy growing be-

tween us we both retreated behind the screens of routine.
Tea in a pot, and cookies set on a plate, the turning on of the
television and the reaching for the crossword book. Clanging truths were quickly muffled in our house. We were both
too happy to sink into the sofa cushions, pass the time with
small talk and minute pleasures. The reassurance that came
from doing things as they were always done.

I wonder now if this makes it my fault as much as his. I
decide not. Because I was only fourteen, and what was I
supposed to know?

It was a summer made of all the wrong people. There was
Bálint and Angelika and no Tamás. The wrong people, right
from the beginning. Including me, I think. I was shifting
on new tides, restless and ready to snap. At home in Devon
the small things irritated me. The sound of my father's teeth
clacking as he chewed his toast. The fact that the flush in
the downstairs toilet never worked on the first pull. That
sometimes when Marika's letters came my name on the envelope was smeared by rain and the print of the postman's
thumb. Finding out that my parents weren't married bothered me a lot less than I thought it might have. I believed
my father when he said it didn't make a difference, because
what difference could it have made? Marika wasn't the sort
to stay put just because a piece of paper said she should. I
already decided that I would never mention it to her.

But Villa Serena didn't turn out to be the perfect world
I'd hoped for, either, that year. Marika began it. She tossed
her words carelessly, as though a handful of grain to bus-
tling hens.

"I think you're going to have more fun this year, Erzsi.

Tamás's friend Angelika has started coming here for English lessons, and I think you'd get along beautifully."

"Angelika?" It was hard to make such a pretty name sound ugly, but I somehow managed it. "Who's *she?*"

Marika looked at me, her eyebrow shooting up in that way she had, with the corners of her mouth not far behind.

"She goes to school with Tamás, and desperately wants to do better in English. He suggested she come and have some lessons with me. What do you think of that?"

I bent my head and chewed furiously. My mouth was stuffed full of sweets that I had bought at the airport. Stretchy candy colors that tied up my jaw like elastic.

"I think she must be quite thick if she can't learn English herself at school. Tamás speaks it brilliantly," I said possessively.

"Yes, he does. And I know how much he'd like the chance to talk to you when you're here, to practice. It'd be nice if you could include Angelika. She's really very sweet."

It was then that I realized I'd heard Angelika's name before. She had been on Tamás's infamous kiss list. After Dora and before Stefanie. I felt the crushing reality of not being here year-round. Marika, Angelika and Tamás, all having a fine old time without me. I found I had nothing to say, so just swallowed noisily.

Marika came and sat beside me, pushed up against me like a friend nudging on a school bench. I couldn't tell if she knew what I was thinking or not. I resisted at first, then offered her my bag of sweets and she plucked a bright pink one. We sat side by side, our jaws working, until our tongues grew dry and our gums ached.

Before I went to sleep that night, a sore throat suddenly

came upon me. It was like splinters of glass when I swallowed. I lay in bed, holding my hands to my neck, with the covers pulled up around my armpits. Marika stroked my hair back from my forehead and said that I'd probably picked up a bug on the airplane. I remembered someone sneezing like the roar of a freight train, not once but countless times, a few rows back. I'd giggled as everyone around recovered from the fright, time and time again, smoothing their skirts and dabbing at patches of splashed coffee. But it didn't seem so funny now. Marika kissed her finger and pressed it to my lips.

"You rest, sweetie," she said. "Let me get Zoltán. He's the man when it comes to colds. He hasn't been ill as long as I've known him. Not once. He'll give you something to make you feel better."

"Zoltán?" I croaked, but she was already gone.

At home when I was coming down with a cold my father would make me mugs of hot black-currant tea. The fumes would rise and make my nose run, but would always draw a sticky smile. At Villa Serena, tastes ran a little stronger, I realized, as Zoltán tapped at my door and entered, bringing "medicine." He carried a glass bottle on a tray, jet-black and swollen like a bauble. My eyes widened, and I swallowed, wincing as I did so.

"Are you ready for some magic, Erzsi?" he asked.

I shook my head.

"Some special Hungarian magic?"

I shook my head again and sank a little lower beneath the covers.

"We must not tell Marika," he said. "She thinks I'm bringing you hot lemon and honey."

"Aren't you?" I whispered, trying not to look at the bottle he'd brought. It looked like something you'd see in a museum, in a glass case, a Victorian sort of remedy for a dastardly affliction. In the light I could see that the bottle itself was green, but as Zoltán lifted it up I saw what looked like black ink sloshing around inside. "Have you got any black-currant tea?" I edged. "My dad always makes it, with hot water, and…"

"One for you and one for me," said Zoltán as he poured the liquid into two tiny glasses. I could see then that it wasn't black. The color lay instead between deep rust and burnt caramel. "Now, Erzsi. I don't think you will like the taste. I've been drinking this for fifty years, for pleasure, and I'm not sure that I even like it. But it will get rid of your sore throat, I promise."

He passed me the glass and I took it. I sniffed. My nose tingled. It smelled like a combination of things, none of which I felt remotely like drinking. The woods in Harkham on a wet day, when every piece of nature—from loosened bark to rotten old leaves to deer droppings—swelled a little with the rain. The very back of our old toolshed, where bags of potting soil nudged up against broken plant pots and spiders' webs hung like lace curtains. And a "special formula" toothpaste my father bought once by accident, instead of our usual brand. It was all and none of these things. Zoltán raised his glass and winked at me.

"Erzsi, darling. Your good health. *Egészségedre!*"

He downed his glass in one swig, and smacked his lips noisily afterward. I shut my eyes and copied him. My throat burned, my eyes stung, my nose ran. In all of my fourteen years I had never, ever tasted anything so foul.

"Good girl, Erzsi. Good Hungarian girl."

For a moment, I wanted very much to be sick.

"I promise you that you will feel better when you wake up."

I stuck out my tongue and panted.

"Good night, Erzsi. Sleep well. And in the morning…" He clenched his fist and grinned, gesturing strength and well-being, *"Szuper!"*

"Okay," I whimpered. "Good night."

I thought the taste in the back of my throat would keep me awake but soon I found myself hurtling toward a deep and dreamless sleep.

In the morning I awoke to the sunlight streaming through the window, painting the walls bright white. I blinked at the glare and, unable to doze a moment longer, leaped up out of bed and made to go downstairs. I was starving, and wondered if Marika had bought some of the cheese with holes that I loved so much, and the salty salami that left greasy puddles on my plate but tasted much more exciting than boring old ham. I was halfway down the stairs when I realized that my sore throat had completely disappeared. And so had the vicious taste in my mouth. I was, thanks to Zoltán's magic potion, in the rudest of health.

"These funny Hungarians," I said to myself.

"Erzsi!"

Zoltán was in the kitchen, slicing salami with a penknife. He held out a slice to me, and I plucked it from the end of the blade and popped it in my mouth.

"Aren't you going to ask if I'm better?" I said.

"Of course you're better."

I nodded. "It worked like magic. Was it very alcoholic?" I asked.

"Just enough," he said.

The kettle began to whistle on the stove. Zoltán took it and sloshed water into two tin cups. He stirred both three times, tapped the spoon on the side, then held one out to me, with the added flourish of a small bow.

"What's this?" I asked.

But the smell was straightaway familiar. Hot black-currant. I saw the box of tea on the counter and the shopping bag folded beside it. So he had heard me, after all. Or perhaps Marika had sent him out, dispatching him with a flick of her hand and an admonishment for giving me hard liquor. But somehow that seemed less likely. Whatever had been in the bottle with the cross was something intensely Hungarian, and that always met with Marika's approval, no matter what. And unlike my father and me, she'd never believed in the restorative powers of hot black currant.

Zoltán held up his mug and nodded.

"Cheers, Erzsi. *Egészségedre!*"

"Eggy-sheggy-dreh!" I toasted in reply, and we both drank.

I saw his mouth screw up at the sweet taste. I licked my lips and smiled back at him. Out the window I saw Marika at the far end of the garden. She was picking flowers, stooping in her long skirt, yellow-headed blooms all about her feet. I imagined her humming, lost in her own world.

"Breakfast?" said Zoltán.

I took another sip and nodded, slipping into my place at the table. Zoltán sat down beside me and together we patched sandwiches together out of gray bread, holey cheese and oily salami. Our black currant went quickly tepid but we drank it all the same. Zoltán pointed out that my tongue had gone purple and I happily confirmed that his had done the same.

My good feeling that day wasn't to last, though. And all because of Angelika. I found out more about her from Marika, asking questions in an offhand way, as though I couldn't care less about the answers I was given. She was, apparently, thirteen years old and lived in the outskirts of Esztergom in a low-rise block of apartments. She was *extraordinarily pretty,* Marika said, with a *very Hungarian face.* I had no idea what that meant but it didn't matter. The problem was that she existed at all. And so this was how it went with Angelika; three times a week she got on her blue bicycle and cycled up our dirt road, her hands gripping the handlebars with determination, her backpack bursting with books. And we were stuck with her until she decided to go home again. I'd watch her arrival from my spot on the sun lounger, sunk low with my book up to my face. She'd drop her bicycle on the lawn, leaving one wheel still spinning, and trot up to the front door. She'd pull the string on the clanking bell and call out, in a voice that managed to be both high-pitched and throaty, *"Szervusz, Marika néni."* She ignored me every time, affecting a complete disinterest in Erzsi All The Way From England. She was there to see Marika, and together they would sit at the dining-room table and speak a singsong sort of English that didn't appear to suit either of them. I'd sidle in and watch from the doorway sometimes, or sit on the stairs with my chin resting on my knees, hearing, *I would like to buy some bread. How much bread? One loaf, please.* The English lessons were paid for with a flagon of wine and a dense honey cake, with jars of homemade plum jam or apple juice bought in the kind of containers that sometimes contained petrol. Angelika dropped her offerings on the table, gave a small curtsy, then fell over her books with unbending enthusiasm for the next hour. It felt like the longest time, and I was at a complete loss for the hour before, and the one after. In the end, the appearance of Angelika meant the ruin of an entire morning for me.

I also didn't like the way she fawned over Marika, tipping her head on one side and flipping her long braids back over her shoulders. I didn't like the way she caught at Marika's sleeve as she spoke, and laughed in a whining, rocking manner at every opportunity. And I didn't like the way that Marika gave her every ounce of her attention, smiled and held her hands together to mime a clap when she successfully delivered any phrase, and occasionally blasted out a *Bravo!* when Angelika had mastered the *th* of *thanks*. More commonly it came out as *sanks,* and I found myself unnecessarily pleased that such a simple word should evade her. I'd wander around the house and garden, checking my watch before she arrived, then sulked afterward, pretending to be asleep on the sun lounger when Marika came out looking for me. Sometimes the hour ran over and then the two of them would stroll in the garden together, Marika pointing out flowers and offering their English names as Angelika beamed up at her. Once they stopped at the *hajnalkas,* my favorite of Villa Serena's flowers, and Marika picked a bloom and handed it to her. *Morning glory,* she said. Angelika twisted it into her braid and slipped her hand into

Marika's. I bit down on my lip and ignored the pair of them. Which was easy as they weren't looking in my direction.

Once, she came to the villa with Tamás. It was my first sighting of him that year, the first proper time since the kiss, and a strange current ran through our exchange. Again, I felt the ache of a year's absence. The miserable fact that our lives ran separately, only colliding for the briefest of interludes.

Tamás and Angelika jostled up the track together, quacking with laughter. I saw Tamás pull her plait and she batted him away, but I could tell even from a distance that she didn't mind her hair being pulled one bit. In fact, she probably wore it like that, in those ridiculous long plaits, just to tempt him to tweak one. I seethed. I saw Tamás glance at me, and even though they were a way off I expected him to wave and call my name but he didn't. I was dismayed to find that my own hand had shot up in greeting. I quickly pulled it back down. Tamás and Angelika laughed some more, and affected not to see me until they were in the garden and couldn't help it.

"Erzsi!" he eventually said.

I was lying on my lounger, and kept my hands holding tightly on to the book I was reading. I made as if to finish the paragraph I was on, as they approached. As their shadows fell over me I made a show of setting the book down with exaggerated slowness.

"Sorry, I didn't see you. Hi."

"I've been away at my grandparents' again," he said. "I only got back today. I thought you and Angelika would be friends by now but she said you haven't spoken properly yet."

I stared at her. She had heavy blond bangs and a snub nose. Her eyes were the color of cornflowers.

"Yeah, well, I've been busy. And I don't speak Hungarian, remember."

"But Angelika speaks great English now, thanks to Marika. Say something, Angie!"

He turned to her and shook her arm. And I could tell from the way he touched her that it was no big deal, and he'd touched her plenty of times before. Angelika smiled and showed her pearly teeth. She said something rapidly in Hungarian, and it was in a tiny bird voice that I found hilarious and stupid but Tamás seemed charmed by. He laughed and pushed at her.

"She's shy. You've made her shy, Erzsi."

I heard Marika's steps on the veranda, and she called out in carefully pronounced English.

"My star pupil is here! Angelika, darling, stay and talk with Erzsi if you like. I will let you be late today. It's okay."

"Oh, no," Angelika twittered. "I come now. Thank you."

And she smiled down at me, in a way that to everyone else probably looked sweet and friendly but seemed shot through with something else, to me.

"Goodbye, Erzsi," she said. And it felt like a dismissal. As though I was the one being asked to leave. To gather up my book, pack my things and get back on the plane to England. *Goodbye, Erzsi.*

I watched her trot across the lawn, toward Marika. I watched Marika put an arm around her shoulders and walk inside with her, brushing through the beaded curtain, side by side.

I felt a new weight on the lounger, and realized Tamás had sat down on one end.

"Careful, you'll tip it," I said. But it came out sounding grumpy, and he wrinkled his nose at me. He stood back up.

"I didn't mean you couldn't sit down," I said, joining him in disgruntlement. I couldn't believe it was the first time we'd been alone together since last year's kiss, and we were both frowning.

"What's up, Erzsi?"

"What do you mean? Nothing's up. It's fine."

"No, I mean, *hello.* Isn't that what people say, to mean *hello,* 'what's up'?"

"Maybe in America." I shrugged. "Not in England."

"Well, that's what I meant, anyway. Hello. Hello, Erzsébet. Hello, Erzsébet Lowe."

"Okay, hello."

"I don't think you're happy to see me this year," he said.

"Of course I am," I said.

"I don't think you're happy to meet Angelika."

"So what?"

"She's a nice girl, Erzsi."

"Oh, is she?"

"Yes, she's very nice."

"Well, why don't you just marry her if you love her so much?"

I expected Tamás to laugh. After all, I'd meant it as a joke. But it didn't have that effect. He shook his head and wrinkled his brow again. He looked a lot older this year, I thought, older and more serious.

"I've got homework to do," he said. "I should go and do it. Why don't you join in the lesson with them?"

"I can already speak English, thanks," I said.

"Yes," said Tamás, "but not always very nicely."

He was already walking away, and had thrown the words over his shoulder, not stopping to hear my reply. I couldn't believe he was going to walk on home, as though it made no difference to him that I was there. He'd judged me harshly, but I felt a prick of shame in knowing that he was probably right to.

"I can still kiss nicely, though," I called after him.

But he either didn't hear or hadn't wanted to, because he was already halfway down the lawn.

"Tamás!" I shouted.

He turned. "What?"

We stared at each other. I swallowed.

"Nothing."

That same afternoon, after Angelika had gone, Marika came over to me where I still lolled on the lounger.

"I don't know why you aren't more friendly toward Angelika," she said.

"I don't think she pays enough for the lessons," I said, thinking of the sweet and clotting honey that I licked from my fingers and the delicious apple juice that I gulped down, my lips like a sucker fish around the carton's neck. "I think she takes up a lot of your time for just a few homemade things."

Marika looked at me. She folded her arms across her chest and I noticed her pretty embroidered blouse. She always wore something nice when Angelika was coming. I glowered back.

"Well, that's a shame," she said, "because I was going to

invite her to stay for lunch next time, so you two could talk together. Perhaps she could teach you some Hungarian. I was going to invite Tamás, too."

"No, thank you," I said.

"Right. No, thank you. Well, I shall have lunch with Angelika and Tamás on Thursday, and you can join us if you like."

She walked back across her lawn, her skirt catching at the heads of the daisies.

"Wait," I called after her. "Please, wait! If you want me to, I will."

"It isn't a question of what I want."

"But I don't mind."

"And it's not a question of what you want, Erzsi. Sometimes we should just do things because it's the right thing to do. I'd have thought you'd have made more of an effort with Angelika."

"But why should I? I mean, why? She isn't anything to me," I said, adding in a lower voice, with my foot kicking at the leg of the lounger. "She shouldn't be anything to you, either."

Marika stomped back then. She stood over me, and her shape blocked the sun like a dark tower.

"I expected more from you, Erzsi."

"It's only because she's Hungarian," I said hurriedly. "You never cared about my friends at home."

"That's not true."

"It is. You never made a fuss about inviting them for lunch. You didn't walk around the garden with them and give them flowers."

"This is different. Angelika comes here to see me."

"She comes to learn English. She could do that at school."

"She's very smart. She wants to go to England one day."

"Well, good for her."

"Erzsi, you're being very rude. I don't appreciate you answering back like this."

"You don't appreciate anything."

"Right, that's it. Go inside."

"Inside?"

"You can go inside and stay there. I won't tolerate this behavior from you."

I stood, and faced her. I folded my arms tight across my chest. I thought for a moment that this would be the moment when I'd say everything that I'd ever been thinking.

"I'm fourteen. You can't send me to my room."

"While you're in my house I can do anything I like."

"It's not your house, though, is it? It's Zoltán's."

"Erzsi, I'm warning you."

"Warning me of what? You can't do anything. You're not my mother, not anymore. You can't live here and still think that things can be the same. You can't live in Hungary and expect us all to just carry on as if everything's just like it always used to be."

She made a fist from her hand and brought it to her mouth. She shut her eyes and I saw that her lids were reddened and her cheeks were flecked with scarlet. I bit my lip, and waited for the storm. But instead she took hold of me, gently. She set a hand on both of my shoulders, her face close to mine.

"This isn't about Angelika, is it?" she said. "It's not even about her being friends with Tamás, and you being jealous of that, is it?"

I didn't reply. I saw her suck her breath in, her lips crisp.
"Erzsi...listen to me, please. I know this is hard for you.
But I've done everything I can to make it easier, honestly,
I have. I said from the beginning that this was your place,
our place. Somewhere we could be together."

"I know," I said.

"Then what is it? What is it that you want? I know it's
difficult, you're getting older. Your father..."

"Don't mention my father. It's nothing to do with him."

"Then what is it, Erzsi?"

"I don't want Angelika to come."

"And that's it? That's all it is?"

"If I can't have you, then why should she?"

Marika was lost then. She stared down at the ground and
I wondered where she had gone. She didn't say anything,
and in the space that gaped between us my words echoed
back and forth. I breathed deeply, fighting the urge to say
more, or to take them back altogether.

"It's just how I feel," I said after a while, quietly.

Marika nodded. A barely perceptible movement of her
head.

"While you're here, I'll ask Angelika not to come."

She smiled at me, but her eyes stayed flat.

I shrugged in reply, finally adopting the favorite Hungarian
gesture that could mean just about anything.

She turned and walked away, a slow pace, her steps precise.
Her arms hung by her sides and I saw her fingers flex
like opening blooms. The buzzing of the summer garden
grew louder and I smacked at a fly that settled on my arm.

Afterward, I stayed out in the garden and Marika remained
inside the house. I stretched out on the lounger

but I felt self-conscious and exposed. Zoltán came out of
his studio and raised a hand in greeting. I waved back, but
flushed guiltily. Victory tasted sour. Marika was as much
a mother to me there as she ever had been in England. I
couldn't shrug her off, as my father appeared to have done.
There was something contagious about her. Her touch was
indelible. Her letters, with their wild scribbled lines and
raggedy illustrations, crossed borders to come to me, each
more precious than the last. I kept them underneath my bed
at home, in a special box, a walnut writing case I'd found
at a school rummage sale. She treated me as an equal, and I
had thrilled to her confidences. But there was still so much
I couldn't understand. Things that maybe someone like
Angelika could.

I thought of the time that I'd been browsing the history section in the school library, looking for a book that
I needed for some homework. Instead, I'd come across a
book about the Hungarian revolution. I'd opened it, and
there on the first page was a picture of a man with a gun.
His hair was shined like shoe polish and his eyes were black
as jet, eyes that said, *Come on, then,* daring conflict. He was
handsome, frighteningly so, and he held a gun to his chest.
Behind him stood a building that was half torn down, its
exposed rooms like a ragged doll's house. I'd turned the
page and stared next at a photograph of a tank. People
were clambering aboard it, a woman with her skirt gathered up in raw abandon, and two young men, scarcely more
than boys, with their hands held aloft, the remnants of a
torn flag blowing. And again, in the background, were the
same dark, hanging buildings, looking as though they were
held together by nothing more than shrapnel and ripped

paper casing. I turned the pages, saw more pictures, until my homework assignment was forgotten and I was lost in the freezing, wet Budapest autumn of 1956. Rain streaked every photograph, dashing hair into black tendrils, sticking clothes to angular limbs and making weapons shine like night. The school bell rang and I clapped the book shut with a gasp. All through my afternoon classes I'd asked myself the same question: If Marika's memories were made of that, how could she have longed to return? What pull was there, when all that promised was the memory of darkness? Perhaps it was something only a Hungarian would understand.

I shifted on the lounger. I looked at the house and it stared back, its red wooden shutters unblinking. Her absence was somehow worse than her fury. I pictured her again, with her eyes closed and color rising. I wished she had slapped me and felt her hand laid hard across my cheek. I deserved it. Then we could both have cried and felt better together.

The argument with Marika had overtaken my short-tempered exchange with Tamás. As a first meeting that summer, it couldn't have gone much worse. But I couldn't shake the angry feeling that he seemed to be reveling in his friendship with Angelika. Making me feel like an outsider, and just another name on the kiss list. I thought of all the other names that had probably been added to it since last year. Or what if it was just Angelika, Angelika, Angelika? Which would be worse, definitely worse.

I left the lounger and put on my flip-flops. I crossed the lawn and slipped out of the gate. Marika had promised that Angelika wouldn't return while I was there, but for all I knew, she could spend the rest of the year at Villa Serena, tramping up the road in the snow or kicking through the

leaves that littered the forest floor to drink hot apple juice
with Marika, sitting at the kitchen table in my seat. And
always calling on Tamás as she passed his house. I thought
I knew everything about life there. The rhythms of the
villa and the people in it: Zoltán with his thick gray hair
and paint-smeared forearms, Marika rousing the house at
sunrise and cheering the arrival of the day. The way the
shadows fell across the lawn as the day turned to evening,
the balcony lamps where the moths tangled in spiders' webs
and midges moved in flitting dance. My world revolved
around my time there, and I would bottle the scent and take
it down and breathe it in for months afterward. It smelled
of perfect summer days, but when clouds passed over they
were unexpected and thunderous. I felt my steps fall out of
time as I squinted at the dark skies.

Kicking down the lane I stopped and hovered near the
entrance to the Horváths' place. Two chickens scratched
about by the gateposts, and I crouched to tease one closer,
rubbing my finger and thumb together. It let out a contented warbling sound and bobbed its head.

"*Szervusz,*" said a voice, and I started. I looked up and
saw Tamás's brother, Bálint, for the first time, properly,
since the occasion in the woods. It felt like ancient history.
I struggled to stand, wiping my dusty hands on my shorts.

Bálint Horváth had darker hair than Tamás. It was cut
short all over, running to a peak at the front. His face
was warmed and brown by years of sunshine, and his eyes
gleamed blackish blue. He smiled and showed perfect teeth,
top and bottom. I hesitated before smiling back. Now that
he was right in front of me, I couldn't be sure if he was the
same person I had seen in the woods two years ago. I had

felt so certain at the time, but now I didn't know. His hair was different, and he was smiling, and when he spoke his tone wasn't nearly as gruff as I'd remembered. It seemed treacly somehow. I didn't think I'd ever heard a voice like it.

"Erzsébet?" he said. "We haven't met, have we?"

He was supposed to ride motorbikes with abandon, lights spraying the hillside at night. He was no use to his father, considered lazy and was only interested in chasing girls. Those were the things I knew about Bálint Horváth. But did he also fold his fingers into a blond girl's hair and pull her onto the ground? Did he yank at his trousers and stride toward the bushes as he caught my look? Faced with him now, smiling in the sunshine, I began to doubt that any of it was true.

"No, we haven't," I said emphatically. "I've heard about you, but I've never seen you."

The way was clear. I had erased the woods.

"Are you looking for Tamás?" he asked. "He's with An-gelika."

"No, I'm not looking for him," I said.

"They've gone to the town."

"It's all right," I said. "I'm not looking for him."

"She's not his girlfriend," said Bálint.

"I don't care if she is."

He nodded. I couldn't tell if the smile that cut his face was one of approval or mockery. I flicked my hair out of my eyes.

"How old are you?" I asked.

"Old? Nineteen."

"Have you got a motorbike?"

"Ducati! You want to see it?"

I felt a strange sense of abandonment. I thought of Marika and wanted her to prickle with worry as she saw the deserted sun lounger. I wanted her to find me with Bálint Horváth, and realize that I wasn't the child she took me for. And more than anything I wanted Tamás to come home and see that I was quite all right without him. That I could find my own fun. And that he'd better watch out that I wasn't having too much without him. So I smiled and nodded and Bálint led me to the barn.

I couldn't see the bike at first. It took a moment for my eyes to adjust to the dim light. The barn smelled of heavy-bellied cows and rangy goats, and beneath it all the dry scent of cold stone. But then Bálint threw out an arm in an extravagant gesture and there, in all its shining yellow glory, was the motorbike. He laid a hand on it and stroked it reverently. He said some things in English that I suppose he had learned from brochures—*horsepower, torque,* words that I didn't know the meaning of but nodded at just the same. I had an image of myself sitting astride it, my arms wrapped around Bálint's waist as we flew down the road, gravel spitting, dust rising. My cry loud above the engine's roar. Marika's mouth shaping an O as she watched us from a gateway, her skirt flapping in the wind as we rocketed by. A smarting Tamás farther down the road, standing with his bicycle, his back pressed against the hedge as we burst past, owning the road. I wondered if Angelika had ever ridden a motorcycle. I was willing to bet that she hadn't. The thought thrilled me and terrified me in equal measure. I turned to Bálint, assessed him again in the half-light. I laid a hand on the seat.

"Could we go for a ride?"

"What?"

"Would you take me out on it? Just down the track?"

He laughed then, a snickering sort of laugh that made me fold my arms tight across my chest.

"No. No way. It's not for children."

"Children? I'm not a child," I said. "Why would you say I'm a child?"

"You're a little girl, Erzsi."

He was laughing still, and his shoulders jogged up and down. The way he said it made me think again of the woods. *What are you looking at, little girl?*

"Oh, shut up, it's not that funny," I snapped, my heart pounding now inside my chest.

He laid a hand on my arm as though to steady himself. He banged his fist on his stomach, brought his laughter under control. I decided he was mad, or drunk. I shrugged off his hand.

"If you got hurt, Marika would kill me," he said, and cut his hand across his throat in quick motion. "Dead."

"Whatever," I said.

"Too risk."

"Too *risky*," I corrected.

"It's different for men," he said. "But little girls...no."

"Stop saying that. I'm not a little girl anymore," I said. "I can do what I want," I continued with sudden ferocity.

He looked at me differently then, as though I'd shared a secret with him. I'm not sure he fully understood what I'd said because I'd spoken quickly and carelessly, but he saw my face. And something flipped inside of me, a light turning in the very pit of my stomach.

"I can do anything," I said in a voice that shook, "if I want. No one really cares when I'm in Hungary."

He stepped close and I smelled him, warm skin and a nutty outside smell, the way my own hands smelled sometimes after a walk in the woods. A deep, living smell. He was much taller than me, and when he touched a finger to my chin and gently nudged me, my eyes came level with his brown chest. I smiled, without necessarily meaning to. He bent down, put both hands on my shoulders and kissed me. Just once, on the lips. He pulled back a little and I stared at him. I couldn't move. So he kissed me again, harder this time. My back pressed into the rough stone of the barn wall. With Tamás, under the dripping canopy, I'd melted at the slightest touch, but there in the barn with Bálint, I froze. An image flashed into my head of the twinkling button flying off the girl's dress, that time in the woods. I twisted in Bálint's loose grip. Whether he felt my awkwardness or lost interest I couldn't be sure but he stopped kissing me and regarded me in the gloom. He shook his head.

"Okay, forget it," he said. Then he turned and walked out of the barn.

I put my hand to my mouth and wiped my lips fiercely, as though his kisses had left a print. I stood there, by the motorbike that I was too young to ride and in front of the empty patch in the straw where he had kicked the ground as he turned. I thought about making a break for it, crossing the yard, making sure my legs didn't tangle in each other, one hand pulling down my hair so it hid my pink cheeks. Then a figure appeared in the doorway and it was Tamás. I felt the heat of rising tears as I realized what I'd done.

"What's going on?" he said.

He was silhouetted, his outline giving nothing away. Only his voice failed him, cracking, as it lifted with its question.

"Nothing," I said to him, for the second time that day.

Then I ran away. The way I always did, apparently, after a kiss. I brushed past him in the doorway and for a moment I felt his fingers catch at my arm. But I shook him off, without even trying. Perhaps he hadn't really wanted to stop me at all.

I sat just inside one of the Horváths' fields, on the rutted dirt of a path torn by a tractor. I suppose I hoped Tamás might find me there, with my legs stretched out on the spiked grass. I imagined me telling him everything, a torrent of apology and declaration. But he didn't come. And as time went on, I convinced myself that perhaps he hadn't seen a thing. He could have thought I was just skulking in his barn, maybe looking for him. But I felt guilty all the same, my cheeks burning at the memory of Bálint's hasty, pushy kiss.

I had nowhere to go other than back to my other worry. Marika. I pulled at a flower that was growing among the barley. A giant daisy. I began to pull at the petals. *He loves me, he loves me not. She loves me, she loves me not.* Around and around. My head swam with Marika, bending over textbooks beside a blond-headed girl, running her fingers along dusty English words that she'd surely almost forgotten. And my father, at home, stooping to shovel earth, his spade turning, his back stiff, his lips clamped tight. And Tamás. With his year-round life revolving happily, just occasional summer interruptions from a silly English girl who maybe wasn't half as nice as she made out to be.

Where did I want to be, really, when I thought about it? At home in England, with the eternal promise of Hungary? Or at Villa Serena, with every day bringing me closer to the time I had to leave again? The problem with a dream is that the only time you know you're in one is when you've woken up. When everything is already over.

I wound my way back to the villa. Halfway up the dirt road I turned at the sound of mewing and saw a tiny black-and-white cat. She had a crooked tail and four trembling feet that dithered in the dust. I could see her rib cage, the brittle lines of her bones. She moved toward me like a ghost and when she mewed again I saw a bright pink flash of tongue and shining eyes like two blue pennies. I bent down and held out my hand and she tottered toward me, rising up to rub her head, twining about my legs with more vigor than I could have imagined from such a tiny frame. I knelt on the dusty path and petted her, smoothed back her feltlike ears and picked burrs from her fur. She thrilled to my every touch, with a deep purring that belied her half-starved ballerina appearance. She followed me home.

Later, Marika drew the cat onto her lap and we called her Cica, which was *kitten* in Hungarian. We gave her pieces of ham and a saucer of milk and her tiny tongue flashed pink again as she lapped up every last drop. I sat watching with my chin resting on my knees and Marika said I had been right to bring her home. We smiled at each other quietly over the top of Cica. I wanted her to know that I was sorry, and I knew she felt the same. We spent the rest of the afternoon sitting beside Cica as she ate and gamboled and finally slept between us, her newly round belly rising and falling.

As the light shifted to early evening a gentle breeze licked the morning glory so its leaves whispered. Marika ran Cica's tail through her fingers like a ribbon.

"Can you keep her?" I said.

"If she'll stay," said Marika.

"Of course she'll stay," I said. "Anybody would be glad to be here." I reached out a hand and smoothed her whiskers, had my touch answered with a purr. "I'd stay, if I could."

Marika said nothing.

"I didn't mean what I said before. I'm really sorry."

Marika scooped up Cica in her arms. She pushed her nose into her fur.

"Perhaps you were right, Erzsi. In some ways, I can't be the same person for you. Things have changed."

"No, that's not true! I was being stupid, I wasn't thinking. I was jealous, that was all. Honestly."

My voice quavered. I caught her hand and held it, squeezing her fingers tightly. I refused to let it go, even when I felt her pulling gently away.

"Things *are* different," I said, "but I like them. I'm used to them. I love being here with you. If we'd all stayed in Devon, and you'd been unhappy, then we'd all just have made one another miserable. Now I'm happy when we're together. And Dad's happy for me."

It was as though the thread that had once bound us all together had loosened and stretched. It had crossed a continent, wound around a new finger, but it still held firm. If I knew this, surely Marika knew it, too.

Zoltán called us then from the kitchen. Marika threw an

arm around my waist and walked us inside. Cica followed, slipping between our ankles.

Dinner was a fish soup, red with paprika and hot like flames, and we ate it with hunched shoulders and lips pursed. There was a quietness to Marika that suggested she had been bitten more by our argument than I was. I watched her over the top of my spoon. She *was* happy, wasn't she? She had everything she wanted, after all. She blew hot and cold but I felt each draft and saw it coming. In that respect she was far easier to read than my father. He didn't seem any more or less content now than when I was eight years old. Back in Harkham he'd never once wailed for his missing Marika. He'd been angry after she went. I'd seen his fingers press white against the edge of the table, the tips of his ears glowing red, but it always felt like it was on my behalf and not his own. As if I was the only one who was alive and mattered, as if he didn't exist at all. I'd covered his fingertips with my own, hugged him so my arms swallowed his head and covered his hot ears. *It's okay,* I'd say. *I'll be seeing her soon.* I felt him then, the very bones of him.

When Zoltán cleared our plates and went to find more wine I decided I would confide in her. Another way to say sorry, a jewel pressed into her hand. I leaned across the table. I told her that I had been really stupid that day. I said how I had met Tamás's brother Bálint and he had been quite nice to me, not at all like I'd imagined. I said how he'd tried to kiss me, but probably only because he thought I wanted it, and he soon realized that I didn't. And it was all just because Tamás was being funny about Angelika, and I was jealous, and now I felt so guilty and stupid. I told her that more than anything I wanted to be Tamás's girlfriend. I told her there had only been the one kiss, the year before, but I remembered every tiny thing about it. I told her I missed him, even though a grown-up would say that I didn't know him well enough, but I missed him all the same. He was as much a part of Villa Serena as everything else. Like Zoltán was to her. And she covered her mouth at that; I couldn't tell if she was smiling or angry. I asked her what I should do. What would be her advice, as my mother? *What should I do?*

She stared at me and opened her mouth to speak, then closed it again. She bit down on her lip and I saw the color rise to the surface, poppy red.

"The same thing I'd say to anyone, Erzsi. Follow your heart."

Was that it?

I had expected her to admonish me for allowing myself to be kissed by Bálint, at least to tell me I was too young to get myself into that sort of position with someone so much older. And with his reputation, too, the wild boy of the Villa Serena hills. Or, to clasp my hand and talk of Tamás and true love, and spin a tale of her own. But she had the spirit for neither. All she did was turn to Zoltán as he appeared with a new bottle of wine and tap the edge of her glass with a smile, then reach up for a kiss. Which he obliged, one hand resting on the table, his fingers splayed.

I stood suddenly, my chair rocking back on its hind legs. "I think I might go to bed, then," I said.

She caught me on the stairs. She took my hand, as I had taken hers before, and drew me back down two steps.

"When I say 'follow your heart,' I mean it. But I get caught up in it sometimes. I forget I even have a head. I always have done, it's a fault of mine. You're not like that,

though, Erzsi, are you? You're like your father in that way.
You're a thinker, a planner."

"I didn't think today with Bálint. Or...Angelika."

"No. No, you didn't. And that's why you feel funny. Because that's just not you. It's *me*. You're trusting and honest
and well-meaning and you don't rush into stupid things.
You should never follow my example, Erzsi. It's never been
any good."

"That's not true!"

Her face seemed to tighten, different forces pulling her.
She carried on. "And your father, he...means well, he does.
But I think sometimes he forgets what's going on around
him. Sometimes, he's not really with us. With you. He gets
lost in himself, doesn't he?"

"Everybody does," I said, "it's not just him."

"No. No, it's not just him. But you have to find your own
way. That's free from either one of us. You have to follow
your heart, and yours alone."

"Could I write to him, do you think?" I said in a hushed
voice.

"Tamás?"

I nodded. I was sitting on the step now, and Marika was
leaning on the banister.

"I want to tell him everything," I said.

"I'll deliver it for you," she said. "Or better still, send
it from England, with a foreign stamp. I'll give you some
Hungarian to write."

"*Szeretlek.*" *I love you.*

"Yes! Where did you learn that?"

"I used to hear you say it."

"Oh, Erzsi. Do you know how to spell it? You must spell it properly."

"No, I mean, *szeretlek*. Not for Tamás, for you."

And she joined me on the stair, the pair of us sitting side by side. I laid my head on her shoulder and shut my eyes. In my chest my heart beat—*tap, tap, tap, tap*—and I listened to it, promised to follow it. Just as she would do.

CHAPTER EIGHT

Somewhere, in a pocket or a handbag, someone's telephone was ringing. Its sound was not immediately apparent, rather it nudged into the edges of my consciousness, like a slow-gathering tide. I turned my head in its direction, to better listen. Then it stopped, cutting dead in the middle of a ring. A silence hummed in its wake. Had my father tried to telephone me? Even now, as I sat in the park, was my house throbbing with an unanswered telephone? Perhaps he was bent over the receiver at his end in Harkham, willing me to answer, knowing the news that came from Hungary could not have been good. For even though some people might write out of the blue with good news, not us, not our people. We didn't write at all.

It would be impossible to tell my father that Marika had died. I knew I could not find the words. And what would he do with them, anyway, once they were given? There was no way in which they could be reordered. The hopeless patterns would persist. He would be of no more help now than he ever had been. I stopped myself then from thinking down this path, but the nip of anger had already helped. I gritted my teeth and rubbed my eyes fiercely with my hands.

I looked down at the book and saw Erzsi looking back at me. *Come on,* she seemed to say, *what are you waiting for?*

In the picture it is 1996 and I am fifteen years old. I am tangled in the drapes of a beaded curtain, their lengths running like braids through my hair, exotic necklaces falling across one sharp collarbone. It is the doorway to Villa Serena and the beads were there to dissuade the flies. I can hear the clacking sound they made, feel the cool run of them over my shoulders as I pushed through to the house.

The photograph has a snappy quality to it, as though I've just turned to face the camera before hurrying on inside. My fingers are splayed and blurred in movement, my smile is crooked. I must have come from the forest pool, because my hair is wet and falls thickly. Look closer and there is a green leaf caught by my ear, or a piece of pondweed, like a fragment of a dyed doily, hanging ready to drop.

The shadows of the interior set me off in bright relief. The snub of my nose and the streaks of my cheekbones are marked by the sun. I have a happy, earthy look. My arms are brown and skinny, like smoothed branches.

There is fire in my eyes, and I know it would have come from that last running descent from the woods, my arms thrown wide as I swept down the hillside. Tamás flying behind me, his head tipped back in song.

It was the summer of the two of us. Where we tripped about together, half children, half something more, without a care in the world.

I ran my fingers over the picture, a small smile tickling

the corner of my mouth. I wanted this girl to climb free of the page, the bead drapes clacking behind her, drops raining from her still-wet hair. She appeared magical. Hungary had lit her, leaving her eyes impossibly bright, her skin brown and polished, her lips stained with love's first kisses. Beside her now, I would appear lifeless. All wrung out. *Erzsi?* she would say, in sweet but disbelieving tones. And I would have to shake my head. Answer, *Not anymore.*

I was fifteen, and life was what happened in Hungary. I had always been split between two worlds, but until that point my home with my father had always held its own. The sunny freedoms of Villa Serena allured me in every way, but our Devon cottage, the place I'd taken my first breaths in, where I'd learned to walk with jammy hands smearing the wallpaper, that had held me in its cocoon as I cried into the pillow after Marika left, was eternally dear to me. But somehow, sometime, it had begun to feel less of a home. There were no striking incidents, no particular occasions that come to mind, that would allow me to pinpoint the moment when this unwelcome feeling began to assert itself. I only know that it did. Perhaps it had something to do with the way I was beginning to feel about Tamás. Left unchecked, my imagination galloped way ahead. Tamás belonged to another world, and I just couldn't picture him walking up the path to our cottage. I couldn't see him shaking hands with my father and taking his place at the kitchen table, to eat pork chops and peas or toast and jam, like we did. He was tall and would bang his head on the low and unexpected doorways; he'd knock his elbows on our curious dark furniture. My father would seem unwelcoming, and limp as a fish. Tamás would mistake his quiet manner for disinterest, his nodding head as nervousness. He would look at my father and think, *Erzsi is half of this man,* and because of that I would somehow diminish in his eyes. A smaller, paler me.

Why these imaginings? Because, just as Marika had suggested, I'd written to Tamás. On a misty September morning in Harkham I took up my fountain pen and began to write—my regret for the wasted summer, the mistake of the kiss with Bálint, the foolishness over Angelika. And Tamás had replied. A precious first missive, the receipt of which I will never forget. And in one sentence he made everything all right again, better than all right. *None of it matters, Erzsi, because I know how you really feel, and I know how I feel, too.* Those words were my treasure.

In the end there were nine or ten letters from Tamás in the year that passed. And I kept them in a special chest with a heavy lock. Not that anyone would have come snooping. My father didn't set foot in my room anymore. It was as though the doorway marked the edge of a cliff drop that he peeked over with extreme trepidation. If he made me a cup of tea he would set it on the step outside, tapping his knuckles on the frame, saying, "When you're ready, Erzsi," as though I needed to summon courage to accept his offerings, when surely it was the other way around. As much as I dared to play the teenager with Marika, with my father I tried hard to be the same daughter I always was, but he eyed me sideways all the same. Perhaps it was because I was growing to resemble Marika with each passing day, my long brown hair uncut and my angular limbs, collarbones like ledges and ankles like blades. Maybe I unsettled him, a dark creature moving through his quiet space, disturbing the shadows with my step. He noticed the way I skidded excitedly down the stairs in my socks as the mailbox clunked. He saw me crouch and pocket any letter from Marika, as I always did, but then continue to sift through, looking for another. I was searching with a new hunger, for an envelope with slanted handwriting, a lanky *Erzsébet Lowe,* written with precision and deliberation, not anything like the flamboyant, careless hand of my mother.

"Another letter?" my father would remark.

"I made a friend in Hungary," I replied, "the same age as me," and then I'd run upstairs to throw myself onto my bed with the curtains pulled hastily across and read in the half-light, poring over every word. I memorized sections, my lips later replaying lines like, *It is not the same when you are not here,* as I kicked through leaves on the way to the school bus, or sat staring from the kitchen window onto a rain-splashed Saturday morning. Our letters were full of the minutiae of existence—friends at school, Saturday weather and then sudden sweeping professions of love, underlined, and with kisses marking the edges, as certain as a row of stitches. There were no knotted, muddled questions or explorations, just lists of what we'd eaten for supper and quibbles and qualms about school and *I love you I miss you I can't wait to see you.*

Once, I'd enclosed the crumpled football stickers that I'd carried with me every year preceding and had always been too shy to give. Tamás had written back saying that he slept with them under his pillow, and for a moment I wondered, *What boy would do that? That's the kind of thing*

I'd do, but then I remembered he was Hungarian and they were different. Marika had agreed.

Perhaps my changing feelings about Harkham also had to do with my father. I think he thought I was growing too fast for him to keep up so he gave me space. Vast universes of it. On a weekend I could go the whole day and barely see him, just the nudging of a closing door or the clink of a teaspoon against a cup giving away his presence in the house. And when I came home from school there would be a supper he had prepared, vegetables from his patch and a slight cut of meat, and we would eat quietly together. Then we'd both drift separately, him to his study, me to my room, or to the garden, or to the copse at the end of the lane where the last of the sunlight fell through the trees and touched it with a kind of radiance.

It earned me a certain respect among my teenage friends that our relationship was dislocated, disconnected. They considered me nonchalant. They thought I found it silly that they were still entwined with their parents, and so they kept quiet about the rhythms of their family lives. The making up of a foursome at the tennis club on a sunny afternoon. The walking of the dog together, the small talk, the swapped smiles between faces that resembled one another. They never knew how much I envied these things that seemed so mundane and childish to them. They seemed to have the idea that I was a rebel, who did just as she liked. The truth was that at home I trod quietly and carefully but need not have bothered, because I was mostly invisible. I breathed on windowpanes just to see some mark of myself. I ran my finger along the dusty top of the piano, the edges of picture frames. I shattered a cup once, letting it fall from my fingers onto the flagstones in the kitchen, but the noise passed too quickly. One cough, one sigh, and you'd have missed it.

Aunt Jessica no longer came to visit. She and my father had a disagreement that he refused to share the details of. All I knew was that one day she sent me a card with a picture of an oak tree on it, and a check for twenty-five pounds inside. She didn't write much of a message, just this: *Dear Elizabeth, Brothers and sisters have a habit of bickering, but don't worry, things will right themselves. Best wishes, Aunt Jessica.*

I wasn't particularly bothered if my father had fallen out with his sister. I didn't think it was any of my business, and I didn't mind that she didn't visit anymore. For as long as I'd known her I felt she'd disapproved of our family but I could never put my finger on her reasons why. I used to think it was because she didn't get along with Marika, but after she left us Aunt Jessica still picked and prodded at us with her lips pursed and her tongue tutting. Whether it was spotting grubby windows or thinking the lawn was overrun with daisies or the sight of my messy handwriting on the cover of a schoolbook, there was always something that seemed to rile her.

"She's been like that for as long as I can remember," my father simply said.

"Is that why she's not married?" I asked once.

And he laughed at that, for the first time in a long time.

At school, things were changing, too. A new boy had started, partway through the spring semester. The rumor was that he'd been expelled, and so had ended up at our school, the only place that would take him. On the first morning break he got into a fight, coming out of it with no more than red cheeks and hanging shirttails and the blood from someone's nose on his knuckles. He spent his first lunchtime in detention. This lent him a kind of notoriety among the girls in my year, for there was a whiff of danger about him. When he was around, they rolled the waistbands of their skirts to make them shorter, and they loosened the knots of their ties and pulled open their collars so that their creamy necks showed. But he remained unimpressed. It seemed that Justin Travers had eyes only for me.

He was a redhead with a spray of freckles across both cheeks, and his eyes were furtive like a fox's. He wasn't particularly tall, but he had a nonchalance that made him seem bigger than he really was. In his first French class, on his second day, he slid into the spare seat beside me.

"Hi," he said, shaking the contents of his sports bag onto the desk—textbook, papers, a once-expensive-looking fountain pen with teeth marks at one end.

"Kate sits here," I said.

"Not today, though. She's out sick, isn't she?"

I adjusted myself in my seat and stared hard at the front of the class. I liked French. I liked Madame Duval, with her pencil skirts and clacking heels. I saw her and imagined rain-soaked Parisian streets by night, cafés with steamed windows and people sharing cigarettes. I pointedly ignored Justin and opened my books. He surprised me by ignoring me back. As the lesson went on, Madame Duval scratched a list of dusty verbs on the chalkboard and I stole glances at Justin's book. He wrote neatly, with an elegant slant to his letters. I've always set store by good handwriting; even now

I can be pleasantly surprised by a man's penmanship, and have him shoot up several notches in my estimation based purely on this fact. But on closer, cautious inspection, I saw that Justin wasn't writing down the list of verbs at all. Instead, he was writing something else entirely. I caught the words at the top of the page: *Dear E.*

I stared hard toward the front of the class. When Madame Duval asked me a question, what the polite form of *venir* was, I stumbled and my mind went blank. Her spectacles lurched on her nose as she raised one eyebrow. *Ça va, aujourd'hui, Erzsi?* she asked, and I reddened, mumbled my reply, *Ça va bien, merci.*

As the bell rang, chairs scraped and chatter instantly rose. I packed my belongings slowly. Justin did the same, a lopsided smile twisting his mouth.

"If she asks to see your book you'll be in trouble," I said.

"What do I care? Anyway, it'll be ripped out by then. I just need to make some finishing touches."

I shook my head and stood. I shrugged on my coat and went to leave. We were the last in the classroom. Madame Duval had already gone.

"Don't you want to know what it says?"

"Not really," I said.

"Suit yourself."

He caught hold of my arm and I looked at him then, straight into his gray-green eyes. They flickered, his pupils swelling as big as black moons, and I stared levelly back.

"I have a boyfriend," I said.

"Oh, really? You do? I've heard about him. He's miles away, Poland or somewhere. I really don't think he's much of a boyfriend, if he's hidden away in Eastern Europe. I don't think anybody can be much of anything, if they're hundreds of miles away."

"What do *you* know?" I flashed.

"I *know*," he said. "I know what it's like, to have parents that screw everything up for themselves and for you, too. To be no more than collateral damage."

"I don't think you know anything," I said.

"I know about you. I know your mother lives on what might as well be the other side of the world. I know you're stuck with your father, in the arse-end of nowhere. I know you hate both of these things, but you're too sweet to do anything about it."

He put out his hands so that he was holding each of my elbows. It was a strange grip, but I didn't move from it. He shook me gently.

"I hate this lousy school, just as I've hated all the others. But the minute I saw you, I knew we had things in common. So I asked around, and I was right. You're as messed up as I am, only you don't know it and I do. Don't you see, I can help you?"

"Get off," I said, finding the will to move, and to my surprise his hands fell away lightly and hung by his sides. His bluster had momentarily blown itself out.

"You don't know the first thing about me," I said, my voice rising. "All that stuff you just said, that's just geography. It doesn't matter where someone is if they love you. It doesn't matter if you don't see them all that much, if you know that when you do it'll be amazing."

"Are you talking about your so-called boyfriend or your so-called mother?"

"None of it matters, if you *know,* and I know."

"Know what?"

"Know that it's fine. That everything's fine."

"Fine?"

"Yes."

"Fine?"

"Yes."

"Erzsébet Lowe. You're going to look back on this day and wish you'd listened to me."

"Oh, really?"

I wanted to tell him that I didn't care what he had to say, but I'd suddenly lost my voice. I was reeling from the fact that I'd already given him too much, that I'd talked about love with a total stranger. And that I'd been in such a rush to tell him all about this love that was mine, that I missed rising to his so-called jibes. *My so-called mother.*

"Takes one to know one, that's all I'm saying," he went on. "My dad left when I was seven. He ran off with his secretary, about as clichéd as you can get. Have I forgiven him? Not a chance. I hate him. I hate him, and I always will."

He sniffed and rubbed his hand across his eyes. I thought of all the girls that liked him, for no greater reason than he was new and he looked like trouble. I imagined them leaning against the wall at the back of the science hall, surreptitiously smoking, hoping to be seen by anyone that wasn't a teacher but especially by him. I wondered what they'd say if they knew that he was there with me, in Madame Duval's empty classroom. I suddenly felt so sorry for him that my stomach twisted and I needed to sit down. I felt so sorry, that I didn't know if I was sad for him or sad for me, or both. I sank into a chair and we stayed like that for a moment, him perched on the edge of the desk, hunched over like a toy that had lost its stuffing, me opposite, with my legs crossed and my head spinning. After a silence, I spoke quietly.

"What's the point in hating someone? You can't change anything. What's the point of making yourself miserable?"

"I'll never, ever forgive him. It doesn't matter that it was years ago, that everyone says I should get over it. I can't and I won't. And you shouldn't, either."

"I don't hate my mother, Justin. And I don't hate being with my father. If I hate anything, it's the fact that anyone ever has to be unhappy. And what's the use of that? I might as well hate the fact that we all die in the end. Which I do, by the way, but it's still futile."

"Futile?"

"You know, pointless."

"I know what futile means. I just didn't expect to hear someone say it at this school."

"So you're a snob, as well as…"

"As well as what?"

"A screw-up."

"Yeah, well," he said, suddenly reaching down for his bag and heaving it over his shoulder. "I'll see you around, Erzsébet Lowe."

And he swaggered out of the classroom, slamming the door behind him so that the glass rattled in its sagging frame.

Curiously I was ready to be friends with him, after that day. But I never got the chance because he was gone by the end of the week. The rumor was that his mother was moving to London and taking him with her. I never got to see the letter he'd written to me when he should have been listing French verbs, even though I searched my locker twice over, in case it'd been slipped inside. And I never got to tell him again that he really was wrong, that miles didn't matter, not if you loved someone. That borders and oceans weren't obstacles, not for the mind. I wished I'd been able to tell him these things, because saying them out loud to someone real, instead of a mirror or a postcard, would have made them all the more convincing.

I thought of him now. Were his words an omen? Did I look back on that day and wish I'd listened, as he said I would? I pictured him as he might be today, angry still, chugging down drinks in a backstreet bar. A reckless high-achiever that couldn't care less. Or perhaps the opposite? The type I see in Victoria Park on a Sunday, sauntering contentedly beside their neat little wife, pushing a stroller with a sweet-faced baby tucked beneath blankets and plush toys. Someone who'd found contentment at last, and valued it above all else. Who looked back on their childhood with a shake of the head and a rueful smile. *I was all sound and fury, signifying nothing,* he'd say, forgetting that a hopeless ache had once been all he knew. Would he be amused that we'd swapped places later in life? If he wrote me a letter, a page torn from a notebook, what would it say today? *Dear E....*

There was a ritual to my arrivals at Villa Serena. At the start of every summer we sat outside on the shaded terrace and drank Marika's homemade lemonade. It was a wild drink I could easily picture her making, squeezing the lemons between her fists with the juice running over her knuckles, heaping sugar and stirring as clouds rose. Then she would crack handfuls of ice and pour it glugging into cut-glass jugs. On that first afternoon, the beginning of my sixth stay at Villa Serena, we drank thirstily, our eyes pricking at the bittersweet taste, our hands leaving their misted prints on glasses. We smacked our lips, the zest lighting up our tongues.

Afterward, Marika usually asked me if I wanted to go off and explore and I always went willingly. I trod my usual paths, marveling at new finds. I knelt to inspect a rat-tailed lizard with a tongue like a viper. I edged close to a zigzagging dragonfly as it alighted on a fence post, its wings like old net curtains. And I stroked the nose of the chestnut-colored horse, trying not to look at its back hooves sprouting like curly toed slippers. Then I wandered into the avenues of corn that ran behind the Horváths' house, my hands trailing. I didn't care if Bálint saw me, and laughed at the thought of last year in the barn, my bluff and rose-cheeked bluster. Or if Mrs. Horváth paused while washing dishes at the sink, the suds reaching her elbows, and looked out across the field, watching me waltz across her field of corn. Or if Mr. Horváth shifted in his afternoon sleep, stirred by the cracking wings of pigeons as they rose from my feet and scattered toward the sky. All I wanted was for Tamás to know that I had returned and that I was ready for him. To kiss my lemon-sweet lips and let the summer begin.

For once, wishing worked. That night as I lay in bed a light snapped back and forth across the opposite wall. I went to the window and leaned out, curled my fingers around the crooked tiles that jutted beneath and looked beyond the dark lawn and over to the steep, black woods. A lamplight flicked between the trees, then panned to the sky and bobbed about like a loose star. *Tamás,* I whispered, knowing that it was him, with the easy faith of those who believe themselves in love. A message, then. A fire-bright code that answered and said, *I know you are there.* I watched it blink yellow, then snap to black, and fell asleep with the window wide open, and the sounds of whispering trees and furtive footsteps moving across the forest floor.

The next morning I took my breakfast out onto the veranda and sat on a dew-wet chair. The early sun showed a blond head passing on the track below.

"Hey!" I called.

I watched the head stop and turn. I couldn't see the face; the tangle of undergrowth at the edge of the lawn obscured my view. An elder tree dripped, nettles straggled; a rhododendron bustled loudly.

"Hey," came the reply.

I stood and leaned against the balcony.

"It's you," I said.

"And you," he said. A soft voice, shyer than I remembered.

"I saw you last night in the forest. That was you, wasn't it?"

"Yes."

"And I suppose you knew I'd be right here, on the balcony, this morning?"

"I guessed."

The head disappeared for a moment then and I heard a rustle.

"I brought you this. Watch out!"

I jumped as a small stone arced through the air and landed on the balcony, rolling under the table. I bent to my knees to retrieve it. I rolled it in my palm and felt the press of a crooked-shaped heart, white like marble. It was smooth to the touch but with unfinished edges. He must have found it on one of his walks, washed it in a stream and carried it in his pocket, waiting for my return. I ran my fingers over it. Later, I would drop a kiss on its cool surface, but not in front of him, not yet. It became my most prized possession, and as I curled my fingers around its shape I resolved to never let it go.

"I love it, Tamás," I said, through the trees.

I love you. That was what I really wanted to say. And we'd said it to each other already, in letters. I'd copied out Marika's writing—*szeretlek.* And he had written it back. "Meet me by the pool in the forest at ten o'clock," I called down to him, through the elder and the rhododendron and the bending nettles.

I heard the smile in his voice as he answered with a single *"Igen,"* yes. And I heard the kick in his step as he ran back to his house. On the balcony of Villa Serena my fingers closed tight around the heart he'd given me.

Marika caught my arm as I ran through the house afterward. She swiveled me around and I spun like a dancer. We both laughed, and I felt a chord pull in me. She kissed the top of my head and stood back, with fire in her cheeks and a flush across her breastbone. She held my arms with fingers that pressed tight. She was a girl again. The Hungarian boy with pale hair and eyes like new sky was hers as much as mine. As I raced upstairs to change I heard her break into song.

I stopped on the last stair and listened with my back flat against the wall. It was a village tune that I'd heard before, seen it sung, as men danced in white cotton shirts and blackened cowboy boots, and the girls strutted with their hands on hips, skirts billowing, throwing coquettish looks and chirpy choruses. It was a song of romance. I listened and thought of Marika, how she could snare the essence of adventure in no time at all. I thought of Zoltán downstairs in his studio, mixing colors and launching them at blank canvases with his lips parted. It wasn't any wonder that they ran together, like quick water cutting a new path. The love that lived in those hills was of the heart-stopping kind. *Passion,* Marika had said once, and now I felt its ripple for myself. There would be some part of Marika with me at the pool, but in the end she would be left behind. The hands that would twine uncertainly behind my back would belong only to me, and the words when they came, misshapen but true, would also be mine. And I would quake for a moment, feeling as though I was stepping away from one thing toward another. I would close my eyes and become something else. Like ice to water in the hot sun.

At the pool, Tamás and I had slipped into the water and kissed, above its surface and below, like deep-sea divers who've abandoned their masks. Afterward, he took me over the hills, so far away that I couldn't even see our slip of red roof. We trod dusty paths until my ankles grew mottled and the soles of my feet sore. We paddled in fast-dashing river water, touching our pruned toes together, laughing wet smiles with our tongues stained red from wild strawberries that we'd snatched from the forest floor. Tamás pointed to a hawk and we lay flat on our backs and watched it circle high above us, a king of the sky. He caught a field mouse and let me cup it in my hand, its beaded eyes jet-black and shining. He kissed me as we hung on a field gate, and as we balanced on a log across a brook and as we ran, tumbling down a hillside that was parched yellow and crackling with our quick steps. His kisses fell like sweet and welcome rain.

I grew brown and happy and undone. My body felt loose in my possession, liable to do things without my full consent. Like diving headfirst beneath a waterfall, turning cartwheels in the middle of the road to Esztergom, or reaching out a hand and catching Tamás, drawing him toward me so our bodies were pressed, top to toe.

We gorged ourselves but I was always hungry that summer. We ate salty steaks of pork, dusted hot with paprika. Butter-soaked sweet corn that we raced to nibble to the end, our teeth flecked yellow. Sausages cooked over a fire, smoky and sweet, that left us thirsty for Zoltán's brown bottled beer that once weaved my steps ragged and sent me giggling across the lawn.

One such night, after raiding Zoltán's beers, I asked Tamás what Marika was like when I wasn't there.

He shrugged. "The same," he said. "Same Marika."

I bit at my fingernails. "Not quieter?" I asked, "Not sadder?"

"Marika is never sad or quiet!" Tamás laughed.

I flinched, and brushed at a prickle of an insect landing on my arm. I took another swig and spoke up over the roar of the cicadas.

"I suppose she thinks it's perfect here. Well, I suppose it is, isn't it?"

He jumped out of his chair and kneeled down in front of me. He took my hands and began to kiss them.

"Nothing's perfect without you," he said.

"But Marika?" I persisted. "She acts and looks the same?"

He dropped my hands gently back into my lap. He shrugged.

"It's okay," I said. "Really. She is what she is, with or without me. It's not like I want her to be anything different."

That same summer I finally saw inside the Horváths' house. I stood in their tiny living room with its green papered walls and drapes embroidered with the heads of flowers, the crucifix on the wall and a clay statue of the Virgin Mary, her head dipped in prayer, her robe chipped and faded blue. I sat on the edge of the sofa and drank a glass of flat Coca-Cola as Tamás pointed things out that I might find interesting: his green-and-white *Ferencváros* football shirt, a postcard from Canada with a picture of a black bear that a distant relative had sent, an old leather satchel his grandfather used for hunting in the Pilis hills behind the house. I ran my fingers over its cracked surface, and when we both bent to smell its tang our hair brushed and we stole a kiss, under the Virgin's eyes. When he disappeared to the bathroom I stared hard at a school photograph propped beside the television set. I picked him out, tall and upright in the back row, his blond hair like a lick of gold, his mouth wide and laughing. It looked like it was taken in the fifties, all the children had an old-fashioned look that I couldn't put my finger on. I imagined Marika in such a class shot, with her uneven braids and steely stare. Likely, she would have moved as it was taken, a blur of motion in the middle row, appearing later like a ghost.

Marika and Zoltán welcomed Tamás, laughing as he coughed through their cigarette smoke, then filled his glass

for him, with bull's blood wine. We sat as strange equals at
the supper table, a couple on either side, and talked long into
the night as fireflies danced at the edge of the lawn. Once
or twice his parents would wander over, which they never
used to do, bringing with them a bottle of moonshine and
a plate heaped high with walnut cookies. The men laughed
loud and long, the women knocked their spoons against
their coffee cups and Tamás and I crept inside to the den,
to fall asleep in front of a German television show, arms and
legs tangled, with the windows open to the night. It felt
like the summer would never end. And my other life, my
childish English life, was far from all my thoughts.

But Marika delivered the reminder.

"You'll miss him, won't you, when you go?"

I was standing in the kitchen, glugging peach juice,
bikini-clad, my feet turned out impishly. I stopped, lowered the glass, a drop running down my chin.

"I can't imagine not being here," I said. I let the words
hang, heavy with expectation. The crooked plates on the
dresser seemed to sing *Stay,* so did the rattling bead drapes
in the doorway, Zoltán's canvases in the hallway, the colors shaping and reforming to paint the words before me.
Stay, then.

"I mean, I've been thinking, maybe I could just..."

Marika set a pot of coffee on the stove. She made a great
show of looking for the sugar. I watched her back and the
way her shoulder blades pointed through her blouse.

"Don't think of it as an ending," she said as she laid out
the saucers. "It's just things changing shape."

"I like the shape of things as they are," I said. "I don't
want anything to change. If I could just stay here..."

"Change keeps us alive," said Marika, and she turned away, her face drawn pale. "We all need change."

I set down my glass and a fly lost no time in settling on its sticky rim.

"Erzsi, just because you're not here with Tamás doesn't mean he's not with you," she said. "Just thinking about someone can be enough sometimes. Knowing where they are and what they're doing and seeing them, in the mind's eye. Memory, imagination, these are the gifts. The power to conjure. This magic…"

"It's not enough," I said. "It might be enough for you, but not for me. And it's not magic, it's just…sad."

I wondered how many years would turn before the past ceased to matter anymore. She was right, change did keep us alive. But it gave us a new life, when the old one wasn't necessarily done yet. When the old one still fitted, even if it was a little thin at the elbow. Hungarian summers with Marika were wonderful, but the time before had never quite faded from my view. I felt an itch behind my eyes. I rubbed them.

"I've always carried you in my heart," she said simply, one hand resting on her chest.

"I know," I said. "But actually being here is better."

We faced each other, and I thought there would be something more, but she just swiped my glass for the sink and finished preparing the coffee with precise gestures. I walked out of the kitchen ahead of her, my bare feet scuffing, as behind me she carried the tray to the lawn.

I wanted change. I'd outgrown Harkham. I felt the top of my head pushing at its low ceilings, the tips of my fingers pressing at the walls. The routine of it all. My father leaving for work each day at the same time, his jacket, his briefcase, always the same. I'd hear the engine of our old car complaining as he teased it into action, then the crunch of gravel as it rolled slowly onto the lane. I then had twenty minutes before the school bus came. I'd exhale, run around the house and shake its cobwebs. Kick back on my bed and throw my legs in the air. Shout until I was hoarse. Then I'd straighten my school clothes and walk down the road to the bus stop. Wishing, suddenly and fiercely and inconveniently, that I'd kissed my father goodbye. On his cheek, as I used to do when I was younger. When he'd scoop me up and hold me high in the air, his hands firmly under my armpits, my legs kicking, my face laughing.

The day before I had to leave I went to Tamás's house again. His parents had gone to the market and the place was dark and cool and quiet. Tamás poured us glasses of cola while I wandered around the living room, picking things up and putting them down. I went over to the windowsill where there was a boxy-looking cassette recorder, with a small stack of tapes beside it. I glanced through them. Most were folk-music recordings, their covers showing men in flouncy shirts and tight black breeches and women with extravagantly braided hair and nipped-in waists. More polished versions of the village dancers I had seen. A couple showed grave older men with bristling whiskers and sorrowful eyes, chins resting on violins, fingers dancing over zithers. And one had a blond man on the cover, with round spectacles, his hair trimmed in a square and bowl-like cut. He wore a pistachio-colored Western-style shirt and a safe smile. *Pure cheese,* my school friends would have called it. But my father liked John Denver. In fact, he had this very cassette; I'd

seen it in the drawer where he kept all his tapes. I remembered the cover, and thinking he looked like a cowboy who
was too soft to ride the range, electing instead to sit by a
fire and strum his guitar. I hadn't heard my father play the
tape for a very long time. In fact, I hadn't seen it for years.

Tamás came back in then, and I felt his warm breath on
my ear.

"Want to play some music?" he said.

"This one." I held out the smiling cowboy.

"That one? It's too sad."

"No, it's not. Go on, play it!"

"You don't think it's sad?"

I couldn't remember it being sad. I couldn't remember it
at all. "No," I said, "I don't think so. I like it."

Tamás took the tape and put it in the machine. He re-
wound it just a little bit, then stopped it, as though at a precise point. He hit Play.

"Dance with me," he said very quietly, his eyes intent
on mine.

As guitar music filled the room he took hold of both of
my hands and moved me into the middle. I began to giggle, then stopped. The cowboy was singing about leaving.
He sang of cases in the hallway, a kiss, a promise, a last embrace. And then a jet plane streaking the sky, its return unknown. Tamás's eyes had turned a watery blue, and I felt
my own prick with tears in ready answer. My toes curled
into the old woven rug that lay on the floor. Tamás moved
me closer to him, and I rested my head on his shoulder. The
cowboy didn't want to leave and neither did I. We danced
very slowly, our arms wrapped around each other. And then,
without warning, I began to think about a different sort of

departure. No planes, but a ferry trip and an opposite shore. A lake black as night, with wine huts running beside and a rolling crowd. A strange and stilted breakfast. My father on the beach, the rash of sunburn across his collarbones. Too much ice cream. Bags in the hallway, Marika's face pale and heart-shaped, me just heartbroken.

With my face nestled into Tamás's shoulder I began to cry. With careful thumbs he smoothed away my tears and kissed my lips. We slowly twirled, our bodies melded into one.

"It's okay, Erzsi," he whispered. "This song always makes me cry, too. I played it all last year when I was waiting for you to come back again. Marika gave it to me, in fact."

I looked up. "Marika?"

"She was throwing out some things, I think."

I remembered then, how I knew my father liked John Denver. Years and years ago, perhaps when I was six or seven, I'd come across a record of his, and my father had put it on. I had a very distinct memory of him operating the record player, as I didn't see him touch it very often. He placed the needle with such precision, his lips pointed, his back hunched. As country music filled our cottage, Marika had sashayed in from the kitchen and swept my reluctant father into her arms. The two of them had danced around the living room, my father's footwork cautious and embarrassed, my mother moving beats ahead of the music. I'd jumped around in their footsteps, before throwing myself onto the sofa, giggling as cushions rained down on my head. The dancing hadn't lasted long and was never repeated, but for one strange and delicious moment, I'd felt like an outsider in my parents' love story and I hadn't minded one bit.

"Leaving is the worst thing that anyone can ever do," I said.

"Not always, Erzsi," he said, his lips warm against my ear. "If Marika hadn't left, how would I have met you?"

The song ended and another began and we kept on dancing. Slowly, and in not quite perfect time.

CHAPTER NINE

I came to the last photograph in the album. It is also the last that was ever taken of the two of us. I ran my hands over it, following the lines of me and of her. It is in this moment, when my guard is let down, that the past reached out its pointed finger and nicked my skin, eliciting a sharp pain that only a cry suppressed. I allowed myself to speak her name for the first time. *Marika.* Just a whisper at first. Three syllables. Until my voice grew louder and I rolled them all together. *MarikaMarikaMarikaMarikaMarikaMarika.*

Around me, the park disappeared from view. The avalanche's roar, the one I first heard in the gallery before I knew no more than old sadness, was upon me, and it was deafening. I was consumed by it. But instead of white light I saw an endless Hungarian lake, its surface cracked and restless. Above it, a bruised sky glowers. A sharp wind was whipping. On the blanket I shivered and curled more tightly into myself, my bare skin prickled with goose bumps. Around me, park life continued, lit by sunshine and blue skies, but I knew nothing of it. I was somewhere else. I was in the last of the summers. And just like it always did, it pervaded and colored all others. What shade? I wonder. Not sepia, although it was a long time ago. Nor red, for no blood was shed. Perhaps it should be the color of flame. Licking and destroying everything around it, drying throats and pricking eyes. Turning once-bright things to ash.

I held my breath, and looked closely at this last photograph. I stared so hard and unblinkingly that my eyes began to water, and for a moment everything swam out of focus.

In the picture it is 1997 and I am sixteen years old. Despite everything that happened that summer there is a photograph included just the same. And as I could have guessed, it is a picture of the two of us. Marika, yanking on heartstrings with all the delicacy of a novice bell ringer.

We are at Lake Balaton, leaning on the balustrade of a promenade. The glittering water is behind us and the breeze lifts our dark and matching hair. Marika's arm is draped around me and my head leans on her shoulder. The sunshine splashes us both golden. We are a comfortable tangle of mother and daughter and are having the time of our lives. We are certain of it, for our smiles run deep and true.

Before I could go to Hungary again, there was a year to pass in England. A restless year, where everything I yearned for felt both extremely close and never more remote. I remember my sixteenth birthday, and how I'd spent the days before it moping. Tamás had sent a package from Hungary but it hadn't arrived yet and I feared it was lost, or stolen by light-fingered postal workers, curious at what could be sent to that faraway country, Anglia. And Marika had telephoned me two days earlier to say that she couldn't call me on my actual birthday, as she and Zoltán were going away. Outside the day was lit with spring sunshine, but I'd felt cold when I set the receiver down. I'd gone to my room and turned up my music, drowning out my father's appeals to adjust the volume. I sulked and painted my fingernails a rotten shade of plum that not even I particularly liked.

On my birthday morning my father made us both poached eggs, two apiece, with extra triangles of toast set at the sides. He had the radio on in the kitchen and turned it up as a classical piece came on. We watched a gang of sparrows attacking the bird feeder. He made me feel as though I'd turned fifty, not sixteen.

"Would you like your present?" he said. "I'm afraid I may have gotten it dreadfully wrong."

"Okay," I said, thinking sorrowfully that he probably had.

He reached into the bottom kitchen cupboard and drew out a brown paper package. It was tied with string and stuck with odd pieces of masking tape. It looked like the packets of string beans he put together for harvest festivals.

"Ooh," I said, "what is it?" Already dreading the moment of discovery. I prepared my features, so that they wouldn't drop in disappointment.

I opened it and inside found a red dress. I held it up. It was made of the kind of dimpled cotton fabric that was in all the shops, that I had run my fingers over and cooed at through windows. It had a full skirt, and capped sleeves, and a neck that came down in a V-shape.

"Is it all right?" he said. "I got it from that shop you always talk about. They helped me pick the size. I didn't know what you'd need. I said you came up to my shoulder and your waist was about the width of a loaf of bread and they seemed to work it out from that."

"Dad," I said, and started crying. I folded the dress in my lap and my tears rained on it.

"Oh, dear, I've gotten it wrong, haven't I? I'm useless." And he came and stood beside me, his hand patting my shoulder as I tried to find the voice to tell him that he had gotten it utterly, perfectly right.

Despite being touched by my father's thoughtfulness, I had a plan that I would not be swayed from. I had spent the year swapping dozens of letters with Tamás, and my flights of imagination had taken me everywhere. I saw us in a Budapest apartment listening to jazz records, the kind that Marika and Zoltán played. I saw us walking beneath a string of lime trees as university students with books clasped to our chests. I saw us tanned brown and lounging by a lazy river's edge, one hand on a pram settled in the shade, a soft mewing accompanying its rock. Or I just saw us as we would be that year, padding around Villa Serena, bare-footed and carefree, as Marika poured wine and Zoltán turned strips of meat on the fire.

I'd decided that I wanted to talk to Marika properly about staying. All I really wanted was to be in Hungary. I was in a hurry to start a new life, but I had no intention of broaching the subject with my father until Marika and I had talked it over. I knew she'd understand, and would love all my impassioned reasoning, offering her own in support. By the time my stay was up I'd have a perfectly constructed argument to take to my father. I knew he couldn't refuse.

As I kissed his cheek at the airport, for a fleeting moment I'd wished I was small again. I'd looked at him then, without the judgment or evaluation of a stranger. But I was back in the present, and I was irritated. He'd said goodbye to me without mentioning Marika or Villa Serena or anything about Hungary. It was nothing new but it smarted still. Instead, he dug his fingers into my shoulder with what he intended to be affection, but felt more like a miser's pinch. He said, *You'll miss the best of the sweet corn, of course,* and as usual I filled in the gaps. I wondered how it would feel to say, *I'll miss you, too.*

Like Marika before me, I knew I was ready to go. It broke my heart that he probably knew it, too.

"Erzsi! So much beauty!"

Zoltán was in an expansive mood. He bent and kissed my hand in chivalric fashion, clicking his heels as the courtly Hungarians once did, the effect slightly dampened by his bare feet. I had just arrived and my suitcases had not even made it inside. My dress was crumpled from travel, my cheeks spotted red with excitement and fatigue. I had barely slept the night before, twisting in my sheets through expectation of the weeks to come.

Tamás emerged from the house carrying a tray of clinking glasses and he set them hurriedly down as I threw myself at him. He had sprouted in the year that passed and was far taller than me now; he lifted me up and spun me around and we all laughed as I yelped. Marika placed a hand on his shoulder and drew us all to the table. I saw the comfortable exchanges, the easy gestures that passed between them. He had seen more of Marika and Zoltán over the year, perhaps even joined them in meals such as this one. I watched him run his fingers through his hair, which fell longer across

his forehead, and cross his legs lazily under the table. I saw
the way muscles flickered in his forearm as he passed a plate
heaped high with peppered pork. He had a tiny white scar
on his chin that was new. Later I would run my finger over
it, kiss its edges. His eyes seemed bluer than before, a richer
vein of color, and sharp like a cat's.

It was just as we were finishing dessert that Marika and
Tamás floated their big idea. We were eating *Somlói galuska,*
a messy bowlful of liquor-doused sponge cake, a nutty chocolate sauce and billows of whipped cream, and conversation
had momentarily subsided. Marika threw her spoon into her
bowl, her finger dabbing at the last of the scattered almonds.

"So," she said, licking her lips, "Tamás and I have been
plotting."

He nodded. "I want to give you the perfect summer,
Erzsi," he said, "the perfect Hungarian summer. And that
has to be Balaton."

I didn't look at anyone, only him, although I felt the heat
of Marika's stare. I smiled. Smiled, then laughed.

"That's a brilliant idea," I said. "When do we leave?"

As it turned out, it had been all Tamás's plan. He had
gone to Marika and Zoltán and explained that he wanted to
take me to the lake, but thought it was too far to go there
and back in one day. He wanted to stay with me there, but
would they allow it? They would, Marika said, but only
if they went, too. She said this with a steeliness, her eyes
unblinking. Things fell quickly into place after that. Zoltán had been asked to tutor a group of summer school students, four days of cover for a friend of his who had to go
to the hospital. The school was in Keszthely, at the far tip
of the lake. He would stride between easels and cock his

head learnedly to one side as the students peeped out at the water from under their sun hats. Marika and Zoltán would find a place to stay, a simple summer house by the shore, and Tamás and I would go, too. The four of us, to Balaton.

We were to leave in two days' time, so each of us began our preparations. Marika took me to Esztergom and bought me a new bikini from a market stall. I tried it on in front of a cracked mirror as she held up a sheet in front of me. I turned to admire myself with my hands on my hips, a pale vision in tangerine nylon. Tamás ferreted in one of his outhouses and retrieved a creased and dusty bundle of yellow rubber that turned out to be a dinghy with plastic oars. He spread it on the lawn, hosing off the spiders' webs and motorcycle grease, and declared it seaworthy. Meanwhile Zoltán wrote a list of places of interest for us to enjoy while he worked. One was a palace, the thought of which fascinated me. I couldn't imagine a glittering mansion on the shores of Balaton, hemmed in by summerhouses, orange tennis courts and banks of waving reed. If Tamás had been an English boy, he'd have rolled his eyes when Zoltán produced his earnest list, but instead he listened intently, and said he'd once been to the library at the palace on a school trip. He remembered the smell of books, the towering shelves that held them. As he spoke I reached for his hand and felt the contours of each finger underneath the table. I squeezed each knuckle, and felt the rough skin at the edges of his nails.

I wondered briefly if Tamás knew what it might mean to me, to return to Balaton. Had Marika warned him of my possible reluctance when he first suggested his plan? In all of our letters and whisperings I had never told him anything about Marika's departure while at the lake, and he in turn had never asked. I wondered if that meant he knew it all, anyway, listening in on Mrs. Horváth and Marika as they chattered like blackbirds over a line of flapping laundry, or even years ago, when he'd seen the Balaton painting that Zoltán had given me and asked if I liked it there. I decided not. It helped that the idea to go to Balaton had come from him, but as soon as he said it I realized I wanted to go all the same. Hungary had become my land of unbridled freedom, and that stretch of endless water was the only place where a shadow still lurked. I wanted to banish it. I wanted to stare at the water like I did at Zoltán's painting, with its daubs of every blue. I wanted to drink in the views without a sharp taste turning my tongue. I wanted to see Marika in a black dress, one that clung to her hips and dipped at her chest, and watch her as she turned and laughed, a glass of wine in her hand, the warm night behind. And I wanted to slip my hand into hers and walk away together, tightly bound.

There was a new feeling rising, too. I wanted to rid myself of a nagging finger of guilt. My father. He would hate the idea of my return to Balaton, the four of us together, a boy with an easy arm around my waist and his own place taken by a man in a long white shirt and sun hat. A man with brown hands and laugh lines.

Although my father was a teacher, he was surrounded by children, not teenagers. He worked at a cloistered prep school, with boys too young and polite to snort behind his back, boast of misadventures or swap loud opinions about the lone female member of staff. They were snub-nosed children who washed their hands and said *please* and *thank you*. They sang in choirs and dreamed of swooping jets and purring engines. They seemed to come from another age, and so did my father. They got along very well together, with the airy detachment of an aging schoolmaster and disciplined charges. As a result, my father managed to stave off reality in every direction. At home I acted like the daughter he wanted, a younger, sweeter version of myself. Not at all the type of girl who vacationed with her boyfriend and her mother's lover in a place that, at home, he and I would never even dare to mention.

A week before I'd left he'd said, *We could go on holiday together, you and I.* And I think I'd laughed. *What would we do?* I'd said, *I can't imagine it.* He'd rubbed his mustache and said, *Well, what we do at home, I suppose.* And I'd laughed again. It was only later that I realized he might really have meant it.

At Keszthely, the house we had rented was nothing like the place in Fenyves, and I was thankful for it. It sat on a tree-lined street of stately houses that had been turned into blocks of vacation apartments. Ours was a buttercup-yellow pile of brickwork, with fancy white-painted balconies. Cars in the driveway had German plates and bulging bumpers. Inside there were red tiles and blond wooden furniture, bright blue bedspreads and a zesty smell that suggested a thorough and recent scrubbing. I felt a palpable sense of relief at its bright newness and distinct identity that drew on nothing I'd hitherto experienced. I sat down at a shiny table, drinking fizzing cherry soda, nose to nose with my boyfriend.

I felt as though the world was at my feet. All I had to do was take a step.

Later, we walked down streets trimmed by picket fences and iron railings, occasional barking dogs making us jump.

We came upon a restaurant, hearing the sounds of knives and forks, clinking glasses, the murmur of lunchtime conversation. It had a tented roof that caught the hot air and broiled it. Vines twisted at the railings and a giant cheese plant curled up and sideways, its thick rubbery fingers clutching at anything it could find. I stopped and stared.

"Hungry?" said Zoltán, nodding at a passing waiter as he delivered his dishes to a table; the sight of the piled-high plates made him involuntarily lick his lips.

"No, no. I just wanted to…look."

I hadn't been to Keszthely before, but all Balaton resorts seemed to have the same air about them. It wasn't like in England, where seaside towns just miles apart had characters all of their own, tumbling pebbles or sweeping sand dunes in bright white or dusty red, landscapes dramatically altering as you rounded a cliff or stumbled upon a new beach. No matter where you were on the Balaton shore, it seemed that if you'd been anywhere at all, you felt like you'd been everywhere. The same flat water, the same hazy hills, the scents and smells and shapes of people moving. The restaurant, which I had never seen before, brought it all back.

I saw myself, nine years old, perched on similar benched seating, my father beside me and Marika across from us. My legs swung under the table, my chin was cupped in my hands. There had been a platter to share, served with a ripple of excitement that had me sitting up straight. It had been heaped with cuts of meat, scarlet sausages, thick-cut potatoes and rice with peas. Across the top, strung out like fans, had been glistening *szalonna,* the roasted fat that Marika so loved. She had snatched it as though she were claiming a prize, her lips shining. I remembered tall glasses of Fanta, which I learned to pronounce as *Fon-toh,* and a cucumber salad dripping in vinegar, dabbed with sour cream and dusted with red paprika. I'd held one of the wafer-thin slices of cucumber up to my eye and stared through it at the restaurant. I had been told off for playing with my food. It was precious in Hungary, Marika had said, and not to be taken for granted.

I could remember the way my father mopped his soup bowl with the gray-white bread from the basket on the table, the way it stained red and dripped on his shirt. Afterward, he had chosen an ice-cream cup laced with strawberry sauce and topped with a lime-green cocktail umbrella, an unexpected moment of frivolity. He had given the umbrella to me, and I had kept it until we were back in England on our own. I had swiveled it in my fingers, seen its lime print blur, then thrown it away, pushing it to the very bottom of the kitchen trash, with the tea leaves and the soup cans and bread crusts.

I became aware of the others staring at me. Marika shifting in her sandals. Zoltán's brow knotted. Tamás linked his arm though mine, pulled me along and said, *Come on, let's go to the water.*

The Balaton worked in mysterious ways. You could be just meters from the water and not see it, its edges fringed with low-dipping trees and hasty beachside settlements. Somewhere, I knew the blue water was waiting, its surface cracked and shifting with waders, bathers and swimmers, and endless stretches farther out, where the currents from the breeze whipped the deep water stronger. The sun was rising high and pounded everything.

I flexed my fingers, feeling stiff in the heat. We crossed

onto the road that led to the lakeside and quickly found ourselves in the resort's flurry. We were on a path hemmed with kiosks and cafés, their wares spilling onto the street, high piles of riotously colored plastic. I scanned the faces around me. There was bare skin everywhere: hard-muscled shoulders, deep brown torsos, skinny stomachs, thick swinging arms, long bandy legs, men and women, boys and girls. There were the smells of sweet suntan lotion or nutty perspiration, all about us sun-warmed flesh, and wafts of frying pancakes and frankfurter sausages, beef burgers and pans of goulash soup.

Tamás pointed to a giant inflatable cola bottle, a raft made for idle drifting, that was propped incongruously beside a rack of painted plates and homespun pottery, strings of dried paprika touching its rubber edges. Beside it there was an inflatable shark with a creased fin, and an island the size of a trash can lid, with a collapsing palm tree, its air escaping.

"It's nice but we already have our ship," he said, thinking of the old yellow dinghy, "the best boat on the water."

Keszthely beach was a stretch of grass that ran beside the lake in both directions, a path marking the edge. Burly willow trees offered some shade but everywhere the sun beamed hard on the holidaymakers. Tiny children pottered at the edges with the tepid water swelling gently around their ankles. Older children launched themselves into the water, leaping against the bright sky. Frisbees skimmed the surface, a Windsurfer teetered with sagging sail, drifting backward, ever closer to the shore. A fleet of candy-colored paddle boats were pulled up on the bank, with four or five more on the water. Knees jumped furiously, the water beneath churning. A fluorescent pink raft bobbed gently, its owner prostrate with an open book across his chest. We stood and watched, feeling overdressed in our dresses and shorts and shirts. I felt Marika's hand on my back.

"Do you like it, Erzsi?"

And I thought it odd, as though she believed I was seeing Balaton for the first time.

"Yes," I said with resolve, "I'm glad we came."

And I meant it, especially as I saw Tamás pull off his shirt and stand bare-chested, looking out over the water. I imagined rolling under the surface with him, our bodies slippery as eels. Then we'd wander home through the back streets hand in hand, our wet footprints dark in the dust.

"A new beginning," I heard Marika say quietly, echoing my thoughts. I stood ready to catch her eye but she stared straight ahead and into the distance, one hand shielding the sun from her face.

That evening we ate in a garden restaurant lit by twinkling lights and a host of people. A twisting staircase led down to the dining patio, each step creeping with ivy and marked by lanterns. It was there that we met four of Zoltán's artist friends, who were also in Keszthely for the summer school. I remembered János Papp, the wolf artist from my first year at Villa Serena. I noted that he had a new woman with him, a plump and dimpled girl called Carla, whom I liked immediately. We swapped kisses and I smelled the sweet perfume of the women, felt the stubble of the men. I was wearing the dress that my father had given me, with its plunging neck and swirly skirt, and enjoyed the compliments that came my way. How Carla took my hand and twirled me, saying, *Szép, szép,* in honeyed tones. I looked for the glint of gold in János's smile and found it.

Later we sat elbow to elbow as cauldrons of soup, roasted meats and whole baked fish were carried to our table. Zoltán held court and Marika shone beside him, her lips painted, her hair glossier than the shining lake beyond. I watched them, my hand resting on the back of Tamás's chair. I wondered if I looked like the daughter of this couple, if Zoltán was passing as my father, a swarthier, burlier influence, but unmistakably mine. It was an illicit thought, titillating to contemplate. For just a moment I dismissed my quiet, stooping father at home, and adopted this noisier, somehow *bigger* man. I felt guilty, but copied Zoltán's easy laughter nonetheless, proffered my own wineglass as the bottle came around. I let my hand drop onto Tamás's shoulder and stay there. He shot me a warning glance and swept his hair uncertainly from his eyes. I sipped my wine and leaned closer in to him. I smiled across at Marika but her attention was elsewhere. I felt drunk with the experience and fought the urge to shout out loud, whether with joy or something else I wasn't sure. I whispered in Tamás's ear, *Szeretlek, szeretlek,* and other things in hushed and breathy tones, English things that I knew he wouldn't understand and I barely did myself.

After supper we walked back to the apartment, Tamás and I dawdling as I pulled back on his arm and Marika and Zoltán walked ahead of us.

"Come on, you two," said Marika, turning, "it's late."

"Maybe we'll keep walking," I said, my hand tight in Tamás's. "If you leave the door open, we'll come in quietly."

"No, Erzsi, not on your own," said Marika.

"I won't be on my own." I laughed.

The Book of Summers

"No, Erzsi," said Marika.

I couldn't account for her change in mood.

"Just because you're tired," I said.

"I'm tired, too," said Tamás quickly. "Let's go back."

Marika and Zoltán went to bed right away, going through to their room at the back. I heard the creak of their bed as they got into it, the purr of the electric fan as they turned it up a notch. I tiptoed back down the hall, my bare feet silent on the tiles.

"The wine they drank, they'll be asleep in seconds," I said to Tamás.

"Maybe we should go, too," he said.

The apartment had just two bedrooms, so Tamás was to sleep on the sofa in the den that also folded into a bed. A pile of sheets and a peach-colored towel had been attentively left on the sofa's arm. I settled myself down among the cushions.

"But I'm not even slightly tired yet," I said.

I flicked on the television and it fizzed and crackled. I turned it down low, and watched as flickering football players ran across a slanting field. I reached out and took hold of Tamás's arm and pulled him toward me. I could feel his body tense, his head turned in the direction of Marika and Zoltán's room.

"Don't you want to kiss me?" I said.

"I just think maybe..."

"Maybe, what? We do what we want at Villa Serena, you don't care there."

"There we're not on holiday with your parents," he said. "I mean, with Marika and Zoltán."

"They're fine," I said, "they like you. Marika thinks you're the best."

But I could have said anything; he wasn't to be persuaded. He stood frigidly, his arms folded across his chest.

"God, come on!" I laughed, and pulled him so he was caught off balance and fell onto me on the sofa. We were tangled, and I trapped him with my legs. "Got you," I whispered, and began to kiss his ear.

I didn't hear the bedroom door open, or Marika's padding steps down the hall. I only heard her stern and exaggerated cough, as she stood in her white nightdress. We sprang apart. In the half-light from the television screen I saw her face. It wasn't anger etched there, or disappointment, but worry. Worry snaking up her neck in a red flush and ruddying her cheeks. In the dim and flickering light there was something of my father in Marika's stare. A craggy brow bent low, a vivid flush and the look of someone swept along by a current that they couldn't control.

"Total overreaction," I said.

It was the next morning, and I was standing in the kitchen in a skimpy vest and shorts, tapping my fingers against the rim of my mug. Tamás had gone to the shops to fetch fresh rolls, anxious to redeem himself as the perfect guest. Zoltán had left early for the summer school, throwing a wave and escaping into the light morning air with a straw hat and his easel. Marika and I were alone in the apartment. She wore a long purple dress splashed with painterly flowers in sun-bright yellow. Her hair was loosely braided. But despite her jolly appearance her eyes were steely. I matched them with my own.

"I mean, talk about being melodramatic. You made me feel really stupid in front of Tamás."

I took my mug and slid into a chair at the table. I rested my elbows and held it with both hands. I sipped the hot, strong coffee. It was more bitter than I liked, but I persevered with it. I needed something to wrap my hands around; otherwise, they would have fidgeted in my lap, or pulled at strands of my hair. I shut my eyes and drank.

"You were showing off last night, Erzsi. I don't know what got into you."

"Showing off? I'm not five years old."

"Oh, aren't you? You're still a child, Erzsi. Although you wouldn't think it to see you with Tamás. You need to slow down."

"Slow down? I don't get it," I said. And I didn't. "At home, I mean at Villa Serena, anything goes. So, why do you suddenly care if Tamás holds my hand? Or kisses me? It's no big deal. He's my boyfriend. We love each other."

Marika was drinking fruit tea and the smell of it was sickly and pungent. I had seen her stir in three spoonfuls of honey and lick the spoon afterward before throwing it in the sink.

"Your father," she said, sipping her tea, "he doesn't know anything about Tamás, does he?"

"What makes you think that?"

"I doubt whether he would approve...."

"You don't care about my father's approval," I said. "You never have! Isn't that the point? You always did just what you wanted."

I expected fireworks, wanted them, but she just dipped her head and sipped again.

"Maybe I'm more like you than you realize," I said.

I thought of that second summer when I'd leaped into the waters of the hidden pool, surprising myself, and most of all surprising Marika. I realized then how the subsequent summers had changed me. With the turning of the years I'd grown bolder.

We looked at each other, our eyes holding the other's gaze. Hers were green—in the pale kitchen light shown as pale moss; at other times, under lamplight, or starlight, glinting emerald. Mine were green, too, but rarely changed their hue. She had full lips, painted deep red, made for kissing and laughing, whereas mine were thinner and straighter and more serious in intent. Her nose was aquiline—it gave shape to her face, a strong shape—whereas mine was snubbed and freckled. But we both had the same slanting cheekbones, and the same set to our jaws.

"I don't think I ever felt even the smallest bit Hungarian when I was little," I said. "But I do now. With Tamás, and Zoltán, sure, but especially when I'm with you. I get it. I get it now. What it means, to have something else inside of you."

Marika's eyes blinked. I reached out my hand. Her fingers were sticky from the honey jar, like a child's.

"I really love Tamás. And he loves me. We've written to each other all year. Now we're together, I want us to really be together." I paused, glanced up at her, met her green eyes. "I don't want to go back to Devon after this summer and that be it. Another year's wait. I'm free to do what I want."

"But, Erzsi, you've got school in the autumn."

"That doesn't matter. I mean, I can delay it. Or I could transfer, couldn't I? There must be places here I could go?"

"No, Erzsi, I'm sorry. I don't think it'd work."

"Of course it'd work! If you're worried about Dad it doesn't matter, he won't mind. He just wants me to be happy."

"It's different, Erzsi."

"How is it different?"

"It just is."

"I'm going to sleep with him, you know. This summer. I'm ready. And I love him. I love Tamás so much. I'm a grown-up, Marika. I can do what I want now. And I know my future's here. It always has been. England seems so… dry, in comparison. It's Hungary and it's you and it's Tamás. This is my life now."

Tamás walked in then, swinging a bag of crusty rolls, a giant watermelon in the crook of his arm. Marika and I turned to him at the same time and he smiled, a bright, white smile.

"Sorry, I'm sorry. The woman in the shop would not stop talking to me. That's why I'm late. Shall I make breakfast? I got eggs, too. Did Zoltán already leave?"

Marika stood and stooped to retrieve handfuls of rolls from Tamás's bag, with excessive diligence. I willed her to catch my eye and smile to show that she understood, but she was caught in a breakfast whirlwind, with Tamás moving at her elbow, for all the world like an attentive son.

I gave up and crept out into the garden. Now that I had spoken my mind, I knew it was really true, every bit of it. I took a deep breath. Marika would understand. Eventually. She knew all about love. She knew what it was to yearn to be somewhere different. I'd seen the fire in her eyes at the thought of me living with her. Her Hungarian girl.

I curled my toes in the grass. From my vantage point in the garden I watched a procession of beach folk make their way to the lake with their rafts pumped and hoisted high, and a bright yellow ball bouncing down the road beside them. The people in the apartment above ours were playing their transistor radio on the balcony, a kind of folk song, joyous and rousing. I walked over to the lounger and stretched myself out, arching my back and pointing my toes. Above me the sky was uninterrupted, like every sky Zoltán conjured. We had read in the paper that it was going to be the hottest day of all. I closed my eyes.

After breakfast, Marika insisted on taking us to the Festetics Palace. Surrounded by resplendent formal gardens, with its iced-cake Baroque styling, perhaps she hoped it might civilize me and instill in me a formality so I'd keep my hands away from Tamás. We traipsed around the lawns that lay baking in the heat, the sun glancing off the white stones and making us squint. Inside was cool and dark and the cloth slippers we were made to wear to protect the delicate floors gave us the appearance of soft-footed, shuffling elephants. We visited the library that Tamás had mentioned, and I sat on a leather seat that stuck to the backs of my legs. I picked at some stuffing that was working its way out of the arm and studied my bright pink nails. Marika bent over the volumes, breathing in their dusty scent, lost in her own world. Through an open window, beyond the fringe of trees and hosed lawns, the dusty town stood in all its crumbling grandeur, with mustard-yellow houses and wobbly tiled rooftops, and sloping streets that led to the lake. I hated being stuck inside a library on such a day but it was important that I stayed close to Marika. I needed to convince her of my plans.

Tamás, meanwhile, was lamblike and trotted about obediently, occasionally offering me his hand but more often walking with Marika. I wanted to shock him deliciously with my dream, catch him outside by the giant fountain and whisper in his ear as the waters tinkled behind. His eyes would widen and a smile would break over his face. Then we would run, hand in hand, fast like thieves, and find our own spot away from everyone, high above the town with the lake falling away behind. Such a place would be ours, someday very soon. But for now, at Marika's insistence, we were in a library, on a broiling summer's day.

Eventually even Marika tired of the books and the three of us walked back outside into the white light. We blinked fast and strolled through the gardens with the sun high overhead. I felt Marika stumble and knock my arm heavily. I turned just as she fell to the floor in a faint, her feet kicking the gravel, small stones peppering the lawn beside. I let out a cry and bent down to her. Her eyes were closed and her head rolled back. Tamás called for help, a Hungarian word that sounded like *sheggy-tenny*. It was a word that couldn't convey the horror I felt as I looked at Marika's still face, one long arm lying beside her, the other thrown up beside her head.

A bearlike man, a passerby, with a short-sleeved shirt and arms of matted hair, bent beside her and fanned her with a museum brochure. He took a bottle of water from his leather shoulder bag. He spoke gently, as though to a child or a sick animal, and Marika's eyelids fluttered. She awoke slowly but instead of kicking and panicking as I expected, she lay quite still and listened, her eyes blinking, her lips forming a dry pout. In time she was lifted gently to her feet, the same man tucking an arm around her, and we walked a few steps to a bench in the shade. She sat with a white face and pink cheeks and drank quietly from the bottle of water, a drop running down her chin. I had my hand curled in the cloth of her skirt. Tamás sat on the other side of her, his head turned to the man who had helped us, watching him reverently.

"He says it is no surprise in this heat that people faint," said Tamás, translating. "He said that there is nothing to worry about. Just shade and rest and some water is what she needs."

I nodded and tightened my grasp of her skirt. Marika added some soothing words of her own, but they were in Hungarian. I felt my own vision twinkle and star, the sweat pricking at my forehead, my view yellowing. A sympathy faint, I wondered. I blinked and concentrated hard on a green tree. I steadied my breathing.

"Erzsi? Did you hear? The gentleman has said he will drive us back to the house."

"That's nice of him," I said, but I was scared and distracted. The image of Marika folding like a pack of cards and flopping neatly to the floor played again and again.

"I'm fine, Erzsi," said Marika in a quiet voice, patting my hand. "I'm fine. No need for fuss. But a lift would be much appreciated. *Köszönöm nagyon szépen, kedves bácsi.*"

We got into a red car that was shaped like an old boat with a pointed nose. Even with the windows wound all the way down, the heat inside choked us. At my feet lay empty cola bottles and candy wrappers; the cracked leather

seating tore at my legs and there was a smell that made
the back of my throat itch. But it was a relief not to walk
with Marika failing beside us, and somehow comforting
to have a stranger involved in our plight. Although Marika
was much recovered, so much so that she conversed all the
journey back with our helpful new friend, I willed him to
stay awhile once we were at the apartment. In case anything else happened. But he simply made sure we were
safe inside, refused the offer of a cool drink and drove off
with a tip of his cotton hat, his dark arms sturdy on the
steering wheel. I watched the car disappear with a strange,
sad feeling.

Marika had gone straight to bed and lay with a single
white sheet loose about her shoulders.

"Don't worry, Erzsi," she said. "I just want to take it easy
for a bit."

"Can I do anything?" I said, my face creased. "I mean,
anything? Can I?"

"No, Erzsi—" she took my hand "—but perhaps don't
go anywhere, will you? Stay close for a bit."

"Of course," I said, settling into a chair at the foot of her
bed. "I won't budge from here."

I saw her face relax and her eyes close. I sat with my knees
drawn up and my arms tight around them, watching her.
Down the hall I heard Tamás settle in a chair and turn on
the television, flicking until he found a sports channel. I sat
listening to the soft pock of tennis balls, played on a faraway
court, never taking my eyes off the sleeping face of Marika.

I wasn't used to people fainting. I'd never fainted myself
and I'd never been close by when someone else had. It felt

like a snatch of death stealing in, like a dress rehearsal for the real thing.

"If I ever lost you again," I whispered to her, "I wouldn't know what to do."

I heard Zoltán returning later that afternoon. He'd have been surprised to find us all indoors. *On a day like this,* I could imagine him saying, *you're crazy.* Tamás must have explained what happened as next he came thundering into the room, jolting me upright and snapping Marika awake with his heavy step and bellowed cry. He gathered her up in his arms and I turned away, slipping from the room quietly to leave them together.

I took up a new post outside in a deck chair by the screen doors, and Tamás came and threw himself down at my feet like a puppy. My hand played with his hair, absently. I imagined the two of them coming out showered and changed, stepping out into the sun of the garden and suggesting a walk before supper. I knew Marika was all right, really. But instead the muffled sounds of raised voices came through the wall. My hand froze in Tamás's hair. They had no reason to argue. Was Zoltán afraid, panicked from Marika's sudden fall and shouting in agitated relief? Was that the Hungarian way? But it was Marika's voice I heard most plainly. Her high notes were the ones that caught my ears. And my name, said over and over, by both of them.

"Tamás, what are they saying?" I said.

"I don't know. We shouldn't listen."

"Tamás! They're talking about me, what is it? What are they saying?"

"I think it's private."

"It's not! Not if it's about me!"

"Okay. All right, Erzsi, calm down. They're saying... something about...telling something. Telling someone something. Or not telling—I can't hear. It's not for us, this, Erzsi...."

But my hand kneaded the back of his neck and he squirmed.

"Tell me, Tamás, come on. If they're saying my name, then I have to know. *Please.*"

He hesitated, then craned his head to listen. But he didn't need to, the words were clear enough as they came through the thin walls. He turned around so that he was leaning against my legs and facing me. He ran his finger along the fabric of my shorts, as if to draw my attention away from what he was saying.

"Okay. Well, it sounds like...Zoltán is saying, 'Erzsi needs to know.' And Marika is saying, 'No, she doesn't. She can't know.' And they are repeating this over and over."

"What else?"

"That, er, it isn't the right time. Marika said that. And Zoltán said that it was already too late. But that you still needed to know."

"Are you sure?" I said, but Tamás just shrugged.

I knotted my hands together in my lap. I cut a crescent in my palm with my thumbnail. When I spoke, my words came like glass, sharp edged and as clear as I could.

"She's sick," I said. "She's sick and dying."

He stared back at me, his eyes wide like moons. I turned away from him, sitting sideways on my chair and facing the wall. I believed it, in the crackling heat of the garden, with my boyfriend curled at my feet. I believed it so hard that

the dizzy feeling returned, the yellow spots fizzing at the
corners of my eyes. Tamás held on to my foot, guilty for
his part in the news, and I sank low in the chair, waiting
to hear my name called. Waiting for Marika to agree that,
yes, I needed to know.

We went for a walk, Marika and I. Just the two of us. The
grand heat of the day was passing into late afternoon, made
less rabid by a breeze tickling the surface of the water. She
wore a headscarf with a splashing poppy print, tied at the
back around her blue-black hair. I had seen it before. She
liked the Romany edge it gave her, but today she wore it
simply for protection from the sun. All I could think was
that it gave her an invalided air. I walked beside her with
my hands plunged deep into the pockets of my shorts. I refused to meet her eye. We settled on a bench, beneath the
canopy of a plane tree. I kicked out my legs so the sun fell
across my calves. Marika's shoulders were dappled with pale
splotches, I looked at my chest and it was the same. I lifted
an arm, and the pattern moved. I squinted upward, knowing it was just the way the light fell through the leaves. But
to me we were both marked. The stain of a wasting disease.

"Thank you for coming with me, Erzsi. The lake's lovely
at this time of day, isn't it?"

It was and it wasn't. I had walked at the water's edge
alongside my father once, our hands held to our faces in
worry. I remembered the way the sun fell off the water, and
the impossible longing I had felt for the faraway sails, the
white triangles of hope tripping the horizon. Sailing away,
worries left churning in their wake.

"Please," I said suddenly. "Please, just tell me. I heard you arguing. I know there's something wrong. Please."

"Oh, Erzsi," said Marika. I had heard "Oh, Erzsi" a lot over the years. She could coat my name in worry, shame, regret, love, just by popping that "oh" in front. *Oh, Marika.*

"There's nothing wrong, Erzsi. You needn't look like that. Really."

"Then why were you and Zoltán arguing? And why have you brought me out here on my own, if it's not to tell me something terrible?"

"Oh, Erzsi."

"Please, stop saying that! Just tell me. Is it about before? Is it because you fainted?"

"No, it isn't. Well, yes. In a strange way, perhaps. But I think I only fainted because I was...*wrought.* Mixed up inside. And the heat was getting to me. It was all getting to me. It was only when I was lying in that darkened room afterward, and my head was darting in all these different directions, that I knew I couldn't keep it in any longer."

"We heard everything, Tamás and I. Zoltán said you should have told me a long time ago. Is that right? Is it too late?"

"There's no such thing as too late," said Marika. "Zoltán doesn't know what he's talking about when he says things like that. It's easy for him. It always has been."

And it felt like she was talking about something else then. I saw her and Zoltán stalking the terrace at Villa Serena, their voices raised and their footfall heavy, the summer trees turning to dead autumn behind them. What was it? I strained to hear. Was it sickness, a secret illness, a shut-up room with its curtains closed? Maybe a baby, an all-Hungarian baby with an artist for a father, born on the hillside, then buried in a tiny casket by the Horváths' fields of barley?

"The longer you go without saying anything, the worse the things are that I imagine," I said, "so if you love me, you'll tell me now. Mum. *Please!*"

"Dear God. Let me speak, then, before you say another word. Let me tell you. Ah...how can I begin?"

She cupped her hands and rocked forward. Her legs were crossed tight, wound almost inside herself. I noticed her veins, taut against the underside of her arm.

"When you were a little baby," she said, "you were in an accident."

She stopped for breath, and looked at me, her hands kneading in her lap. Her face was cut with pity. I saw it welling in her eyes, her lips bitten and pursed, and a flicker at her temple.

"The car you were in, Erzsi, it skidded off the road and hit a tree. You were very lucky to be alive. A gift, your father always said."

"Why hasn't anybody told me about this?" I asked in a whisper. Vulnerability caught ahold of me. I felt limp, as though my baby limbs had never recovered.

"Why hasn't anybody told me about this?" I asked again, louder the second time.

"It wasn't easy for your father, Erzsi. You must forgive him. I'm not sure he's ever gotten over what happened that day. In fact, I know he hasn't, and I doubt he ever will. Erzsi, listen. Everything sounds straightforward, but it wasn't. It really wasn't. Not at the time. Not then, not now."

"Please!"

"Erzsi, there was a person driving the car. And she died.

Erzsi, it was your mother driving the car. And she died that day. In the car, with you. But you lived, Erzsi. A gift, a wonderful gift. I was there almost from the beginning, you see. But your mother, your real mother, your natural mother, she died. When you were very, very small. I'm so… sorry for that. I couldn't be sorrier, Erzsi. I wish we never had to tell you. I mean, I wish there was a way for you to have known, and for it to have all been all right, long, long ago. It'd have been easier, in a way, if you'd remembered it happening. But you were so very tiny. And your father was so very sad. And we were both so very…afraid."

I didn't speak. I was sitting on my hands, hunched over. If you'd have passed me, I'd have looked sick sitting like that. I'd have looked small, and sick. Marika went on, and every word she spoke seemed less likely than the one before. She talked breathlessly, as though fearful of interruption, or silence, or reaction of any kind.

She told me that we'd lived in Oxford then. She'd been working at a college library and had come to know my father. He was at the edge of a circle she had found herself belonging to, of high-minded folk that stood stiffly in suits and dresses on summer lawns and swapped opinions in taut voices. Compared to the rest, my father seemed peaceful and gentle, a kind of respite among the clamor. He kept his intelligence to himself, and she liked that, she said. She never met my mother, but she heard about the accident. It was in the paper. It sent ripples—no, it sent shock waves. Marika had brought my father flowers, a card offering condolences, and then she began to visit him regularly, making a pot of tea and laying out cookies. She stuck her finger through the bars of my crib once, and I grasped it tightly.

"Erzsi, you had such a strong grip. You clung to me. You looked right into my eyes, and you wouldn't let me go," she said.

That was then. Now, I couldn't meet her gaze. She reached out for me and I pulled away. I curled into myself, at the end of the bench. But I still felt the proximity of her body, its heaving, heard the choked-back sobs in her voice. She wasn't even trying to contain herself. I clenched my teeth, made myself granite, through and through.

She told me how my father moved to Devon, without so much as a farewell, taking me with him. And Marika, in a fit of spontaneity, left the lawns and the dinner parties and the boyfriend with gray whiskers and the high ambition, and followed the grieving David Lowe. Followed us. She said she never fit in her old world; it was too straitlaced, and all the things she'd once found charming about it, the comfort, the calm, the measure, ended up suffocating her.

"Erzsi, it's like I've always told you. I followed my heart," she said.

I thought of how I'd thrilled to her stirring advice about Tamás, how I'd copied her lines of Hungarian—the words for *I love you*—and listened as she spoke in wild and beautiful torrents. *Follow your heart, Erzsi.* The words stank of betrayal now. An excuse, disguised as romance. She blundered on, thinking I was hearing her.

"And, Erzsi, I found you in the end. Just like I knew I would. Like I knew I should."

She said we'd taken a cottage on a dark, wet Devon lane, with chestnut trees that nudged the thatch and a run of untidy garden ending in a splintered wooden fence. We were hiding from the world, she said, and no good ever came of that.

"I took care of you. In the beginning that was all it was," she said.

I dug my nails into my leg. It felt foul, to reduce her existence in our lives to practical necessity. Her voice bubbled now, like the contents of an out-of-control pan on the stove. Perhaps she realized she was losing me, because her words fell over one another. She said my father trod through the house like a ghost, creaking boards and shifting curtains. And I lay in my crib and wailed, my arms thrown up, as if I knew there was someone there just waiting to hold me. Someone who would never let me go. Who would be a mother to me, she said. And she spoke without edging or uncertainty. Seemingly oblivious.

"You were called Elizabeth, but one day I called you Erzsébet and your father heard me say it. He said he liked it, that it was better, that it could be a fresh start. And so forms were filled out and you became Erzsébet. Just as you are now."

So that was me. Erzsi. A little half-Hungarian baby, apparently. Even my name was a lie. On the bench, I kept my head bowed. I couldn't look at Marika as she fought on, a new thrill in her voice. Perhaps this was a part of the story she liked. She said how I was rosy-cheeked and rambunctious. And love grew in that house, she said. It sprang up like daisies on a lawn, suddenly and profusely.

"And, Erzsi, I believe your father loved me, too," she said. "As much as he ever could. Which wasn't very much, in the end. But it was all he had left, and I knew that. And for a long time it was enough, until in the end it wasn't, but, well, that's a story you already know."

But they'd never made a pact not to tell me, she said. It hadn't been anyone's doing. It had just…happened. If the truth was to come at all, she said, it had to come from my father. But it was as though he couldn't cope with it, that even the thought of framing the words, of describing what happened that day when the wheels skidded and the car buckled and the tree threw up its arms helplessly, was more than he could bear.

"He never stopped loving her, you see. He never stopped loving his wife. And saying that she had ever existed was the same as saying she existed no more. That she was in the past."

I was silent.

"I couldn't not tell you, not this time," said Marika. "I've always thought you should know the truth but ever since you got here this summer you've been talking about moving to Hungary, of being with me here. Of, in a way, choosing me over your father. And then there's Tamás. You and Tamás are moving so fast, and I know you love him—I believe you when you say you do—but I realized we'd let things go too far. That your time with me in Hungary was taking you in directions that weren't necessarily the right ones. Or, at least, not fully considered ones."

"Lies, then?" I said, finding my voice and feeling the edge of every letter. "You lied to me every day of my life and so did my father."

"No," said Marika, "we just didn't tell you the truth right away." Then, she said, in a barely audible croak, "No. We lied to you."

"And this time with you in Hungary. Villa Serena, and all those summers. That's the biggest lie of all. You, pretending to be something you're not. And making me pretend that I'm something I'm not. Hungary this, Hungary that. As though this place has something to do with me, when it's nothing to me. It's worse than nothing."

I got up. My legs quaked and I was on board the boat again, sailing for the horizon. I felt the sickness rising. I started to walk away.

"Erzsi, come back."

I walked past a family; they were licking ice creams as though their lives depended on it, yellow running down their wrists. I walked past the man selling giant buttered sweet corns, and I ignored his entreaty, the wave of his tongs. I only started to run when I got to the roads that led up from the lake, my sandals slapping on the pavement. I ran until a cramp bit at my side and my breath came in wheezes. I ran until my throat hurt, and the air I gulped in was hot and dry. I knew I was crying, because my lips were salty and my view smeared. But the sound of it, the sobs that tumbled one on top of the other, seemed to come from some other source.

An old man with a stick stared at me and I stared back at him, my lip jutting, as though he were the one making a spectacle. As though he were the one whose world had collapsed, tangled all about his feet. I ran until I tripped and the road drew a long graze down one knee and on one elbow. I didn't stop to pick out the grit, didn't try and arrest the trickles of bright blood that ran to my wrist and to my ankle. But my running fell to a faltering stumble, and for a moment I leaned back against a wall, the stones hard against my back. The ache in my side and my leg and my arm, the pain in my chest, my head, full and dizzying. Sweat sticking my bangs to my forehead and running down my back. Cheeks wet and inflamed, feverish and blaring.

How quickly I'd felt the physical pain. The discomfort coursing through me, not one part of me spared. All she had spoken were words. No knives were thrown, no axes wielded. Maybe, just maybe, I had gotten it all wrong. I thought of April Fools' Day, and a prank I'd once played with a sheet of plastic wrap and a toilet seat. I wondered if they had a day like that in Hungary, a day that fell deep in the summer, and demanded that tricks were played at every turn. I put a hand to my head. Then everything sparkled and turned yellow and the pavement suddenly seemed to be all at the wrong angle, and very, very close.

So that was how the world tilted. I came around probably only seconds later, with a pain in my side and a fluttering in my chest. The street was empty, no gentle men in cloth caps stooping with assurances. No Tamás by my side. I was all alone. I got to my knees and then slowly to my feet. I put both hands out, as a tightrope walker might. The jolt had given me an odd sense of clarity. My flight had been ragged and without direction but now I walked steadily, with a dogged sense of purpose.

The telephone booth was on a street called Tánya Utca. The name of the road was set on a plaque in the wall and I could see it through the smeared glass. Inside it smelled of old summers, stifling and dusty. A knot of spiders sat clumped in their straggling web in one corner and a giant fly bumped noisily against the pane. I dropped in coins but I took too long about it and they fell back through, a metallic cascade as though I'd hit the jackpot in an arcade. I started again, quicker this time, my movements deliberate, and then began to dial. I heard the ring tone at the other end. On it rang. And then finally he answered. Hearing his voice I lost my own, and for a moment I could only croak into the receiver.

"Erzsi, is that you?" he said.

"I need to come home. Now."

I didn't mean "home." I simply meant that I had to leave Hungary, that I needed to escape Marika's duplicitous clutches at all costs. Home, I now knew, was no more than a collection of letters, the Devon cottage as much of a sham as Villa Serena. Card houses that toppled and fell with a single breath, delivered sixteen years too late. In spite of my father's own role in the deception, I needed him. I told him that I could be at Budapest Airport in four hours if I got on the next train. I said that I wouldn't mind sleeping on a bench in Departures, just that he had to do anything to get me on the first flight back to England. It was only when I'd had his assurance on this, when I'd dropped the receiver back into its cradle, that I realized that he hadn't asked me what was wrong. As though he had been waiting for this day to come, and he had been ready. The old snake, I thought, and this image was so at odds with my picture of my father that a crackling laugh escaped my lips, and again I was startled by the sounds I made, the things that came from me. "The old snake," I said, this time out loud. Yet somehow, his measured assistance and calm tones were a refuge beside Marika's raw, straggling misery.

As I left the telephone booth my head was filled with train timetables and clattering train cars and the blinding polished floor of the airport. Action was a comfort, and I tried to dwell on the practicalities of a getaway. But Hungary invaded, its rude heat taunting me. *I shouldn't even be here,* I thought. *I don't belong here and I never did.* Everything that had been, in the past and in the present, was sullied. The horses with the chestnut manes and the Horváths' goat. The first taste of *Tokaji Aszú* and the waters of the forest pool. Zoltán with his multicolored apron and boom of laughter, spinning me in dance. Tamás, with his polished heart that I'd caught and cupped, and all the things that we were supposed to do together and now never would. The fireflies at the edge of the lawn. The rattling gypsy music that flooded the kitchen and rolled out over the yellow green hills. Even the morning glory that twisted its blooms at the foot of the steps, and closed up again by nightfall.

It was the end of everything.

The one thing I clung to, the only rock-solid thing, was that I would never, ever return to Hungary. I made that vow so I could draw a line around my heartbreak, like a border on a map. My own iron curtain, drawn tight, with no light escaping. And Marika on the other side in swathes of darkness.

At the summer apartment, I opened the gate very quietly and slipped inside. The lawn was deserted, and through the doorway I could see the polished tiles of the living-room floor, uninterrupted by the lolling legs of people watching television or catching a snooze in the cool. Perhaps they were at the lake, the men leaving the women to their drama. Had Zoltán told Tamás? I wondered. Were they even now at a picnic table by the beach, whispering over their beers, froth painting their lips?

After I'd phoned my father, my breathing had steadied and I'd walked back to the house with calmer steps. A quiet resolution had been switched on inside of me, one that I knew would be short-lived but for now was necessary to my survival. My escape. I stood inside the living room as my eyes adjusted to the dark. The shutters were closed, and the sunlight in the doorway was blinding. Neon dots and dashes swam before me.

I went through to the hallway and opened the door to Marika and Zoltán's bedroom. I saw the crumpled sheets where she'd lain. The blinds were still half-drawn. And the room smelled of her, the perfume she'd worn the night before, and another indistinct scent that I only knew as hers. I started as I saw a figure across the room, for a moment thinking it was Marika, that she'd somehow beaten me back to the house and was waiting in the shadows. But I realized it was only my reflection, caught in the dressing-table mirror. I walked toward myself, my hands reaching to the bed for steadiness. I stared hard, and I saw the flush that cut across my cheeks, my black hair hanging in ragged tendrils, my red-rimmed eyes with the whites turned gray. I took hold of the mirror and held it in both hands. I used to think I looked so like my mother. That every summer, as the sun browned my skin and my eyes were opened to life in Hungary, I grew truer to my roots. Was I that stupid? So much a fool, that I only ever saw what I wanted to see, believed what I wanted to believe? I was no more Hungarian than Aunt Jessica, with her shortbread cookies and cans of Spam. And I looked no more like Marika than any girl in any street in any town. I was nothing. The girl in the mirror looked like no one. My cheeks flushed with shame and I threw it to the floor, the glass shattering on the tiles. A spot of blood trickled between my toes, but I couldn't feel its sting, not then. I still have the mark today, a fine white line across my foot. I've told lies about how I got that battle scar—a tangle of barbed wire, a fierce cat's claws, anything but a dashed mirror. I remember the sound that the soles of my sandals made as they crunched across the glittering shards.

"Erzsébet," Zoltán said from the doorway.

"No," I said, and pushed past him, running toward my own room, the soles of my sandals crunching in the glittering shards of broken mirror. I began to pull clothes into my suitcase feverishly as Zoltán's cautious tread came down the hallway. What had I done with my passport? Did I even have it with me, or was it on the bedside table of my room at Villa Serena, beside Marika's bunch of liar flowers, and the miniature copy of one of Zoltán's falsely cheerful landscapes? I panicked and yanked open drawers wildly.

"Erzsi." I felt Zoltán's hand on my elbow and I leaped away from him. "Erzsi," he said, "please, talk to me. Are you hurt? From the glass?"

I found it, my hands closing gratefully around its maroon cover. I'm British, I thought, not one bit Hungarian.

"Zoltán," I said, clutching my passport, refusing to look at him, "will you please, please take me to the airport?"

He didn't answer, so I turned to him. He was standing with a hand on each hip. His shirt hung open, showing his dark and burly chest. His head was bent. He didn't know what to do any more than I did. I remembered him suddenly, years ago, in the forest. When he'd stood a little away from us, kicking pinecones, as Marika hugged me and I called her "Mother" and he'd refused to look at either of us. How later he'd told me I was his friend, too, and I could always come to Villa Serena. I felt tears pushing at my eyes. I let them fall, tickling my cheeks. I touched his arm.

"Please, Zoltán, I have to go. Please do this one thing for me."

"Where is Marika?"

"I don't care."

He rubbed his chin, and his stubble crackled.

"If you don't take me, I'll find some other way. If we don't leave now, I'm going, anyway."

"Is Marika at the lake still?"

"I told you, I don't care."

"Tamás is at the shops."

"I don't care!" I shouted, and shoved at him with both hands. He barely shifted on his feet, a rock, and so I fell into him, my head on his chest. I began to sob. His arm curled around my back and he held me tightly. It was suffocating, but it didn't matter if I stopped breathing. I heard him speaking, but couldn't make out the words. I cried harder, and eventually he peeled me off him, and taking my hand in his, my case in the other, he led me outside.

The metal of the car smoldered in the heat. When we opened the doors I felt the hot draft of escaping air. I climbed inside the backseat, with my case hugged beside me. The leather of the seats stuck to the backs of my legs. I closed the door, but the seat belt caught in it. I pulled it open, fought with the belt and slammed it again. I saw Zoltán go back inside the house and for a moment I thought

he'd changed his mind, but then minutes later he came out
again. He strode across the lawn, past the car to open the
gate. He got in the front.

"Don't you want to sit here?" he asked, turning, his hand
patting the passenger seat.

Without thinking, I'd left it for Marika. I remembered
another departure from Lake Balaton, where I'd sat beside
my father up front. How small I'd felt, with the seat belt
cutting just under my chin. How beside him there'd been
nowhere to hide, so I'd turned to the window and watched
the lake pass by in a blur of tears until my neck was cricked
and aching. *I've done this before,* I thought. *I can do it again.*

"No," I said, steadily, "no, thank you."

The engine started without any of its usual fuss, and we
pulled out of the gateway, onto the road. We rolled past
all the summerhouses, with their shining fences and satellite dishes, *zimmer frei* signs and neat lawns. We passed the
dusted orange tennis courts and the restaurant on the corner with white and blue Zipfer umbrellas. We slowed to
let three skinny children in swim shorts cross ahead of us,
their shoulder blades poking from their backs like wings,
their skin coffee colored and wet from the lake.

"Can't we go faster?" I said.

"There's Tamás," said Zoltán, taking his hand from the
wheel to point, slowing down suddenly.

Tamás had a stuffed shopping bag in each hand. He was
walking down the street on my side, the shaded side, with
patterns of the plane trees falling across him. I stared at
him for a moment, taking in the prickle of blond hair, the
long brown arms and legs, the baggy shorts that scraped his
knees. I thought how childlike he looked, how innocent.

But was he? Did he know, just as Zoltán had known? Perhaps they were all complicit. I sank down in my seat.

Zoltán half turned. "Do you want to say something?" he asked over his shoulder. "Do you want to say goodbye?"

I shook my head, fiercely. "Please drive faster," I said.

As we passed Tamás I turned, peeping from the back window. I thought of our song from last summer, how we'd danced together, and he'd quietly sung along to the words that were all about leaving, leaving but remembering. I watched him until he grew smaller and smaller, then was out of sight altogether. I turned back, resting my chin on the edge of my case. The soft and smiling cowboy had sung of loneliness, and Tamás and I had held on tightly to each other. How little we knew.

"Well, I left him a note," said Zoltán, his gray eyes catching me in the mirror.

It took us two and a half hours, and we drove largely in silence. At a roadside kiosk somewhere away from the lake Zoltán pulled in and left the car without saying anything. He came back with a string bag containing a bottle of Fanta, a salami, three rolls and a bar of chocolate that was already melting. He passed it to me, clasping my hand in his bearlike paw as I took it. We drove on. At the first sign for the airport, I spoke. My voice was querulous, and each word was an effort, as though my mouth was stuffed full of marbles. I swallowed, fearfully.

"Zoltán, why haven't you tried to persuade me not to go?"

He glanced at me in the mirror. He shook his head.

"You're like Marika. Once you get an idea, there's nothing anyone can do about it."

"I'm nothing like her. She's a liar."

"No, Erzsi. She always wanted to tell you."

"Oh, yeah? I thought you said that once she got an idea there was nothing anyone could do about it?"

"With your father it was different."

I didn't answer. Instead, I stared from the window at the yellowing hills and reedy verges. The sky was fading, and shadows from the telephone poles fell like spears. I shut my eyes.

"Please let's not say anything else," I whispered.

Budapest Airport was bathed in a kind of white summer light, as though dusk was moving in but everything still held the sun of the day. We pulled in to the area by Departures. Zoltán turned off the engine and we sat for a moment, listening to the motor click and sigh. A fat-bellied jet climbed the sky overhead and a tourist coach passed us, its windows pressed with faces. A taxi cut in front of us at great speed, and two businessmen leaped from it, running into the terminal, with their leather-soled shoes slapping.

"I've got it from here," I said. I climbed out with my suitcase bumping my legs behind me. He met me on the pavement, stopping me with a hand on my shoulder.

"If I don't put you safely on the plane, Marika will kill me," Zoltán said. His hand rubbed his chin. "But then, if I do put you on the plane, Marika will also kill me."

"I don't want to get you into trouble," I said.

"We're all in trouble," he said.

The sun had faded but I screwed my eyes into a squint. I didn't really know what he meant.

"I suppose we are," I said.

"Erzsi, it will get better, you know."

"I don't see how," I said.

"Because things always do."

I thought of my father and his dead wife.

"No, they don't," I said.

"Erzsi, I don't need to tell you how much Marika loves you. How much I love you. And Tamás. How much we all love you, and especially Marika. I don't need to tell you, do I?"

I looked at him, knowing it was for the last time. My heart swelled like a balloon and I dared the tears to fall.

"No," I said, "no, you don't. Because it's already in the past."

I walked toward the terminal building, dragging my suitcase behind me.

"Erzsi!" he shouted.

I hesitated, then turned. He was standing with his arms held wide. As though he was ready to catch something huge, falling from the sky.

"We love you!" he cried.

I nodded.

"I loved you, too," I said.

CHAPTER TEN

I held the book on my knee as around me the park flitted
back to life. In the boughs above me a blackbird chattered,
downwind the leathery football smacked on skin resound-
ingly, and beyond the green a police car wailed in put-out
fashion. These were the sounds of the living. I carried on
staring at the book, unflinchingly. There were no more
summers. I turned the remaining pages—five, six, seven
brown paper leaves…each one blank and staring. Marika
and I had simply run out.

Perhaps I should have gotten up then. Stalked across the
grass to a bar and downed a stiff drink. Then walked home
past the cemetery, and whispered a quiet and unaccustomed
prayer to anyone who would hear it. But instead I lingered. I thought about the empty pages and how I would
have filled them with the pictures that came afterward, the
ones that weren't Marika's to see. Me at Budapest Airport,
straggle-haired and red-eyed, clinging to my suitcase like a
life raft. Me landing in London late in the night, wandering blankly into Arrivals as a sea of expectant faces stared

past me, keeping an eye out for their returning beloveds. Me curled in a seat on a charter bus bound for Exeter, my arms hugging myself in a pose of contortion, messily shaking my head at the offer of a bag of jelly beans from the stringy old lady who sat behind. Me facing my father in the weak dawn light, him reaching for my bag as though that was what was burdening me. As though that was the right thing to do and the only thing to say.

These are the images that I have carried with me. The ones that, if asked, have made me who I really am. In them I am pale and wanting, not sun-kissed and merry. My lips are two thin, hard lines, reshaping only to form the sad words.

On the evening flight to London Heathrow people kept to themselves. As the plane climbed skyward a hush descended, and everyone dropped low in their seats, pulled blankets over their knees and gave way to dreaming. I was sitting in the back, tucked in by the window with nobody beside me. Below, the Budapest lights blinked once, then were gone. We whirled deep into the night. Somehow, I fell asleep. But my dreams were of the rabid kind, where I jolted and fell, waking with my eyes wide and my hands balled into fists. Unease nipped me like a sickness, and I sat fretting with it. I stared from the window into nothingness, the occasional swathe of cloud passing like a ghost. But when we hit the runway, bouncing once, engines screaming, I cried out, clapping a hand to my mouth quickly. I hadn't wanted to arrive. The night sky had felt like a refuge. Its emptiness, its blackness. I could lose myself there, I'd thought. I could disappear and no one would ever find me.

Later, on the bus to Exeter, I was impervious. A look

I've since perfected. As I lined up to get on, my eyes had a glassy look. I prayed that no one could hear the clatter of my heart in my chest. I remember the driver that I handed my ticket to. He wore giant spectacles, and I saw myself reflected bleakly in them. I wanted to send them the way of the mirror. He tipped his head with fatherly concern but I climbed the steps, kicked my feet onto the seat and pretended to chew gum, my jaws working nothing. *I can do this,* I thought. I can keep moving, always forward. I remember how we sped down the highway by night, the jagged arms of pylons, robotic against the sky, and stopping off in shadowy towns with blockish buildings, shot through with rectangles of light. I remember thinking that this was an England I didn't recognize. That I didn't recognize anything anymore.

I had telephoned my father from the airport to tell him the time that my bus would arrive. Even in my misery, the old habits died hard. I'd had to dial the number three times because my hands were shaking and clumsy and my voice had been machinelike when it came, an automated message stating an arrival time. We pulled into Exeter in the early hours of the morning, just as a pinkish sky was lifting in the east. The place looked deserted, until my father stepped from the shadows. He stood with his hands pushed into his pockets as the bus turned in a wide, slow circle. My legs were stiff from my curled-up posture, and I staggered down the aisle, past the hunched forms of sleeping passengers bound for Torquay and Plymouth. I envied them, their slow release into the dawn, for the sun would be quite risen when they arrived at their destinations. The light of a summer's day would be on their faces and they wouldn't mind that they'd traveled all night. They'd revel in the morning, taking a coffee from the vending machine, biting down on the polystyrene cup with a sleepy smile.

I left them and walked toward my father.

As I approached, he reached out for my suitcase. I stared at his hand.

"Erzsi, let me take that," he said.

At home I flew through the door and wheeled around to face him in the hallway, my feet skidding on the flagstones, my arms flung out in remonstration. I threw words like knives. And I watched him sink, first against the wall, his face turned flat against the rose-patterned wallpaper, then dropping to his knees before me. His whole body shook, as though set to explode. The sound that came from that ragged bundle, all elbows and bent back, was a barking sob. I stepped back, horrified. I turned to run upstairs, then stopped myself, one hand resting on the banister. I took a breath, knowing that my next move would come back to me, time and time again. So I made a decision. I tiptoed up to him. I knelt down and placed my hands gently on his shoulders, and eased him back up.

"Dad, Dad, listen, it's okay. Really, it's okay. It's okay."

He clung to me with both hands. He shook me gently.

"It's not, though, Erzsi, none of it is. I can't even begin to say sorry. I can't find the words. I don't know how to say it so you know I mean it. But I am sorry. So very, very sorry."

"I know you are," I said. "I know. Let's not talk anymore, let's just not talk."

Then I folded myself into him, adding my own soft sobs and words of assurance to his rough, shrill cries.

The heap we made on the floor that day became our pact.
For in sorrow, we were matched. I could not leave him, as
I had left Marika, so instead, I mended things. I made tea,
and we sat side by side on the couch, as we used to when I
was small. Except my teeth were set. I did not sink into his
side, offering and seeking comfort. I did not yield to any
embrace. I'd done those things to save him in the hallway,
but I wasn't capable of doing them again. Instead, I turned to
him and made sure he understood one huge and vital thing.
I handed him a piece of paper, folded once in the middle.

"I'm going to bed," I said, "but I want you to read this.
This is the only way things can be now."

And so I left my father with a torn piece of paper, and
my scribbled writing telling him that we never could talk of
Marika. She was gone. And his wife, the woman who gave
birth to me, was gone also. *For me,* I wrote, *she never existed.*

Upstairs I lay in bed with my eyes wide open. It was the
middle of the day, and even though the curtains were drawn
the sunlight crowded into my room. Downstairs I heard
the telephone ringing. It rang on and on incessantly. *Good,*
I thought, *he's leaving it. Good, good, good.* Then it stopped.
Moments later, I heard a cautious tap at the door.

"I'm awake," I said.

He trod softly into my room, and I sank lower beneath
my quilt. He didn't sit on my bed, but instead stood beside
it, half-bent. He reached for my hand.

"What I wrote," I said, "I don't mean to be unkind, but
I do mean it."

He nodded and squeezed my fingers. I knew then that
he understood. That silence would be his way, too. With
his wife it was the price he'd already paid, in denying her

so long. In my room that afternoon he didn't ask for forgiveness, and nor did I offer it. He just said sorry—*I'm sorry, sorry, sorry*—until it was a word I never wanted to hear again. And the thing I didn't say, the thing that not even I could bring myself to write down, was this: I knew that when he saw my torment it stoked the fires of his own. That when he collapsed weeping in the hallway it wasn't just through anguish at having let me down, but it was desperate grieving for his long-dead wife, and the cruel swipe that took her from his life. Knowing this, knowing how my unavoidable misery affected him at every turn, I had no choice but to absent myself. It was the only way I could save the pair of us. Our healing, if it came at all, would be separate.

"Dad, I want to go to sleep now. I'm so tired, I haven't slept."

He began to apologize again.

"Dad, *please*," I said.

"Erzsi, the telephone," he said, suddenly startled, as though he'd just thought of it. "Do you want to know if anybody calls?"

"No. You mustn't answer it."

"I can't just leave it, it could be anyone."

"You have to just leave it, Dad. Or just…don't tell me. I think you can manage that. Not telling me, I think you'd be good at."

He closed the door quietly and I listened to his retreating step on the stairs, until all I could hear was my own muffled sob and the miserable echo of a cheap shot.

They tried to reach me, and I turned from each of them. Hungary was a place I quite simply erased. In later years

it would be the everyday details of this life lost that would
catch my breath and floor me when I was least expecting
it. The thought of Marika in her dressing gown, spelling
out my name in raspberries. Zoltán standing in the door
to his studio, waving his brush in cheerful, paint-splashed
salute. And Tamás. How would it have felt to have finally
done it, slept with him, a new light warming every part of
us? I'd left the heart he gave me, wrapped in a handkerchief
on the bedside table.

One great lie takes everything with it. There are no sur-
vivors among the wreckage.

The telephone calls were easy to ignore, and I made a
fine art out of my selective hearing. My father struggled
with this. He'd stand wringing his fingers in front of the
telephone, then march to the bottom of the garden with his
hands clapped to his ears and dig furiously. I'd watch him
from the window, my nose pushed to the glass. When I was
certain he was occupied I'd go to the phone and press the
buttons that let you see who called. I'd listen to the numbers listed in a cool anonymous voice. They always began
with a Hungarian area code. I knew exactly where the
telephone was in Villa Serena. It was on a side table in the
hallway, beneath a hook from which hung Marika's floppy
sun hat. There was a bronze statue of a rearing horse, and
a vase that commonly held sunflowers, their giant heads
pushed together as though they were gossiping and kissing. A white-painted wicker chair offered the caller a place
for repose. I wondered if these things were still in place.
Or whether they had been swept away by fire or flood or
quake. Then I stopped imagining, and had the automatic

voice read me the numbers again. I always slammed down the receiver before the last was reached.

Letters came, too. Each one trashed. *Are you sure?* my father would edge, hovering with an envelope in his hand. *Surer than sure,* I'd say. And the communion over the fate of the letters became a sort of bond. If it was winter they went directly on the fire, me raking the embers, making sure every last piece was gone. If it was summer they'd be ripped to tatters and pushed to the very bottom of the kitchen trash. When I undressed one night for bed I found a fragment of paper stuck to the underside of my sock. It said *iss.* It was in Tamás's tight-knitted scrawl. I balanced it on the tip of my finger and inspected it with my breath held, as one might a butterfly that might take flight at any moment. It could have been a torn piece of any number of words. *Kiss? Miss?*

I spent most of the remaining days of that summer two villages away, in Ashridge. BMXs and skateboards circled the parking lot at dusk. The lit ends of cigarettes glowed in the dark. A long stretch of field was a late-night hangout, where lolling bodies flattened the damp grasses, and empty cider bottles were scattered like skittles. I made friends with people I'd never bothered with before. *We thought you were a Goody Two-shoes,* they said, *but you're even worse than us,* as fingers teased under my blouse and smoky breath met mine. It was supposed to have been Tamás but instead it was Gary. Gary with a slither of ponytail and cherry-red Doc Martens. Gary with a puckered scar where his appendix had come out, and fingers that pinched. After such nights I'd bike home, screaming down the middle of the lane, the wind whipping tears from my eyes. I'd throw my bike against the porch, and slam the front door behind me. My noisy entrances did nothing to stir my father. Only once did he take me aside.

"Erzsi, you need to tell me if you're going to be out late."

His voice was strained and I worried that it'd break. I couldn't bear another scene in the hallway, all the tears, the apologies. I didn't have the heart to take us back there.

"I did," I snapped, "but you weren't listening."

It was a lie, of course, but we both knew it could have been the truth.

Somehow, the time passed. In the fall I went to study art. Not to Exeter, as I'd planned, but to a place near Torquay, instead. A whole new crowd, and I had them call me Beth, not Erzsi. The English Riviera, as it ambitiously claimed, was a world away from Harkham. I traveled by bus and train every day, leaving earlier and coming home ever later. I started staying over with new and different friends, who lived in cramped rows of houses blown by sea spray, or bungalows with thick carpets and new cars in the driveway. I ate other people's suppers. I took a seat beside other people's brothers and sisters. I made polite conversation with different fathers, and helped other mothers with the dishes. My backpack had a toothbrush stuffed permanently in its side pocket. I washed my bra and underwear in sinks and my T-shirts bore the imprints of radiator stripes.

At weekends I mostly made it home to Harkham. I shut myself in my room and drew the curtains. I dragged the head of my lamp toward me, so my eyes saw white dashes. I hunched over my easel and desk, working hard so that my teachers gave me excellent grades. As long as I was achieving, I thought my father could not fault me. The time away from home made sense, because the commute was too tiring to do every day. And the hours I spent secreted in my room working were because I wanted to do well, I told him, and it was true. We left each other alone, and as an artist, I began to find my style. Zoltán's lavish, lurid fairytale scenes and Marika's attempts at abstract flourishes sent me firmly in the direction of realism. I made tight and intricate drawings. Perspective, scale, form—I was a willing slave to them all.

I went through a photography phase, as just about every young artist does. I loved the weighty feel of the camera in my hands, its cool metal against my forehead. I shot scenes of normality—a trio of old ladies licking ice creams on the blustery seafront, an elderly gentleman dragging his scotch-patterned briefcase up a steep and endless hill. I stole through the streets of the town, capturing people, feeling purposeful and brave. I never photographed Harkham, even though in spring the apple blossoms danced in the air like confetti and in autumn the fallen leaves shone rubber-duck yellow out of the mud. Even though in the hard winter, the garden glittered with crystals, and trees held up their gilded arms for all to admire. And summer, summer when hip-high cow parsley bloomed in the hedges and buttercups dusted my ankles yellow. I never photographed the cottage with the tawny thatch and broken gate. I sought reason everywhere except at home, a place that I left as abstract and imprecise.

At eighteen I won the place I wanted at art school, at the London College of Printing, as it was known then. At last, I could leave. Harkham was caught in an Indian summer that year, and it was a September that burned hot and fragrant. My father insisted on cooking me a last supper, an unseasonal beef stew with baked potatoes. It took him hours to prepare, and we ate late, sweating our way through the meal as the oven behind us threw out heat and our jaws labored at the meat. He opened a bottle of red wine, brushing a cobweb from its neck. It was French and expensive and I could barely manage three sips. I was restless and got up to open the window, hoping for a whisper of cool air. I knocked my glass over, and a pool of red soaked the tablecloth and dripped to the floor. I apologized madly, and my father joined in, as though no matter what happened, the fault was always his. After supper I made my excuses, yawning and stretching with an amateur's emphasis. But in bed I lay with my eyes wide open. It was three o'clock in the morning before I heard his tread on the stairs. He hesitated by my door and I held my breath. And then the floorboards creaked and he passed on.

The next day I stood in the lane outside the cottage, the overgrown hedges forming an arch above my head. The light was green and dappled as I waited for my father to drive me to the station. He pulled the car out of the driveway, and for a moment it looked as if it were underwater. I took a breath and got in. He sat with the engine ticking over, idling in the heat.

"Dad?" I said. "What are you doing?"

He turned his head to me, a look of faint surprise on his face, as though he'd forgotten our journey had a purpose.

"I have to show you something," he said. "Before you go."

He reached into his shirt pocket, and took out a photo-

graph. I wondered if it had always been there, only I'd never
noticed. It was black and white and deeply grained. It had
rounded corners and a thick, greasy feel to it. I saw a woman
with pale hair pulled back in a ponytail, a polo sweater ac-
centuating her swan's neck. She had long, slim arms that
held a baby against her chest. Its small face was folded, its
eyes two creases, a wisp of black hair on its forehead. The
woman looked down at the baby, her mouth working into
a smile. But the camera had snapped too soon. A moment
later and it would have been the perfect shot of an adoring
mother and child. Instead, the woman looked uncertain, as
though the baby wasn't really hers.

I looked at it, then placed it back in his hand. He spoke
her name, very quietly. *Sarah.*

We both started as a honking sounded behind us. It was
a tractor, with its trailer piled high with bales. My father
pulled over with an apologetic wave, and it passed us, accel-
erating quickly. The air before us filled with wisps of hay.

"Please," I said, "I'll miss the train."

All the way to London, I was trailed. Not by my father
and his sad and groping memories. Nor by the pale ghost
of Sarah, the thief of his happiness and my rightful mother.
But always and relentlessly by Marika. It was as though she
was riding on the back of the train, with her black tresses
flying behind her. As before me unspoken things blew back
and forth, like strands of hay falling in a country lane.

CHAPTER ELEVEN

My legs were stiff from sitting. I stretched, catlike, then stood. I had inhabited the park for hours. The sun had warmed my skin without burning. My fingers had an earthy scent. I felt light-headed. Many hours had passed since my early morning coffee, my only sustenance, but the scent of a nearby barbecue turned my stomach. Despite this, I felt a sudden sense of purpose and resolution. I picked up *The Book of Summers* and placed it carefully in my shoulder bag. My hand lingered for a moment on its cover, and I traced my fingers over the letters that Marika had once painted. It had been hers, and yet now it seemed to belong to a different life altogether. I rolled up my blanket and began to walk toward home, crisscrossing residential streets, taking the back alleys.

I passed a scrawny lilac tree, a gust of summer wind catching its branches. There had been lilac in the woods above Villa Serena. I'd pushed through it on my first day's explorations, purple halos dancing above my head. Later I'd found a teacup beside my bed, filled with mauve blooms.

There have always been moments something like this. Ordinary, everyday things that whispered, *Marika*. Jewelry, when it caught the light and gleamed, gem-bright. And perfect fried eggs. She used to tip them on my plate with a triumphant cry, as though she'd caught the yellow sun itself. And poppies, always poppies. In autumn, when people pin paper flowers to their lapels I've never thought of the bravery of fallen men. Instead, it's always been Marika, sitting on the edge of the veranda, stitching flowers onto the hem of a skirt, a needle with red thread pulled high toward the sky.

Some would say memory brings life after death. Perhaps there's truth in that, but only if we're content to enjoy our recollections at soft distance, as passing flickers or occasional sparks. If we're grasping and desperate, if we want it all too much, if we reach out and try to touch it, what happens then? It fades so fast from view that we're left wondering if it was ever there at all. Perhaps the trick is to find a gentle use for memory. Learn to cup the small and glorious moments in our hands and treasure them, finding some solace this way. Otherwise, all they do is remind us that we are too late. That what is lost is lost forever.

I used to think it was Marika that was the shape-shifter. The flighty hell-bent Magyar, who blew with the wind, her heart's compass spinning wildly. Whereas I was rock-steady, a hard shell with a made-up mind and lips clammed tight—my father's daughter, whether I liked it or not. For almost every year I spent in Harkham, for every summer at Villa Serena unknowingly living a lie, I've matched it since with a year of my own making. I swore a life of truth. When Marika told me that I wasn't who I thought I was, my simple answer was to become someone else. I gave myself a lens to see the world through, with a focus I could adjust. I threw myself into the waters of a city of millions, and drank in its depths. I kept my regret hidden, like threadbare underwear beneath a party dress. And for fourteen years I've stayed true to my original impulse: to flee, then wash Marika away with silence. Now, white noise has turned to a deafening roar.

In the park, with Marika's book beside me, for the first time in the longest time I had allowed myself to think of these things again. Somewhere, Tamás was smiling as he always smiled, easy as he ever was. I liked to think I could still pick him out in a crowd, but I know for certain that he would not know me. I suppose mine is an ordinary sadness, a typical lament for lost love. Maybe no one loves anybody like they do when they're sixteen. But its hurt is no less fierce. Despite the distances between us, of ocean and land and language, Tamás and I knew and believed in each other. And every single time I saw him, from the first day with the goat on the path up to Villa Serena, to the last day, walking on his own down the Balaton road, something in me always shifted. What is it, that indescribable feeling that the lucky among us have? I believe I've forgotten it. I certainly know I've never felt it since.

What of Zoltán? The man who wisely never tried to be my father but gave me something cherished all the same. I delighted in all the ways that he was so different from anything I'd ever known. He played jazz too loudly and drank inky shots of savage liquor even when he didn't have a cold. Paint was ground into his skin, under nails and in the creases of his knuckles. His hair was often standing on end, brushlike. And in the offering of his friendship he asked for nothing in return. His was a simple equation; he loved Marika, and so he loved me, too.

A few years ago the strangest thing happened. I saw a painting, reproduced in a catalog of abstract expressionists from a Munich gallery. It was an obscure publication to find among a stack of arty periodicals in a Shoreditch bar. Before I saw his name, *Zoltán Károly,* I recognized his landscape. It showed tumbling hillsides of yellow and green, with a tiny little brown-haired girl in the foreground, watching as the earth fell away before her. It was similar to the painting I'd seen in the gallery in Szentendre, but it wasn't identical. In this one, the shining dome of Esztergom's basilica wasn't in the distance. In fact, there was nothing to root it in Hungary at all. A line of trees, skinny like poplars, gave it a faint Mediterranean feel, just as the dim blue outline of a mountain range suggested more exotic climes. Looking at it more closely, the only thing that hadn't changed was the small brown-haired girl, who was still lying on her belly, her chin cupped in her hands as she watched all that was before her. I gaped, and for a moment my world tilted on its axis. Everything threatened to slide. I tore the page out, my back turned to the bar so no one would see. But I didn't slip it between the leaves of a book, a safe place where later I would marvel at its finding. Instead, I went straight to the bathroom, ripped it to shreds and flushed it down the toilet, watching it disappear into swirling neon-blue waters. A cigarette butt bobbed in its wake. Then I leaned my head against the wall, shaking like a daytime drunk.

Zoltán's letter deserved a reply but I knew I couldn't conjure one. What could I possibly say? I have no practice in words for the bereaved. I only know that death can either

kill the people left behind, or be the greatest force for life of
all. My inclination is for the former. Again, I am too much
my father's daughter. But then I thought of Zoltán's loss.
I pictured him on the hillside behind Villa Serena, where
Marika lay in scattered ashes. I saw him with his head tipped
to the sky, a sky that's blue like a chapel ceiling. I heard all
the birds in Hungary joining him in song.

The word came to me then. *Hiányzol*. It meant *I miss
you* in Hungarian. I've seen it written, in letter after letter,
as scratched characters that ached on the page. I've heard it
on the telephone, the way it pitched and died on the line.
I've whispered it into the cup of my hand, on London buses
and in the dark of my apartment, day after day, year after
year. One word, to carry all that regret, that loss, that love.
One word, for all those precious people, but for Marika
most of all.

Hiányzol.

In the mess of it all, it felt like the only thing left to say.

Could she hear me? I wondered. I liked to think she
could. I liked to think she always could. Marika believed
in the things she wanted to, and the peace she found was of
her own making. Perhaps in that there was a lesson I could
learn, a comfort I could draw. To be both like her, and not
like her. It felt unreal, to imagine living like that. To have
conflict resting evenly within me, like rock strata, instead
of grinding away at my insides until I'm quite undone. But
perhaps it is the only way to be. A solid footing, a heart kept
steady, despite the mistakes of the past.

After all, anyone could learn the truth. It was what you
did with it that mattered.

I reached my front door and as I turned the key in the

lock I knew what I was going to do. I would be inside for just moments; all I had to get was a change of clothes, leave a note for Lily and make a quick phone call. I needed to tell my father I was coming home to see him, that very evening. And that Marika was the reason. *Wasn't she always?* I imagined him saying. And we might each of us smile sadly at that, and know it to be true.

CHAPTER TWELVE

Marika always believed in following her heart, no matter where it led her. Mine took me to Devon. I arrived that August evening just as the dropping sun was rolling over the hills in swathes of gold, and the dusky shadows stretched and pointed. My father's aborted visit, only the day before, seemed a lifetime ago. He was standing at the garden gate as my taxi pulled in, holding a bouquet of country flowers, big-headed daisies and gangly marigolds and wilted harebells.

I couldn't wait until we moved through to the lamp-lit house. I couldn't wait until the sound of the taxi's engine had faded from the evening air. I couldn't even wait until he'd finished hugging me, the flowers crushed between us.

"She died, Dad," I said into his neck. "Marika died."

I felt his body tense. He held me very tightly. The embrace had been for me, but now I knew it was for him, too.

"Oh," he whispered. "Oh, Marika."

After some time, he let me go. Collected, he cupped my face between his hands, wiping my tears with his fingers.

"It was from Zoltán, the letter," I said. "He wrote to tell me."

"Beth, I didn't know. I would never have left you alone with that," he said. "Not if I'd known, not ever, Beth. Poor, dear Marika."

"She had a heart attack. There was nothing anyone could do."

He stroked my hair, his hand against my head feeling so sure and steady. I shut my eyes. This was my father. I remembered this man.

"What can I do now?" he said. "What can I do to make anything better?"

I shifted lightly in his embrace, and drew *The Book of Summers* from my bag. I handed it to him, and our hands touched. I moved in closer again as he bent his head to look.

"She made it," I said.

"A photo album?" he said.

I hesitated. It was a photo album. Every house in Harkham no doubt had shelves and drawers and wardrobes packed with them. Books full of holidays and parties, birthdays and family events; pictures snapped and pasted, albums opened and shut, as people laughed at bad haircuts and worse clothes, grew wistful over former glories and simpler times. How could I explain that Marika's book was different? That once you fell into its pages you grew wings.

"It's me and her," I said. "It's us."

As night was falling, we stayed out in the garden. We sat opposite each other and drank cold white wine from tall glasses. Instead of the porch light I'd lit candles and they'd begun to melt into a puddle, the last of their flames guttering. The whole evening had a Marika-ish feel about it. The meal my father had prepared was hotly peppered. The Devon night was kind and warm. Strains of music drifted from the living room's open window, a classical piece I've never known the name of but I knew I loved.

My father spent a long time looking at *The Book of Summers,* turning each page with solemnity. I watched him, seeing it all again through his eyes. A world that he was never a part of, one that I'd purposefully kept hidden from him, thinking that it was the right thing to do. He'd never probed, I'd never offered, and we'd moved along without question or answer. I thought of all the secrets, the barely dared thoughts, the never-finished poems, the scribbled wishes. Our house had always been stuffed full of them, beneath baseboards, misted writing on mirrors, the creases of pillows that were flattened from punching and damp from tears. The three of us always hid things because we thought it was somehow better. We were dreamers, I suppose. And the worlds we inhabited were of our own fierce making.

"Seeing you happy was the most powerful, unexpected, precious thing, Beth." My father looked up from the pages, speaking suddenly, as though I'd just asked him a question.

I stared at him—the familiar grooves of his forehead and the little tight creases at the edges of his mouth. He began to speak, in a gentle but unfaltering stream, words that had been cooped up for too long but retained dignity and measure in their flight.

"After Marika left I kept thinking, *I need to tell you, it has to be said,* but then another letter would arrive, or a postcard, and you'd fall on it like it was Christmas morning, devour it and be buoyed by its contents for days and weeks. Or she'd phone you, and afterward you'd sit there hugging yourself. Then you'd be giggling at dinner, adorable, giddy. You'd even excuse my terrible cooking because you'd spoken to Marika. Whatever she said to you, or wrote to you, gave you hope. She gave you joy. And that was in rather short supply in our house, I'm afraid."

The last candle died, and we sat in near-darkness. I smoothed my skirt with my hands, digging a thumbnail into its edge. I thought, *I will remember this moment; this is a moment that will matter.* He went on.

"And then you went to stay with her for the first time. All the way to Hungary, on your own. I fretted for the entire week that you were away. I must have dug the garden over five times. I didn't know if I'd done the right thing in letting you go. But you'd been so earnest, Beth, you wanted to go so very much. And of course you came back and you'd had the most wonderful time. It became a routine after that, I suppose. Every summer you'd go to Hungary, to Marika, and it made you so happy that I couldn't bring myself to take it from you."

"But you must have known it would all come out one day...."

"Why? Marika didn't want to lose you. She loved you. She'd already taken a huge risk in changing things by leaving us. She was so fearful that she wouldn't see you again. You thought she was so assured, so fiercely confident, but I know what it meant to her to have you there. How the two of you became friends, in a way you never were when we were all at home together. She was a good mother to you, a loving mother always, but it was you and me who were the pals. It wasn't always like that, but Marika had a way of separating herself from us, as though she felt she never really belonged. So it was you and me. Helping me pick beans in the garden. Watching our silly television shows. Going to choose library books. When you were little, Marika used to say you were a daddy's girl, which of course was true. But, Beth, something changed. When you started going to Hungary and you saw how happy she was, just as she wanted to be, you wanted that, too. At the end of the vacations I got my girl back, and you were brown as a berry and bright-eyed, bubbling with adventure. And you were always wonderful to me, far sweeter than I deserved. And I was just so relieved that you could be happy, that you *were* happy."

I was silent. When I spoke, it was as a whisper.

"But it was all a lie," I said.

"No. Not all of it. Some parts of it were very, very true. Weren't they?"

"Maybe. Perhaps some parts."

"You've never really forgiven me, Beth. And although that's terrible to live with I accept it, I've deserved it. But Marika…"

"Don't say anything more, please. You can't be silent for fourteen years, then start talking as if you can't stop. It's too late."

"Yes."

"So, just don't."

"Just, this last. We hurt you in the most awful way, I know that. We never meant to, but that doesn't matter— we hurt you all the same. But Marika… She was the one who told you the truth. She was the one who wanted you to know. That was why I never could understand why, afterward, you treated us so differently."

I wanted to tell him all the things that I'd told myself. That she'd betrayed me twice over. That she'd torn apart our family but how, even at nine, I'd forced myself to understand her reasons, assured of her continuing love. But then she'd ruined everything all over again. The bond that had grown between us, all the secrets I'd shared with her in that Hungarian dreamland she made me believe in—it was all a mockery. Everything that I had some claim to, through bent of being her daughter, I'd lost. Villa Serena was gone. Tamás with it. Zoltán, too. Because of Marika, everything had ended, and all that was left were terrible things. Not least of all shame, a searing, breath-stealing sense of humiliation that I had gotten everything wrong. I'd tried to play a part that simply wasn't mine—the carefree half-Hungarian girl, with love in her heart. But if I wasn't her, who was I? What remained?

But I didn't say any of these things. Because they were old, and tired, and I was fed up with them. I wanted to feel something different.

"You needed me more," I said. "I knew that she would be all right. Marika understood leaving, she knew how it worked."

"But it didn't work, did it?"

He reached his hand across the table and I took it. I hung on to it, and it felt like such a solid thing. So real, so warm. So very *important,* that I decided in that moment that I'd never let it go.

That evening, he brought out two photographs of his own. The first was one I'd seen before, the one that he'd tried to show me as I left for London, on a sweltering summer's day when I was at once so desperate and afraid to leave.

My father's fingers shook as he handed it over. I looked at it steadily, then I placed it gently back in his hand.

"She looks kind," I said. "She looks like a good mother."

"Yes," he said. He was just a little drunk, I could tell; his eyes had a faraway quality. "You've been lucky, Beth, in that way. To have had two. Because she was, wasn't she, Marika? In her way."

I nodded.

He held the photograph between his finger and thumb. He looked at it, shaking his head. He said her name, very quietly. *Sarah.*

"I never stopped loving her," he said. "I couldn't let her go. Once the past gets you in its clutches, well, you've got to want to fight to be released. I never did. That was my mistake."

He put the photograph in the breast pocket of his shirt. I wondered where in the house he kept it, and if there were others like it. I hoped there were, for his sake. Sarah had been his great love, the one that surpassed all others, including Marika. Even then I couldn't bring myself to ask him questions; I never could. I didn't know if she preferred jam to honey, if her laugh was high and bright or muffled and low. If she loved summer more than winter. She might have been my mother, for a brief time, long ago, but more than that she was the thief of my father's happiness. A sad and pale ghost.

"Marika and you were so different from each other," I edged. "Was that why you liked her?"

My father nodded. "I did love her once, Beth," he said,

"just…not enough, I suppose. The fault was mine. I remember the day she turned up, you know, from Oxford. It was the strangest thing, seeing this striking, bright and noisy woman on my doorstep, when we were hiding ourselves so quietly, you and I. I don't think she knew what she was doing, and I certainly didn't, but all I knew was that I was glad to see her because when I opened the door, something in me shifted. Only I mistook it. I thought it was affection, that one day it could perhaps become more than that. But it was, I think, *relief.* Because she was so full of life and that was what we were missing. We were suffocating, crying ourselves to sleep, drowning in air. You were a baby, but me? I was just pitiful. I asked her once what on earth she saw in me. What possessed her to follow us as she did? And she said she couldn't explain it. She said she followed her heart, and her heart had told her it was the right thing to do. It baffled me, eternally, but that was Marika's way. She didn't offer explanation. And she didn't demand it in return."

"So, for a while—" my voice cracked, I took a breath "—she saved us?"

"I don't know what would have become of us without her. Not in those early days."

I pictured us both weeping, me as a baby, my father with grief. I heard the knock at the door, that uncertain Devon night, then her song and her laughter. I felt her quick-dashed kisses and her sweeping embraces. Then I thought of the later days, the days without her, when I'd cut her from my life. The jagged edges that were left behind.

"What's the other photo?" I whispered.

"Ah," he said, "I came across this in a box. I thought I'd

thrown away everything from that holiday, but I must have forgotten this one." He reconsidered this. "Or kept it. Perhaps I kept it, after all."

It showed a family of three, sitting at a table on a starlit terrace. I recognized it as our first night in Hungary, before we got to the lake. Behind us the night was looming, but we couldn't see its darkness because our faces were beaming and upturned. I choked, for our easy looks couldn't have been anything more than a trick of the light. My father was dressed in white cotton, the very cut of the Englishman abroad. He should have been triumphant; he had traversed Europe with his family, bringing them safely to that table. But he was never one for basking. Instead, he allowed himself a cold beer, the froth of which painted the quiver of his mustache. Marika sat upright, her long sweep of hair framing her pale heart face. Her collarbones gleamed, the hollow between was a scoop of shadow like a pendant. She looked lithe and poised, the still photo containing her energy but only for a moment. Glance away and she would surely up and run. And me? I was between the pair of them. My T-shirt shone bright white. I had a red clip in my hair, pinning back unruly wisps. My arms were draped lazily around my parents' shoulders. The fool I was. It was so casual a touch, when really I should have been gripping tightly. Holding on for dear life.

How would it have been, if things had been different?
That was the question I asked my father, as we sat there in the garden's darkness, the hillsides rolling in behind us. Before he could answer, I told him all the things I'd ever thought.

If things had been different, I said, I would have had every summer, including the last one, but in the end I wouldn't have run. In the face of truth I would have stood firm. I would've felt sadness, I would've felt hurt, but then would've come mending, forgiveness and faith again. And years on, what would have been my secret? What would have been my hidden place? That I was not my mother's daughter, nor my father's child, but someone of my own making. Someone who could forgive without forgetting. Who knew that if you looked for something in the right place, you'd find it, no matter how trying the hunt.

If things had been different, I said, you and Marika would have lost your way just the same, but you would have told me every truth you knew when I was nine years old and wet cheeked, anyway. The new sorrows would have washed into the old sorrows and I would have one day emerged from it all. I'd have seen Marika as the woman who loved me still, if not to the ends of the earth, then at least to Hungary and back, and so I'd have gone to Villa Serena just the same. Zoltán, Tamás, they'd have been there, waiting for me. And together we'd have had our days in the sun, as behind us, the shadows fell away. Afterward, you'd have met me at the airport, with a straight back and strong hands. You'd have taken my suitcase and said, *So what did you bring me back?* And there would have been something for you. A small wooden horse or a string of chili peppers.

If things had been different, I said, we'd all have gone to Hungary the first time, and we would've loved it. We'd have loved the big things, like the shining Balaton and the sun-beaten plains, the iced palaces and the seven bridges across the river, made of stone creatures and heavy neck-

laces. And the little things, like Zita Szabó's honey cookies, sweet curd cheese and knowing that a stork nesting on
your chimney meant good luck for all under the roof. And
we'd have gone back for our holidays, not every year, but
most of them. And back home, here in Harkham, we'd have
had the photographs from our vacations displayed around
the house. On the piano top, beside the clock, on bedside
tables. Sunshine and memory caught and held and put in
a nice frame.

   If things had been different, I said, we would never have
gone to Hungary, because Marika would have had everything she felt she ever needed right here with us. She'd have
talked about the country sometimes, the place of her roots,
but as one discusses the contents of a dream, with distance,
and no inclination to go back. When I was older, long
legged and wide smiled, I'd perhaps have taken a vacation
to Budapest, a cheap flight with friends, after Prague and
before Munich. I'd have telephoned her later and said how
it was *the Paris of the East,* or some other line taken from a
guidebook. We'd have agreed that perhaps it'd be fun to
go together one day, for the twinkling Christmas markets
or a cruise on the blue Danube. When her hair was striped
with gray and I had a child of my own perhaps. A baby girl.

   If things had been different, I said, you, my father, would
have rallied and found a bravery in your grief. When the
bright and daring woman you knew from Oxford followed
you to Devon, you'd have brushed her politely off and sent
her home after an afternoon, with a jar of local honey and
a promise to perhaps write. Or, if you'd let her stay, in the
end you would have managed to love her more. You would
have loved her like a person who wanted to be loved back.

Like someone who knew that proof of love was love itself. There would have been furtive kisses in the pantry as I fell around on a play mat. You would have pushed her back and forth on the swing that hung from the apple tree, as I picked daisies and clutched them in my pudgy fist. And we would have grown together, as tightly wound as morning glory around a veranda. Our love for one another would have given each of us a strength that we couldn't see but feel, like music, in our fingers and our toes. And so when I'd been old enough to speak and think and see the world, you would have told me something that for a while would crush everything I knew. But I would be resilient; I would have inherited the best of you, all of your courage, all of your fight. I would have cried for Sarah Lowe, but it would have been into the breast of Marika that I wept. And with your arms wrapped tightly around the pair of us. Never letting go, for we were living. We were living.

If things had been different, I said, Harkham would not have raised its eyebrows when my mother wore scarlet leather sandals and swirling skirts, because instead she would have dressed in navy blue with a neat comb tucked in her pale blond hair and been someone else altogether. We'd have taken holidays somewhere damp and misty, not hot and dusty, braving no more than rain splashes, in our raincoats and knee socks. We'd have been a huddle of three under the canvas of a campsite or sitting around the table of a farm cottage, eating scones noisily and with our mouths open, not knowing or caring that the word for that was *csámcsog* in Hungarian.

If things had been different, I said, the Oxfordshire rain would never have made the roads slick. The dark would not have fallen so quickly, and the stout oak on the corner of the lane would not have loomed so large and stayed so strong, when weaker things, hard metal and soft bodies, crumpled and fell.

If things had been different, I said, I would have died beside my mother that night. A mere dot of pencil, smudged out.

"I'd have known no misery," I said. "No pain. No regret. If I'd died that night, I'd have left all of that for you. A dreadful legacy, but a true one. What if that was what should have happened?"

"Oh, Beth," he said, smiling sadly.

His look stopped me. I lost my thread.

"We can't talk of what might have been. We only have what was, and what is."

"I know…" I began, but he carried on.

"*And* what will be. You know, things can always be different, Beth. I'm coming rather late to that realization and I'm not sure I'll ever forgive myself for it, but it's true."

"Marika's dead, Dad," I said, and the words winded me. "And there's nothing I can do. There's no way I can tell her that I loved her."

My father stood. He moved slowly to the edge of the terrace and gazed out into the night.

"Beth, I wish to take a liberty," he said, his head half turned. "A long time ago, when you were very small, I took a similar liberty. Do you remember? I gave you an airplane ticket to Hungary. And despite all the things that happened, before and after, I still think it was the right thing to do."

"Dad, it was," I whispered.

He turned around, one side of his face lit by the glow

from the window. His cheek shone wet with tears. It was only the second time I'd ever seen him cry, for his were tears for behind closed doors, pushed into the heels of hands, or blinked away before they fell. They were not something he showed me, not since the first time. When Marika went away.

"I want to do it again, Beth. I want you to let me buy you a ticket. It's easy to say it's too late, but I don't think it is, not really, not completely. I think something can still be saved."

I stared at him. I wiped my eyes, and saw him do the same. We looked at each other afresh.

"Hungary?" I said.

He nodded.

"What, Villa Serena?"

He nodded again.

Maybe, in so many ways, we were too late; but wasn't it worse somehow, to make that the end of it? Perhaps my father was right. Marika wasn't lost to me forever. If we knew where to look, we'd be able to find each other again.

In the past I've often wondered what I'd have said if anyone asked me if I was at all like Marika. After all, we'd grown up together, as mothers and daughters do. I used to think of all the things I might have answered, about her departure and then mine, about her efforts to reach me afterward, her resilience and passion, and my dismissal, my equal strength and vigor. Then once she eventually fell quiet, how I'd assumed the same stillness. At least on the outside. How I'd waded through the days that followed, the days that still came. And then I would have lied. I'd have said we were as different as two people could possibly be.

If I was asked now, I'd say something different and it'd be more like the truth. Because apart from the big things, there were all the little things, as well. I'd say that we both liked peanut butter, the crunchy kind that sticks your teeth fast together. I'd say that sometimes when we both laughed you couldn't tell whose peal belonged to whom. And I'd say that we both considered sunny mornings were something to be celebrated, to feel glad of on waking.

It was such a morning when I left London to fly to Hungary two weeks later.

Marika would have sung for it, in a simple, bright key. A morning to be thankful for. To be glad to be alive.

Before I'd left Devon, over a week ago, I'd telephoned Villa Serena. I dialed each digit carefully, as though one misstep would send me plummeting into a booby trap. I waited with my breath held as it rang in long, continental drones. Zoltán answered, sounding exactly like he always sounded. It was a miracle, and my cautious faith grew a little stronger. I found my voice. I said that I was so very, very sorry. For Marika, for…everything. *Oh, Erzsi,* he'd said, *just for Marika, nothing else. I understand everything else. But for Marika…ah, yes. She had too much life for it to be taken away like that. No one deserves to die, but she, she was the most unlikely person. To just disappear one day.*

It was true. And yet in the same breath, it wasn't. Because it had been her way, all those sudden movements, all those flashes and bangs. Just as, in the end, it had been mine, too.

Once, when she was trying to explain why she'd returned to Hungary, Marika said, *Sometimes if you don't go backward, you can't move forward.* I'd repeated this to my father, hoping he'd be able to unravel her words. But he'd just muttered something about stubborn cars meeting on country roads and I'd thought it best to ask no more. Now, though, I think we both know what she meant.

I told Zoltán that if he were willing, if he could bear it, I would love to see him. To stay with him again, just as I always used to. The line went silent and I listened for the slightest sound, a breath, a sigh, anything to let me know that he was still there. When it came, his was a cheer that blew me off my feet. I leaned against the wall, awash with relief, regret and another feeling that I knew so well but had almost forgotten. Long after he'd hung up I kept the receiver clutched to my chest. For it had been easy, in the end, the picking up of the phone.

On the train to the airport, I reached for my bag and took out *The Book of Summers,* laying it on my knee. I opened its pages, alighting on the picture of me posing in front of Villa Serena, that first year, where my whole being appeared to shine with joy. *Erzsi, All The Way From England.* I said it out loud, trying it on for size. It felt odd, leaving a strange taste in my mouth. But not as foreign as I expected, not as bitter as I might have thought. Perhaps that was how I was to come back. A few words at a time, with feeling hands and eyes wide open.

I thought of my father, and the day he'd taken me to the station a little under two weeks ago. In the brief time I spent with him we'd found more words than I'd thought there could be between us. The image I was taking of my father to Hungary was a lovely one. He saw me off at the train station, and for a few brief steps he'd moved beside the train as it pulled away. His corduroy trousers were blown back by the gusting draft and he appeared faintly comedic, fated to fail in this racing of the train. But his eyes had stayed on mine and he'd waved his hand and smiled, and I had done the same. I realized that I missed him already. I knew that I would see him again soon.

And now, I lifted my head and stared out at the city's sprawl. The edges of London spun away from me. The tight-packed houses and teetering towers turned to the rampant forests behind Villa Serena. Among the office buildings and smeared satellite dishes I saw red tiles and crooked gables. The grimy railway sidings turned to white paths flocked by rhododendrons, in eye-popping pink. Even the sun appeared to burn more brightly, and with greater intent.

Back to my book and I turned the page. The next. And the next. The more time I spent with them, the pictures began to take on a life of their own, no longer confined to two dimensions, to sticky tape and a brown paper page. And as I looked, another came to me. It was not a photograph, but it assumed its place like one. Marika and I were walking down a lane, and I knew it to be in England, because the trees were dark and the ground was wet. Our fingers were wound tightly together, our feet fell in step. It must have been before the letter arrived from Hungary, before we ever went there. That would have made me eight or nine years old. And yet I was standing shoulder to shoulder with her, and our waists appeared similarly shaped. Her hair was graying, ebbing at her shoulders in wintry waves, and her lips shone berry red. Marika was a person at once strange and familiar. Everything I ever wanted and perhaps some things I could have done without. In time she would turn to me, and after a moment's start, we would meet in a smile. But for the moment I simply watched her, and I felt the press of her hand in mine. My heart fluttered, then righted itself. Her beat went on.

Epilogue

It is on days like these, when the gray rain streaks the window and the earth seems flatter than it really is, that Beth takes down the book. She turns the pages and she disappears into all the sun-filled days.

There she is in the early mornings, when soft light kissed away the dew and tempted them all outside, with blushed cheeks. There she is in the late afternoons, times when a ruder heat descended, flattening them, sending them sprawling—on the yellow lawn, in the forest pool, beneath the canopy of acacia trees. There she is in the slow-ebbing evenings, when the spent sun dipped toward the faded hills, and they lounged on the terrace, basking in the last of the glow.

She looks at the pictures, and, fleetingly, she feels them looking back.

Her relationship with the book is curious. It has taken time for her to understand it, to wish to bask within its pages. Now she knows that it isn't just its *world* she loves, but the fact that it exists at all. That Marika sat down and made it, with searching fingers and ink-smudging tears and

dreamy smiles, and paint and glue and snippets and fragments. That she took photographs when no one knew photographs were being taken, so the pictures within its pages
appear like whispered secrets. *The Book of Summers.* A name
that came from the delight of the first, and the anticipation
of all of the others to come.

Beth loves the book, for when she turns the pages she is
a time traveler. It thrums with life, and tempts her closer.
She smells coconut cream streaked on pale skin to ward
off scatterings of freckles. She smells wood smoke lingering in hair, as though there had been a dance through licking flames. She smells cherry sherbets with a taste like a
sweet prickle. She dips her head over the pages, caught in
the moment, and the scent she catches is a balm. Restorative and heavenly.

She often hears voices as she studies the book. They call
her name and something in her answers, as it always does.
Even after she has closed its cover and set it back on the
shelf, her face is splashed with sunlight, spangles catching
in her hair, and the murmurs stay with her.

No matter where Beth is, she can close her eyes and feel
Marika all around her, and when she opens them she knows
she's still there. Neither one has fled. This is the book's quiet
work. This is its treasure.

She has grown to like this, the fact that she is never alone
anymore, her heart and mind a patchwork of infinitesimal
fabrics. And now she is adding new memories to the old
ones—the gauze-green pool she found again, where she
slipped from her traveling dress and ran and jumped and
burst into the water's kiss, then floated like a lily pad, se-
rene and lovely; an improvised waltz on a sloping lawn in

the arms of a dear, now elderly, artist, watched over by a house whose once-shuttered windows now smiled open; a fire-bright exchange with a handful of earth, a patch of sky, a thousand tiny fragments scattered on the wind and settled in the grasses. A laying to rest.

And not yet a memory but nonetheless: Beth has begun to write a letter. She has been writing it for days, haltingly, uncertainly, with none of her one-time belief in rows of kisses and proclamations in copied Hungarian. She should probably just finish it and mail it, for its recipient already knows to expect it. Already knows, in fact, what he will write in reply, because Zoltán, it seems, cannot keep a secret so well, after all. But she lingers over it. She chooses her words carefully. Because there is so much to say, and there is so much still to be done.

★ ★ ★ ★ ★

Acknowledgments

Thank you to everyone who has helped bring this book to life; somehow I've landed the dream team, for which I'm truly grateful. I'm indebted to Rowan Lawton and PFD for taking a chance on me—I simply couldn't imagine a better agent. I'm incredibly lucky to be working with Leah Woodburn and Headline, whose care and conviction is amazing. And in the U.S., I owe great thanks to Beth Davey and my brilliant editor at MIRA Books, Erika Imranyi—*Köszönöm szépen.* Along the road, I was touched by the legendary magic of the Arvon Foundation, inspired by Louise Dean, Bidisha, Patrick Neate, Harriet Evans and Polly Clark's Fielding Programme. I'm ever thankful for the unequivocal support and encouragement of my dear friends and family, especially Kate Haines, one of my earliest readers. I doubt I'd be writing at all if my parents hadn't instilled in me the belief that a life lived imaginatively is the richest kind there is; for this I owe thanks to my mother, whose passion for Hungary led us there in the first place, my father for always providing creative inspiration and my sister, my ally on all of our childhood travels. And finally, Robin. My husband, my love. Thank you for always believing. And everything else, besides.

1. Cultural identity is an important theme in the book. It's a factor in motivating Marika to leave her family, and at one point Erzsi claims she is starting to feel "more Hungarian." To what extent do you think we "feel" our nationalities? And is this sense of belonging something that we are born with, or something that we develop willfully?

2. Memory is depicted in the book as an incredibly powerful force—a source of great pleasure and immense sadness. Discuss the relationship that Marika, David and Erzsi each have with their memories, and how their lives have been affected as a result.

3. Villa Serena is a bohemian idyll—a place where Erzsi can run free and be joyful, but the "real world" does still manage to intrude. Discuss some scenes in the book where Erzsi

feels her paradise is threatened. How many of Erzsi's concerns stem from her own feelings of vulnerability, as she moves between her father and her mother's homes and becomes a teenager?

4. Marika is a free spirit, who amazes and disappoints Erzsi with equal vigor. Is she a good mother? Is she a bad mother? What characteristics does she have that define her one way or another?

5. Zoltán is a quiet figure in the book, yet a powerful one. Discuss his relationship with Erzsi and his importance to the story.

6. During the last summer in Hungary, Erzsi is looking ahead to shaping a life with Tamás— she is deeply in love with him. How real do you think the love is that we feel at sixteen? Is it too fanciful to imagine that their romance could be rekindled many years later?

7. Marika's revelation comes as an absolute shock to Erzsi. What do you make of her coping mechanisms in the immediate aftermath and the years that follow? How do you feel about the differing ways that Erzsi treats Marika and her father, from that moment onward?

8. When Erzsi cuts ties with Marika, she also loses Tamás, Zoltán and, to an extent, the whole of Hungary. To what degree are our perceptions of

a place shaped by the people who inhabit it? Is it ever possible to separate the two?

9. David Lowe's path is a difficult one; first as a widower, then a single parent and guardian of a secret he cannot bring himself to share, then finally a father who loses the trust of his only child. How much should he blame himself for the way events unfold? Is he right to allow Erzsi to spend time with Marika every summer? And how honest should we be with our children when they are young?

10. Making peace with the past is a major theme in the book, notably for Erzsi, but also for her father. By the end, how successful do you think they have each been in achieving this?

In many ways, *The Book of Summers* is a love letter to Hungary. What initially drew you to this setting? What do you think is so alluring about Hungary that makes Marika choose it over her own family?

When I was a child, my family vacationed in Hungary. We'd spent time abroad before that, in France, Germany and Austria, but Hungary was the first place I visited that felt truly foreign. My eleven-year-old self was entranced, exhilarated and a little unsettled. My memories, from that first trip and all subsequent ones, have proved indelible. I believe fervently in the influence of childhood on our later lives. When Marika returns to Hungary after many years of absence, her passion for the country is reawakened. And although she left Hungary at age ten, she feels innately Hungarian—she believes she is more herself there. Would Marika have chosen Hungary over her family had she and David been in a satisfying relationship, if her life in England felt complete? Possibly not. But circumstances conspire and, for the restless Marika, Hungary offers the temptation of a newer, truer life.

What inspired your idea for the story and characters in *The Book of Summers*?

I wanted to write a novel set in Hungary because I felt it was a place that few people were familiar with, much less visited. The country had imprinted itself on my mind, not necessarily because of my heritage—my mother is Hungarian—but because of the summer vacations I'd spent there, growing up. I had such precious memories of those trips that the thought of stepping back in time and weaving a story that evoked the places I'd been and the things I'd seen was very seductive.

You've created such an emotionally rich and memorable cast of characters in this novel, especially Marika, a passionate bohemian who is larger than life. When you started the book, did you have her story and personality already in mind? How did she surprise you along the way?

The idea of someone being drawn to another country was undoubtedly inspired by my own mother, but she has always put her family first and wouldn't have dreamed of uprooting us all. With Marika, it had to be plausible that she would leave her family, and for a long time I struggled with that, especially as it was important to the story that she remained appealing despite her imperfections; someone who was as infuriating as she was lovable. Then I decided to fundamentally change her relationship to Erzsi—which was not part of my original plan, but rather a plot point that revealed itself as I was writing. It was a real lightbulb moment, because it not only provided a genuine twist but also helped add a rationale to what was, for me, still a problematic piece of behavior—a mother leaving her child.

Cultural identity is such a powerful theme in the book. Has culture been an important force in your own life, as well? If so, how?

I grew up knowing some Hungarian words, eating Hungarian food every so often, celebrating Christmas on both Christmas Eve, continental-style, and Christmas Day... To me, these were things that added color to everyday life. The time we spent abroad when I was younger whetted my appetite for other cultures more generally—my association with all things foreign was one of absolute pleasure. And I think that's something I take into my writing. When we're in another country, we're somehow more ready to find things marvelous. We notice the details, the idiosyncrasies that we believe are definitive of the place we're in. I once read that poets are like babies, because they find the everyday world wonderful. I certainly identify with that perspective, whether at home or abroad. The more prepared we are to take pleasure and interest in life, the richer it becomes.

If thirty-year-old Erzsi could tell nine-year-old Erzsi anything at all, what do you think it would be?

To accept that life is imperfect. To take joy in the small things, as well as the big. And that when you find love, you hold on to it and you don't let it go.

What was your greatest challenge in writing *The Book of Summers*? And what gave you the most pleasure?

My greatest challenge is probably a common one among writers—the balancing act of sufficiently liberating myself in order to get lost in the story, while keeping a cool, critical head. I like to write in quite an organic fashion— allowing characters to develop on the page—while still recognizing the need for a structured approach. I rewrote a lot throughout the process, making wrong turns, realizing my own mistakes, finding new directions, but was always sure of the heart of the story, and that remained my guiding light. I took most pleasure in transporting myself—exploring real memories, real places, and meshing them with many imaginary ones. To me, writing is a kind of magic. I delight in it.

Do you read other fiction while you're writing, or do you find it distracting? What do you enjoy reading most?

Good fiction is always inspiring, and I think of it as essential fuel for the writing process. Reading an amazing book just makes me want to raise my own game. I remember how I felt after finishing Barbara Kingsolver's The Poisonwood Bible. Humbled, yes, awed, definitely, but also a thrill; that when you sit down with a pen and paper, anything is possible. I also find it helpful to read poetry, for the rhythms of language and the bottling of *big ideas into small spaces—that sense of economy. I read widely, but the books I enjoy the most are where writers show their understanding of human nature; the barely there gestures, the sideways glances, the unspoken thoughts. Last year, I started reading Anne Tyler, and I think she's particularly brilliant in this respect.*

Can you describe your writing process? Do you write the scenes consecutively or do you jump around? Do you have a schedule or routine? A lucky charm?

I always, always write consecutively. The only time I'd consider jumping forward would be if I was describing a setting or place. But if it's people...never. I think that's because I have faith in the natural process of character development. That's not to say I don't go back and forth in the editing process, but at the first-draft stage I write as "naturally" as possible. I like to experience events as they unfold, just as the characters do. I write best in the mornings, aided by several cups of coffee, always in my same bright orange Santa Fe mug, bought from a five-and-dime store on my honeymoon in New Mexico. That mug is the closest thing I have to a charm. If it broke, I think I'd have to get on the first flight out to replace it.

Can you tell us something about the book you're working on now?

I can. It's set in Switzerland, among a crowd of ex-pats and international students on the shores of glamorous Lake Geneva. I'm taking great pleasure in creating a portrait of a city, and painting it as vividly as I can. I want to capture the feeling of being young and abroad, the excitement and trepidation. I'm exploring the idea of deceptive veneers; the places or people that seem perfect to us, and what happens when we discover that they're not.

♥